THE ICE MIRROR

Robert Wishart is a born climber with a brilliant international reputation. But there is one terrible flaw in that reputation. For Wishart has led two companions to disaster on the North Wall of the Eiger: and now he is afraid . . .

Wishart has to conquer that fear together with the mountain that so brutally tore away his self-confidence. He is helped by Jo, the girl he loves, who has her own reasons for hating the mountain. Her father – a man in his fifties – is planning a winter climb on the North Wall. Gradually, as if in a nightmare, Wishart is drawn into the scheme and the living nightmare of pain, cold, snow, ice and utter exhaustion begins . . .

D1189106

Available in Fontana by the same author

Send Down a Dove

CHARLES MACHARDY

The Ice Mirror

FONTANA / Collins

First published by Wm. Collins 1971
First issued in Fontana Books 1973

© Charles MacHardy 1971

Printed in Great Britain
Collins Clear-Type Press London and Glasgow

TO MY FAMILY, GORDON AND CLAERWEN,
AND THE C.D.M.C.

If I am not for myself
Who shall be for me?
But if I am for myself alone—
What am I?

THE TALMUD

CHAPTER I

This early in the evening the small *Bierstube* was nearly empty. Apart from the slow hiss of escaping steam from the ancient percolator standing on the counter there was only the low buzz of sound from a group of locals seated by the bar.

Robert Wishart finished his beer and fished out a packet of cigarettes from the top pocket of his thick woollen shirt and lit up. He watched the slow curl of smoke spiral upwards, wondering how many he'd smoked that day. Twenty? Thirty? He couldn't be sure, but one thing was certain: it was too many. At the age of forty-two, health wasn't something to be taken for granted.

Pushing his glass away he caught the eye of the waitress. Blonde plaits bobbing, she came over right away. He ordered another beer and then in a moment of extravagance a whisky. The waitress looked at him oddly. Whisky and beer? Waiting for her to return he sat worriedly fingering the ridge of pale scar tissue on his temple. Within seconds she was back, her plump hands deftly removing the glasses from the tray to set them down on the table.

He thanked her and watched her go, noting the precise way she walked, the strong legs, the military-stiff back. The Swiss? So precise, so mercilessly efficient, with minds like cash registers. What was it that Harry Lime had said about them in *The Third Man*? A thousand years of peace and all they'd managed to produce was the cuckoo clock. But he was letting his bitterness cloud his thinking again. How could he forget the rescue teams, the doctors and all the others who'd helped? If it hadn't been for them he wouldn't be here now in the *Bierstube*.

He drank some beer and lifted his whisky glass. The first sip caught at his throat and he reached for his beer again, coughing. Alcohol and nicotine, the twin crutches of civilised man. It was perhaps fortunate the price of whisky was prohibitive. A man could handle beer all right, but whisky? What was it his grandfather had said about it? 'A guid friend but a hellish sore enemy'; and since the old man had drunk nearly a bottle every day of his adult life his words had some authority.

Wishart turned to look out of the window, his face looking

beaten and weary in the slanting rays of the late sun. It was the face, with its deep lines and nut-coloured skin, of a man who'd spent much of his life outdoors. A strong face, though the grey-green eyes were cloudy and bruised with pain.

Outside in the street small groups of tourists were taking their evening stroll before dinner. They reminded him of well-fed prize cattle, but he gave them little attention, shifting his gaze to reach across the rooftops on the opposite side of the street. Beyond the rooftops, rearing up into the sky, a rocky snow-covered barrier, nearly two miles high, walled in the valley. In the middle of the great barrier a dirty greyish-brown mass, ugly as a tobacco-stained tooth, stood out ominous and aggressive.

With a bleak expression Wishart stared for a long minute upon the precipitous North Wall of the Eiger.

The Eiger?

Even now in the quiet warmth of the *Bierstube* he could feel its oppressiveness, and he shivered slightly as if a cold hand had been plunged down the back of his woollen shirt.

The North Wall? How he'd dreamed about it. The hours of planning, the discussions that went on long into the night, and then the moment when the dreams had finally become a reality. He shivered again at the thought of the three terrible nights and days they'd spent on the Wall. A short period of time and yet within it had been the sufferings of a lifetime.

Staring at the North Wall of the Eiger he found it difficult to believe that only a few miles away from the warmth and safety of the *Bierstube*, a place could exist that was as alien and inhospitable to life as the surface of the moon. Behind those deceptively soft little gatherings of cloud, the temperatures on the Wall would be sub-zero and the rock encased in an iron hard shell of snow and ice.

At the beginning everything had gone well. Clear skies and firm snow had enabled them to get as far as the third ice-field by evening of the first day. But next morning, after a night's bivouac, the sky had darkened and taken on an ominous disturbed appearance. Dennis and Joe were all for going on, but he'd hesitated a long time unable to make up his mind and looking up anxiously at the sky. Joe had argued, pointing out rightly that they were still fresh and strong, but he'd still hesitated, his mind full of doubts and uncertainties. Finally he'd suggested a compromise: go back down the ice-field, and if the weather broke they'd be near the safety of the railway tunnel which opened out on to the face. From there, if the threatened storm didn't materialise, they wouldn't have lost all that much and could still complete the ascent. He stressed the point that too many people had been killed on the Wall simply because they hadn't taken sufficient precautions. Reluctantly Joe and Dennis had given in to his arguments.

Just below the second great ice-field the storm had hit them; impenetrable thick blankets of freezing snow driven by a madly howling wind. For three whole days and nights they'd been pinned to the Wall. When the storm finally blew itself out to leave no more than gently falling curtains of soft snow they were nearly dead from hunger and exposure. How they had been able to get back over the near vertical ice-glazed slabs of the Hinterstoisser Traverse had been a miracle.

They'd reached the tunnel where Joe and Dennis had collapsed. It was only his awareness of his responsibility as leader of the party that had given him the strength to stumble down the mountainside to reach the Kleine Scheidegg. Luckily a rescue team had been ready and were just waiting for the snowfall to clear before setting out. They went up to the tunnel that evening and brought down Joe and Dennis; an action that saved their lives.

Then the long days of delirium in the hospital followed by the sickening moment when the surgeon had told him he might have to lose his hand. But he'd been lucky. Lucky Bob Wishart. He'd got away with the removal of two finger-tips. Joe hadn't been so lucky. His leg had been badly frostbitten. They'd had to amputate it from below the knee. Joe of all people. He'd felt like crying when he'd heard about it. His life-long friend who'd climbed with him all over the world, the man who'd shared his last crust and last fag with him. It was cruel. After the operation he'd gone to see Joe, terrified of what he might discover in the frank brown eyes. But Joe had managed a grin. It could have been worse, he'd said. What the hell, he'd be the first one-legged climber in the world.

To Wishart, the knowledge that he'd been responsible had been like a knife plunged into his insides. In an agony of self-recrimination he cursed himself for his decision to turn back, knowing only too well the real reasons that had caused him to make it.

He felt he'd aged ten years after visiting Joe. And then there had been Dennis. That hadn't been easy either. Fortunately Dennis had been spared the brutality of surgery but something visibly had gone out of him. He was going to live, but . . .?

God, what a terrible price his two friends had had to pay for their trust in him.

A long time later he'd managed to screw up his courage sufficiently to return to the hills. He'd recovered his hard fitness, but his first climb left him shaking inside and his legs turned to jelly. The experience shook him. All the thoughts he'd been holding in check – even before their attempt on the North Wall – had come back at him with renewed strength. Like mist rising from the ground on a chill damp morning doubts and uncertainties seeped into his mind.

But even before their attempt on the Wall he'd known in a vague kind of way that there had been something wrong. He'd struggled stubbornly against the feelings, trying to ignore their significance.

And then, the night before they'd set out, camped in the shadow of the Wall, he'd been forced to come face to face with the truth. The revelation had brought him out of his half-dozing state to sit bolt upright, his heart thumping wildly, his body soaked in sweat.

What he'd seen was as recognisable as the reflection of his own face in a mirror.

At that moment he'd known he was afraid!

CHAPTER II

He ground his cigarette into the ash-tray. If he'd had any sense he would never have returned to Grindelwald. Why had he come back anyway?

He signalled the waitress again and lit a fresh cigarette, staring out of the window again as if hypnotised. The light was beginning to fade. High up on the tops, in the angled rays of the sun, a deep roseate hue had spread like a seeping dye over the blue-white snow. It reminded him of the colour of blood flushing down a sink.

He turned away from the window thumping his empty glass down on the table. Immediately a few heads swivelled round. He returned the stares with a look of hostility as the waitress came hurrying over, her eyes clouding with anxiety. He pushed his empty beer glass towards her. Ja, ja, she understood. More beer. She made off quickly.

Some of the locals were still looking over in his direction. He glowered back. To hell with them. What did they know about it? He got his drink, hoisting the glass up to watch the light diffuse softly through the pale-coloured liquid.

Alcohol? 'A guid friend, but a hellish sore enemy.'

He took a deep gulp, little driblets of beer running down his chin. He wiped them away with the back of his hand. So what if they did notice? What were they anyway? A bunch of penny-hoarding, over-cautious, small-time burghers. What did they know about the Eiger, about the North Wall? All they knew was how to make money out of it. They didn't know what it could be like up there – the awful cold, the loneliness, the sheer terror of that great bulk. The nearest they'd probably ever been to it was on the mountain railway or viewing it safely through the end of a six-inch telescope when fools like himself had been struggling for their lives.

He rubbed the scar on his temple, conscious for a moment of his missing finger-tips. Not much was it? Only two finger-tips. Not like an arm – or a leg. At least he could still climb?

Could he? The thought caused him to laugh with silent bitterness.

He belched slightly, feeling the taste of the whisky come back at him sourly. He glanced at his watch, screwing his eyes into focus. At least he knew the time, though he couldn't be sure what day it was. He counted off on his fingers. He'd arrived Monday, that was two days ago, so it must be Wednesday.

Wednesday? He sat up. To-morrow would be Thursday and the day after that Brian was due to arrive.

God, how could he have been so stupid? He must have been drunk. What else could have made him ask Dillon to join him for a few days. So what was he going to do now? Tell Dillon he'd sprained his ankle? That he was sickening for a cold? He'd have to think of something better than that.

He had a few more beers before settling his bill and going out into the street. It was quite cold and a full moon glittered frostily in the clear air as he made his way up the street towards the camp site where he'd parked the Dormobile.

What the hell was he going to tell Dillon?

If only they hadn't met that day in Besançon. And of course, Cornforth had to be there shooting off his big mouth, asking questions like why hadn't he seen him in the hills recently, was he still climbing, and things like that. The drink had loosened his tongue and boosted his confidence. To counter Cornforth's insinuations he'd asked Dillon to join him for a couple of days' climbing. Dillon had jumped at the chance. Cornforth had been silenced. But now he was going to have to pay a price for trying to prove to Cornforth that he was still as good a climber as ever.

Reaching the end of the village he turned right and headed towards the river. Soon the metalled roadway gave way to a loose covering of gravel. No lights were to be seen on the site and the only sounds were the soft crunch of gravel beneath his feet and the lonely howling of a dog.

Threading his way between the parked caravans and tents he reached the Dormobile. Unlocking the door he stepped inside and switched on the light, pulling the door shut after him. The coffee pot was on the stove. He lit a match and turned on the gas ring. In a few minutes the coffee was boiling. He poured himself a cup and, reaching into a cupboard above the bunk, produced a bottle of whisky. He uncorked it and poured a stiff measure of the spirits into his coffee cup.

He sat down, about to take his boots off, but he felt nervous and uneasy. He went outside to sit on the step of the Dormobile. In the moonlight the site looked as if it had been sprayed with aluminium dust. It was quite bright. He looked upwards, reading the weather signs. Only a few rags of clouds, drifting slowly like flotsam on an ebb tide, scattered the sky. The whole of the valley was bathed in a soft luminescence and to the south the bluish-white peaks were gathered together like a group of cowled monks surrounding the glistening black wall of the Eiger.

Trying to think clearly, he lit a cigarette. Dillon would be arriving in thirty-six hours. What was he going to do? He suddenly felt the cold. Flinging away the remains of his coffee he stubbed his cigarette on the grass, climbed back into the Dormobile and closed the door behind him.

A few minutes later the chink of light showing round the curtained windows blinked out. From a distance the dog began to howl again.

He awoke with a groan. His mouth felt as if it had been stuffed with cotton wool. Easing himself out of the bunk he pulled on a pair of slacks and a thick woollen jersey. For a moment he sat on the edge of the bed, running his fingers through his hair and mopping his face with his hand. His head ached and he had a hollow sensation in his stomach. He looked at his watch. Only seven o'clock. Pulling on his boots he felt his head throb protestingly as he bent down. He got to his feet searching round the confined space of the Dormobile for his toilet gear. At last he found it and, wrapping a towel round his neck, stepped outside.

The grass was soaked in dew and the chill of the morning air caught at his lungs, but he inhaled deeply, pulling his head back and flexing his arms before setting off for the toilet-rooms at the bottom of the site.

In the shower-room he tested the water with a cautious toe. It was boiling hot. Stripping off he soaped himself thoroughly and let the water run over him, relaxing in its warmth. He had to steel himself to lean over and reverse the tap. The cold water hit him with the strength of an electric shock. Gasping for breath he turned off the water and emerged from the shower, his lightly tanned skin turning to a deep coppery red. After a vigorous rub down he felt warm again.

There was still no one about. He had the shaving booth to himself. Though each bowl had its own separate electric razor fitting he preferred to shave the old-fashioned way. There was something peculiarly satisfying about the feel of sharp steel scything through the thick creamy lather. He broke out a fresh Wilkinson Sword blade from a pack he'd remembered to buy and fitted it to his razor before soaping his face.

He took his time shaving, stretching the skin with his fingers and varying the angle of the blade. When he'd finished he paused to examine his face in the mirror. The eyes which stared back at him were dull and without lustre and the surrounding skin had run into a myriad of tiny wrinkles. The lines in his forehead reminded him of the cracked leather of an old shoe.

Moodily he returned to the Dormobile and cooked himself breakfast. It was still cold but he decided to eat outside; the air would help to clear his head. He took his time over breakfast. It wasn't till he was having a cigarette over a cup of coffee that he heard the first signs of life on the camp site.

He made up his mind. What he needed was a long, bruising march in the hills. After that he would be better able to decide what he was going to do about Dillon.

He cleared up his breakfast things and folded back the table, before getting out his pack. He wouldn't need much for the day: a flask of coffee, a couple of fruit bars and some spare clothing. He checked the pack. The whistle, compass and torch were where he always kept them. From the back flap he took out a map of the district and stuffed it in his anorak pocket. Though he knew the surrounding country well it was always better to take a map. But these were routine habits and required no thought. There was nothing else to do now but check whether he had cigarettes and matches. He thought about taking his pipe but put it back in the drawer. He hadn't smoked a pipe for months now. Making sure he had his keys he slipped on his anorak and stepped outside. It was a pleasant feeling to be setting out for the hills again. The early hour of departure, the dull sound of his boots on the grass, the light tug of the pack straps all combined to improve his mood.

Clearing the camp site he followed the road which would take him across the river to the other side of the valley. As he plunged into the early morning shadow cast by the Schreckhorn, he felt the temperature drop noticeably. He didn't mind. When he reached the top of the valley and turned towards the north he would have the sun with him for the rest of the day.

Walking with an oiled rhythm he made his way along the path, long strides never varying: a pace which he could keep going all day – and night – if necessary.

By noon he had crossed the head of the valley and stopped to have a smoke. Clear of the shadow he felt the strength of

12

the sun's rays . . . it would be hot later on. Slipping off his pack and anorak he lay down on the grass. Underneath, the earth had a comfortable, soothing feel.

He finished his cigarette and got to his feet, dusting off the loose vegetation that clung to his clothing. All around him was a deep silence broken only now and again by the cry of a mountain bird. He took a deep, lung-filling breath of the pure air and flung his pack on his back.

An hour later, walking with the same unvarying stride, he looked back. He'd come quite a distance. The Grosse Scheidegg was a matchbox village at the head of the valley. He stopped to take his bearings. Above him and to the right the rocks rose steeply. The snow slopes he could see above the buttress marked the ridge of the Schwarzhorn.

He made up his mind. Leaving the track he began cutting up towards the foot of the buttress, stopping only now and again to take in the line of its contours. Soon he saw what he'd been looking for. At the foot of the buttress a large broken slab of rock rose to terminate in a natural platform which led to a deep-cut chimney. It would do.

His pulse quickened as he made his way upwards.

Reaching the base of the slab he looked up again. It was as he'd thought. The chimney forty feet above was quite wide; there was no danger of the pack getting snagged up.

He patted his shirt pocket making sure his cigarettes and matches were still there. He gave the pack another hitch and took a deep breath.

The slab was quite steep but the holds were plentiful and sound. It gave him no trouble and soon he reached the platform. Above his head the chimney stretched upwards; a deep cleft in the rock. He leant back as far as he dared in an effort to see what lay beyond, but the angle was too abrupt. He'd just have to take a chance he didn't come up against an overhang. Alone and without proper equipment he'd be forced to come back down.

Before starting on the chimney he paused to look down. Far below was the valley. With the sun directly in his eyes the soft green meadows and the clumps of woodland had an arid, colourless appearance as if overlaid with a coating of fine ash, the river twisting away like a sliver of precious metal. The old thrill and excitement of a climb came back to him. His body felt light, almost weightless, his muscles like strands of powerful elastic.

He reached up into the chimney. The wall to his right was

13

smooth but the left wall was broken and offered the best line of attack. Straddling his legs he got a purchase on both walls and began to ascend. When the holds on the left wall began to thin out he had to use considerable muscular effort to make progress. It was hard work and he was thankful he'd kept himself fit. Half way up the chimney he stopped for a breather, craning his head back to see if he could make out what lay ahead, but he was too close to the rock to get any length of vision. He started up again. Near the top he had one bad moment. A slight bulge had forced him outwards, and as he leaned out balancing on small holds he felt a sudden stab of panic. He moved quickly, not giving his limbs a chance to freeze; and he was over the bulge. He climbed a few more feet, his breathing returning to normal as he kept telling himself to relax and not think about it. At the top of the chimney the walls fanned out. Above that a huge block barred further progress.

He looked around him. A narrow terrace ran to the left. To the right the rock leaned out from the vertical. He took the terrace, suspecting it would lead him off the buttress and back to the vegetation-covered slopes. He was right. The terrace ran along forty feet before petering out into a series of shelves marking the extremity of the buttress. He climbed back down on to the easier slopes and sat down on the grass.

It hadn't been much, but he'd satisfied his impulse. But more than that he'd proved to himself that he could still climb with all his old skill. Apart from that one bad bit . . .?

He got quickly to his feet again not wanting to think about it. The sun was beating down strongly now, and he was beginning to feel hungry and thirsty. He headed up the hill away from the buttress. Shortly after, he reached the top of a slope. Here the ground flattened out forming a sort of plateau. He wasn't far from the restaurant on top of the mountain and for a moment he was tempted to head for it, but he changed his mind and instead made for the loch that lay at the back of the plateau.

The water was deliciously cool as he splashed cupped handfuls into his mouth. It ran down his neck and the front of his shirt, but he didn't mind. He sat back and removed his boots and plunged his feet into the waters of the loch before reaching into his pack and bringing out the flask. After coffee he munched a fruit bar and then lay back. He felt a warm glow of pleasure seeping over his body: the feeling that comes after hard physical exertion. He must have dozed about an hour. When he awoke he looked at his watch. It was time to start back if he wanted to head along the tops and come down through the woods above the village.

Nearly two hours later he picked up the road, and within a quarter of an hour was back in the camp site. Dumping his gear he made for the wash-room and had a quick shower. Changing into fresh clothing he went back up to the village.

The *Bierstube*, as usual, was fairly quiet at this time of evening. He ordered a beer, gulping it down thirstily before examining the menu. The waitress smiled as she took his order. After the meal he sat back in his chair feeling relaxed. He smoked a cigarette and then went outside. Crossing the street by the car-park he heard the familiar sound of English voices. He stopped. A small man with tinted glasses and wearing a cream-coloured alpaca jacket was surrounded by a group of tourists. He was smiling and pointing across the valley as he spoke.

Wishart heard snatches of what was obviously a rehearsed speech as the man in the alpaca jacket described for the eager tourists the features of the North Wall.

One of the tourists had interrupted to ask a question about accidents on the Wall. The courier responded enthusiastically as he delved into the long history of fatalities.

Wishart turned away angrily, ashamed at his own race that they could be so morbidly curious. They reminded him of dull, sheep-faced crowds gathered to watch a public hanging. He felt like shouting at them.

It was the first thing they all asked. Was that the Eiger? Where was the North Wall? Was it true it was known as 'the killer face'?

Thrusting his hands in his pockets he walked away angrily. He must have walked for about an hour before turning back. It was getting dark as he re-entered the village. Crossing the open railtracks he made for a stumpy little brick-built *Gästhaus*.

Pushing open the door he stepped into the hallway. In one corner above a doorway an illuminated sign indicated the bar. He went in. A handful of people looked round in mild curiosity, but ignoring their glances he got himself a drink and sat down at a table.

It was the first time he'd been in the bar, in fact he didn't really know why he'd chosen to come here. There was nothing distinguishing about it, just one of a thousand bars like it. On the wood-panelled walls there was the usual collection of sporting trophies and above the open-hearth fireplace on the mantelshelf a pair of stuffed mountain birds stared beadily at each other. He noticed the large painting eventually. Inside the ornate gilt framing, the artist had conceived a highly romanticised 'tourist's picture' of the Alps. In the foreground, standing by a mountain stream, a guide was gazing up at the sculpted white Alpine peaks with resolute blue eyes. At his feet a St Bernard looked up at him with an expression of sad loyalty. It was all there, the Tyrolean hat, the heavy hemp rope, the cumbersome ice-axe and of course the long-stemmed pipe sticking out from the guide's mouth.

He looked at it with distaste. Tourist junk. A picture of a happy peasantry secure in their mountain world. An idyll, and just about as real as a bunch of air-borne cherubs circling round the crowned head of the Saviour.

He drank his beer, feeling his edginess mount. To-morrow Brian would be here and he still hadn't been able to think of a way out of his dilemma.

If only he could regain something of his old confidence, like this afternoon. He'd been all right then except for that one bad moment. But that was the trouble, he couldn't afford bad moments. It would be unfair to Dillon. If you couldn't keep your head climbing, it was asking for trouble.

He was just about to get up and get another drink when he heard a shout and turned to see a bulky figure in a blue anorak filling up the doorway.

'Hi here, Bob!' Dillon's face was split in a wide grin.

Wishart's jaw dropped. 'Brian? What . . .?'

Dillon came up to him. 'I know, you didn't expect me till to-morrow. And you know something, I didn't expect to see *you* here. I just got off the train this minute and was going to have a beer before heading up to the camp site. Well, say something, don't look so surprised.'

'But . . . I mean, what happened?'

'The weather. That's what happened. From the moment we arrived it pissed down. You know I'm sorry I didn't team up with you that night we met in Besançon. If I hadn't promised to go to the Chamonix with Johnny Cornforth I'd have come along there and then. Anyway, I'm here now and that's what counts, so how about getting me up a jar instead of standing there looking as if you'd seen a ghost.'

'Sure . . . sure, Brian. I wasn't expecting you so soon, that's all. You took me by surprise. What is it you're having?'

'Oh, just a pint or whatever it is of their local wallop.'

16

Dillon grinned again impulsively. 'How're you doing, anyway? It's good to see you, mate. Okay, okay, you get the beer up first and you can tell me all about it.'

Wishart got two beers and they sat down at a table.

Dillon took a swig and let out a long sigh. 'Whatever else they might be good at they bloody well can't make beer. So how's the weather been here? It was bloody awful down in Chamonix. All we did was sit around all day and get stoned out of our heads. After that lot I'm just raring to go. It's my first time here, you know. S'funny, and yet I've always wanted to have a look at the Eiger. In fact last year Vic Dinsdale and I were going to have a bash at it, but he went off to Canada and I couldn't get anyone else in time.'

'Listen, Brian . . .' Wishart began guardedly.

'Yeh?'

'I thought, I mean, you've been travelling. I thought we might just have a bit of a walk to-morrow. We could go up to the Jungfrau and maybe have a walk over the tops.'

Dillon put his glass down. 'You must be joking, Bob. What do you mean, a walk? Look, I've been sitting on my backside swilling beer for the last few days. And that's another thing, remember I don't have very long here, I'll have to be heading back the weekend.'

Wishart rubbed his forehead. 'I just thought . . .'

'Don't worry about me, Bob. I'll be all right to-morrow. Drink up, mate, and I'll buy you a beer.' Dillon finished off his own glass and went over to the bar counter. He came back with two beers. 'Well, cheers my old son . . .' He held up his glass. 'Here's to the Eiger.'

CHAPTER III

Wishart sat down on a rock to wait for Dillon who was coming up behind him. Down below in the valley of Grindelwald he could hear the distant sound of a train. From where he sat the train wasn't visible, but the long winding track flashed in the rays of the sun.

It was early in the morning and still chilly. He got up and stamped his feet, taking in deep breaths of the pure mountain air, trying to fight off the nervous feeling that seemed to spread outwards from the region of his solar plexus.

It was too late to say anything now. He'd had his chance last night to tell Dillon and he hadn't. He had to go through with it, but he despised himself for his weakness.

He looked up at the sky. At least it was going to be a good day, it was clear up top and only the faint wisps of snow spuming off the cornices indicated the presence of the wind higher up.

Dillon was still a long way below, his blue anorak showing up brightly against the grass-covered lower slopes. Wishart sat down again trying to control his nervousness. He glanced back and upwards. Like the spiny, serrated back of a primordial beast the North-East ridge of the Eiger rose at a sharp angle to end in the snow-capped peak 6,000 feet above. Directly under the peak the great expanse of the North Wall plunged as steeply as the sides of a steeple.

He lit a cigarette and almost immediately flung it away again. The taste of nicotine and beer still lingered in his mouth from the previous evening, and his head throbbed slightly. Feeling the cold, he thrust his hands in his pockets.

Dillon was getting nearer, forcing his fourteen stone up the hill like a steam engine. He stopped when he caught sight of Wishart, then with a wave of his arms started up again. In a few more minutes he'd drawn level.

'Jesus,' he sank down on the rock beside Wishart. 'It's some haul that. Whew!'

'Take a breather. You'll be all right when you get your wind,' Wishart said.

'I don't know how you can do it, mate,' Dillon said, still struggling to get his breath back. 'Don't you ever get tired?'

'Just take it easy. We've got all day in front of us. Have a blow.'

'Bugger that,' Dillon rose to his feet. 'Let's get going.'

Wishart picked up the rope and straightened up. 'It'll be easier when we get on the rock. We haven't far now to go to the ridge.'

Dillon gave a grunt and nodded.

Once started, Wishart soon drew ahead again. Heading upwards towards the ridge he had to stop constantly to allow Dillon to catch up.

Eventually the ground began to get steeper and he shortened the length of his stride to meet the incline. They were nearing the rock now. In front of them the slope was strewn with huge boulders, detritus from the steep slabs above. They threaded their way between the boulders and soon the shadow cast by the ridge cut them off from the sun.

'It's got a bit bloody cold hasn't it?' Dillon's voice echoed off the rock.

'It'll get colder, ' Wishart said, as he weaved his way through the boulder field. 'There's a bit of wind coming up.' Even as he spoke a puff of cold air swirled round the foot of the mountain causing him to shiver. At last they came to a broad patch of snow. It was covered with a thin windcrust but was soft underneath. He plunged into it feeling the familiar chill as he sank up to his knees. Ploughing through the patch he bore left and within a few minutes stood at the first rocky buttress that supported the foot of the ridge. He unslung the full-weight nylon from his shoulder and heard it thump down on the wet grass.

Dillon came up a few minutes later, his features red with exertion.

"Whew! Thank Christ for that. I never thought I'd make it. Must be the bloody beer. I just don't know how you do it, honest I don't.' Twisting his arms behind him Dillon unshipped his ice-axe, plunged the point into the chill earth and seated himself on the blade.

Wishart sat down on the coiled nylon. 'Better have a breather before we get going,' he said.

'Yeh. It was a bit of a slog, that.' Dillon bent down to massage his calf muscles, cocking his head round to grin at Wishart. 'You'll have to let me in on the secret of how you keep fit. Mebbe I should drink whisky and lay off the beer.'

Wishart made no reply. How ironic it was that Dillon envied him his fitness. If only he knew the state of his mind.

19

But he couldn't afford to let himself become introspective or he would seize up like a machine that had run out of oil. He got to his feet. 'Okay, Brian,' he said. 'We won't rope up yet. We can travel Alpine style for a bit.'

'Suits me,' said Dillon tugging his ice-axe out and replacing it in his pack. 'Let's go.'

Wishart led off. The rock was broken and afforded easy climbing even though it was quite steep. They'd climbed a few hundred feet before he decided it would be better to rope up.

'We'll rope up here.'

Dillon nodded. His movements had become less laboured since they'd started on the ridge. He grabbed the end of the nylon which Wishart passed to him and tied on. 'That's me,' he said. Wishart passed him the loose coils and tied on himself.

'We'll lead through, if you want?'

'Okay. Off you go. I'll take the next pitch.'

Dillon slipped a loop of free rope round the small of his back and backed up against the rock. 'I'm ready when you are.'

Wishart began to climb, the rope lengthening between them as he gained height. He found a suitable stance and brought Dillon up. Dillon took over on the next pitch. The rock had steepened, but here and there it had formed into stratified bands creating a series of shelves. A few hundred feet up they stepped up on to a wide grassy platform. Wishart kicked some of the loose snow away, looking upwards at the curving ridge critically.

'All right, Bob?'

'I think we've come a bit too far to the right.'

Dillon followed his gaze. 'Think so?'

'Mmm. Looks a bit loose to me. Try and keep to your left. If you meet anything you don't like, come back down again and we'll work our way farther round.'

'Okay, Bob.' Dillon hoisted himself up and a few minutes later he'd vanished as he followed the curve of the pitch.

Wishart waited in silence, a frown of concern on his features as he heard Dillon's boots scraping for holds. He didn't like it. He ducked quickly as a small pile of stones shot past his head. He heard Dillon shout, and immediately tensed to check a fall.

'Watch it, up here. It's a bit dicey.' Dillon's voice sounded distant.

Wishart swore softly to himself. 'Keep to your left,' he

20

shouted. 'If it doesn't get better, come down.' A boulder, the size of a football, sliced through the air with an angry whine. He flattened himself against the rock. Bloody fool. What the hell was he doing climbing on that stuff. He was about to shout again when he heard Dillon's voice, and felt a tug on the rope round his waist. The voice was faint.

'Come on up. I've got a good belay.'

Good belay? He started to climb. He hadn't got far when he found himself on loose rock. It was like climbing over the tiles of a derelict building; every hold threatened to come away in his hand. He'd always hated this kind of climbing and moved with extreme caution.

'That was a bit shitty, wasn't it?' Dillon was grinning as he took in the slack of the nylon. He looked as if he were enjoying himself.

Wishart joined him on the ledge. 'I told you to keep over to the left. That bloody stuff's dangerous.'

The grin cleared from Dillon's face. 'I didn't think it was all that bad, Bob. I mean . . .'

'Okay, okay,' said Wishart snappishly. 'Let's get on with it.' He cast about him. 'Look, I'm going to see if I can find a way out of this. Keep your eye on the rope, will you.'

Dillon nodded silently, paying out the nylon as Wishart traversed to his left. But a few minutes later he was back.

'No go. We'll just have to carry on up.'

The next pitch was even worse. It seemed to Wishart that the whole structure was about to collapse and hurl them both to the bottom. Every slab and every block seemed to quiver independently of the main mass, held together only by adhesion. Nervously and indecisively he found himself slowing up when he should have been moving quickly never allowing his full weight to rest on any one hold longer than necessary. But a paralysis had gripped his limbs. Nerves jumping and his forehead damp with sweat he reached a snow-covered terrace. He stretched his arm up, thrusting with his feet. He felt something go underneath as he mantelshelfed on to the platform.

'Gardyloo!' He let out a yell.

Seconds later there came a dull heavy thump as the dislodged boulder landed on the slopes below. He held his breath, but seconds later he heard a reassuring cry from Dillon. He got to his feet shakily. Christ, that could have smashed Dillon's skull in. He looked round for a belay, but found nothing that would do. Biting his lip he made a closer inspection of his stance. Everywhere the rock seemed as if it would

21

break off at the slightest touch. He began to curse in a low monotone. If he'd had any sense he wouldn't have been here. Why hadn't he just told Dillon that he wasn't feeling well and got out of it that way? Dillon would have been disappointed, but at least it would have been the truth. And the truth was that in his present state he should never have allowed himself to climb. He bit his lip again. There was no point in going on about it. The first thing to do was to get out of here and reach something sound.

He looked about him again. This time he noticed a small crack high up on the slab that formed the back of the plat-form. He put his weight on the slab. It moved fractionally. But he had no choice. It would have to do.

Searching in his anorak pocket he found a wedge block. He jammed it in the crack, slipping a sling loop round the wedge and hooking himself on to the snap-link. He gave the sling a tug. Again the rock moved but the wedge was solid in the crack.

Secured to the block he squatted down on his heels so that if Dillon came off the force of the fall would be transmitted in a direction least likely to disturb the block. Settling into his position he had another look at the wedge and called out to Dillon.

He felt the rope twitch in his hands and began to take the slack in. Conscious of their insecurity he offered up a silent prayer. The block, if it ever came free of its anchorage, would crush them both as easily as flies. Though the air was cool he found himself sweating freely, the nylon running oilily through his damp palms. Soon he heard the sound of Dillon's heavy breathing and the scuffling noise of his boots on the rock. From below Dillon appeared to be sending down a hail of stones. Wishart tensed to take the shock of Dillon's fourteen stone. But then Dillon's head appeared. He pulled himself up on the platform.

'Bloody great thing that was,' he said, getting his breath back. 'Just missed my head, it did.' He leaned against the rock and took a step back, his eyes widening. 'Jesus Christ,' he said, 'the bloody thing's loose. Is that what you were belaying me on?' He touched it again gingerly.

'The whole place is falling apart. I . . .' Wishart stopped. There didn't seem to be any point in saying I told you so. Instead he said: 'If you're ready, let's get cracking. I'll be glad to get out of this place.'

The phlegmatic Dillon looked impressed. He edged his way

round the block, testing it carefully. 'Well, if this bloody lot comes loose at least we'll have our own headstone.' He shot Wishart a grin and stepped up on to the block. Wishart felt a tremor run through it. He half closed his eyes and paid the rope out as Dillon began to gain height.

A few hundred feet farther they came to firmer rock. Wishart halted. He could now see the route clearly. It was as he suspected, they'd come too far right. The problem now was to get back on to the route. A traverse was impossible and in front of them was a steep wall. Craning backwards he could just see the top of the wall. It was steep all right, but it looked sound, and from the top a long finger of snow ran towards the ridge. There was no alternative. It had to be the wall.

'That's it, Bob. From the top we'll be able to traverse along to the ridge by the look of it,' Dillon read his thoughts.

Wishart nodded without enthusiasm.

'It's a piece of cake. You'll be up it in no time.'

Wishart was fingering the scar on his temple as he stared upwards. 'I'm not so sure. It looks pretty tricky there, at the top.'

Dillon was also looking. 'Aaagh. It's nothing. Bash a couple of pitons in on the way up. It'll be a walk-over.'

Wishart still hesitated.

'Would you like me to lead it?' suggested Dillon, a little surprised by Wishart's hesitation.

'What's that?'

'I said, would you like me to take the lead?'

Wishart's brows came down and his lips tightened. 'It's my lead, isn't it?'

'I know. I was only suggesting . . .'

'We'd better get going,' Wishart cut in sourly. 'Give me a belay, will you?' He looked up at the wall again as Dillon belayed him. He didn't like it and inwardly cursed himself again for getting himself into this mess. And he was really in it now. It was impossible to back out and suggest calling the thing off; equally it was unthinkable that he should turn the lead over to Dillon. He had to go on. With a sickening feeling in the bottom of his stomach he reached up and found a handhold on the wall. Just keep going, he told himself. You can do it. There's nothing all that difficult about this. Just keep going and don't think about falling or anything else and remember you've done a lot harder climbs before. Yes, but the trouble was could he do them now? Now stop it, he warned himself angrily. Just think about what you've got to do, and no matter what happens keep going . . .

Right from the start he knew he was in for something that was going to test him to the limit. The holds were thin and sparse, calling for widely spaced movements and delicate balance. Bitterly regretting his folly he eased himself up the near perpendicular wall unable to check the tightening of his muscles. Relax, relax, he kept telling himself, you can do it. Just breathe easily and smoothly. And don't let Dillon see there's anything wrong. Forcing himself on he found a small stance about a third of the way up. It wasn't much, only a small step cut in the smooth wall and no more than three inches deep, but it enabled him to rest for a minute. Breathing heavily he squirmed around till be was able to free a piton from the sling round his shoulders. His whole weight supported on his toes, he reached up above his head and banged a piton into the rock. He let out a sigh of relief as he slipped the rope through the gate of the snap-link he'd hooked into the eye of the piton. For a moment he was safe, but he couldn't really rest here. Already his calf muscles were beginning to ache from the effort of supporting his body.

He moved off again. He hadn't gone more than a few feet when he began to feel sick inside. With fevered intensity he unshipped another piton from his sling and banged it home. It gave him a momentary sense of security. But he had to move again soon. Once again the holds began to thin out, but he forced himself to go on, only his pride preventing him from hammering pitons in every few feet. He was getting near the top now. The angle of the wall was so steep that he couldn't see what lay ahead, but glancing down between his legs he was able to get a rough idea of how far he'd climbed. Far below he caught a glimpse of a pale featureless smudge framed against a background of bright blue as Dillon peered upwards.

It was a long way. A long way to fall.

Immediately he killed the thought, concentrating on his next move. The sparsity of holds had forced him to adopt a near spread-eagled position, and he was finding difficulty getting enough leverage on his right foot to enable him to thrust himself upwards. Fighting back thoughts of a fall, he stretched out his hand, fingers groping at the rock. He found a hold and eased himself up another few feet. His whole body was aching now from the tension in his muscles, but he was near the top. Only a few feet now, he whispered to himself. Just take it easy.

The wall seemed to have become as smooth as a piece of polished marble, but above his head he could just see a small crack running vertically. He had to reach that crack. The sweat ran from his armpits and down his chest and he could hardly breathe. His whole body felt as if it were gripped in a vice, but he had to reach the crack.

He was standing tip-toed now, his frame stretched out, his fingers inching up the wall with crab-like movements. He licked the sweat from his lips. He couldn't stretch farther. Already his feet were dangerously insecure. But just a few more inches.

His heart gave an outraged jolt as his foot slipped. Instinctively he threw everything into a mad leap for the crack. His fingers found it, dug in and held.

Working slowly, half-blinded by his own running sweat, he levered his fingers into the crack till he was able to jam his whole hand in. For one blissful moment he was able to take the weight off his protesting calves. But only for a moment. He still had to move quickly.

Scraping the wall with his feet he was able to find sufficient purchase to enable him to reach up with his other hand into the crack. He felt the rock bite into his knuckles as he heaved with all his strength to bring his feet up. Higher. Now he was able to get his whole arm in the crack. Wriggling his way up he jammed in the toe of his boot. He was safe – for the moment.

It seemed to him that he was incapable of moving another inch as he clung to the rock, like an infant monkey to its mother. He was jammed close to the rock and he could feel its cold chill against his cheek. It was impossible to see what lay above and he couldn't move his head more than a few inches to survey his position.

Now with his free hand he felt the rock above his head. His searching fingers found a fissure. It was small but it would take a piton. He would have to move up farther – but how?

Down below Dillon gazed anxiously upwards. He could sense Wishart was in trouble, and planted his feet firmly, prepared for the worst. From the very start, he'd suspected there was something wrong. Wishart's moves had been oddly nervous and clumsy. He could hardly believe it was the same man he'd climbed with before. And now Wishart seemed to be glued to the rock, unable to move. But there was nothing he could do to help. Methodically he checked his stance, calculating how much rope he'd be able to get in before the enormous weight of a body in free fall hit him. The more he got in the less distance Wishart would have to fall and the less strain there would be on the rope. It wasn't the first fall Dillon had held, but he'd never have guessed he'd find himself in that position with Bob Wishart in the lead.

Wishart took a deep breath. His heart seemed to be leaping about wildly in his rib-cage. His left leg had gone into spasm and was shaking uncontrollably. He tried to move again but a great weight seemed to imprison him to the rock. Trying to shift his weight, his left leg slipped, and he started convulsively. He ran his tongue over his lips and glanced at the nylon rope stretching away downwards into space. How far out on the rope had he run, eighty feet? A hundred feet? He had no way of telling, but he knew whatever it was it was a long way to fall.

Forcing air into his lungs he struggled to control his breathing. If only he could get his breathing right the muscles would lose their tension. He knew he was dangerously near to panic and tried not to think about falling.

Again his leg began to tremble violently.

He had to move and get that piton in before it was too late!

Biting deeply into his lip he stretched upwards. With most of the weight on his toes he slipped again.

His boot skidded out of the crack with the force of a released spring. Thrown out of balance he lost his other foothold. A searing pain hit his arm like a red-hot poker thrust into the soft flesh as it took the whole weight of his twelve stone. Pushed out by the angle of the wall and hanging by one arm only his body began to revolve slowly like a sack on the end of a rope.

Sweat burst from his forehead in great globules. He felt like crying out. For a moment the temptation to let go was almost unbearable. It would be one sure way to end his problems. All he had to do was let go and that would be the end of it all. No more worries about the future, about the past, no more waking up in the night, heart pounding and struggling for breath, no more cares, just one brief moment of pain and then . . . merciful oblivion.

'You bastard, Wishart,' he heard himself shout. 'You cowardly bastard . . . move . . . get back up there!' He wasn't aware that he was shouting and down below Dillon could only hear a confused echo of sound.

Chest rising and falling like a pair of bellows he put all his strength into his arm and heaved. His scrabbling boots found some sort of hold. One more hefty pull and he was back in the crack.

Breath coming in great aching sobs he cradled his head against the rock, utterly exhausted. For a long minute he hung on till the wild flutter of his heart eased. He tried hard to force himself to face up to his situation. Without a piton to help it was only a matter of time.

He just had to get that piton in!

The sweat ran down into his eyes causing them to smart as once again he reached. Almost immediately his leg renewed its trembling, but his fingers found the fissure in the rock above. Fumbling with the sling round his shoulder he managed to unship a piton. Next the hammer. With the piton in his free hand he found it awkward to get at the hammer. He wasted a few valuable seconds before he had the sense to seize the piton between his teeth. With his hand now free he was able to release the hammer from the pocket in his breeches. He turned his head fractionally to call out over his shoulder to Dillon.

'Brian . . .'

The piton fell from his mouth. He heard it sing through the cold clear air and then the sharp upward change of pitch as it struck the rock below.

'Look out, Brian,' he called belatedly, cursing himself for his stupidity.

A faint but reassuring sound floated back up. Then silence.

Idiot, he accused himself. The piton could have gone right through Brian's skull. He swore and turned to face the rock. He was doing everything wrong. Slipping the hammer back in his pocket he loosed another piton. He was tiring again and had to work hard to concentrate.

With the piton in his hand he reached up and inserted the point of the metal spike into the small crack in the wall. It went in far enough to hold. Good. Now the hammer. He unshipped it once more and hefted it in his hand, unable to dispel the idea that every move he made threatened his delicate balance. Breathing heavily he tested the piton again. It seemed to be all right, but would it take the blow from the hammer without shooting out? He stretched up and with his hand wriggled it back and forth in the crack to get a greater purchase. Little granules of rock fell away from the crack, getting into his eyes and half-blinding him. He shook his head, the hammer poised in his hand preparatory to making a blow, and . . . slipped.

The muscles in his shoulders cracked audibly as they took the shock of his fall. Sobbing with pain he hung from the rock, feet dangling in the air without even the strength to call out to Dillon.

It looked all over now.

He would hang on as long as he could; as long as his failing strength allowed. He could do no more than that. It wasn't fair that more should be expected of him. He'd tried his best and it hadn't been good enough. He felt as if a clock were ticking away in his head, chopping away at the few remaining seconds of his life. Lights were flashing in his head, strange formations of colour that waved and swayed like marine growths in clear water.

The world of recognisable and familiar things was fading farther and farther into a remote distance and from somewhere he could hear a voice calling. It grew stronger and stronger, and he could almost make out the words. It grew wild, shouting at him in a torrent of language. It seemed that something was expected of him. What? What was this angry, thundering voice saying? What was he supposed to do? What had he done to cause such anger, give such offence . . .?

His head cleared and the colours vanished to be replaced by a blinding white flash. His body was being stretched on a rack, each turn of the screw sending fresh waves of pain along his already tortured nerve paths. He felt like screaming out in one final burst of anguish. Somehow his remaining energy was channelled to his leg. He heard the sound of leather scraping the coarse rock with a feeling of detachment and almost smiled at the thought. He was dead but his legs were still alive. And then he was back up in the crack, his head pressed to the rock and his chest heaving violently.

It seemed to him that a long time later he came back to a state of consciousness. He was shaking all over and every cell in his body was fired with pain, but he was to be given another chance. From the bottom of his misery a truth welled up: it was his duty to stay alive!

The hammer in his hand felt enormously heavy. It was all or nothing now. If he failed there would be no further chance. He wouldn't have the strength – or will – to make another try.

Gritting his teeth together he swung the hammer.

Clang! He could have cried out with joy at the sound of metal meeting metal. The piton bit into the rock.

28

With renewed strength he swung at it again . . . and again.

He slipped the hammer back in his breeches pocket and reached up. The piton was firm. He put his weight on it. It held. He cried out with relief.

The karabiner almost slipped from his trembling fingers but he slipped the opened gate through the eye of the piton. With a final effort he hitched on his sling.

He was safe now.

It was a long time before he was able to move. At first he had an almost overpowering temptation to rope down and let Dillon take over the lead. But, though he was still trembling and felt like being sick, his stubborn pride wouldn't let him back down now.

Using the piton as a handhold he pulled himself up. He found a fresh hold for his feet. He could look up. Only a few feet to the top of the pitch. Just one more effort, but first a long and awkward stretch.

It happened so quickly he had no time to think about it.

His foot slipped again. Supported only by his arms he hadn't the strength to hang on. His body came away from the rock to drop like a stone.

A sharp tug at his waistband told him the piton had come out. Everything depended on Dillon now.

Falling backwards his body described a somersault. The white snow, the mottled grey rock, the brownish-green vegetation merged together, colours flattening out in the whirling centre.

He was sorry about Dillon, but for himself he had no regrets. All his life he'd climbed, and now it had come to this. Up till the moment his self-confidence had begun to drain away like sand in an hour glass his life had been full, and enjoyable. He'd known hardship and suffering, cold and hunger, but he'd loved the mountains with a great passion. If he'd suffered, he'd also known great joy. He'd also found a sense of peace and the deep warmth of human companionship. He'd discovered things within himself he hadn't known he possessed. In the end it was fitting that as he'd lived his life in the mountains he should die in them.

But it was too bad about Dillon . . . and Joe. He'd let them both down. He'd also let his ex-wife Penny down. He hadn't really tried to share his life with her, had never given her the chance to understand his need to climb. But she'd get over it in the same way Carole would. It might just take a little longer.

Dillon's face was a white blur as it leaped up at him before dissolving in a mist.

With a shock that knocked every breath out of his body he landed on Dillon's half-crouched form. The force of the collision knocked him momentarily senseless.

It seemed a long time later before he was able to open his eyes. By some miracle he was lying on the platform, but there was something wrong with his sight. He couldn't get his eyes to focus properly. Dazedly he got to his feet, shaking his head, conscious something was wrong. He shook his head again, trying to think. Then it hit him.

Dillon. Where was he?

He saw the rope. Dillon's sling had broken and the heavy nylon hung over the edge of the platform. With a cry he stretched himself out to peer over the edge. He could see no sign of Dillon, but the steep snow gulley below the platform was heavily ploughed up.

Springing into action he grabbed the rope, tied a loop and belayed it over a projecting rock. It would do for the moment.

He began pulling on the nylon but he hadn't taken in more than a few feet when it jammed.

He shouted down the gully but his voice seemed lost in the emptiness of space. He shouted again and tugged at the rope. Still no reply.

What could have happened to Dillon?

He kept on calling in the eerie, cold silence, feeling sick at the thought of having to climb down the gully. He got the spare nylon out of his pack and doubling it slung it round the rock as he prepared to rope down the gully. At the point where it petered out he could see the meadows far below. His legs felt shaky as he lowered himself. He'd just got his feet firmly in the snow when he thought he heard a cry.

He hesitated. He was sure he heard it again. He shouted back and this time the cry was clear. Thank God! Dillon was still alive. He bent down and pulled on the climbing rope again, and this time was able to gain a little slack. He gave it a jerk and felt an answering tug.

'Brian,' he called out, 'are you all right?'

The voice was faint. 'Okay, Bob.'

'Do you want me to come down?'

'Stay where you are. I'm okay.'

He felt a sense of intense relief. 'Right, Brian.' He stepped out of the abseil rope and back on to the platform. Sounds came from the direction of the gully, and a few minutes later

Dillon's head appeared. He eased his bulk back on to the shelf.

'That was a bit bloody close,' he said. 'Are you all right?' Wishart ran his hand over his damp forehead. 'A bit shaken, but nothing broken,' he said in a shaky voice.

Dillon sat down with a nervous laugh. 'I saw you come off . . . that was bad enough, but when you hit me I thought we were both goners. I was arse over tit before I could do anything. The rope must have caught up because the next thing I knew I was dangling in thin air. Just as well I was able to get back on to the rock.'

Wishart coiled up the spare rope. He hoped Dillon didn't notice his shaking hands.

A few minutes later Dillon rose to his feet. He brushed the loose snow from his breeches and stockings, glancing up at the pitch. 'Okay, do you want to have another go, or do I have a bash at the bugger this time?'

Wishart flicked his cigarette away. He had to tell Dillon he couldn't go on. His nerves were strained to breaking point. He'd taken enough. Exhaling deeply, he lied deliberately. 'I think I gave my leg a bit of a knock when I came off,' he said, rubbing his knee. 'It's a bit wonky.'

Dillon frowned. 'Is it bad?'

Wishart shook his head, hating himself for lying.

'It could be worse.'

'Will you be able to move?' Dillon's voice sounded genuinely anxious.

'It'll probably be okay. But I wouldn't like to chance it by going on.'

Dillon hid his disappointment. 'We'd better get back down. Mebbe you should see a doctor?'

'It's not that bad,' Wishart said.

'Sure?'

'I'll be okay.'

'Let's go, then, if you're ready. No point in hanging around.'

An hour later they'd reached the grass meadow that led down to the bottom of the valley. Once on easier ground Wishart stopped limping. It was impossible to keep up the deception.

In silence they reached the camp site and let themselves into the Dormobile. Wishart flung off his things as Dillon lit the stove.

'I'm just going to have a shower, Brian,' he said. 'Help yourself to anything you want.'

'I think I'll have a sandwich. What about you, want one?'

Dillon was lying on the bunk when he got back, drinking coffee. He rose. 'Cup of coffee?'

Wishart waved him back again. 'Stay where you are, I'll get it myself.' He poured himself a cup and sat down on the edge of the bunk alongside Dillon.

'How's the leg?' Dillon asked.

'Did you have anything to eat?' Wishart ignored the question.

'I had a sandwich, but to tell you the truth I'm still starving. I could eat a horse. And what I could do to a pint. How about it, Bob?'

'You go on ahead. I'll have a rest and join you later.'

'Oh, come on. I mean, I don't even know where to go.'

'No. You go on, Brian. It's easy to find. Just go down the main street and right opposite the car-park on your left there's a café. I'll see you in there.'

Before going, Dillon splashed some water on his face and ran a comb through his thick black hair. 'Okay, Bob. But don't be long, will you?'

When he'd gone, Wishart lay down on the bunk, his nerves jangling. Much as he liked Dillon he just wanted to be left alone. Drawing the curtain over the window he lay flat on his back staring at the roof of the Dormobile.

When was it going to end? That afternoon he'd nearly killed Dillon and all because he refused to face up to the fact that he was no longer able to climb as he had in the past. His life was a lie and he was making others suffer for it. Recently he'd even begun to take it out on Carole. It was impossible to go on like this.

Dillon found the *Bierstube*. Feeling uncomfortable on his own he sat down and ordered a meal, puzzling over the behaviour of Wishart. He found it difficult to believe in retrospect that Wishart had really hurt his leg. Why then had he refused to go on with the climb? And that was another thing. Just look at the way he'd been climbing. It was difficult to believe it was the same Bob Wishart he'd known in the past.

How long was it since he'd last seen him? A couple of years? No, nearer three. He remembered because at the time Wishart had been in company with Joe Baillie up in North Wales and they'd been talking about the Eiger then. What had happened since then? Wishart was behaving as if he were hiding something, and further it was obvious he was as nervous as a kitten.

32

Dillon shook his head. He felt it was a betrayal to think in this way about his old friend, but there was no point in trying to ignore the facts. Wishart had changed.

He finished off his meal. Maybe it had something to do with Wishart's divorce. That must have upset him. Or was he still feeling lousy about what had happened to Joe?

He waited another ten minutes and, as Wishart didn't show up, made his way back to the camp site.

CHAPTER IV

Thick grey clouds hung low over the valley. A soft rain had been falling since early morning, seeping into the meadowlands, filling the tributaries of the mountain streams and clinging to the foliage of the trees. From the earth a heavy pungent aroma rose and the farm animals made swishing sounds as they waded through the long damp grass. Since dawn birds had kept up a steady chatter reminding Wishart of a gathering of village folk on market day.

The birds had woken him after a fitful night's sleep, and he'd got up and had a shower. Later, around eight o'clock, he gave Dillon a shout.

Dillon sat up yawning, rubbing his fingers through his hair. 'Wharsatime?' he asked reaching out to take the cup of coffee which Wishart handed him.

'Near eight.'

Dillon yawned again. 'Eight? What's the weather like?'

'It's been raining all morning,' Wishart answered.

Dillon blinked and screwed his features up. 'All morning? How long have you been up?'

'An hour or so. What would you like for breakfast.'

'Huh? Oh, breakfast. What are you having?'

'Boiled eggs and toast.'

'Great. How're you fixed for eggs? I feel a bit peckish.'

'You can have three if you want.'

Dillon grinned happily and putting his cup down wriggled out of his sleeping bag. 'I'll give you a hand,' he offered.

'No, you go and get washed.' Wishart lit the stove and filled a pan with water. 'I'll have it ready by the time you're back.'

The table was laid and the folding bunk and sleeping bags stowed when Dillon returned.

'Mmm . . . smells good.'

'Sit down, the eggs will be ready in a minute,' Wishart said, opening the door of the oven and putting a plateful of buttered toast on the table. Dillon poured out the tea. They had breakfast.

Dillon pushed his plate away and smacked his lips. 'I enjoyed that.'

'There's more if you want?'

34

Dillon shook his tousled head. 'No, that's fine,' he hesitated, 'Well, mebbe another couple of slices of toast.'

He finished off another three slices of toast before jerking his head in the direction of the door. 'Looks as if it might be on for the day, what do you think?'

Wishart leaned back and lit a cigarette. He'd been thinking about what to do since he'd risen. Climbing was out, and as Dillon was due back in a couple of days they might as well leave now. The rain had been a blessing: the excuse he needed.

He blew out a puff of smoke. 'Doesn't look too good. The wind's from the west too.'

'It might last then?'

'Looks like being on for a couple of days, I would say.'

Dillon was silent for a few minutes. 'I've to be back Wednesday.' He pulled a glum expression. 'Might just as well head for home if it's going to be like this. What are you going to do?'

'I've been thinking about it myself.'

Dillon sat up. 'You mean you're thinking about going back?'

'Well,' Wishart shrugged, 'it's not much fun in this. I've a lot of work to catch up on anyway.'

'Hey, that's great. I'll be able to get a lift all the way back. Let's get going, will we?' He got to his feet. Once a decision was reached Dillon didn't hang about. Wishart envied him. It was a quality he himself no longer possessed.

'Right, we'll have a clean up and get cracking.'

Half an hour later they pulled out of the camp site.

Wishart stopped the Dormobile at the Post Office and wired Carole in London.

As he got back in the driving seat Dillon noticed the tired lines and dark shadows round Wishart's eyes. 'Would you like me to drive?' he offered.

Wishart shook his head. 'Later on mebbe.'

Reaching the sharp bend leading out of the village he had to swing the wheel over sharply. A chocolate-coloured 300 SL had entered the bend from the opposite direction, taking a big bite out of the road.

'Silly bastard!' Wishart swore, catching a glimpse of the driver through the slicing arcs of the windscreen wipers.

Dillon, who'd been flung heavily against the doorway, swung round to look in the direction of the vanishing car. 'Bloody squarehead. You'd think they owned the roads.'

Wishart said nothing, concentrating on his driving. But he couldn't help thinking, if anyone had looked less like a

35

German it had been the driver of the Mercedes. In fact the face had seemed typically English to him: upper-class English, with its air of haughtiness.

Dillon was still muttering. 'Arrogant bastards. You'd think it was *them* who won the war.'

Wishart felt he had to make some kind of protest. 'Everybody who drives a Mercedes isn't a German, you know.'

'Aaagh. Don't give me that, Bob. I know a bloody squarehead when I see one. Bloody madman . . . never even saw us.'

Wishart glanced at Dillon out of the corner of his eye, wondering what was behind the big man's reactions. 'Seems you don't like Germans,' he said.

Dillon muttered to himself under his breath.

'What was that?'

'Nothing,' Dillon growled, and fell silent. But a few minutes later he spoke again. 'They can't all be bad. Some of them must be all right. You been to Germany much?'

'Once or twice.'

'I was over last year. I don't know about you but I wouldn't go back again. One night we went into this kind of café. We were starving after driving all day. It was going like a bomb, lots of cars and everything outside. Anyway we were told we couldn't get anything to take away, we'd have to sit down. The place was packed to the door and you should have seen some of the looks we were getting. Johnny spots a couple of blokes getting up from a table and he goes over. Obviously they were just going, but when they saw we wanted the table they just stood there grinning at each other. I says to Johnny, who's going to thump them, you or me, but he grabs my arm and drags me back to the counter. After a bit of an argument we managed to get something to take away. We're on our way out again when I sees these two blokes standing by the door still grinning at each other like a pair of goons. They wouldn't get out of the way. Right, I says, and thumps one of them. When his mate's getting him to his feet Johnny and I are off at the double. A big gang of them followed us but we got off our marks. But it was like that all over. No sooner did you open the door of some boozer or café and they'd all be looking at you as if you were something the cat dragged in. I tell you they're just dying to have another go at us to get their own back for the last lot.'

Wishart shrugged. He'd met that sort of thing himself, especially in Bavaria, but he was too tired to argue. He drove on, trying to keep his attention on the road. The cloud had gradually been sinking lower and lower, thick grey stuff that shut off the light. All the way down the long valley it continued to rain heavily, adding to his depression. In a way he was glad he was returning to the UK. He'd left London badly in need of a break, and it hadn't worked out. If only he'd gone across to Austria or some other place where he could have had long walks in the hills instead of going back to Grindelwald with its disturbing memories. But it was too late now.

Leaning over he asked Dillon to hand him out his lighter from the glove compartment. Amongst a pile of old maps, fuses and spare sparking plugs Dillon eventually found it. 'When do we hope to get to Interlaken?' he asked, handing over the lighter.

'Don't tell me you're hungry again?'

'Well, I feel a bit peckish.'

'I was hoping to get as far as Neuchatel before stopping for petrol,' Wishart said squinting at the gauge.

'How far's that?'

'Have a look at the map. It's in the scuttle.'

Dillon pulled out the maps but he seemed to be having difficulty, spreading the maps out and peering at them closely.

'Forget it, Brian,' Wishart said, 'I'll stop at Interlaken if you're really hungry.'

Half an hour later they pulled into the car-park of a roadside café on the outskirts of the town. Locking up the Dormobile he followed the eager Dillon into the café. He had a coffee while the heavy-weight Dillon ordered a couple of rounds of sandwiches, finishing off with a hefty slab of cheesecake.

'That should do you till we reach Paris,' Wishart said.

Dillon gave a self-conscious grin, burying his teeth into a slice of cheesecake.

Brigadier Iain Grant, DSO, MC, after a shower, brushed his iron-grey hair into a neat side-parting. Dressing in dark grey flannel trousers and a sports jacket he went downstairs into the lounge of the hotel. After motoring across the continent with very little sleep during the journey he still managed to feel quite fresh. But the Brigadier was accustomed to going for long periods without proper sleep and in fact had conditioned himself to the state where he only required a few hours at a time.

At the age of fifty-three he was as fit and healthy as most

men half his age. But apart from certain hereditary gifts he also worked hard at maintaining his condition. Walking briskly into the carpeted lounge he rang the bell for service.

A waiter appeared. Grant was about to order coffee then he changed his mind. He felt unusually thirsty and decided to have a gin with lots of lime.

The waiter spread his hands and shook his head regretfully. Sorry, but there was no lime. Gin, of course, but no lime.

Grant frowned. 'What do you mean, no lime?' Though he had perfectly good German, he preferred to use English.

The waiter shrugged again, and tried to explain the difficulties of obtaining lime-juice in Switzerland. Apparently the Government had set such rigorous food-control standards that few manufacturers were able to meet them.

Grant listened patiently to the explanation. He made no fuss but accepted the position as a fact. 'Very well, then. Bring coffee for three, will you.'

When the waiter had gone Grant rose and walked over to the large bay window which fronted the lounge of the hotel. Outside, the thick mist and driving rain had cut down visibility to a few yards. He shook his head and walked away from the window, glancing at the clock on the wall and checking it against his wrist-watch. He noted the clock was three minutes slow and also that it had been seven minutes exactly since he'd left his room. He frowned again, wondering where his daughter and Osborne had got to. Impatiently he strode over towards the window again. Unlike the common soldier, Grant had no brief for the maxim that you should never stand when you could sit, never sit when you could lie down. He felt that since man had gone to the trouble to learn to walk on two feet then he should remain on them at all possible opportunities. It was an important factor which distinguished mankind from lesser animals. One of Grant's few disturbing thoughts was that one in which he thought he might die in his bed. He fervently hoped that when death came it would find him erect and on his two feet – like a man!

Where in heaven's name were Joanna and Osborne? Young people, they had so little sense of time. They didn't realise it was an expendable commodity like everything else. Something that had to be measured out like food or water rations. What a day to arrive. He peered through the window at the deserted main street, watching the rain bounce heavily off the bodywork of the Mercedes. He was half tempted to go and put the car under cover, but remembered he'd returned the keys to

Osborne. He cursed the weather again. They had only a few days before he had to get back and he wanted to make sure Osborne would have an idea what they would be up against. Suddenly he remembered he'd seen a barometer in the hall.

He'd just reached the door when it swung open. He stopped, half expecting the waiter with the coffee, but it was a girl who opened the door. She was quite a striking looking girl, with a high forehead, fair hair and a pair of extraordinarily calm grey eyes. She was wearing a pair of olive green corduroy slacks and a black roll-neck jumper.

'Ah, there you are, Joanna. Have you seen anything of Osborne? I've been waiting here wondering what had happened to you.'

Grant's daughter shook her head and smiled tolerantly. She was accustomed to her father and his attitude towards time. Since childhood she'd been taught that time was something wrapped in little usable bundles and units: so many minutes to wash, to brush her teeth, to have a bath, to practise her music lessons. As a result it had bred in her a refusal to be ruled by the mechanical dictates of the clock, and if she was punctual in her habits it was only out of a real consideration for others. But it wasn't only with regard to time that Joanna Grant refused to be ruled. She had an exceptionally strong sense of independence which showed itself in a number of ways.

'Where are you going?' she asked her father.

'I've ordered coffee. It'll be here soon,' Grant replied, looking at his watch. 'I'm off to have a look at the weather; there's a barometer in the hall.'

Joanna went into the lounge and sat down. The door opened and a waiter came in with a tray. He looked about him hesitantly before coming over to her table.

She smiled reassuringly and motioned with her hands as she explained her father had ordered coffee.

The waiter put the coffee things down on the table. Her voice and appearance had caused a little galvanic thrill of pleasure to shoot through his nervous system. It was an unusual voice, having a definite sexual quality about it without being in any way coquettish. A strong voice and yet very feminine. He returned her smile.

She had just poured coffee for herself when Osborne arrived. With a long lazy stride he crossed the floor of the lounge – a tall man in his early thirties, dressed in a houndstooth checked suit and wearing suède boots. His auburn-coloured hair was brushed straight back from his forehead to curl over his collar. He was the sort of man seen at point-to-point meetings carrying a shooting stick and wearing a rubberised coat.

'Ah, coffee. Just what I could do with. I must say I'm a bit whacked after that journey. Where's your father?'

'He's gone to have a look at the barometer in the hall,' said Joanna, pouring Osborne a coffee. She'd only met him recently when he'd arrived at her flat in London with her father. From the moment she saw him she hadn't liked him. She knew it was a fault of hers to make instant and instinctive judgments and sometimes she'd had cause to regret them, but she felt absolutely sure about Osborne. He seemed to represent all the things she hated in her own class with his stylised manners and inborn arrogance.

She'd been surprised when Osborne had turned up with her father, expecting instead to greet one of his old climbing friends.

Osborne sipped his coffee and offered her a cigarette.

'No thank you,' she said. 'I try not to smoke before lunch.'

He lit one for himself. 'Golden rule, eh?' Osborne squirmed round in his chair to look out of the window. 'Must say the weather looks pretty foul. It's not going to be much fun for you if this keeps up.'

'Oh, I'll be all right. I've brought plenty to read with me,' she said, but he'd been right. She had been hoping to be able to have some long walks in the countryside. As Osborne had said, it wasn't going to be much fun if the weather didn't improve. At first, when her father had phoned her from Scotland to say he was going to Switzerland for a few days and would she like to come along, she had said no, knowing her father would spend most of his time climbing. But then she'd changed her mind. She hadn't seen her father for some time and London hadn't seemed to have recovered from a long asthmatic winter. The more she thought about it the more the idea of returning to Switzerland even for a few days appealed to her. She hadn't been there since she was a child, that had been nearly twelve years before and her mother had been alive then.

It was something she remembered clearly. It was the last holiday they'd had together before her mother had died of cancer. Her father, who was still in the Army, hadn't married again. Shortly after the death of her mother something had happened to her father, and when he'd been asked to join an Army expedition to the Himalayas it seemed to Joanna he'd vanished from her life. From that time onwards he would be off for long periods on some expedition or other. It was as if he was desperately trying to fill the gap in his life caused by the death of her mother.

While her father was chasing about the world she got on with her own life and quietly took an Arts degree at University. Just a straight degree; no honours. It was all she wanted. University life had little appeal for her. It seemed to her a narrow and confined world divided into two camps: one of precocious adolescents continually in search of new excitements, and the other camp a group of bespectacled monastics with no sense of life and adventure.

She was glad when she finally left Edinburgh and got herself a job with a publisher in London, though she'd often suspected the real reason she'd got the job was because of her father's fame and reputation.

She fell in love with the world of books and soon discovered she had a real talent for editing. At first she missed Scotland very much but she was sensible enough to realise she couldn't have her cake and eat it. But there were days, particularly towards the changing of the seasons, when she was stricken with longing to see her native hills again and the sight and feel of snow in winter could still make her ache with nostalgia.

Her head turned as the lounge door swung open again.

Her father strode over towards the table. 'I've just been having a look at the glass. It seems to be rising.' He sat down and she poured him a cup of coffee. 'I don't suppose we'll be able to get a look at much to-day, but I suggest we have a try anyway. What do you say?' he said, addressing Osborne.

'Well, I suppose it will be a jolly sight better than sitting around,' Osborne agreed.

'How about you, Joanna? What are you going to do? You could come along for the train ride if you feel like it.'

'No-o. If you don't mind I'll stay here, Father. You go on.'

'Are you sure?'

'Yes. I'll be all right. I can write a few letters and read.'

'Well, if you're sure.' Grant turned to Osborne. 'Right. See you in the hall in ten minutes. I wouldn't take much but bring your ice-axe.' He finished his coffee. 'If we're not back by seven, Jo, don't bother to wait ... you don't mind dining alone do you?'

She laughed. 'Of course not. Now off you go and don't worry about me. I'll be perfectly all right.'

Grant paused to give his daughter a concerned look, and

with a muttered: 'See you in ten minutes' to Osborne, went off.

Osborne rose to his feet. 'Mustn't keep your father waiting,' he said. He hung about for another few seconds as if expecting Joanna to say something. When she was silent he said: 'Well, must go . . . hope to see you at dinner this evening.'

Joanna moved over to the window when both men had gone. Her forehead was creased in a little frown. She was worried about her father. He looked well and appeared to have regained all his usual strength and vitality since returning from a trip to the Andes. But she knew instinctively it had taken a lot out of him. He wasn't a young man, and top-class mountaineering was a young man's sport. But he was so determined. She was frightened he might take too much out of himself one of these days. His very strength might prove to be his weakness.

In a few minutes her father and Osborne had appeared in the driveway. They were both dressed for the hills and it was typical of her father that he should be carrying the rucksack. He always had to be proving something or other. Both men turned round and waved. Next moment they were off down the driveway. She watched till they'd vanished from sight and made her way to her room upstairs.

There was a train standing in the station. Grant and Osborne climbed aboard and found they had the carriage to themselves. The rain had discouraged the tourists. Grant sat down, gazing out of the window as if he hoped to change the pattern of weather by force of will.

'It seems to have eased off,' Osborne remarked stretching his legs out.

'Hmm. We'll see,' Grant replied. 'It's pretty thick.'

A smooth tremor ran through the carriage. A few moments later a whistle sounded and the train slid away from the terminal, picking up speed as it dipped down into the sloping floor of the valley before beginning its long journey up the mountain.

When it stopped at Alpiglen breaks had begun to appear in the overhang of cloud. The clouds seemed to tumble over themselves as a strong wind pushed them to the north.

Grant looked out of the window. The station buildings hid his view and he leaned back in his seat. He couldn't do anything about the weather so there was no point in worrying about it. The only things worth worrying about were those that could be influenced by action. Thinking about problems in general, his daughter Joanna came to mind. It was a pity her

mother had died so young. He could see now that she had been
left too much on her own. But why in heaven's name hadn't
she married someone? She'd be twenty-five years of age soon,
and in a few more years thirty. He frowned. There were some
things about his daughter difficult to understand. Well, next
year, when this was behind him, he'd take it more easy.
There had to be an end sometime, and he'd still have his fishing and shooting, and he'd still be able to climb at home in
Scotland. He'd make sure he spent more time with Joanna
then. But first . . .

The train came to a halt at Kleine Scheidegg. They got out.

Grant stood for a moment on the platform looking up at
the sky, his head thrown back and his nostrils spread as if
sniffing the weather. He turned to Osborne. 'Let's have a spot
of lunch and see what happens then.'

At the entrance to the railway hotel he paused again to
look upwards. 'I hope to heaven it does clear. We have only
a few days and I'd like to get as much done as possible. I
shan't manage to get back now till late in the year, and
after that there won't be much time left. I can't tell you how
important it is that you should get the shape and feel of the
whole thing . . . but remember, not a word to Joanna. I'll tell
her about it nearer the time. As far as she is concerned we're
only here for a few days' sport.'

They had lunch in the hotel. After coffee the Brigadier went
out to have another look at the weather. The thick heavy cloud
was rolling away down the valley. Up top, patches of blue
sky had appeared behind light muslin wisps of cirrus. He went
back in.

'I think it's beginning to clear,' he said to Osborne. 'The
wind's changed and the glass is still rising slowly. We might
be all right yet.'

Osborne got to his feet. 'Shall we go?'

'Yes. We'll make for the ridge. If the weather clears we
should get a good view of the territory. To-morrow we can
have a look from the other side. After that we can do the
top and see what the problems are there. We'll be able to
get the train, so we'll have time that way. Of course what
you have to bear in mind is that the whole thing's much
different in winter.'

Osborne laughed. 'I can well imagine.'

Leaving the hotel they followed the curve of the path that
ran alongside the railway track.

Half an hour later Grant, who was in the lead, stopped.

The heavy rain cloud had magically parted to show a large triangular area of clear blue sky. Before them, in the sudden flood of sunlight, rock gleaming wetly and ice-fields sparkling, lay the whole of the North Wall.

Grant stabbed with the point of his ice-axe. 'Well, there you are. What do you think of it?'

Osborne let out a low whistle, his eyes narrowing in the sudden burst of strong light. 'Looks pretty fearful, I must say!'

Grant laughed shortly. 'Fearful? Wait till you see it in winter.'

Fresh trailing curtains of rain, a mile high, swept down the mountainside. In a moment the North Face was hidden from view. Heavy drops of rain fell and a chilling wind swept along the base of the wall to gust over the ridge, sending the temperature down by degrees.

The two men, bending forward to counteract the force of the wind, shivered and began making their way slowly up the ridge.

CHAPTER V

At Neuchatel they had a meal. Dillon ordered sandwiches, and had the vacuum flasks filled with coffee. After that they drove round to a garage and filled up with petrol, checking the oil and tyre pressures.

Wishart was determined to get as far on the road as he could that night, but by the time they crossed the border and reached Mulhouse he felt all in. He wondered if it was the delayed shock effect of his fall.

In the darkened cab, lit only by the glow of the instrument panel, Dillon seemed wide awake as he munched a sandwich.

'Feeling a bit tired?' he asked, his mouth half full.

Wishart shook his head. He felt all in, but he knew the moment his mind was released from the need to concentrate on driving it would screw itself up into little knots. But by the time they had gone some forty miles beyond Dijon and on the road to Paris he couldn't keep his eyes open. The lights of the oncoming traffic seemed to hypnotise him; he knew he was driving badly.

He pulled into a lay-by and got out of the cab feeling his legs buckle under him. He felt as if he was going to be sick.

Dillon wound down the window and leaned out. 'Are you all right, Bob?'

Wishart waved a hand. 'It's all this driving in the dark. I'll be okay in a minute.'

Dillon got out. 'Let me take over. You need a spell.'

Wishart shook his head. 'I was thinking we might stop here for the night.'

'Suits me. But I'll take over if you want.'

Wishart went round to the side of the Dormobile and unlocked the door. He handed the keys to Dillon. 'Lock up front will you? I'll get the sleeping bags out. Don't forget to switch off the lights.'

'Okay, you turn in. I'll be back in a minute. I'm just going for a slash.'

Wishart crept wearily into the living quarters of the Dormobile and let the bunk down. He was undressed in seconds and into his sleeping bag. He heard Dillon come in and a few seconds later the light went out and the bunk creaked as

45

Dillon lay down.

For a long time he lay awake before falling off into a broken sleep. Towards dawn he was awakened by the sounds of the *camions* thundering past, the Dormobile shaking violently in their slipstream.

Climbing over the sleeping form of Dillon he dressed quietly. He filled the small wash-hand bowl and splashed water on his face. The icy water helped to shake off the drugged feeling that seemed to paralyse his limbs. He dried his face, deciding to shave later, and lit the stove. Dillon was still sound asleep and snoring softly. He waited till the coffee was ready before he woke him.

'Here you are . . . drink it while it's hot.'

'Uhmmm . . . whatsat?' Dillon grunted, flopped around for a bit, and raised himself on an elbow. He blinked and knuckled his eyes. 'Oh, coffee . . . thanks.' He reached out and the cup seemed to disappear in his large fist. 'What . . . what's the time?'

'It's early yet. Half past six. I thought we might get on the road early. Have breakfast later on.'

Dillon had sat up. 'Half past six? Mmm.' He took a mouthful of coffee, and smacked his lips. 'Okay, I'll be with you in a minute.'

Outside, low layers of cloud hung over the land, and the earth had a damp musty smell; the air was heavy with moisture. It was cold.

Wishart started the engine and let it warm up for a few minutes. Dillon had cleared away everything in the back.

'Do you want me to drive?' he asked.

'Okay,' Wishart slid along the bench seat. 'I'll give you a break later.'

They had breakfast on the road, and by late afternoon were approaching Paris.

Wishart was driving again. Dillon laughed.

'What's the joke?'

Dillon shook his head chuckling to himself. 'Oh, nothing. I was just thinking.'

'Come on.'

'You remember Willie Barr and Jock Rollo? Well, it was just us getting near Paris that reminded me about them. It seems they were coming back from Chamonix once and they had to stop outside Paris. They'd spent most of their dough and hadn't enough to pay for a camp-site . . . have you heard the story?'

46

'No, but I'm prepared to believe anything about that pair.'

'Well, as I said, they're on their way back home and they've no money. It's not far from Paris when they decide to kip down for the night, so they get off the bike. At the side of the road there's a bloody great wall all covered with barbed wire and broken glass, so thinking they'd be better off the road they get out the sleeping bags and shin up over the wall. There's a sort of park the other side of the wall and it's a good night so they decide to doss it down right there. They get into their bags and in no time are fast asleep.

'Willie's the first to get up in the morning. He gives Jock a nudge and Jock wakes up yelling blue murder and waving his arms about like a madman, shouting: "Get off. Get off, you bastards!" "What's the matter with you, Jock, have you flipped your top?" Willie asks. But Rollo just shakes his head and says he's had an awful dream. During the night he kept waking up imagining strange creatures prowling about, sniffing, growling and licking his face.

'When Willie hears this he can't believe it. He's had exactly the same dream; furry things, like beasts, padding about and sticking their snouts in his bag.

'They decide to get away from the place in a hurry, and in no time at all they're back on the bike and away at the double . . .' Dillon had another fit of laughing.

'They only got a few hundred yards up the road when they come to a big gate. Guess what's written on it?'

Wishart waited to be told, one eye on the road.

'It's a big sign saying it's the entrance to some kind of open zoo . . . they'd been sleeping out in the wolf park with a bloody great pack of wolves sniffing round them all night.' Dillon roared and slapped his thigh. 'Just imagine that . . . camping in a bloody zoo.'

Wishart couldn't help smiling. Thinking of Barr and Rollo again was enough to warm his heart. They were a pair of life's great indestructibles. A couple of rough-necks who half-worked, half-bummed their way round every known continent in search of adventure and new mountains to climb. The pair of them had even had a go at Everest, and there wasn't a climbing centre in Europe where they weren't known; especially Switzerland. They'd been run out of Zermatt by the guides for dragging tourists up the Matterhorn, but by that time they'd had enough in the kitty to keep them going for another three months in Europe.

And those wild nights with them in Glencoe. Wearing

voluminous ex-WD gas-capes – to hide the rifles – they'd hunted the deer. The long nights on the river after the salmon when they'd find themselves hunted by the bailiffs till the early hours of dawn. And what about the time when, as a protest against the rising cost of drink, they'd decided to distil their own whisky. He could smell the pungent fumes of the burning peat, the tang of the heather and the gentle murmur of the mountain burn, see the great blackened cast-iron pot and the glint of the copper coil in the sunshine and Barr telling Rollo to get it to hell out of sight before the Redcoats (Barr always referred to authority as Redcoats) saw it. In the end they'd produced a distillation which Barr described as a mixture of dirty water, sheep-dip and bird-shit, and the worst bloody drink in the northern hemisphere. But they'd all got roaring drunk on it just the same.

Great days. No fear then, only the excitement of living as the body responded to the stimulus of the charged nervous system.

They came to a sign. Ten kilometres to Paris.

'We'll be in Paris soon,' said Wishart. 'About five miles from the centre, there's a camp site. I think I know where it is but I wouldn't like to miss the turning. Get the map of Paris out, will you?'

Dillon got the map out and spread it on his knees.

'Is that the right one? If we miss the turning we'll finish up in the Champs Elysées.' He took his eye off the road for a second to look at the map. 'That's it.' He stabbed with his finger. 'That's where we turn off. Keep your eye open for the sign.'

Soon the traffic began to get heavier. Wishart drove on keeping his eye open for familiar landmarks. He stopped at lights. A bus pulled out from the side road. He looked at the sign on the front. It was a city bus. They must be getting near. He reminded Dillon of the importance of spotting the sign as they started up again. A mile along the road he began to feel uncomfortable. They should have been there by now. The traffic was getting heavier and they were having to stop longer at each set of lights. Wishart's nerves began to jump. At this rate they'd soon be in the heart of Paris. He stole a glance over in Dillon's direction. The big man seemed to be having trouble with the map.

'Never mind the map now,' Wishart cried, 'just keep a look-out for the signpost!'

The traffic was really heavy now. Wishart felt as if the

48

Dormobile was penned in on all sides. They must have gone too far. A few minutes later they came to a bridge. He was in the wrong lane. With a sickening feeling he realised they were caught up now. They had to go on. Over the bridge they had to turn left. Wishart gave a groan as he caught sight of the Eiffel Tower looming up in the distance.

'We've missed the bloody turning, Brian,' he cried angrily.

Dillon peered at the map. 'No, I think we're all right. We haven't come to it yet.'

Wishart mopped his forehead as he pulled up on the red at a traffic light. 'Where are you looking?' His finger jabbed at the map again. 'That's where we are. We're miles past the turning.'

There was a blare of horns as the lights changed to green.

He banged the Dormobile in gear and let the clutch out fiercely in exasperation. They shot forward and the map slid out of Dillon's hands.

'We've got to get out of this. Find me a turning to the right, so's we can get off the main road.'

Dillon still didn't seem convinced.

Wishart felt his temper rise. 'Look!' he cried, pointing ahead at the Eiffel Tower. 'What do you think that is — the British Museum?'

A little flush of colour spread over Dillon's features. 'I don't know how we could have missed it. It was . . .'

'Never mind that, now. Just find a route out of here. Any right turn will do near enough.' He looked anxiously out of the side window. He was in the middle lane. How the hell was he going to get back to the outside? He could see nothing but vehicles on all sides. They were trapped.

'Now!' Dillon cried excitedly as they stopped at lights again. 'Turn right here. Quick.' He waved the map urging Wishart to turn.

Wishart gasped. 'How do you expect me to turn here? I'm in the wrong lane.'

Both of them were getting excited.

'It's your last chance for nearly a mile,' Dillon cried. 'Now, before we miss it!'

Wishart's nerves were in such a bad state that he was hardly conscious of what he was doing as he swung the wheel over, crossing three lanes of traffic as they moved off on the green.

Instantly the air was filled with the blare of horns, and from somewhere came the shrill sound of a gendarme's whistle. The car on the inside lane just scraped his rear bumper as he swung across its path. He felt like shutting his eyes and letting the Dormobile drive itself, as he put his foot to the boards and roared up the side-street feeling it buck as it hit the cobbles.

'Right again,' shouted Dillon in his ear above the roar of the engine. 'Keep going right!'

He no longer cared where he went as long as he got out of this nerve-shattering environment. Again he swung the wheel over. Immediately he found himself in a narrow street lined with stalls. Crawling through the market place at a few miles an hour, the shoppers screamed at them, shook their fists and pounded the sides of the Dormobile with rage. It was like a nightmare.

They got to the end of the street and he turned left, deaf to Dillon's shouted instructions. They seemed to thread their way through a labyrinth of back streets for miles before he found a main road again. But it led to Versailles and he had to make another wide detour before finding the road they had originally entered Paris by. He followed it for a mile going as slowly as he dared in the traffic and eventually they picked up the sign they had been looking for. He turned off down towards the river.

The site was pretty crowded but they booked in and found a quiet space for the Dormobile.

Wishart cut the engine and slumped across the wheel. He felt absolutely sold.

Dillon wisely said nothing, but reaching over fished the keys out from the ignition switch and went out and opened up the side door, got his toilet gear and headed for the wash-room. When he came back Wishart had got out of the cab and was lying on the bunk at the back.

'Look, I'm sorry about that cock-up . . .' Dillon began.

Wishart sat up slowly. 'Forget it. Everyone gets lost in Paris.' He massaged his forehead. 'That bloody traffic. My head's still splitting.' Reaching up behind him into the locker he brought out the whisky. 'Want a drink?'

Dillon shook his head. 'I'm more in need of something to eat.'

Wishart poured himself a stiff whisky. 'There's a café just outside the gate.'

'Aren't you eating?' Dillon asked.

'Later, mebbe. I'm too tired right now.'

'Well, if you don't mind . . .'

'Sure, off you go. You'll find it just outside the gate.'

Dillon went off. He found the café without any difficulty.

He had some trouble ordering as he had no French, but he managed to make himself understood. After his meal he walked along the river bank and found a café with tables outside. He had a few drinks and made his way back, surprised to find it was getting dark. Passing the check-point on the camp site, he made his way towards the Dormobile. At first he couldn't believe his eyes. It was gone. But it was impossible. Wishart would never do a thing like that: just pull out and leave him. He searched round the vicinity of the toilets again without success. Then he saw another group of buildings down by the far end of the site.

Feeling a fresh surge of hope he almost ran across to the other side of the huge field. He recognised the Dormobile right away. With a sigh of relief he went up to it and gently squeezed open the door. Wishart was still sleeping. He called softly once or twice. Wishart turned over, appeared to murmur something and was still again.

Dillon called again but got no response.

Throwing a blanket over the sleeping form, Dillon undressed and got into his sleeping bag.

He was first up next morning. He made a pot of tea and shook Wishart. 'Wakey, wakey, Bob.'

Wishart sat up and ran his fingers through his hair.

'Here, take it,' Dillon handed him a cup of tea. 'That was some sleep you had. You must have been out for near eighteen hours.'

Wishart screwed his features up. 'Eh, what time is it?'

'It's near eight.'

'Have I . . .?'

'All the time. We just arrived here and you were away. I tried to wake you but you were dead to the world. You must be starving.'

Wishart shook his head as he sipped at his tea. 'I'll just finish this and go and have a shower and we'll be on our way. We can have breakfast once we get outside Paris, okay?'

'Suits me. But let's get cracking, eh? I could eat a horse.'

By eleven o'clock they were clear of Paris and heading for Boulogne. Wishart felt the better for his sleep and drove all the way.

Fortunately when they arrived there was a ferry already in the port. They boarded it, and, parking the Dormobile on the car deck, made their way up top. Within minutes the ferry boat cast off.

They found a seat in the lounge. The ferry, no sooner had

51

it cleared the mole, began to roll and heavy spray whipped across the observation window, obscuring the view.

'Looks like being rough,' Dillon remarked.

'I think I'll go up top,' Wishart said. 'Get some fresh air. How about you?'

'I think I'll have a pint first. I'm just dying to get some good old English beer down my gullet.'

'Okay. I'll be up top on the fore deck.'

The wind was blowing quite hard when he stepped out on deck. Not many people were up top braving the weather. Hair blowing all over the place, Wishart crossed over to the weather side and grabbed at the rail as the ferry rolled wildly. Below his feet huge waves roller-coasted the length of the ship's side, threatening to turn the high deck awash. He stood by the rail a long time watching the channel water work its way up into a dirty grey turbulence.

Dillon came up but after a few minutes said he was going below again. Wishart remained where he was, a bleak expression on his face as he gazed seawards.

A small coaster hove into view, battling her way north, seas bursting with explosive force over her decks. She passed within a few cables' length. Looking at her wild contortions he had a sudden feeling of sympathy for her crew. He'd known something of hardship himself and his heart went out to them. Within minutes the boiling water seemed to have swallowed the coaster up, and all he could see of her was her wildly gyrating masthead and an occasional glimpse of her deck-house.

Dusk was falling as they entered Dover harbour. In the fading light, the houses and buildings were barely visible, but the sea front was a string of lights, lit up like the runway of an airport.

Dillon came up on deck. They stood together in silence enjoying the sharp thrill of voyagers returning to their native land, before going back down below to the car-deck.

They were at the very back of the line. It took a long time to clear the ferry. After that they ran into a hold-up at the Customs' barrier. Some kind of flap was on; every vehicle was being systematically searched. They crept forward at a snail's pace. Wishart looked at his watch.

'We're going to be late by the time we get to London,' he said. 'When's your last train, do you know?'

'I've no idea, Bob. I think I'll be all right. They run till about midnight.'

It was an hour before they reached the barrier. A Customs officer stepped round to the driving side. Wishart wound down the window. The officer asked what dutiable goods they had in their possession. Wishart told him and the officer waved them on.

They drove out of the gates and winding their way through Dover picked up the London road. Three hours later, almost to the minute, Wishart dropped Dillon at Euston Station. He got out of the driving seat and opened the side door of the Dormobile.

'Are you sure you've got everything now?' he asked as he handed Dillon his pack.

'Yeh, that's the lot. I checked everything was in the pack before we left Paris.'

'Okay. Just leave the pack here and nip into the station and make sure you can get a train. Off you go, I'll look after the pack.'

'No, don't bother. I'll get a train all right . . .'

'Look, off you go, Brian. If you've missed your train I can put you up for the night. Now, chop chop.'

A few minutes later Dillon came hurrying back. 'There's a train in five minutes, Bob. I'd better dash.'

Dillon stuck out his hand. 'Well, thanks for everything, Bob. It's been good seeing you again . . . next time you come up to North Wales, give us a buzz. See you.' He turned away, hurrying towards the station entrance looking bulkier than ever with the heavy pack on his back.

Wishart climbed back into the driving seat. He waited till Dillon had vanished before pressing the starter. Ten minutes later he was home. Parking the Dormobile round in the mews he got out. He was too tired to bother about removing all his gear. He decided to clean out the Dormobile thoroughly in the morning before returning it to its owner. But he took his pack out, making sure he'd locked all the doors.

In his flat he dumped the pack in the hallway and made for bed, feeling absolutely worn out by the long journey from Paris.

CHAPTER VI

He came out of the Underground station. A thin drizzle of rain was falling as he cut through the back streets towards the pub where he was to meet Carole. Thinking how bloody awful the weather was for July he turned up his coat collar.

Half way there he stopped to look at his watch. He didn't want to be too early. Some of Carole's B B C colleagues were bound to be in the pub and they bored him with their trendy talk. En route he stopped for a quick drink. His stop had taken longer than he'd calculated and when he arrived at his destination Carole was already there. She was seated on a bar stool. Two men dressed in tweed jackets and leather elbow patches and wearing open-necked shirts were with her.

'Sorry I'm late,' he apologised.

She smiled without humour. 'Just as well I had someone to keep me company. You know Peter and Tony?'

The faces were vaguely familiar and he nodded. He waited for a moment, but neither of the men offered to buy a drink.

'Anyone drinking?' he asked, a note of aggression in his voice.

One of the men smiled. 'No thanks, old chap. Must be off. Got work to do.' He excused himself and the other man followed him out.

'What about you, Carole,' Wishart asked when they'd gone.

'Really, Bob. You're the limit. I've been waiting here for ten minutes and you breeze in as if . . .'

'Look, I said I was sorry. You know what it's like in the rain, everything's held up. Now what are you going to drink?'

She made a tut-tutting sound and put her empty glass down on the counter. 'You're sorry. Supposing I'd have been by myself . . . I'll have a gin and tonic.

'Did you remember to get the tickets?' Carole asked when he had given the order.

'Of course I remembered,' he said, patting his pocket. 'You don't think I'd forget a thing like that, do you?'

She shook her head. 'I don't know, you seem to forget so many things these days.'

He let it go.

'Well,' he said, when the drinks were served, 'what sort of a
54

day did you have?'

She made a mouth. 'So-so.'

'One of those, eh? I've had a pretty rough one myself. I've been trying to get hold of some pictures for this book they want me to do on the history of mountaineering The publisher was supposed to get them, or get somebody to get them. That was about ten days ago and nothing's happened so I decided to get the damned things myself. 1 think I've been round every agency in London. Anyway I think I've got something fixed up . . . what happened to you?'

She shrugged indifferently. 'One of those days. Have you a cigarette?' He gave her one and lit up himself. 'Remind me to get some before we leave, will you . . . oh, and another thing. Daddy's mebbe coming up Friday . . . for the day. We might have lunch or something together and he wants to take me to dinner at night. I must phone him about it this evening.'

'Why didn't you phone from the office?'

'The office? You know Daddy's not at home all day Tuesday.'

'Mmm. Well, you can phone later this evening after the concert.'

She shook her head. 'I must phone before then. I'll phone from the hall?'

'Yeh, I suppose so.' He finished off his beer and glanced at his watch. 'Well, we haven't all that much time, if we're going.'

'Didn't you bring the car?' she said with a frown.

'Come off it, Carole. It's raining.'

'You *could* put the hood up.'

He sighed inwardly. When he'd met her first she enjoyed travelling in an open car. But later she began to complain, saying it messed up her hair. And yet she knew one of the things that used to delight him was to see her leaning back in the seat, her long black hair streaming out in the wind like a pennant. 'What about the draughts? You're always complaining about the draughts.'

Her eyes flashed. 'That's just nonsense. I've never complained . . .'

He leant over and put his hand on her arm. 'Okay, Carole. Don't let's quarrel about it. Drink up and we'll get going, time's getting on.' He'd have to get a taxi. Carole didn't like travelling in buses or tubes.

But she refused to be hurried and sipped her drink slowly. He'd finished his own drink and was waiting. But she merely

55

slid round on her stool letting her coat fall open. 'Do you like it?'

'Huh?'

She opened her coat wider. Underneath he could see she was wearing a domino-patterned woollen jumper and a leather mini-skirt. She was showing a lot of leg. He frowned and glanced round the bar.

'It's real chamois, it cost a fortune,' she said.

He was sure everyone was looking at her. 'It sounds a lot to pay for so little,' he said dryly.

'Oho! A note of disapproval!' She clicked the rim of her glass against her even white teeth sensuously. 'You're nearly as bad as Daddy. I'm sure it's got something to do with that Puritan background of yours. Can't you enjoy yourself without suffering agonies of remorse?'

'I didn't know they taught psychiatry at Roedean . . .'

She waved her glass in front of him. 'Ah-ah. You're being nasty now, Robert. And anyway I didn't go to Roedean. Daddy couldn't afford it.' She put her glass down and coolly rising offered him her arm.

It was still raining and they had to wait for a taxi. When they reached the Festival Hall they had only a few minutes to spare before the concert began, but she insisted on phoning her father.

The concert had started by the time she returned. They waited till the overture was over before taking their seats.

'Did you get a programme?' she asked.

He shook his head. 'I know what they're playing.'

'What?' she asked, making no effort to keep her voice down.

'Sibelius: the second,' he answered in a half-whisper, irritated by her upper-class assurance.

But when the music began and she moved closer to him he forgot everything else as he felt the warmth of her body pressing against him. Sibelius was so graphic; so visual. The music seemed to arise out of the land itself. The harmonic structure was the earth, and the melodic line the soft brush of wind in the trees; the rushing sound of white water coursing down a hillside, the wild cry of a mountain bird. Lost in his private imagery he was unaware that Carole was speaking to him as the first movement ended.

'Ssshhh!' he warned.

'I was just saying about Daddy –'

'Later,' he whispered fiercely and felt her body stiffen and draw away from him. After that the music wasn't the same.

The sounds that had elated now depressed him, bringing feelings of dark premonition. At the end of Sibelius she announced she wanted to go. People around them stared angrily as they began to quarrel. He gave in.

'Stay there,' he snapped when they'd reached the foyer. 'I'll get the coats.'

She was standing in an exaggerated model's pose, a cold expression on her features, when he returned.

He handed her her coat. 'What was all that about?'

She eyed him coolly. 'I had a bit of a headache.'

'Headache? I suppose you want to go home now?'

'That's a good idea, if you insist on behaving . . .'

'If *I* insist? Who was it . . .?' he broke off defeatedly. 'Okay, Carole, if that's what you want. I just wish you'd make up your mind. If you didn't want to go to the concert you should have let me know in the . . .'

She flung her head back. 'I've told you what I want to do. I want to go home.'

He went off to get a taxi. He was soaked by the time he returned. It hadn't improved his temper.

'Aren't you coming with me?' she asked as she got in, her dark eyes glowing against her pale skin. For a moment she looked lonely and unsure of herself. He hesitated and then taking a deep breath got in after her. He gave the driver her address in Knightsbridge.

'Carole . . .' he began, but she snuggled up close to him. He knew he was being weak but he was unable to resist putting his arm around her. They travelled in silence.

They were nearing her flat when she turned round, gazing up into his face with her big glowing eyes. 'I don't really want to go home, Bob,' she confessed.

He stared at her in the dim light of the cab. Christ! Would he ever understand women? He'd thought he'd understood his wife, but he hadn't. The result of that was the divorce court. What did they want? A husband, a lover, a breadwinner or all three in one? Who was it said that a woman required a husband who was a cross between a stevedore and a brain surgeon?

He compressed his lips. 'Where do you want to go?'

She reached out her hand and touched the scar on his temple.

'Poor Robert,' she said, and leant over and brushed the scar with her lips. 'You've never really told me how you got that, have you?'

'Where . . .?'

'Why don't we go and have something to eat and you can tell me all about it? We could go to that place off Sloane Street. You know?'

He shrugged. 'Okay.'

The restaurant was crowded but the head waiter remembered them and they were able to get a table. Carole went off to the ladies' room. He noticed the number of admiring glances she drew. It made him feel slightly jealous and proud at the same time. His own reaction had been the same the first time he'd seen her at Broadcasting House. He'd done a programme on mountaineering in Britain for schools, and she'd been the production assistant. From the moment he saw her he was fascinated. They'd met afterwards in the producer's office. She hadn't said much but her large eyes had been alert and expressive. He'd been very conscious of her womanly body and the way she moved. In that brief meeting he knew he had to see her again.

Lacking his old confidence, it took him nearly a fortnight before he phoned. To his relief she welcomed his call. It was around about their third or fourth meeting that he learned she was waiting for her divorce. He'd already guessed that such an attractive woman must have been married, but it shook him to hear it. It wasn't all that long since his own divorce. Even now he could remember the pain and anxiety, the solemn-faced lawyers and the cold austerity of the court-room. That was something he never wanted to go through again.

In spite of this he continued to see her. She'd come into his life when he needed something tangible to keep him from flying apart. His life came and passed in a daily grey uniformity of time. He was living without hope; without challenge; and without confidence.

He stopped drumming on the table and his hand went up to finger the scar on his temple. He felt so empty and powerless at times, just letting everything slide in the hope it would work itself out. He knew he was going to have to try and reshape his life somehow. Whatever happened it was important to him that he should climb again.

If only Carole could understand. But like everyone else she accepted him as a success – not a failure. She'd never know what made a man want to drive himself to the very limit of his capabilities, to go always that little farther. Carole was too close to her own problems to see his. In a month or so she would be divorced and though neither of them had spoken about marriage he knew she thought about it. Carole needed a husband, even in name. Despite all her self-assuredness he was aware she needed some cornerstone to her life.

But what kind of future would they have together? They were always quarrelling. The sort of quarrels that couldn't be patched up in bed. And that was another thing he'd have to do something about. He'd told her it was only a temporary thing, but how long was she likely to go along with that? It was asking too much.

Maybe he should stop seeing her until the divorce was over. After that they could always try living together and see how it worked out, but even as he considered this idea he knew it was hopeless. He was too committed to the idea of the sanctity of marriage. It was his old style Calvinism raising its suffering head again perhaps, but that's what he believed and he wasn't going to change in that now.

She came back. Her humour appeared to have improved, and over the meal she chatted quite freely. Later she spotted a couple of friends. The man, an airline pilot whom Wishart had met once and didn't like, came over and asked if they'd care to join them. Wishart made some excuse, saying he had to be home early as he'd work to do. Carole was immediately furious.

'Why couldn't we have joined them?' she said, when the pilot had gone back to his table. 'It's because you don't like Eric, isn't it,' she accused. 'You don't like any of my friends, but of course I have to like yours.'

'Aw, Carole, cut it out, will you?'

'But it's true, isn't it?'

'I'll have to ask the waiter where they got that wine from. It appears to be pretty powerful stuff.'

Carole sat back, breathing heavily. A moment later she got to her feet. 'I want to go home,' she said, and without a further word headed for the cloakroom.

He got up and followed her.

He paid the bill and went outside. She was standing in the doorway. It was raining quite heavily. Wishart spotted a taxi. Brushing past her he stepped out on to the roadway and signalled the cab. It pulled up outside the entrance, its black coachwork gleaming wetly in the rain. Giving the driver an address he opened the door for her. She got in and he followed her.

'You don't have to bother, you know, I can manage myself,' she said, drawing herself away from him.

He offered her a cigarette, but she refused, staring out of the window of the cab coldly.

They hadn't gone very far when there was a mad squeal of brakes and the next second they were flung to the floor of the cab in a wild tangle of arms and legs. Wishart picked himself up. His head ached where it had struck the corner of the folding seat. He helped Carole back on to her seat.

'You all right?' he queried as he peered anxiously into her face.

'What happened?' she gasped, her eyes wide with shock.

'Just stay there,' he said. 'Don't move. I'll be back in a minute.'

He got out of the cab, prepared to give the driver a blast. And then he heard it. It was an awful wailing sound and seemed to come from somewhere near the front of the cab. It was only then he noticed the driver was leaning over the wing, his face a deathly colour in the light of the dipped head-lamps.

'What is it?' Wishart rasped. 'What the hell's the matter?'

The driver turned round, his mouth trembling. Wishart heard the unearthly sound again. The driver finally muttered something but Wishart pushed past him. A screech filled his eardrums as he bent down.

Then he saw it.

Pinned under the front wheel of the cab was a small dog. Saliva dripped from its mouth and its eyes were red with pain.

Wishart felt sick as he straightened up. 'Move your cab back,' he said.

But the driver shook his head as if he hadn't understood. He mumbled something. Wishart grabbed him by the shoulder. 'For Christ's sake, man, move it back will you. There's a dog trapped under . . .' and then he heard the back door open. He took three quick steps and was able to grab Carole before she got out.

'Didn't I tell you to stay where you were,' he said angrily. 'Now . . .'

'What is it, Bob?' she asked, trying to keep the fear out of her voice. The dog howled again. Instinctively she clapped her hands to her ears. 'For God's sake, what is it?'

He pushed her back into the cab. 'It's a dog,' he told her. 'It's trapped under the wheel.'

'Oh my God,' her eyes widened with horror. 'Oh,' she gasped, 'is it . . .?'

'I don't know. Just stay there, will you? I'll be back.'

She sat down and buried her face in her hands. Wishart went back to the driver. He'd recovered sufficiently to speak and grabbed Wishart's arm.

'It wasn't my fault . . . it just ran out in front of me . . . I didn't have a chance . . . I couldn't . . .'

'Get out of the way,' snapped Wishart impatiently. Opening the front door of the cab he climbed into the driving seat. The keys were still in the ignition switch. He started the engine, ignoring the protests of the driver. He wriggled the gear lever round and felt the slight pressure of the retaining spring. The dog's howls were getting louder. He pushed the lever home and let the clutch out very gently. Reversing a few feet he stopped the engine, and, having pulled back the handbrake, he jumped out.

The driver was moaning softly to himself and repeating over and over again that it hadn't been his fault. Wishart saw for the first time that he was quite an old man, his face covered in tired wrinkles. He put his hand on the man's shoulder.

'All right, all right,' he soothed. 'Now just tell me where the nearest phone is.'

The man blinked for a moment and shook his head. 'Phone? I don't know,' he said, 'I don't know round this way. I was just coming back from a fare . . .'

'Okay!' He saw it was hopeless. He went forward again. The dog had stopped howling, but a low breathy moan came from its half-opened mouth. In the reflected glare of the cab lights, Wishart saw a dark stain spreading across the road. He bent down on one knee. Instantly the dog bared its teeth and its eyes glowed angrily. The dog had a funny look as if the two halves of its body had been separated and crudely rejoined.

He stood up. The driver had come up behind him to peer over his shoulder.

'Honest . . . it wasn't my fault . . .'

Wishart turned and put his hand on the man's arm. 'Don't go near it. It's probably mad with pain and shock.'

As if to confirm his words the dog bared its teeth again till its gums showed black in the artificial light, then brought its jaws violently together with a loud and anguished yell.

Wishart felt the sound pierce his ears. 'Listen,' he said urgently to the driver. 'I'll stay here, you go and find a phone. Get the police . . .' he broke off. The driver was muttering something about he wasn't allowed to leave his cab. Wishart tried to think. He didn't want to leave Carole and the driver

61

alone with the dog. God knows what Carole might try and do. She couldn't help – the dog's back was broken, he was sure of that – but he knew she might try.

There was no point in prolonging the dog's suffering. He took the driver by the shoulder again. 'Listen,' he said. 'Have you any tools with you, something heavy, like a spanner?'

The driver looked at him blankly. 'A spanner? What do you want . . .?' His eyes widened as understanding hit him. 'Oh no, you can't . . .'

Wishart shook him roughly. 'Look, it might be half an hour before the police or anyone else arrives, even if we can phone them. The dog's back's broken. There's nothing that anyone can do for it, understand. Now, just get me that spanner.'

The driver still hesitated. Wishart flung open the cab door and stepped aside. The driver gave him a beseeching look and then bent forward inside the cab to fumble around underneath the seat. Turning round he handed Wishart a large shifting wrench. 'Listen . . . don't you think . . .?'

Wishart grabbed the wrench from his shaking hands. 'Stay here,' he warned. 'See that the girl doesn't come out . . . understand? Don't let her leave the cab.'

He hefted the wrench in his hand. It would do. Grasping it firmly, he rolled up his coat sleeve.

The dog was whimpering quietly now as if exhausted by pain. Wishart stole a glance behind him and caught a glimpse of the driver's ashen face.

He took a quick step forward.

The dog looked up at his approach. The savageness had gone from its eyes to be replaced by a strangely sad look. Its mouth was working slowly and a thin dribble of blood and saliva ran from its jaws down on to the roadway. Poor little bastard. It was almost as if it were trying to speak to him.

He wished he could have shut his eyes.

Taking a deep breath he tensed his arm.

The dog gave one brief, lonely howl of despair – then silence.

He stood up and took a step backwards.

He turned away. To his horror Carole had got out of the cab and was standing behind him. 'What the hell,' he swore, and stopped. 'Look, just get back inside, Carole. I told you not to come out. There's nothing you can do.'

Her eyes were dark and big with accusation: 'You've killed it, haven't you?'

'Yes,' he said wearily, 'now go back, will you?'

Without another word she went back into the cab.

Wishart wiped his forehead with the back of his hand and handed the driver back the wrench.

Only one more thing had to be done. The small lifeless bundle seemed surprisingly heavy as he took hold of it by the neck and dragged it over towards the gutter. He left it lying there, pathetic in its stillness: a small creature that belonged to no one. Poor little bastard without a soul to grieve for it.

He walked slowly back to the cab feeling sorry for one small dog which had just happened to get itself in the wrong place at the wrong time.

He got inside the cab and told the driver to make for the nearest police station. At the station he reported the incident to a bored-looking desk sergeant, and took Carole home.

He paid the cab-driver and let him go. The man was visibly shaken and Wishart didn't want to drag him all the way back to Hampstead. He could get another cab.

Standing in the doorway at the top of the steps, fumbling in her handbag for her key, Carole suddenly flung her arms round him. He felt her body tremble.

'Oh, Bob,' she moaned. Her face was pressed to his chest and sounded muffled. 'Don't go,' she said, 'I was angry and you were so . . . so . . .'

He put his arm round her shoulders. 'Okay, Carole. Just take it easy.'

She sniffled once or twice and searched for her handkerchief.

He took her handbag from her, extracted the key and opened the door. She smiled up at him wanly as they went into the hallway.

He lay awake, quietly smoking. Carole had fallen asleep. She was breathing as softly as a mouse, her long hair startlingly black against the stark white of the pillowcase.

He stubbed out his cigarette in the ash-tray by the bedside and lay back, reflecting on the tragedy and suffering of all living things.

CHAPTER VII

For the next two weeks he was busy and didn't see much of Carole. He was trying to get a firm grip on his life. He'd cut down his drinking and was working hard on the book about the history of mountaineering. It meant a great deal of research and he spent most of his days in the local library rooms making notes and working them up in the evening. It was to be an expensive production with lots of colour plates, and though there were other contributors he had something like 25,000 words to get out.

He'd met Carole once or twice for lunch and one evening they'd managed to see a film. Afterwards, during supper, she'd given him the name of a producer who wanted a dramatised script of the first ascent of the Matterhorn. He hadn't been so sure about this. A straight documentary or a blow by blow account he could handle, but a dramatisation . . .? But he promised to follow it up. A few days later she asked him how he'd got on. He had to confess he hadn't done anything about it. She was very annoyed and he made a firm promise to phone the next day.

This time he did phone. The producer was full of enthusiasm when he went along to see him and spoke as if it was all arranged. Wishart reminded him he was only going to think about it, but the producer ignored this and began to talk about programme planning and dates. Leaving the office Wishart had the vague feeling he'd committed himself.

Later in the evening, after he'd phoned Carole to tell her how he'd got on, he settled down to do some work and write a few letters. For some time he'd been thinking of having a few days in Scotland and taking Carole with him; she'd often said she'd like to go. He wrote to the proprietor of the local hotel reserving accommodation. He finished work before midnight. He wanted to be up early in the morning. Getting into bed he realised he'd once again forgotten to see his bank manager. He'd have to do something about that before he went on holiday. He'd also have to think seriously about the radio script.

'Well, what did you think of Appleby?' Carole said as they sat down to lunch the next day.

'What was that?'

'Appleby, the producer.'

'Oh. He was all right. Bit theatrical, but pleasant enough.'

Carole tutted impatiently. 'But what do you say? Are you going to do it or not?'

'I'm not sure,' he said.

'Not sure? I suppose that's supposed to be an answer. What did Appleby have to say?'

'He seemed quite keen . . .'

'It's more than you do.'

'It's not as easy as all that.'

She pursed her lips. 'What's so difficult about it? I would have thought it was right up your street.'

'Well, it is and it isn't. He wants a kind of dramatised version of the thing.'

'So?'

'Look, Carole, I'm no dramatist. It's not a straight documentary he wants, you know.'

'You mean to tell me you think you can't do it?'

'I didn't say that. I just don't want to rush into it, that's all.'

'I don't know what's happened to you, Bob. Where's your self-confidence gone?'

'Just let's forget it for the moment, Carole. I told you I was going to think about it,' he said irritably. 'Anyway I've got a lot on my plate just now.'

They were silent during the meal. He ate sparingly, no longer feeling hungry.

At last he said to her: 'I've been thinking of going up to Scotland for a few days.'

'That should be nice for you,' she said.

'How're you fixed?' he said, ignoring the sarcasm. 'Could you get time off?'

Her eyebrows went up in surprise.

'We could travel up by car,' he went on. 'I have a friend up the glen who has a hotel, he'll fix us up.'

'You've got it all arranged, have you? And when do you propose to go?' she answered.

'About the end of next week, say Friday.'

'And you expect me to go in and say I'm going on holiday next week? You might have given me some warning. Really, you're the limit, Bob.'

He leant over. 'Look, Carole, I want you to come. You'd like it. You've never been there before. I think it would do us both good.'

She gave him an arch look. 'And what's that supposed to mean?'

'Are you going to try or not? You could fix it. Say your old granny's ill or something.'

'The last time when *I* suggested something like that you said it was dishonest, remember?'

He leant closer. 'Look, Carole, I want to get away from London for a few days and I want you to come with me. I can't be plainer than that.'

She looked away for a moment and then turned to face him. 'And what would I be supposed to do with myself up there when you're clambering up and down those mountains of yours? I'm not going to hang around some little country hotel discussing the weather or the moral degeneration of teen-agers with a bunch of middle-aged frumps in long tweed skirts and pink twin-sets.'

He put his hand on her knee. 'I won't be doing any climbing, Carole, if that's what worries you. And anyway,' he gave a small grin, 'in case you mightn't have heard, the mini-skirt hit Scotland some time ago.'

She was silent for a minute and then she said: 'Oh, Bob, why do you have to spring these things so suddenly on me? How on earth am I supposed to get away at such short notice ... how long did you say we would be away for?'

'I'd like to make it a fortnight, but I'd settle for ten days.'

'You'll get me shot, you know. I can just see old thing-ummy's face when I ask him.' She got to her feet. 'I'll have to go.'

'You'll try then?'

'I can't promise,' she warned.

'But you'll try?'

'I said I would.'

When she'd gone he returned to his flat, collected his brief-case and headed for the library. It was nearly eight before he left. He felt tired but he still had work to do.

After a light supper he took his notes into the study and switched on the radio hoping to be able to pick up a few ideas on the use of dramatic technique. The only thing he could find was a Third Programme high-brow play full of heavy lines and obscure meanings. He switched it off, remembering he had to phone Carole.

He dialled the number. There was a long wait before he got any reply. She sounded breathless as if she'd just been running.

'Hullo, hullo, Carole?' the line was so bad he could hardly make out her reply. 'What was that?' She was just about to have a bath, the water would be overflowing if she didn't get back. The words poured out in a torrent. He put the phone down. Why the hell hadn't she just turned off her bath? Still, the important thing was that she'd been able to get time off. But what was that about not being able to leave till Saturday, as she'd promised to go to a party Friday evening? A party? What the hell did she want to go to a party for?

CHAPTER VIII

The garage door was half open. He stepped inside and the first thing he saw was the big P. 100's of the Aston Martin, a pair of giant eyes encased in thick chromium plate. Tony, the mechanic, was working at the bench at the back of the mews garage. He was alone.

He dropped what he was doing as he caught sight of Wishart and stepped over towards the door wiping the grease from his hands with an old rag.

'Looks good, eh?' he grinned, his teeth showing whitely against his grease-stained face.

Wishart ran his eyes over the lines of the car.

Tony leant over the cutaway door. 'Wait'ya hear this,' he said pressing the starter. The big engine turned smoothly in its bearings and jerked into life. 'The tappets were all over the place, and the carbs were out.' He straightened up and walked forward to undo the bonnet strap. Unfastening the studs he flipped one side of the bonnet up. Underneath, the alloy castings and the brass and copper tubes gleamed, reflecting the light from the single naked bulb overhead. There was a strong smell of oil, grease and petrol. Wishart sucked it in, as Tony flipped the throttle linkage. The big two-litre engine burst into a healthy roar.

Wishart bent over, listening.

'I think that's an exhaust valve beginning to go. If I'd more time I'd have had a look at it,' the mechanic shouted above the noise of the engine.

Wishart signalled with his hand, 'Okay, okay.'

The sound of the engine died to a quiet rhythmic gurgle. 'Sounds like a bloody bloodhound lapping up soup, doesn't it,' the mechanic grinned.

The chassis of the Aston Martin was rocking gently in unison with the softly thudding pistons. Wishart stepped back admiringly. 'She sounds great.'

Tony wiped his hands again. 'You know, if I was you, I'd have her bored out a bit. You'd get that bit extra poke. A skim off the head and a bore out and you wouldn't know her.'

Wishart shook his head. 'No, she's original, Tony, I'd like to keep her that way. There's not a lot of them about.'

The mechanic shrugged, 'I suppose you're right. Anyway it's up to you.' He wiped the door capping. 'Going up to Scotland are you for a few days?'

'To-morrow.'

'I've always been promising myself a trip up there. The wife's old man came from Scotland. She's always on to me about it. They say it's a great place for scenery and that. Anyway have a good trip. I've done the batteries, tyres, and I topped her up with petrol. You shouldn't have any trouble.'

'Fine. I could give you a cheque now, or do you want to wait till I come back, I can pay you in cash then.'

'That's okay, Mr Wishart. Just you pay me when you get back.' The mechanic bent over and wiped the seat. 'She's all yours.'

Wishart climbed in, feeling the warmth and comfort of the thick leather as he snuggled into the bucket seat. He stabbed the throttle enjoying the sound as he watched the rev counter climb.

'Well, have a good holiday. Mind how you go.'

'See you when I get back.' Wishart released the handbrake and slipped into gear as the mechanic swung the garage doors open. Wishart let the clutch in and nosed out into the courtyard, stabbing the throttle. At the end of the mews he stamped on the brakes and swung the wheel over, with a quick glance back and a wave to the mechanic.

Parking the car outside his flat, he got out and looked up at the sky. A smattering of grey cumulus was growing overhead. It might rain. For a moment he thought of pulling back the tonneau cover but with another glance upwards decided it wouldn't rain, if it was going to, for some time.

In the flat he stripped to the waist and had a wash down, changing afterwards into a soft grey hopsack suit. When he'd dressed he phoned Carole. She was nearly ready.

Taking a mac with him he went back down to the car. The cloud had thickened, sooner or later it would rain. He undid the cover and put the hood up.

The traffic was heavy and it took him a long time to get to Knightsbridge. Carole was ready and had been waiting ten minutes by the time he arrived.

She came down to the car looking magnificent in a black cape, her hair done in a chignon style.

'You're looking good to-night,' he said warmly as he helped her into the car.

'Thank you,' she said, her annoyance vanishing at the

compliment. 'I'm glad you think so.'

The party was crowded when they arrived. A dozen voices greeted Carole as he helped her off with her cape. Underneath she was wearing a plain white woollen dress; its starkness and simplicity was set off by her dark skin and jet-black hair, giving her the appearance of some ancient Hellenic beauty.

Leaving their coats in the hall, Wishart led the way into a large room. He felt his feet sink into the thick Oriental carpet. It was an even bigger room than he'd first thought, with a high ceiling, heavily ornamented, and wide bay windows overlooking the street. The windows were hung with plum-coloured velvet curtains and even the Regency striped wallpaper had a rich velvety sheen. From the ornate rose in the centre of the ceiling hung a large crystal chandelier and the period style furniture glowed with a dull waxy sheen reflecting the softness of the lighting. In one corner of the room, and set at an angle to the wall, was a modern Bechstein grand. The room had the unmistakable smell of wealth about it.

Carole introduced him to their host, Tony Cruft, a television director. He'd met him before on one or two occasions, the last time at Aviemore when he'd been doing a documentary on skiing in Scotland. Cruft was a short thickset man with a mop of iron-grey hair. He had a girl with him who looked like an actress.

They spent a few minutes chatting before moving off. Wishart spotted a table covered with a white cloth in a corner of the room. Behind it a man was serving drinks. He steered Carole towards the table, and was just about to ask for a drink when there was a loud cry from behind. He turned round to see a woman approach. The woman, who was dressed in a wildly patterned trouser suit, flung her arms out to embrace Carole. Wishart stared. He'd never seen anyone with such an enormous pair of eyes; they were so large they dwarfed the rest of the woman's features. To add to their startling appearance she was wearing a pair of false-eyelashes which must have been an inch long.

'My dear, I haven't seen you for ages,' the woman boomed in a loud theatrical voice. 'Where have you been hiding?' She took hold of Carole's hand in both her own, clasping it for a long second before letting go and standing back admiringly.

'You're looking so well, dear.' She turned to Wishart. He saw the long eyelashes make a butterfly motion as she looked at him with frank interest. 'So this is your friend?'

'Oh, I'm sorry, Bob, this is Marulka,' Carole said.

Wishart took the plump hand that was offered and was immediately surprised by its strength and vibrancy.

'Yes, I've heard lots about you and I must say it's very wicked of you to keep Carole to yourself for so long.'

'Can I get you a drink?' Wishart asked. 'I was about to get Carole one.'

'You know, I think I'm going to try the punch.'

'How about you, Carole? A gin and tonic?' But Marulka interrupted.

'Why don't you have a glass of punch? I always have it at Tony's parties.'

'Why not?' Carole said laughing.

Wishart had a whisky. Marulka smiled. 'I might have known you'd have whisky.'

'Punch can be pretty strong stuff.'

The smile became arch. 'Whisky isn't?'

'Well, I know how much whisky I can handle.'

'You're just being chauvinistic,' the woman said.

He wasn't quite sure whether she was being serious or not. 'I'm not that kind of a nationalist,' he replied.

She laughed and he could see for the first time that above the eyes she had thick black eyebrows like pieces of felt glued to her forehead. For a moment he thought they might have been false like her eyelashes.

'I tell you what I'm going to do, darling,' the woman turned to Carole. 'I'm going to borrow this Bob of yours for a few minutes. I promise you he'll be quite safe, and anyway I'm sure you've lots of friends you want to see . . .'

Wishart frowned. He didn't want to be left with this strange woman. He'd already sensed she was the type who had a compulsion to ask questions; an inquisitor who probed to discover what people were really like underneath their manners and conventions. To his surprise Carole merely smiled sweetly and with an enigmatic glance in his direction said: 'Look after yourself, Bob. Marulka practises witchcraft. She sticks pins in wax figures and all that sort of thing, so be careful not to say anything to offend her, will you?'

She sauntered off. Wishart felt annoyed with her. He always felt a bit shy and clumsy with people he'd met for the first time, especially strongly extroverted types like this woman.

'She's very beautiful, isn't she?' Marulka's voice broke in on his thoughts.

Wishart took a sip of his whisky and nodded slowly.

'You don't enjoy these things very much, do you?'

The question didn't surprise him. He'd been half-expecting the direct approach.

'Not much,' he said levelly.

'I wouldn't have thought you did. You're not the type.' The dark eyes glinted mischievously as she noticed his glance. 'How do I know what your type is – that's what you're wondering, isn't it? You see, I know Carole. Very well. I don't have to see her to communicate with her.'

She was extravagantly fey – deliberately so. She made him feel edgy.

'I think you're a very lonely person, aren't you?' He frowned at the next question, as he looked over her shoulder to see where Carole had gone.

'Never mind Carole. She'll be perfectly all right. I was saying you're a very lonely person, aren't you?'

'Am I?'

'Oh yes, I can see that. I wonder what it is you're looking for?'

He decided to make a joke of it. 'Mebbe I've found it,' he replied raising his glass.

She shook her head. 'That can only be a substitute. Perhaps its immortality you're looking for. Do you believe in immortality?'

He shifted his feet uncomfortably.

'You should, you know. Such beliefs can be a great help. They can offset that awful feeling that time's running away and it's too late to achieve your ambitions.'

There was an underlying tone of seriousness in her voice that made him feel ill at ease.

She laughed easily. 'I can see I'm upsetting you. You mustn't take any notice of me. Come now, I see Anna's arrived, and I want you to meet her.'

He was about to protest but she gave him no chance as she shot off.

Anna Vogler was a tall willowy sculptress. She had a dramatic way of speaking.

'Ah,' she said, 'so you're Robert Wishart, the famous mountaineer.'

He shook hands feeling the colour mount to his face. The sculptress waved her hands. 'I've heard about you. Now tell me what it is that makes you want to climb . . . is that how you got that scar?'

He nodded briefly, too embarrassed to speak.

'But it's so dangerous. Don't you think so, Michael?' she turned to address a man who had just come up, glass in hand.

'Think what? What's so dangerous . . .?'

'I see you don't know each other,' the sculptress said. She introduced them, adding: 'I'm surprised you don't know Robert, he's quite famous, you know.'

The man called Michael looked unimpressed. 'Really?' he said, looking at Wishart.

The sculptress took his arm. 'Robert's a mountaineer, silly.'

The man sipped at his drink. 'What in heaven's name for?' he drawled.

'I beg your pardon?' said Wishart taking an instant dislike to the man.

'Why do you do it? It all seems rather pointless to me. You go all that way up and then have to come down again. Seems such an extraordinary waste of time and effort.'

'I suppose it does to some people,' he replied evenly, noticing that Marulka was watching his reactions closely.

'I mean, what was it that chap said about wanting to climb mountains because they were there? Seems rather silly to me. The B B C tower's also there but I've never heard of anyone wanting to climb it for that reason. And then you get into all sorts of trouble and all those chaps have to be dragged out to rescue you.'

Wishart's eyes narrowed. 'You may not know it,' he said, 'but when we do get into trouble those chaps that rescue us are climbers themselves. Now if you'll excuse me, I have to find someone.' He turned and walked away, but not before he caught a glimpse of Marulka. She had her glass up to her mouth, but he saw she was smiling as if she'd enjoyed the exchange.

He found Carole. She was standing over by the piano in the centre of a small group. She detached herself for a moment. 'What are you looking so black about?' she asked.

'Oh, some idiot over there. A couple of drinks and some people have to shoot their mouths off.'

She looked over in the direction from which he'd come. 'Which one was it?'

'Aw, forget it. He was just a blabber-mouth,' he answered sourly.

'There's no need to get bad-tempered with me, just because someone upset you.'

The others were listening. 'Okay, okay, Carole, let's forget about it, eh?'

73

She gave him a cool look, and without another word turned and rejoined her company.

Angrily he headed back towards the bar and got himself another drink. Moodily he circled the room to find a quiet corner where he could be by himself. But he wasn't alone for long. Marulka spotted him and came over.

'How did you manage to do that?' she asked.

He hadn't realised he'd been fingering the scar on his temple. 'I fell.'

'You make it sound as if it happens all the time. Do people who climb often fall?'

'Not good ones.'

'You're being modest. Perhaps I shouldn't tell you but I overheard someone say you were one of the best climbers in the country.'

He flushed with irritation. 'I wish people wouldn't talk such damned nonsense. There's no such thing as the best climber in Britain or any other place.'

'Don't be so sensitive.'

'Well, that sort of thing annoys me.' He suddenly felt as if he wanted to get away from all these people and their smart talk.

'Are you superstitious?'

'No, nor religious either.'

'You don't believe in an after-life?'

He was growing more irritated by her persistent questioning. 'When you're dead, you're dead. I can't stand all this mystical nonsense.'

Marulka smiled indulgently. 'Let me see your hand . . .'

Before he could prevent her she'd reached forward and taken him by the wrist with surprising strength. He felt embarrassed but hadn't sufficient strength of will to draw it away. Marulka was looking at his palm with a serious, intent expression.

He felt like an idiot standing there in a crowded room with this strange woman reading his hand. 'What is it?' he asked sarcastically. 'Do I win the pools or do I get run over by a bus?'

She shook her head slowly, her large eyes searching his face. 'There are some things you shouldn't joke about,' she said.

'Look,' he began, but at that moment a burst of music filled the room and within seconds the whole of the party seemed to erupt in a wild thrashing of bodies. He caught one brief glimpse of Carole before she vanished somewhere.

Marulka grabbed his arm again. 'Dance with me,' she shouted above the noise.

He shook his head. 'I don't dance.'

She looked at him despairingly and went off to find another partner.

Everybody appeared to be dancing. He skirted the floor clear of the dancers and made his way to the unattended bar. He helped himself to a whisky at the same time as he reminded himself he'd better be careful as he was driving. He looked at his watch. It was near midnight. He'd have this drink and go. He had a long drive in front of him next day.

There was a break in the music and he took advantage of it to look for Carole. She was standing only a few feet away, her head thrown back. He heard her laughing. He put down his glass and went over to her.

She looked round at his approach, smoothing out her dress and patting her hair in a challenging manner.

'It's getting late, Carole. Remember we've got a long journey in front of us to-morrow,' he said.

Her look was cool.

'Oh, come now, old chap.' For the first time Wishart noticed her partner. It was the man the sculptress had introduced him to earlier. 'The night's only just begun, you know,' he went on.

Wishart ignored him as he continued to wait. Carole still made no reply. He felt his temper mount.

'Carole . . .?'

'Perhaps the lady doesn't want to go.' The voice cut in again.

Wishart held his temper. 'Carole,' he said in a quiet voice, 'are you coming or not?'

She returned his gaze coldly.

'Well, Carole?'

The voice interrupted again. 'I said perhaps . . .'

Wishart swung round. 'I'm not interested in what you said. I wasn't speaking to you.'

Carole's face had gone white.

'Now just hold on there,' the voice was angry with indignation. 'You can't talk to me like that. I'm not . . .'

'Keep out of this, will you?' Wishart snarled. 'Now, for the last time, Carole, are you coming or not? Make up your mind because I'm leaving here in three minutes flat.'

The music had started up again. He waited. Still Carole made no reply.

'Okay,' he snapped and turned on his heel, conscious that a few of the dancers had stopped to stare at him. He'd only taken a few steps when he heard Carole's partner say something in a loud voice. He turned round, his fists bunching aggressively as he slowly walked back.

'What was that you said?'

The man smiled insolently. 'I said that . . .'

'Shut up!' Choking with rage he asked Carole once more if she was leaving. She didn't move. He'd just turned to go when he felt a hand clutch at his sleeve. He swung round on the balls of his feet, body tensed. 'Take your hands off.'

Instead of letting go the man clung the more tightly, thrusting his face close to Wishart's. 'You are a bit of a boor, aren't you?'

Wishart tried to pull away, but the man tugged at his sleeve again. 'I said . . .'

He lost all sense of reason. Jerking his arm away he brought it up in a low arc and gave the man the back of his hand. It was a strong blow. The man staggered and fell, blood slowly trickling from his bruised mouth. There was a sudden shocked silence and a woman screamed. Wishart caught a brief glimpse of Carole's white face as she ran off, and the next moment he was surrounded by an angry crowd of people all talking excitedly. Someone had helped the man to his feet. Cruft, the producer, pushed his way through the crowd.

'That was a damned nice thing to do, wasn't it?' Cruft said angrily.

Wishart felt his cheeks colour. 'I'm sorry,' he said, 'but he asked for it.'

'Asked for it?' Cruft turned to point to the man, who'd been helped to a chair and was sitting with a shocked expression on his blood-streaked face. 'Just look at what you've done . . . I think you'd better go.'

Wishart made his way to the door, conscious that everyone was staring at him. In the hallway, he collected his coat. There was a couple standing by the front door. They looked at him oddly as he asked if they'd seen a girl in a cloak leave. They muttered something about having seen a girl in a white dress dash out.

He brushed past them, ran down the steps and out into the street. At the far end of the street a taxi was turning the corner. He ran after it but by the time he reached the corner it had vanished. Slowly he made his way to where he'd parked his car. His anger had subsided and he felt a sense of shame. He knew he shouldn't have struck the man, but he'd been so infuriated by Carole's behaviour that he'd just lost his head completely.

He put the hood down and got into the car, wondering if he should drive round to her flat. He looked at his watch. It was past midnight, she would probably have gone straight to bed. He lit a cigarette to calm his nerves and drove off.

He'd just got through Kensington and was heading up towards Notting Hill Gate when he saw a torch flash in his direction. It suddenly struck him as he pulled in to the kerb that he'd had quite a few whiskies. He felt himself go cold inside. It was all he needed now – the breathalyser test.

The policeman seemed to take an eternity to walk the few yards to the car. He walked slowly round the front looking at the registration plate and then flashing his torch on the licence disc on the windscreen.

'Evening, sir,' he said, coming round to the driving side. 'Can you tell me the number of your car, sir?'

He told him.

'Can I see your licence, sir?'

He fished it out.

'And your insurance cover, sir.'

He searched in his jacket again and pulled it out. The policeman unfolded the scrap of paper and examined it carefully, nodding his head slowly. Wishart kept silent, scared the policeman might catch the smell of whisky on his breath. The constable handed him back his licence and cover note.

'Got to be careful, sir. There's a lot of cars stolen, you know.'

Wishart mumbled agreement, as the policeman stepped back to allow him to go. He'd just started the engine and was about to slip into first gear when the policeman held up his hand and bent forward. Wishart's heart gave a thump. He waited, rigid with suspense.

'Better switch your lights on, sir.'

'Lights?' he exclaimed stupidly.

'You were driving without lights, sir.'

Cursing himself for his folly he flicked his sidelights on. 'Sorry about that,' he mumbled through half-closed lips, 'I must have forgotten.'

'Hmm.' There was a sudden authority in the policeman's

77

manner. 'You realise it's an offence, sir?'

'Yes, of course, but . . .'

'Have you been drinking, sir?'

He felt himself stiffen. This was it. Any moment he'd be asked to take a breathalyser. Trying to keep his voice even he replied: 'I've had a couple of whiskies.'

'Only two, sir?'

He made a pretence of considering the question. 'That's right, only two. I remember now.'

'How long ago, sir?'

'Oh, about a couple of hours . . . yes, about that.'

'And you drove off and forgot to switch your lights on. I see . . .'

Wishart scarcely dared breathe. A long silence followed. To his astonishment the policeman stepped back again.

'Very well, sir, but I'd be a bit more careful in the future.' The torch flashed again to signal him on.

He could hardly believe his luck. With a mumbled good night he slipped into gear and drove off. He was still shaking inwardly by the time he got to West Hampstead.

He drove into the mews and parked the car. Switching off the ignition he checked to see he'd left nothing inside. He was too tired to bother putting the hood back up. He didn't even trouble to button down the tonneau cover, just pulling it over the seats.

Footsteps sounding unnaturally loud in the narrow cobbled mews, he headed for his flat. It had been a hellish night. He'd quarrelled with Carole, struck a man at the party and had been fortunate not to get himself arrested.

CHAPTER IX

The air was still and humid. By the time he arose, the first few heavy drops of rain had spattered the streets. He peered out of the window and swore. If only they had left on Friday they'd have missed all this.

Half way through his breakfast he heard the dull rumble of thunder above the sound of the early morning radio programme. He rose from the table hurriedly and went over to the window again. Rain was coming down in torrents, bouncing back off the roadway in a heavy spray. With a sickening feeling he tried to remember if he'd put up the hood of the car the previous evening.

He finished his breakfast, and, slipping into an old mac, dashed round to the mews.

It was worse than he'd expected. The unfastened tonneau cover had collapsed under the weight of rainwater, spilling its contents over the upholstery.

He grabbed the cover, dragging it back, trying not to spill more water into the car. The rain was bucketing down as he fought to get the hood up. Water ran up his sleeves and down the back of his neck. He cursed himself furiously for his folly as he got the clips home and buttoned the hood up tightly. He was drenched to the skin.

From the tool locker he extracted an old towel and some rags and began mopping up the pools of water that had formed in the hollows of the bucket seats. It took him the best part of half an hour before he managed to get most of it mopped up, but the seats and floor carpeting were still damp. He imagined how Carole would react to having to sit on a cold, wet seat. Still there was no point in worrying about that now.

The rain was still lashing down as he fixed the sidescreens. Protected from the worst of the weather he drove round to the flat. Back inside he changed his clothes and packed all his gear. He made up a couple of flasks of coffee and checked everything over again before picking up the phone and dialling Carole.

He got the engaged signal. A few minutes later he tried

again. Still engaged. Who could she be phoning at this time in the morning? He looked at his watch to check the time. It had only gone half-past eight. Who in the hell could she be phoning at this time? She might have known he'd call her early. What was she playing at? He picked up the phone again. This time he got the ringing sound, but though he hung on for a long time there was no reply. He tried once more and still no reply. With a curse he flung the instrument back in its cradle. It was near nine o'clock, they should have been on their way by now, and instead he was going to run into all the early morning traffic. The thought of having to drive through town made him furious.

Once again he picked up the phone and dialled her number and once again there was no reply. His exasperation mounting, he dialled the exchange to check out the number. It was ages before he got a reply and when they did check it out it was only to tell him there was no reply from the subscriber.

It was still raining heavily when he took his gear out to the car and packed it into the rear compartment. He was about to drive off when he remembered he hadn't switched the electricity off at the mains. Breathing heavily he went back into the flat, only to find he had in fact switched it off.

About to drive off again, he remembered he'd left the letter from the B B C producer on his desk. He'd intended to reply to it all week but kept putting it off. He couldn't let another fortnight go without a reply.

At last he got away, but by then it was nearly half-past nine. The rain was still heavy and the windscreen wipers struggled to cope with it. He thrust himself forward in his seat, face close to the windscreen. The traffic was very heavy. Everything seemed to be at a standstill and still it rained. It took him nearly an hour to get to Carole's flat in Knightsbridge.

He ran up the steps and rang the bell, pressing close to the doorway to shelter from the rain. The house seemed silent and empty. He was about to ring again when he saw a curtain being drawn from one of the windows on the ground floor. A few minutes later the front door opened and a woman stuck her head out.

'Were you ringing Mrs Greenwood's bell?' she asked sourly, her lips pinching into an expression of disapproval.

'Yes, I . . .'

'Are you Mr Wishart?'

'Yes –'

'Just a minute.' The woman vanished. When she came back she had a letter in her hand. 'It's for you.' She handed it to him.

He frowned. 'For me?'

'You said your name was Wishart?'

'Yes, but . . .'

'Then it's for you. Mrs Greenwood asked me to give it to you if you called.' The next minute the door was shut in his face, leaving him standing dazedly on the steps before he had the sense to rip open the envelope.

The message from Carole was short and to the point. After his disgusting and unwarrantable behaviour at the party the previous evening she felt she could not go on holiday with him. And further, his behaviour had recently become so unpredictable and irascible that it would be better if he didn't try and get in touch again.

He couldn't believe his eyes, and read the note over again. Even then he found it difficult to accept. He was just about to ring the door bell again when the truth hit him: she'd actually gone. She wasn't there. The note contained a few lines of postscript he'd missed. She'd gone to live with a friend in the country for a few days, there was no point in trying to get in touch with her.

In a fury he screwed the letter up into a ball and flung it wide into the street. Gone off to the country with a friend: no point in trying to get in touch with her: unpredictable, irascible. That was pretty good coming from her. And she hadn't even bothered to phone that morning to tell him of her decision. Instead he'd been forced to come half way across London to be told by a soured-up old spinster. Okay, to hell with her. Let her go and stay with her friend in the country, whoever she was. *She* was? An uneasy thought struck him. How did he know it was a she?

He went back down the steps and got back into the car, lashing through the gears as he drove off at speed.

The rain hadn't stopped and the traffic was crawling. It took him over an hour to clear London and by that time he felt as if every nerve in his body had been scraped bare.

Once on the motorway he gunned the Aston Martin, driving the car with a cold fury as he watched the needle climb dangerously near the red segment on the rev counter. The engine note rose from a low throaty growl to a fierce crackle. He'd gone nearly ten miles before he looked in the mirror.

When he did, his heart gave a little leap. Behind him and coming up fast was a white Jaguar. Immediately he throttled down and eased over into the middle lane. The last thing he wanted was another brush with the law.

The white Jag swept past. Breathing a sigh of relief he settled down to a steady seventy mph, the long, grey, monotonous ribbon of motorway unwinding before him. The M1 was quiet, and without the need to concentrate on his driving his mind was free to think about Carole again. His hot rage had been replaced by a slow, smouldering anger. He'd never forgive her for treating him so meanly.

He motored nearly fifty miles before he noticed the skies had cleared and already patches of blue were appearing to the west. At the first lay-by he pulled in and, getting out, unshipped the sidescreens and folded back the hood.

On the road again, the wind whipping into his face and throwing his hair about wildly, his mood cooled. What had happened between him and Carole had been on the cards. If he'd allowed himself to think straight he would have realised it a long time ago, and spared them both the dramatics. What he'd really wanted was in fact a modified version of Carole, but you had to learn to accept people as they were with all their faults and insufficiencies. He hadn't been prepared to do that and he knew Carole well enough to realise that neither had she. Their relationship had been close, but not close enough. For each of them it had been too easy to find faults and too difficult to excuse them.

He would have liked to have told her this, frankly and without malice, but it was too late now. Whatever he and Carole had had together was finished. Perhaps if he'd had the strength and courage to tell her about himself and what had happened to him she would have understood and tried to help. Perhaps, but he'd never know now.

If only he'd been able to tell her the truth about himself. He hadn't, and it had been just as damaging as a lie. But it would have been impossible for him to confess his fears to her. There was only one person in whom he could have confided – and Joe was dead. He'd been killed in a car crash on his way to North Wales.

He remembered reading somewhere that everyone had only a fixed amount of courage at their disposal, expendable like a bank balance. Once that was gone you were in the red.

He didn't believe this but the thought worried him.

If it was right, there was little hope for him.

He'd left the motorway and was heading up the A1 towards Scotch Corner, when he spotted a couple of hitch-hikers. Glancing behind him, he pulled in to the side of the road. They were about two hundred yards away and, burdened by enormous packs, were running clumsily. He could hear the dull thud of their boots above the engine tick-over. He reversed.

'I'm going to Scotland . . . any good?' he shouted above the sound of the engine as they came within hearing distance. He switched off the engine and stepped out of the car as the two men drew level, their faces red with exertion.

'Scotland?' one of them gasped out. 'Did you say you were going to Scotland?'

'That's right. One of you will have to sit in the back. Sorry, it's a bit of a squeeze.'

'Never . . . never mind about that . . . we're just glad to get a lift . . . thanks . . .'

'Okay, take it easy. There's no hurry,' Wishart said. 'Just climb aboard and I'll hand your packs to you . . . just a minute,' he leant over into the back of the car and moved his things over to one side. 'There you are, you can get in now.' He turned round to look at the two men. 'Here,' he said to the smaller one, 'I think you'd better go in the back.'

The man made to climb over.

'Just a minute.' He stopped him. 'You got a sleeping bag in your pack?'

'Sleeping bag. Yes, but . . .?'

'Well, get it out and put it under you. Go on, I'm not kidding, that back seat's as hard as iron, you'll need it.'

The lad did as he was told. Wishart waited till they had both got aboard and then handed them their packs. 'Okay?' he said. They grinned back at him.

Two hours later they were approaching the border. With the noise of the engine and the roar of the wind, it hadn't been possible to talk but he'd seen enough to know that his two passengers were climbers. He wondered where they were eventually heading for – Glencoe, Skye or the North-West. How lucky they were, to be young and healthy with nothing to worry about; nothing they couldn't take in their stride. He recalled his own younger days when he and his mates had hitch-hiked all over Scotland, England and eventually Europe.

Carefree days when the world had been their pillow.

One of the lads offered him a piece of chocolate. He shook his head, but realised he hadn't eaten all day. And when had they last eaten? He decided to stop at the next roadside café.

Three miles along the road he saw a sign announcing there was a café 300 yards on. He slowed down and in a minute saw the entrance to a car-park. A few heavy vehicles were scattered around, left facing in all directions as if the drivers hadn't been able to get out of them quick enough. He pulled in to the park and cut the engine. For a few seconds all three sat without speaking in the unnatural silence which fell.

Wishart was the first to get out: 'I don't know about you two,' he said, 'but I could do with something to eat. How about it?'

They both nodded eagerly and climbed slowly out of the car, massaging their stiff limbs.

'Chuck the packs in the back,' Wishart said, 'and I'll pull the tonneau cover over.'

'Will they be all right?'

'We'll keep an eye on the car from the window,' he said.

The packs were put back in the car and he pulled the cover over, fastening the buttons, and then all three headed for the café.

As he pushed the door open they were met with a blast of sound from the juke-box in the corner. It was almost deafening. Wishart felt it come up all the way through the floor. He grimaced and walked over to a table by the window.

'Well,' he said, feeling his nerves jump as he sat down, 'we might as well get acquainted. My name's Bob, what's yours?' He had to raise his voice to make himself heard.

The smaller one of the two lads introduced himself. 'My name's Robin and this is Jimmy.'

'Good,' said Wishart, relieved that neither of them had offered to shake hands. In Scotland shaking hands was a custom reserved for weddings and funerals.

A man in a grease-stained apron and with red, roughened hands appeared at the table to take their order. Robin and Jimmy ordered sausage, egg and chips, but he settled for a plain omelette.

By the time they'd finished their meal the café had almost emptied and the big glittering juke-box over in the corner was silent. The man who was serving them cleared away the plates and returned with three enormous mugs of steaming hot tea.

Wishart took a sip and put his mug down to wait for it to cool.

'That should keep us going for a bit,' he said.

They smiled back contentedly. 'That was great.'

'It fills a gap,' he said, lighting a cigarette. 'Where are you heading for, by the way? I'm going through Dundee if it's any good to you.'

They looked at each other uncertainly. 'Dundee? We're going to Skye. Dundee's on the other side, isn't it?'

He sipped his tea again. 'If you're going to Skye the best place to head for is Edinburgh or Glasgow. I could take you as far as Dundee and you could get a lift to Perth, but you'd be better staying in Edinburgh. I have to go that way.'

'I don't suppose there would be much chance of getting to Skye to-night?' Robin asked.

'To-night? Not a hope!'

'How about Glencoe?'

He smiled. 'You'd never make it. Not to-night.'

They looked glum. He understood their feelings. They were bursting with impatience to get to the hills. He'd felt like it himself, once.

'Well, drink up and let's get on the road again. We've a bit to go yet.'

They finished their tea and got to their feet, searching their pockets for change to pay the meal.

'I'll get it,' he said. 'I'll see you outside at the car.'

'Oh no . . . we can't let you . . .'

He waved aside their protests. 'Look, if it makes you feel any better you can buy me a pint when we get to Edinburgh, okay?'

They looked at each other hesitatingly.

'Better get going,' he said. 'Time's getting on.'

He went over to the counter and settled up the bill. The tonneau cover had been stripped back and neatly folded, and the two lads were sitting inside the car, their packs on their knees, when he got outside.

He suddenly felt warm towards them as he climbed in. They were good kids. He hoped he hadn't embarrassed them too much with his offer to pay the meal.

'Let's get this show on the road, eh?' he said with a grin as he started the engine.

It was evening by the time they arrived in Edinburgh. It had been raining earlier and there was a fresh smell in the air carried by a soft westerly wind coming down the Firth. Dark patches stained the pavements and the grey-coloured buildings. The sun was low in the sky as he drove along Princes Street. High up on the hill the gables and turrets of the castle were patches of bright colour against a sombre grey, and below the castle inky black grooves cut into the glistening rock. To the west the sky was bright rose, the impressive width of the capital's main street a dull, metallic blue strip arrowing away towards a cluster of lights at its far end.

Up on the hill at the back of Rose Street he found a place to park.

Rubbing the back of his neck where it ached from driving, he said: 'Well, this is it . . . the capital of Scotland.'

His two passengers grinned at each other, eager to explore their new environment.

'I'm not sure where the hostel is, but if I drop you here you shouldn't have any trouble finding it,' Wishart said. He went round the side of the car and lugged out the packs. Out on the pavement Wishart's passengers made no attempt to move but stood looking at him, an expectant expression on their faces.

'I hope . . .' he began.

'Aren't you going to have that drink?' Robin cut in.

'Drink?' he said, remembering he'd promised to have a pint with them. He hesitated and yet he couldn't let them go without the opportunity to buy him a drink. 'Okay,' he said, 'but we'll have to make it a quickie.' Once he'd made the decision he was glad. Of course he had to have a drink with them. They were good lads. The sort you so often met in the hills; trustworthy and dependable. 'Come on then. Let's go.' They walked down the street together. 'One thing, you've never far to travel to find a pub in Edinburgh,' he remarked.

They found a quiet bar behind Rose Street.

'Well, what is it going to be?' asked Robin.

'I think I'll have a pint,' Wishart said, 'a pint of heavy.'

'A pint of . . . what was that?'

'Heavy,' Wishart smiled. 'Just ask the barman, he'll know,' he said, experiencing the peculiar kind of satisfaction a native has when he introduces a visitor to a strange custom or feature of his country.

'Is that like bitter?' Robin asked.

'Sort of. Why don't you try it?'

The barman was waiting patiently for the order. 'I think I will, how about you, Jimmy?' The barman pulled three pints, topping the tumblers up and measuring the froth with an expert air. He slid them along the counter with a beefy hand, leaving dark glistening trails on the polished mahogany.

'All right?' Wishart asked, as the two lads drank up.

They nodded. 'Not bad, is it?'

'Not bad. I can tell you it's pretty strong stuff, I wouldn't like you to have a hangover in the morning.'

They were silent for a minute and then the one called Jimmy, who was the quieter of the two, said: 'How far is it to Skye from Edinburgh?'

He thought for a moment. 'I'd say it was about two hundred miles.'

'What's our best way from here?'

'Well now, that's difficult to say. If you intend to hitch I'd suggest you get to Perth and make for Glencoe and then Fort William.' He thought for a moment again. 'On the other hand, if you were lucky enough to get a lift all the way to Inverness you'd be just as well going that way and coming back down the other side of Loch Ness.'

'You know Skye well?'

'Fairly,' he said guardedly. He didn't want to reveal he climbed himself. 'I've been there.'

'Where's the best place to stay?'

'Depends on what you want to do,' he answered.

'We want to go to the Cuillins.'

'Well, if you're going to the Cuillins, I would suggest Brittle. There's the hostel there or you could camp down by the lochside. Are you camping?'

Robin nodded. 'We've got the tent with us.'

Wishart raised his tumbler. 'It's a long way to the nearest pub from Glen Brittle. Here's hoping you get good weather.'

'Have you done much climbing there?'

It was the question he'd been expecting. 'A little,' he said, trying to make his voice sound casual. 'Just a bit of a scramble here and there.'

'We haven't climbed in Scotland before. We spend most of the time either up at North Wales or the Lakes, but we've heard a lot about Skye . . . and Glencoe.'

He nodded. 'Excuse me, will you?' he said, fishing out a pound note. 'Get another round up, will you? I'm just going to the toilet.' He waved aside their protests: 'Look, I have to go after the next round, so let me get it.'

He left them still arguing about it.

On his way to the toilet his mind went back to Skye and

all the happy times he'd spent there. The mountains had given him everything in life he'd really wanted – adventure, the joy of physical effort and a peace of mind.

He thought of his old friend Joe. It had been an essential part of Joe's philosophy that you never really possessed anything: even life was something you were only temporarily in charge of, and either you looked after it well or you didn't. They'd argued such questions on their first trip to Skye. Lying on a catwalk stretched out between two giant boilers in a distillery, with the rain lashing down and the wind howling they'd contested every human belief, the subjects ranging from sex, politics, philosophy and Buddhism to the Douglas credit system.

It seemed such a long time ago when he and Joe had set out from Glasgow in an old fabric-covered Riley 9 Joe had bought for twelve pounds.

When they finally got over to the west, Skye had been invisible from the mainland, blotted out by dense rain cloud stretching half way out into the Atlantic. Soaked to the skin they reached the head of Glen Brittle to find that the road had become a tumbling stream of water.

The road was impassable, so they headed a few miles farther west down to Carbost. To pitch their tent in the torrential downpour was unthinkable and they made for the police station. The constable suggested they'd be going to see Mr McArthur up at the distillery.

They headed for the cluster of buildings at the end of the village, found the manager's house and knocked at the door. It was McArthur himself who answered, and from the start he treated them as if they'd been destined to appear that very night. An old raincoat over his head and shoulders, he'd led them down from the house to the distillery.

After an exchange in the Gaelic between McArthur and the night watchman, Lachie, it was explained that the boiler-room was the very place for them to stay.

They couldn't believe their luck, in all the wild expanse of wind and rain they'd miraculously found the warmest and driest place in the whole of the island.

Joe had been quick to see the advantages of the boiler-room. Washing a shovel under a stream of boiling water, he piled it up with potatoes, onions and steak. Adding a half pound of margarine and a dash of salt and pepper, he opened the furnace door and thrust the shovel inside.

After their meal, armed with mugs of hot tea laced with

whisky, they retired to stretch out on the catwalk spanning the big boilers.

The storm had lasted two days, and during that time they'd lived like Turks, lying about in the luxurious warmth of the boiler-house, drinking pints of tea mixed with whisky at all hours of the day and night.

Since that time both of them had retained a fondness for Talisker whisky, claiming it came from the finest distillery in the whole of Scotland.

He came back from the toilet, suddenly feeling his energy drain from him. It was time to get on his way.

He refused another drink, but offered to buy them one. It was obvious his insistence was only embarrassing them. He dropped it and, finishing off his beer, picked up his cigarettes and matches.

Having exchanged farewells with the two young lads he left the pub and headed up towards where he'd left the Aston Martin.

'What's the funny look for?' Robin turned to Jimmy when Wishart had left.

'You might think this is crazy, but I'm sure that was Robert Wishart.'

Jimmy expressed a contemptuous disbelief.

'I'm not joking, I thought I knew his face. And there was the bag in the back of the car with the initials R.W. on it. And what about the pair of climbing boots we saw?'

'I don't believe it.'

'Please yourself.'

Jimmy was silent as he sipped his beer. A minute later he said: 'You know, you could be right.'

'I am right.'

Jimmy seemed to be thinking. 'Funny how you never hear about him much these days. Do you think he's mebbe packed up climbing?'

'Don't be so daft,' Robin scoffed. 'What, him?'

'Well, mebbe not. Tell me, what would you do if for some reason or other you had to give up the hills. You know, if something happened.'

'Me? I'll tell you what I'd do. I'd climb up Cloggy and throw myself off the top, that's what I'd do.'

'I think I would too.'

CHAPTER X

Joanna lay for a long time by the river bank, sucking on a blade of grass and listening to the gentle sound of the rippling water. Lying fla on her stomach she let the sounds come to her passively, imagining herself a leaf borne on the slowly flowing river.

The heat was intense and now and again she had to turn on her side to protect the back of her neck from the sun. Looking at the river in the bright white light, the waves and eddies swirling over the rocks reminded her of a shoal of tiny silver fish engaged in a magic dance.

For a moment she felt like casting her shoes off and joining the dance, but her impulse was checked when she thought of her father and what he'd told her the previous evening.

Ever since their return from Switzerland earlier in the year, she'd known instinctively there was something on his mind: something he'd been hiding from her. The knowledge of what he'd since told her was deeply disturbing, and she'd been unable to recapture the feeling of quiet elation she usually experienced on coming back to Scotland.

The warm air, rising from the long curving bowl of the glen in a thermal stream, created a softly moving breeze that ruffled her hair, spilling long gossamer strands across her wide forehead. Brushing the strands back she cupped her chin in her hands and gazed quietly at the river, wondering how it could change all the time and yet remain the same.

The ancient Greek, Heraclitus had said: 'No man steps into the same river twice.' How true. Everything changed; nothing ever remained the same. The grass under her and the earth with its feeling of warmth and security were also in the process of changing; the flowers came up and they withered away. Even the hills, their shape and form which she'd known since childhood were also subject to the same laws.

Living in a city it was difficult to retain a sense of awareness of this. Man had so propped his senses up with artificial aids that he'd lost his ability to recognise and accept the growth and change of nature. He'd filled his only real house with so much gadgetry, papered and painted its walls so heavily that now he could hardly distinguish its separate rooms, far less

90

its general shape.

The skin on her smooth wide forehead furrowed as she thought again of her father. He was so bed-rock sure of himself, so determined and able to convince himself what he was doing was right. It frightened her, this ability of his. Often she wondered how her mother might have handled him had she still been alive. She would have had her problems with him, but perhaps not. It was possible that this ceaseless determination of her father's was no more than compensation to make up for her loss. Maybe if ever he stopped it would be to find life so empty that he would simply drift into the cosy vacuum of London club life.

But how wrong it was not to be able to give; to bend at times when the wind blew.

Softly woolly clouds floated languidly overhead, partially obscuring the sun. It grew cool and she rose to her feet. It must be getting late and she wanted to have a bath before dinner.

Brushing the grass from her jeans she smoothed her hair in place and set off across the field, threading her way between the listless groups of Ayrshires which had been gathering near the water all day. At the far end of the field the ground rose steeply, a sharp wooded rise leading to the road. The heat of the sun had taken some of the strength out of her, and by the time she'd climbed up to the road her calves and ankles ached. There was still a good mile to walk before reaching the house.

The unsurfaced road was baked hard by the long, recent spells of sunshine and her feet were sore by the time she reached the point where the road diverged from the path of the river and ran into a little wooded copse which sheltered the house from the worst blasts of winter. Feeling tired and hungry she was glad at last when she cleared the trees and the house came into view.

Standing at the head of a sloping lawn, the old mansion house where she and her father were staying was solidly built from granite blocks, and though it was square-shaped the severity of its architecture was softened by the huge sycamores – which leaned protectively towards it – and its thick covering of ivy and creepers. At its easterly end was a collection of outhouses and a stone-built barn which at one time had been converted into stables. Colonel Farquharson, who owned the house and neighbouring farm, had been a keen horseman until a spinal injury, incurred in a fall, had ended his activities.

Now the stables were used to store winter feed for the cattle.

From the moment when she'd first set eyes on it, Joanna had liked the house. It was strong and robust without being grim, and like the surrounding hills it had been made to last. All her life she'd had a fondness for big houses with spacious rooms and large windows. Her father's house in Glen Isla only a few miles away was much smaller and, typical of its day, had tiny windows and lacked the disarray of outhouses and barns of the mansion house.

With the death of her mother, her father had sold their house in the village of Swanston outside Edinburgh and moved down to Tonbridge in Kent, leaving her to finish her schooling in Scotland before going on to University. But, five years since, he'd once more returned north to take up residence in their present house with its small acreage of arable and stock farming.

She'd hoped at the time he'd take an interest in the farm, and for a time he had, till the need for excitement and adventure called him again. And now, at the time when he should be learning to settle down, content with his achievements, and concentrating on the farm, he was actually considering something which she sensed was bigger and even more hazardous than anything he'd done before.

The little worried frown still on her features, she walked up the driveway, noting that the Land-Rover wasn't about. That meant her father was still fishing and wouldn't be back till he'd caught something. It also meant he would probably be late for dinner, and Colonel Farquharson's wife would be forced into her role of smiling martyrdom. Joanna didn't particularly like their host's wife. She was a soured up woman who was always complaining and could produce a headache at the slightest disruption of her daily routine. She wondered how Farquharson had been able to put up with her and still manage to retain a fairly cheerful manner and outlook. Apart from his rather archaic views she quite liked the Colonel.

She had her bath and afterwards lay down to read the current issue of the New York Review of Books which she'd brought with her from London. Half an hour later there was a quiet knock on the door.

'Who is it?'

'It's me, Miss Grant. Molly.'

'Oh, come in, Molly,' she said, getting up from the bed and putting her magazine down.

The door opened a foot and the maid put her head round

cautiously. Joanna couldn't help smiling, poor Molly, she was frightened of her own shadow, and Mrs Farquharson didn't help the girl with her domineering ways.

'Come in, Molly. What is it?'

The door opened a little farther, but the girl didn't dare to come into the room. Clutching the door knob as if she needed it for support she said in a breathless voice: 'It's Mrs Farquharson, miss, she told me to tell you your father phoned to say he'd be late and you've just to have dinner without him. Mistress said it'll be ready for eight o'clock if that's all right.'

Joanna wasn't surprised by the message from her father, but she felt rather annoyed that he'd left her to dine alone with their hostess, who wouldn't be in the best of moods as a result of his absence. 'Thank you, Molly,' she said. 'I'll be coming downstairs in a minute or two . . . I'll see Mrs Farquharson myself.'

The maid's head bobbed and the door was closed softly.

Joanna tidied a few things away and, after a quick inspection in the mirror, made her way downstairs, thinking she'd have to try and appease Mrs Farquharson in some way for her father's behaviour.

On reaching the hallway she heard voices from the drawing-room. That was odd, there was no one else staying in the house, but a moment later she heard the sound of the phone being replaced and the door opened and Mrs Farquharson stepped out.

'Ah, there you are, Joanna,' her hands fluttered nervously. 'I told Molly . . .'

'Yes, she's just told me. When did father phone?'

'Oh, just after tea. He said he and Craig were going farther down the water or something, and not to bother about dinner as he wouldn't be back till late. Not that I mind, but I've got to go in to Forfar this evening, and had I known we could have had dinner much earlier. This has been the most awful day. John's not coming back now till Wednesday and I've had people phoning him all day; really I wish he wouldn't do this sort of thing. He knows I've enough to cope with and . . . oh, I don't know . . .' she gave up in exasperation. 'It's really too much.'

'It looks as if father and Sandy haven't had much luck with the fish,' Joanna said.

Mrs Farquharson frowned. 'Fish? What fish . . . oh, I see what you mean. No, I don't suppose so.' She glanced at her watch, her frown deepening. 'We could have dinner in about twenty minutes if that's all right . . . you don't mind it being a little earlier, do you?'

'No, not at all. To tell the truth I'm rather glad. I'm absolutely starving.'

Mrs Farquharson glanced at her as if she'd just said something rude. 'Good. I'll be able to get away early then.'

'Can I help?' Joanna asked.

'Help?'

'Yes. Is there anything I can do?'

Mrs Farquharson's stare was disapproving, as if Joanna had implied she was incapable of running her household. 'No, no. I'll call you when it's ready,' she said, passing her hand across her forehead distractedly as if she'd suddenly recalled something else in a situation she was bravely trying to cope with. 'Oh yes, I'd almost forgotten, your father said he was going up to the hotel later if you'd like to join him . . . now I really must dash.' She went off at a great striding pace, making for the kitchen.

Joanna exhaled deeply and made a face to herself. What a woman! She hated to think what was in store for the poor cook. She went into the drawing-room and sat down, idly picking up a magazine which seemed to contain nothing but pictures of huntsmen and stately homes. The others in the pile weren't much better, and she got to her feet again and made her way across to the piano, lifting the lid and placing her hands upon the yellowing keys. It was a good instrument though it needed tuning. In a moment she'd sat down and begun playing a few of the Chopin preludes, but her memory was at fault and she kept running into phrases which seemed to go nowhere and she was forced to go right back to the beginning again. Eventually she rose and, opening the piano stool, found some Beethoven sonatas. She had just begun the *adagio* from the Pathétique when Mrs Farquharson returned to say dinner was ready.

For most of the meal Mrs Farquharson gave Joanna a detailed account of her many and varied complaints. Joanna could only nod silently. She was glad when the meal was over and her hostess excused herself and dashed away to get ready for her meeting in the little market town of Forfar.

When she'd gone, Joanna helped a horrified Molly to clear away the table things.

'Don't be silly, Molly. I do it myself all the time in London, you know. And anyway, why shouldn't I, I'm not doing anything else.'

94

Molly shook her head, torn between the fear of her mistress and what she would think if she ever found out, and the equally unforgivable crime of showing disrespect to a guest of the household. She got herself into such a state that Joanna gave up in the end and went back up to her room to get ready to meet her father at the hotel. Joanna was beginning to feel she couldn't stay there much longer. It was all right for her father, who didn't have to listen to Mrs Farquharson's continual whining or deal with her feudal mentality. He and Colonel Farquharson had done nothing but fish or else tramp around the farm since their arrival.

Suddenly she made up her mind. The very next day she would go back to Nanga Parbat – her father had renamed the house when he'd bought it – and he could please himself.

From the window of her room she could see across the fields away down to the river. The shadows cast by the trees were beginning to lengthen, and the little black, white and sometimes brown dots down by the river bank had begun to move perceptibly as the cattle, drugged by the long day's heat, headed back up the meadow land. It was still warm, but thin clouds had blanketed the sky, and a gentle breeze coming down the glen lazily stirred the tops of the conifers. Joanna decided to walk rather than take the car.

Changing out of her dress she put on a pair of faded needle-cords and a black, high-necked jumper. It was quite warm and, even if it did rain, which was unlikely, they would be coming back in the Land-Rover. She looked at her watch where it had hung on the mirror support of the dressing-table since she'd arrived; it had just gone half-past eight. It was three miles and a bit to the hotel, she'd be there long before ten and by that time her father should have arrived.

The strong smell of the fields was heavy in the air as she followed the road down by the river, and she could hear the deep lowing of the cattle as they moved up to higher ground like a band of dust-stained pilgrims chanting an ancient hymnal to the mother of all things. Now and again a calf would break away from the herd in a mad gallop of hooves, beating a drum-like tattoo on the baked ground, and in a moment a small stampede would start, only to die out as the herd came to an embarrassed halt as if ashamed of their own foolishness.

She adored cattle and their warm animal smell. They gave her a feeling of peace, and often she thought how wonderful it would be to get away from the city with its noise and dirt.

But once back in her office, surrounded by the world of books and the magic of publishing, she'd sigh in a sad-cheerful way, knowing it wasn't for her and wishing, as people did, that she had two lives. One wasn't sufficient for experimenting.

She'd thought about marriage, having had one or two proposals. The last was from the son of a wealthy farming family in Kent. But though the experience had been gratifying, she was aware the feeling was also transient; no more than a momentary gratification of the ego. But it was comforting to know that, if she never did get married, at least she'd had the opportunity. A girlish thought, but she allowed herself such things on occasions.

She and her friend Henrietta had spoken about marriage. Henrietta felt as she did. Lots of people got married out of a sense of duty or boredom. The former especially applied to their wealthier friends. Their association with horse meetings, hunt balls and parties reminded her too much of the marriage market.

No, if she ever married, the man would have to be sure of what he wanted from her and from life. Only then could she hope to give herself freely and without reservation. She neither wanted to possess nor be possessed: she wanted to share. Her friend Henrietta was in agreement with her.

She'd reached the end of the driveway, and, turning left along the main road, had only gone a few yards when she heard a car approach. It drew past her and then stopped. There were two men in the car. One of them wound down the passenger window and leaned out.

'Can we give you a lift?' he said with a smile.

She saw the driver was leaning over the seat, peering round the door pillars to get a clearer view of her. Both men were well-dressed and in their early thirties. She walked up to the car and, pausing for a moment to smile politely, she replied with just a touch of coolness in her voice: 'Thank you, but I'm walking.'

The man leant farther out of the window. 'We're heading for the hotel. We could give you a lift there,' he said with an easy confidence as he eyed her up and down.

'No thank you,' she repeated and walked on. She felt their eyes boring into her back but it didn't upset her unduly. Living in London she'd become well accustomed to men's approaches and felt perfectly capable of handling the situation.

She heard the car slip into gear and a moment later it drew up alongside her again.

She stopped this time as the man leant out of the window. Without giving him a chance to speak she eyed him coolly: 'I've already told you I prefer to walk. Now please don't ask me again.'

Out of the corner of her eyes as she walked on she saw the man shoot a glance at his companion in the driving seat, as if to say 'we're wasting our time with this one,' before the car started up again.

Passing her, the car slowed for an instant. 'Okay, ducky. See you up at the hotel.' She just caught the words before the car roared off in a burst of speed as if to demonstrate in some vicarious way the virility of its occupants.

Joanna exhaled deeply. She hoped for their sake they didn't approach her in the hotel. With her father around they would be in for a rude shock.

But walking along the road in the quiet of the evening she soon forgot the incident, her mind absorbed by the beauty of the countryside. To her left the road was bounded by a forest of dark green firs, but on the other side she had an unrestricted view of the fields, quilt-like patterns of greens, russets and the yellowing heads of the ripening corn, ascending gently in blanket-like folds towards the foothills of the Cairngorms. For a moment she was able to forget her worries as she enjoyed the smells and sights around her.

It was half an hour later before she reached the road fork. Turning to the left she walked on another few hundred yards and, rounding a sharp curve in the road, began to climb a steep hill. A number of cars passed slowly, as they dropped down a gear to negotiate the hill. Mercifully none stopped to offer her a lift.

At last, passing a handful of houses, she came to the hotel. It was a medium-sized building standing back from the road, with a large sun-porch fronting its entrance.

A number of vehicles were drawn up outside the hotel and there were more in the car-park opposite. Outside the entrance to the public bar a Land-Rover was parked close to the wall. Good, her father and Sandy had at least arrived. She was just about to push open the door when something caught her eye. At the far end of the hotel, near the solitary petrol pump, an open car was parked. There was something so unusual and distinctive about it she paused to have another look. It looked like an old Bentley and yet it didn't. She was almost on the point of going to have a closer look when she heard the door open. Turning round, she saw it was being held open for her.

'Oh, thank you,' she said, and stepped quickly into the sun-porch.

'Fine night,' the man holding the door open said, giving her a warm smile. Joanna puzzled for a second as she went inside. There had been something familiar about the face. Where had she seen him before? And then it came to her, it was the local postman. Without his uniform she hadn't recognised him; he'd looked quite different. It was true she didn't spend much time at home, but she should have recognised him.

Swing doors at the rear of the sun-porch led into the hotel. She pushed them open and stepped directly into the lounge. In front of her and to the right was a bow-fronted bar with a display of bottles cemented into the under structure of the counter. A group of people were gathered round the bar and at least half of the tables in the lounge were occupied. Heads turned to stare at her as she entered. Neither her father nor Colonel Farquharson's gamekeeper, Sandy Craig, appeared to be there, and she began to wonder if the Land-Rover she'd seen parked outside the public bar had been the Colonel's. There were so many Land-Rovers in the glen she could easily have been mistaken.

Leading off the lounge there was another bar. She'd just decided to have a look in there, and was walking towards it, when out of the corner of her eye she caught sight of one of the two men who'd stopped to offer her a lift. She saw him exchange a quick glance with his companion and he half rose to his feet. Just as she was preparing to make some discouraging remark she heard a cry, and turned to see a short, stout man approach her from behind the lounge bar. It was John Mitchell, the proprietor. He was dressed in an old pair of trousers and a shirt open at the collar.

'Ah, there you are, lass,' he said greeting her. 'Your faither and Sandy's in the ither bar. He told me to keep a look out for you. Here, I'll tak' you ben.' Mitchell took her by the arm and led her through.

There were a few men gathered round the bar but she recognised her father instantly, the broad shoulders stretching the checked tweed jacket to its limits, and the silvering grey hair rising from the short thick neck. He was standing at the bar counter drinking with the gamekeeper and turned as she came in.

'Joanna,' he greeted and stretched out his hand to take her by the arm.

Sandy, the gamekeeper, pulled up a bar stool. 'Would you like a seat, Miss?'

She sat down. 'Thank you, Sandy.'

Her father looked at her, his eyes filling with pleasure, proud of his one and only daughter. 'What would you like to drink, Joanna? Just a minute, John,' he caught the proprietor as he was about to leave. 'You'll join us for one, won't you?'

'Later perhaps. I've to get back to the ither bar. We're a bit short-handed the night,' Mitchell replied.

'Well, don't forget now,' Grant warned. 'We'll be expecting you.'

Joanna looked at her father. She could see he'd been drinking. His face was slightly flushed and his eyes were twinkling. She knew he drank heavily at times but he had such immense capacities it never seemed to have much effect on him.

'What did you say you were having, Joanna?' Her father spoke again. 'How about a Scotch? Have you tried Old Parr? Or what would you say to a Chivas Regal?'

Joanna shook her head. 'I think I'd rather have a glass of bitt –' she almost said 'bitter' but corrected herself in time, 'I mean a draught export. Yes, that's what I'd like, I feel quite thirsty.'

'Sure now? You can have one or the other, but I'm not going to encourage you to have both like Sandy here. It's a disgraceful habit to mix beer and whisky.'

The gamekeeper laughed. 'Aye, you're right there, Mr Grant. A "hauf and a hauf" is no exac'ly the drink for young ladies.'

Grant ordered a fresh round of drinks. 'Well now,' he said to his daughter, 'what have you been doing with yourself all day, eh? What have you been up to?'

Joanna took a sip of her beer and smiled at her father. He was addressing her as she imagined he would have addressed one of his junior officers. Even in retirement he hadn't lost the habit. But it wasn't all that surprising, she supposed. He couldn't help it, and at least he didn't insist on that archaic form of snobbery that demanded he should be addressed by his rank. 'Oh, nothing much,' she replied, 'I just had a walk, but I can see what you two have been doing.'

'Eh? What do you mean?' Grant frowned questioningly.

'You've been catching fish, haven't you?'

Sandy lit his pipe and gave a little dry chuckle, blowing smoke in the air. 'Aye, you might say that, Miss. Your father did manage one or two.'

'Well, aren't you going to tell me about it?' she asked.

Her father hrrrmphed. 'Well, we did get a couple. Yes, I suppose they were good fish, would you say so, Sandy?'

'Aye, they were that . . . a fine puckle o' fish.'

Joanna sat back a little and looked at them both. 'Is this some sort of conspiracy? Is that all you're going to say?'

Grant lifted his whisky and winked across at the 'keeper. 'I think you should tell her, Sandy,' he said.

'Aye, mebbe I should, your faither's sic a modest man, Miss Grant. Well now, we had a couple o' guid salmon . . .'

Joanna waited, knowing it was expected of her as part of the ritual.

'. . . aye, as fine a pair as I've clapped eyes on for many's a day. Wouldn't you say so yourself, Mr Grant?'

'Oh yes, fine fish, fine fish.'

Craig sucked at his pipe again to get it going and took another sip of his dram. 'You know, I've been on that water man and boy and I don't think I've seen better beasts. I think it was way back in '53 since I saw the like, and that's when there was a sicht mair fish in the water than there is now, I don't mind telling you. Mind you, going back before the war . . .'

'Are you going to tell me, Sandy, or do I have to ask someone else in the bar, because I'm certain that pretty near everyone else knows by this time . . .'

Sandy looked across at Grant as if asking permission.

'Yes, I think you'd better tell her, Sandy,' Grant said with a wink.

'Very well. As I said, they were a fine pair of sea-trout. Good clean fish and well taken if you don't mind me saying so, Mr Grant. Though mind you for an awful minute I thought you were going to lose the second one when he went off down to the foot of the pool yonder with the speed o' lightning, I fair thought he was . . .'

'Sandy?' Joanna warned.

'Aye, of course, you were asking what size they were. Well now,' he stroked the grey stubble on his chin, 'I'd say the first one was all of eighteen pounds . . .'

'Eighteen!' Joanna gasped delightedly.

'Oh yes, all of that I would say. John Mitchell's to put him on the scales just to check, but I'd say it was a good eighteen if not even more.'

'Eighteen pounds, why that's wonderful,' Joanna clapped her hands together, so pleased that her father had had such a good day on the river.

'Aye, but just wait a minute, Miss, there's more to follow . . .'

'You mean?'

'Oh aye, there's more to follow. After that your father got a good ten-pounder,' Joanna's features registered a little disappointment, 'Oh, I know, it's hardly worth bothering aboot but then, just as we were thinking of calling it a day, he hooked this big fellow . . .'

'Yes . . .?'

'Man, he was big. And off like a boat when he was struck. But your father had him. Oh, he had him all right; good and true. And what a bonny fecht he put up before he was landed. But he was on the bank at last, lying there as fat as a calf and weighing . . . oh, I wouldn't like to say just, you can call me a liar if I'm wrong, but yon fish was all of twenty-six pounds.'

'Twenty-six,' Joanna's hands shot to her mouth. 'Twenty-six pounds.' She turned to her father, instinctively putting her head on his arm. 'But that's wonderful. You know, I think I'm going to have that whisky, after all.'

Her father smiled back at her, feeling his heart warm to his daughter. 'By all means, but I'm going to insist you drink your beer first. I'm sure you've enough bad habits as it is, I wouldn't like you to get started on this "half and half" business of Sandy's.'

They looked at each other for a long moment, each proud of the other in their own way.

'Excuse me, Mr Grant,' Sandy interjected. 'There's someone wants me in the bar. I'll be back in a few minutes.'

Joanna waited till he had gone. 'You know, I should really be very angry with you.'

His eyebrows went up. 'Why?'

'Going off and leaving me with Mrs Farquharson like that.'

'Was she terribly upset?'

'Upset? She was near crippled with silent indignation. I had to spend a most uncomfortable hour with her.'

'Oh I am sorry, my dear. But we were on the water and we knew the fish were there. I just couldn't go off and leave them, now could I? Was she really very angry?'

'I think she was near the foaming at the mouth stage.'

'Oh come now, Joanna. I phoned her around five. That's not too bad, is it? It cost me half an hour off the water too. Tell me the truth.'

'Well, let's say she wasn't very pleased. You know what she's like . . . and that's another thing I want to talk to you about.'

CHAPTER XI

Robert Wishart threw for the double three, and missed. The dart landed with a solid *plonk* in the segment bounded by the double and treble spaces.

'Christ, man, that's three to split,' his partner exploded.

'Sorry, Jim,' Wishart grinned.

'Sorry, you hooer! You'll be a damned sight sorrier if we lose this game. Of a' the bluidy partners.'

Wishart grinned again as the next man stepped up to throw. He'd joined in the game nearly an hour before. A game in which he'd been partnering the spare-time barman, Jim, against one of the local shepherds and his mate. They were playing for pints, but in this, the last game, the stakes had been upped to pints and nips. With the opposition needing double sixteen the game had reached a critical stage.

He walked over to the table where he'd left his pint.

'Aye, you fair buggered it there, didn't you, Robert,' said old Sandy Craig who'd come into the public bar a few minutes earlier. 'Just look at Jim's face. If Ian gets his double wi' this throw he'll no speak to you for a week.'

Ian, the shepherd, was taking great care lining up the dart, his hand pawing the air in a series of practice movements. For a moment the hubbub in the bar was stilled as everyone turned to see the result of his throw.

Ian steadied himself for the last time and with a sideways flick of his hand launched the dart. It landed in the sixteen space just missing the double. He cursed and turned to his partner and shook his head irritably. He threw again and got an odd number.

It was Jim Anderson's turn. He picked up his darts from where they lay on the table.

'Come on, Jim,' Wishart encouraged, 'you can do it.'

'I'll bluidy well have to, won't I?' Anderson said. He stepped up to the mark and spat on the floor, working the saliva in with his boot. The bar was silent. Anderson was a good player and had a knack of carrying off the long shot, often coming from behind to win the game.

Wishart buried his head in his pint, scarcely daring to look. There was a shout.

Anderson's first dart had found its target. He had two left

to get the double, with the opposition breathing hard down his neck. But Anderson was nothing if not a showman. Instead of throwing his next dart right away he crossed over to the table and finished off his pint at one gulp, saying to the shepherd: 'Might just as well get them up now, Ian.'

The crowd in the bar liked it and roared their approval as he stepped up to the mark again. His next throw grazed the wire landing outside the scoring area. One dart left!

He took his time over it, rubbing his hand over his leathery features and shuffling his feet about till he got settled in position.

There wasn't a clink of glass to be heard and even the barman on duty stopped for a minute to watch Anderson throw. The dart seemed to glide through the air, approaching the top of the board at an angle before dropping down to make contact. It found the space like a homing missile. In a moment the bar erupted and half a dozen hands slapped Anderson on the back with cries of: 'You've done it again, you bugger!'

Everybody was laughing and joking as Wishart and Anderson went over to the bar to collect. Wishart first toasted the opposition, knocking the whisky back at one go, and then with pint in hand went over to where Craig was standing.

'Well Sandy, how're you keeping? I haven't had a chance to see you since I arrived.'

'Oh fine, Robert, just fine. Canna complain. And how's yourself? Are you staying for long?'

'Oh, a bit yet. I only arrived the weekend.'

'Man that's fine, so we'll be seeing a bit more of you, then.' Wishart smiled. 'I would think so. I'm staying here.'

'Here? At John's? Whit's the matter you're no' staying up at the cottage?'

'I was going to, but I've got a bit of work to do and it's handier here.'

'Dinna tell me you're getting a bit o' a toff. You've worked up at the cottage afore,' Sandy said with a grin.

'That's all right when I've got time. Here at John's I don't have to bother with cooking or clearing up.'

Craig nodded. 'Aye, I suppose that's richt enough, but man, though I like John Mitchell's place fine, I widna think it's the best place in the world to get work done.' He chuckled into his drink. 'There's a gey lot o' temptations here, Robert, though I don't have to tell you that. But tell me are you no' daen' any climbing, that you're up here? I remember the time when we couldna keep you awa' from the hills. Winter and summer you'd be up and doon that road as regular as the clock.'

Wishart's eyes clouded for a moment and he held his pint mug up to his face so that Sandy wouldn't see his expression. Almost everyone, since he'd arrived, had asked the same question and he'd had to make excuses.

'Dinna tell me you've stopped climbing a' thegither. I widna believe that.' The old man looked at him shrewdly.

'What? No, no.' Wishart shook his head in denial. 'It's just that I've a lot of work to do, that's all. Anyway I need a bit of a rest just now, I've got plenty on my plate for next year.'

'Oh. One o' they expeditions again, is it?'

'Mmmm, you could say it's something like that,' he replied, the lie leaving him with a sour taste in his mouth.

'Ah, well, if it's like that, Robert, I'll no' ask any more questions. Here drink up and gie's your glass, I'll get you a drink.'

'No, no. I'll get you one.'

'Haud on there now, Robert, it was me that asked first, wasn't it?' Craig waited till Wishart had drained his tumbler.

Wishart hated himself at that moment. What had made him hint at a thing like that when he knew damn well he wasn't going on any expedition next year . . . nor the year after, nor the year after that? Why did he have to do it? Why couldn't he have told old Sandy the truth or even half the truth. All he'd had to say was that he was concentrating so much on writing that he didn't have time for climbing and left it at that. But no, he'd had to hint that something was brewing, and though Sandy wasn't a gossip he would see no harm in mentioning the fact that 'Robert was planning something abroad again, something he was keeping a secret for the time being.'

Again, and for the hundredth time, he cursed himself for his stupid pride. Up to that moment he'd slowly been beginning to learn to enjoy life again. It was as if he'd been able thought of Carole didn't seem to disturb him so much, though the night after he'd arrived he'd had so much to drink he'd tried to phone her. But long walks during the day, the good food and the company in the hotel had done wonders for him in a few days. And now the old sour feeling had returned to threaten his newly found peace.

Sandy came back with the drinks. He'd got Wishart a whisky to go with his beer.

'Are you trying to get me drunk, Sandy?'

'Drink it up, it'll do you the world o' guid. Whisky never harmed anyone yet that wasn't already harmed by something else. Well, now that you're here and you're not to be wandering aboot the hills, whit would you say to a bit o' fishing? You'll be able to spare a few hours for that surely?'

'Fishing? On the Colonel's water?'

'Och, you're no' to worry aboot that. It's a long time ago and you were little more than a laddie then. Anyway you're a bit of a celebrity now; picture in the papers and on the telly an' a' that. I think Colonel Farquharson might be richt glad to give you a day on the water. Say the word and I'll put it to him when he comes back from Edinburgh.'

'But I don't even have a rod.'

'I've a couple o' spare rods doon by, at the hoose. You'll no' be short o' gear.'

'It's very good of you, Sandy, but you're sure you want to ask the Colonel? It might be a long time ago but poaching's poaching and I've never met a laird yet that didn't have a long memory.'

'Tsk, tsk. I've no' muckle time for poachers myself, but you took a fish for a bit of devilment, that's a'.' Craig put his hand on Wishart's arm. 'Now you just say the word and leave the rest to me. Mind you, I canna guarantee you ony fish, though we had a richt bonny pair the day. Man, they were grand fish.' Craig raised his glass, his blue eyes twinkling at the memory of the day's catch. 'Damn near fifty pounds 'tween the pair o' them.'

Wishart whistled softly.

'Aye, as near as dammit.'

'I heard you had a good day, but I'd no idea . . . who were you out on the water with?'

'A Mr Grant from over Isla way. He's staying wi' the Colonel for a day or twa. Mebbe you'll know him?'

Wishart shook his head. 'No, I don't think so.'

'Mebbe not, but man, he's a richt bonny fisher. No' like half they English loons, flinging awa' at the water as if they were trying to whup the fish to death. Aye, he's a fine man, Mr Grant, with as bonny a dochter as I've clapped eyes on. A fair charmer o' a lass she is, with never ony o' your high and mighty airs even if she does come from London.' Craig threw his head back and finished off his dram. 'Well, must awa' back, Robert. I'm in the ither bar wi' Mr Grant . . . I just came in to see Andra Scott for a minute, so if you'll be excusing me . . .'

'Hang on, Sandy,' Wishart protested. 'I haven't bought you a drink yet.'

But Craig shook his head. 'I promised to be back. I've to see Mr Grant to see if he's ony plans for the morn, and he'll be wanting to get awa' to his supper as he hisna had a bit a' day. But I'm just next door, so I'm no' that far away if you're keen to put me up a dram.'

Grant and his daughter appeared to be having a serious discussion when Sandy returned. He hesitated, but Grant caught sight of him over Joanna's shoulder.

'Ah, there you are, Sandy. I was just wondering if we'd lost you for the night. You've arrived just in time. I'm just going next door for a quick bite, are you joining us?'

'Oh no, Mr Grant. I had my tea this afternoon, you remember, when you went to make your phone call. And the wife'll have my supper ready when I get hame.'

'Right, in that case I'm going to leave you to look after Joanna. Apparently she's not hungry either.'

'It's only a few hours ago since I had dinner, father. What do you think I am?'

'All right, all right. Now, Sandy, you don't mind, do you?' Craig's eyes twinkled. 'It's a rare pleasure, Mr Grant.'

'Good. That's settled. I won't be long, Joanna. Sandy will keep an eye on you.' Grant patted his daughter's arm. Joanna watched him go, the broad back almost filling the doorway as he made for the dining-room, his stride – despite the fact that he'd been drinking quite heavily – firm and purposeful.

There was a sound of a match being scraped and a volume of thick blue smoke enveloped her head. She turned, coughing. Craig was just shaking a match out, puffing at his pipe with studied concentration. He got it going, waving his hand to dispel the clouds of smoke. 'Sorry, Miss Grant,' he said, 'but I canna be daein' wi' they fags. You don't mind, do you?'

Her eyes stinging, she shook her head vigorously as if trying to clear the air around her. She blinked once or twice, taking out her handkerchief to dab her eyes. Craig took a step back, switching his pipe to the other side of his mouth. 'If you'd like I'll put it out . . .'

'No, no, no,' she said, stopping him. 'It's all right, it just caught my breath for a moment. Please don't stop.' She put her handkerchief away.

'Are you . . .?'

'Yes, of course. Anyway, considering what I've to breathe every day in London, your pipe's probably harmless.'

Craig pushed his deerstalker back and scratched his head. 'You know, Miss, that's a place I've never been. I've heard a fair lot aboot it but . . . och well, I'm too auld to go now.'

Joanna looked at the stolid old man before her, dressed in his heavy tweed plus-four suiting and thick-soled boots. She smiled to herself at the thought of him in London; at a publisher's party for instance. He'd stand out like a man from Mars.

Suddenly a thought struck her and she tried to recall which houses, if any, had published titles about gamekeepers or stalkers. She knew she'd seen one or two somewhere, but there might be an idea here. Sandy Craig was an intelligent man with a lot of wisdom and knowledge packed into his – good heavens, she looked at him again, unable to believe he was seventy-four. Seventy-four years of age and as spry and as healthy as many people half his age. He must have lots and lots of stories locked away in that independent mind of his. It might just be worthwhile following up. She must remember to approach him – but 'gey cannily' to use the expression he would have used himself – before she went back. She wondered how it might appeal to him. Perhaps it would be better to get her father to raise it. He and the old gamekeeper got on very well together. She'd have to think about it a bit more before doing anything. 'London, Sandy?' she said. 'I don't think you'd like it, you're much better off up here. It's a dreadful place in many ways.'

Craig shook his head. 'Aye, mebbe you're richt, but I'd like to have seen it. A man should see what's going on in the ither half o' the world, gie'n the opportunity.' As he spoke his gnarled hand delved into a pocket of his waistcoat. He hauled out a great turnip of a watch, thumbing the cover open to glance at the time before closing it again and putting it back in his pocket.

Joanna, noting the action, half-rose from her stool. 'Am I holding you back?' she asked. 'Why don't you just go? I'll be all right here by myself, and anyway father will be back soon. Please, you don't have to stay because of me.'

'No, no, no,' Craig frowned and shook his head. 'Just bide where you are. There's nothing to worry aboot, Missie. I was just wondering if your faither'll be wanting to stay on after he's had a bite.'

'You're wondering about how you're going to get back,' Joanna said, thinking about the Land-Rover outside.

'Oh, I'll get back all right. Andra Scott'll gi' me a lift, but he'll be leavin' the back o' ten.'

Joanna made to glance at her own watch before realising she'd left it off. Grasping the counter she tilted her stool back to glimpse the clock above the bar. It was nearing ten. She half got to her feet but Craig stopped her.

'No, no, you're no' to disturb your father when he's at his meal. We'll give him a few minutes yet and not to worry, Andra widna go without first telling me.'

'But –'

'Please now, Miss Grant. I wouldn't like you to bother your faither when he's at his supper.'

Joanna saw that the old man was determined, and reluctantly climbed back on her stool.

'Would you be wanting another whisky?' Sandy asked.

'No thank you,' she replied, feeling that the old man had better things to do with his money than throw it away on whisky. She would have liked to have bought him a drink but she'd left the house without her purse.

Toying with her glass she became aware that a man had entered the bar. He was standing in the doorway looking over in her direction. The old gamekeeper caught her glance and, removing his pipe from his mouth, swung round. He held his pipe up, gesticulating.

'You've come to buy me that dram, Robert?' he called out. 'Come awa' in, man, and dinna stand there.'

Wishart hesitated, unsure now that he could see that the girl was with Sandy. 'I'll come back later.'

'No, no, man. Come awa' in. I'm sure Miss Grant widna mind you joining us, would you now?' he said turning to her.

Joanna shook her head slowly as she eyed the tall figure in the doorway. 'Not at all, Sandy.'

Wishart came over.

'This is Miss Grant, Robert,' Sandy said. 'Mr Grant's daughter.'

'How'd you do,' Wishart said, finding himself looking into an unusually calm pair of grey eyes.

'Robert, like yourself, is just up from London, though nane the worse o' it by a' accounts,' Sandy said with a chuckle.

'Really,' Joanna replied with a smile, noting at the same time the man had made no attempt to shake hands, and she wondered if it was because of shyness. And yet he didn't look

109

shy. In fact he was looking at her steadily. She returned his gaze, noting the little worried creases round the eyes and the unmistakable air of sadness. She sensed it in the same way she could often sense the identity of the caller when the phone rang. It had happened too often, especially with her father, to be argued away by such explanations as 'coincidence' or 'chance'.

The stranger was speaking to Sandy in an accent that, though anglicised, she suspected was alien to him. There was almost a hint of self-consciousness about it, giving her the impression that his native speech would be much more like Sandy's than her own.

The barman had come over and was waiting to take the order.

'That'll be two whiskies and two halves . . . I'm sorry, what would you like?' he added, speaking to her.

Joanna was about to ask for a fruit juice but changed her mind. 'I think I'll have a whisky, if you don't mind.'

The barman served the drinks. 'Will I put them on your bill, Mr Wishart?' he asked.

Wishart paid and Sandy raised his glass. 'Well, here's health,' he said, tossing off his whisky, and looked at his watch again with a shake of his head. 'Did you see Andra through there, Robert?' he asked.

'Oh, I meant to tell you, he left a few minutes ago, I . . .'

'Whit?' Craig's brows came down. 'He's awa', you say?'

'Yes, he told me to tell you.'

The old man's face filled with anger. 'Just wait . . .'

'It's okay,' Wishart cut in. 'I said I'd run you home if you needed a lift. Andra was going to come through and tell you himself but I said I was on my way to see you anyway.'

Craig turned to Joanna. 'I'm sorry, Miss Grant, but I'll have to go. I promised the auld wife I'd be home by the back o' ten. Mebbe you could tell Mr Grant I had to go. I'll see him in the morning at the same time again. I hope you don't mind me leaving you on your own . . .'

'Don't worry about it, Sandy. I'll be perfectly all right. Father shouldn't be very long now . . .'

'Mebbe I should pop in and see him for a minute . . .?'

'Now,' she reminded him. 'remember what you said, you mustn't disturb a man when he's at his food.'

'Would you like to hang on for a bit?' Wishart interjected.

'Oh no, man, no. I promised the wife faithfully. We'd best get going now.' Craig turned to Joanna once more. 'I'm sorry to leave, but I'll be seeing you again before you go, surely.'

Wishart asked the barman to put his drink aside till he returned. 'I'll say good night now, in case you're gone by the time I get back,' he said to Joanna, his mouth twisting in a lop-sided smile.

Left by herself Joanna glanced around. There was still no sign of her father. He'd probably met someone in the dining-room. She was glad to discover she wasn't the only female in the bar. Since her arrival earlier quite a few more people had come in.

She sipped her whisky. What was that name again? She was pretty good at remembering names – in her job she had to be – but Sandy, in the strange way the Scots had of seeming reluctant to make proper introductions, had only mentioned his first name. And yet for some reason she seemed to know his second name. But that was impossible, how could she when they'd only just met? And then she remembered: the barman had mentioned his name when he'd spoken about putting the drinks on his bill. She hadn't been paying attention at the time, but she was sure it was a short name and began with an 's', or was it an 'f'? Fisher, was that it? No it wasn't Fisher, it was a Scots name that reminded her of something. It reminded her of . . . of . . . of . . . she gave up trying. What did it matter anyway? She was going back to Glen Isla next day and had told her father so. She put it out of her mind and once more returned to thinking about her father. The more she thought about it the less she cared for what he had in mind. It sounded difficult and dangerous to her. It was all right for him to say that a man had to live danger-ously at times or he'd become no more than a hothouse plant, protected from the realities of the outside world, but he was no longer a young man. And another thing, all the expedi-tions he'd been on up to now had been full-scale assaults with a large team of experts to back them up. This scheme of his sounded too much like a 'do-it-yourself' effort. It lacked the authority and safety of numbers. She'd climbed herself a little and understood that climbing, especially at extreme heights and in severe weather conditions, was always attended by a certain amount of risk, but it didn't seem so bad some-how if it was a proper expedition.

She sipped at her whisky again, wishing she had a cigar-ette, but she didn't have a penny with her. It was funny, she seldom smoked and now at this moment she felt like a cigar-ette, though she didn't feel like asking the barman for one even though she could return it later. That was out of the question. But she could ask him for a packet. That would be different. It wasn't just like borrowing one cigarette, was it?

The barman was wiping the counter. He wasn't serving. All she had to do was lean over and ask him. She lifted her glass, encouraging him to wipe the counter in front of her.

'Gets in a bit of a mess,' the barman said, swabbing the dark rings left on the wood by the glasses. 'There you are, that's much better.'

'Excuse me . . .?' With a shock she checked herself in time. Instead of asking for a cigarette she'd nearly asked the barman the name of the man who had bought her a drink. Horrified, she forgot all about her desire for a cigarette, stunned at the thought of what she'd nearly done. Not that it was such an awful thing, but that it had been so unexpected and impulsive, almost as if some other person had taken possession of her mind.

What had she had to drink? Only two whiskies. Not even two, she hadn't finished her second. She heard a sound behind her and turned to see her father.

'Sorry to have been so long. I bumped into Graham Findlay in the dining-room. He was telling me all about his revolutionary ideas on sheep. Very interesting. We must have him along some evening. He's a good chap, Findlay; lots of drive and obviously capable of using his mind. He'll be able to help a lot next year when I really get down to it.'

But she was only half-listening. 'Father,' she said, 'can you let me have a cigarette?'

'Eh? What?' Like his daughter Grant seldom smoked. He gave her one, a surprised look on his face.

'Where's Craig?' he asked as he lit it for her.

'He had to get home. His wife was expecting him and he'd promised not to be late.'

Grant frowned.

'He left his apologies and said he'd see you at the same time to-morrow,' Joanna explained.

'Uhmm.' Grant looked displeased. 'He might . . .?'

'Father! You were only to be away a few minutes, remember. You've been gone nearly half an hour and he *did* promise to be home at a reasonable hour.'

'I suppose so,' Grant said, 'now that I think of it. Well now, have you been enjoying yourself?' He glanced at the glass in her hand. 'I hope you haven't been drinking too much, have you?'

112

'Only a bottle of whisky.'

He sighed. 'I wish you'd be serious.'

'I was, earlier on,' she reminded him.

'We've gone into all that, Jo,' he said irritatedly. 'Why do you have to keep worrying about it? You wouldn't deny me my last fling, now, would you? After it's all over I promise you I'll settle down to the life of a gentleman farmer.'

'I'm not sure if I approve of that,' she mused.

'I don't suppose you do. It's all that Bolshie nonsense of yours. Perhaps you think we should turn the land over to the masses, eh? As if it isn't bad enough as it is with their infernal picnics; tramping about, littering the countryside.'

'If you're so concerned about pollution, why don't you have a look at what industry's doing to the land?'

'That's nothing but scaremongering. Anyway, I'm not going to argue with you, Joanna. I can see the Marxists at Edinburgh University have done a thorough brainwashing job on you.'

Joanna laughed. 'Oh, father. Most of the Marxists I know hold me as a sort of woolly-minded bourgeois liberal . . . and anyway I'd like a drink please.'

'I can see I'm going to have to have a serious talk with you one day, Joanna,' he said. 'Is that a whisky you're having?'

It was past closing time but John Mitchell, the proprietor, had a strong dislike for the licensing laws. He was an innkeeper and felt it his duty to look after the needs of the hungry and thirsty at all times. As a result, his hotel had a happy relaxed atmosphere about it and in all his years as licensee he'd never had cause to evict a single person.

'Do you know, Joanna,' Grant said when he'd got their drinks, 'that in spite of all your theorising and philosophising the world is, and always will be, divided into two kinds of people: the rulers and the ruled. And whether you like it or not we are the class that rules. It is our duty and responsibility to lead. Natural selection – you should know this – has produced us.'

'Like prize cattle?' Joanna said.

'In a way, yes. Take these chaps here, for instance. Good chaps, the salt of the earth you might say, but they are born to be toilers. They need someone to lead them or they'd become extinct, like any other species that has failed to keep pace.'

'But you just mentioned Graham Findlay, isn't he one of the toilers you speak of?' said Joanna, beginning to feel the gulf that separated her from her father.

'I admit Graham is an exception, but just the same . . .'

'He's not quite officer material,' Joanna interjected.

Grant frowned. 'I wasn't going to say that, Joanna, but since you put it that way, I agree. It's a rare quality, you know. You spoke about prize cattle a moment ago, well, we are a special breed and that's what it's all about – it comes down to breeding in the end.'

'I wonder what you'd think of special breeds if I married a bus-conductor, or a farm-worker. That would be treason from your point of view, wouldn't it?' She regretted the words the moment she'd spoken them. She loved her father. In his own way he was quite humanitarian and hated snobbery and pretentiousness as much as she did, but it was his lack of flexibility, his ability to convince himself that what he did was right that frightened her. He had the sort of strength that could so easily be abused. But then, all his life he'd been brought up in the traditions and strict codes of military life. He was a product of his environment just as much as she was of hers, and now she'd hurt him.

Grant looked at his daughter with an expression of pain and resentment.

'That was hardly a nice thing to say, Jo. You know you're free to marry whom you choose. But you know my feelings on the subject. I won't say more than that.'

Impulsively she leaned over and touched his arm. 'I'm sorry, Pops. I didn't mean to hurt.'

Pops? She hadn't used the word since a child, and it brought a smile to his face. For an instant he could see her, long-legged and gawky, pigtails sticking out from beneath her school uniform hat, face freckled and the grey eyes wide open in a kind of breathless sincerity. He smiled again. Pops? 'I'm afraid you're much too clever for me with your feminine cunning. Shall we go after this one? Mustn't be too late. Craig will be round first thing in the morning.'

'Oh yes, he told me to tell you.' She was silent for a minute. She'd just remembered the name of the man whom Sandy had introduced her to.

'What are you thinking about?'

'Oh, nothing. Just dreaming, that's all.'

'A waste of time, my dear. You should plan, not dream. I told you I had a word with Graham Findlay. Next year he'll be able to help me a lot with the farm. You've got to plan in advance.'

114

'Won't you miss . . . I mean it's going to be such a big change for you.'

'Oh, I don't know. I'll be able to do a bit of shooting and fishing. And then of course there's some climbing to be had here. It's quite good in winter. I'll even get in a bit of skiing. In a way I'm quite looking forward to it.'

'You're going to miss a lot of your old friends, staying here.'

'Perhaps. But there's John Farquharson and . . . well, I've got to know quite a lot of people around.'

She thought for a moment. 'A lot?'

'Quite a few.' He looked at her shrewdly. 'Why do you ask?'

'Oh, nothing. I just wondered if you'd heard of someone called Wishart?'

He shook his head slowly as he considered the question. 'Wishart? Can't say I have. I could always ask John Farquharson if it's important, he knows everyone around.'

'It doesn't matter.'

'Come now, Joanna. You must have a reason for asking,' he said looking at his daughter quizzically.

'Well, it's just that a man called Wishart came in to see old Sandy when you were at supper. I wondered if you might have known him.'

'And that's all?'

'He *did* buy me a drink, father.'

'What was his name, did you say, I mean his full name?'

'Robert. Robert Wishart.'

Grant shook his head again. 'No. I don't know anyone of that name in these parts.' He stared at the bar counter for a moment. 'The only Robert Wishart I know, in fact the only Wishart I know, is the mountaineering chap. Done a lot of stuff abroad. The Himalaya, Karakorum and that sort of thing. Writes books and articles. I'm sure you must have heard of him. He was involved in a nasty incident a couple of years ago. It was in all the papers. Not his fault, of course, but I don't like all this publicity nonsense. It's all right perhaps for show business, but not for mountaineering. No, I don't like it.'

'Mmm.' Joanna had a strange intuitive feeling. 'You know him quite well?'

'Not exactly. In fact I've never really met him, though I know of him, of course. He's quite well-known in mountaineering circles. Supposed to be a brilliant snow and ice man,

115

though I haven't heard much of him recently. A rather odd sort of chap. Bit of a lone-wolf, or so I understand. But I don't know why I'm telling you all this.'

Joanna's feeling of intuition had grown stronger as her father spoke. Her curiosity had been aroused and she had a mental image of the face again with its far-away, lost look and the hint of bitterness round the mouth.

'Shall we go?' Her father's voice broke into her thoughts. 'I don't know what time you're planning to leave in the morning, come to think of it I don't know why you're going at all. I don't like the thought of you staying all alone in the house. Why can't you stay till the end of the week and we can go back together? I know Farquharson's wife can be a bit of an old dragon, but you don't have to spend all your time in her company, do you now?'

'Hmm. I've been thinking about it. Perhaps you're right. After all it *is* only a few days. Maybe I will stay.'

Grant looked at his daughter uncomprehendingly. 'You mean you've changed your mind. What's happened to you?'

She rose from her stool. 'Let's say I'm thinking about it.'

He shook his head. 'I'll never understand you. Not long ago you were saying . . .' he gave up.

She linked her arm in his and together they went outside.

CHAPTER XII

He rose at seven and, after a quick wash, slipped out of the hotel and, picking up the narrow winding path, made his way down to the river.

The only sounds from the hotel had been the soft clink of plates and cutlery being laid out in the dining-room and the faintly muffled noises coming from the kitchen. But down here, by the river, life had begun since early dawn. The trees were alive with birds, noisy and chattering, filling the air with their sounds like a gathering of busy housewives.

Standing on the wooden bridge which led across to the old sawmill on the other side of the river, he gazed down at the slow run of water beneath his feet. The long period without rain had lowered the level of the river. Like the hulls of up-turned boats on a foreshore, the rocks lay exposed, their top covering of dark green lichens beginning to turn brown with exposure to the sun. The river had grown so thin and starved that in places it could have been forded by the simple means of jumping from rock to rock.

It was difficult to imagine that the same river, after the melting of the spring snows, would be swollen and fat, tugging greedily at its banks like a captive animal trying to break free. But that was in the spring and now it was well into summer. Even at this hour of the morning there was a warmth in the air as if the land was returning some of the heat borrowed the previous day. The cattle and sheep had begun to stir, foraging about in the green fields as if they knew that, come midday, with the sun high overhead, it would be too hot to stir.

Everyone was enjoying the long spell of good weather. Everyone but the fishers. By evening in the public bar of the hotel the air would be filled with complaints about the state of the water as the anglers drowned their sorrows and prayed for rain. And yet there was fish to be had in the right places. And in the right places inevitably meant that you needed to know the right people or have the right money.

He was one of the lucky ones. He'd been offered a day on the best water. The deep, olive-green pools where the big ones lay, quietly resting, and waiting for the day when the

117

rains would come and they'd make their way up water, driven by an instinct as old as time itself.

The last time he'd been down at the pools it had been at night with the moon low down and the snapping of every twig and branch a thunderclap in his ear. That had been a long time ago. He and Drew had caught fish that night and the fact that they were there without the knowledge or permission of the laird had made it all the more exciting.

In those days he hadn't met Joe or even known of his existence. But Joe would have treasured that night. You had only to say the word and he would be at your side, ready and willing. And now it was too late. There would be no big fish for Joe. No creeping soft-footed through the night, voices hushed and scarce daring to breathe. Joe had gone out into a bigger, darker and much more silent night. A night without end. And yet this sunlit morning there was something of Joe right here in the song of the birds, the sound of the river, and the deep rich smell of the earth. Perhaps he came up every morning with the sun to go down with it again in the evening.

Somewhere in one part of the world or another the sun always shone, perhaps carrying with it Joe's strong spirit and his smiling conviction that it was all worthwhile.

Wishart bent down and, picking up a stone from the bridge, dropped it into the water below. The stone seemed to hang for a long time before descending at speed to hit the water with an audible plopping sound. For an instant it left a record of its passage into another element in a series of ripples, short-lived as trace patterns of atomic particles – then no more.

Was that all that life was: A stone cast into water, a brief transference of energy, a fleeting micro-second of consciousness – then nothing?

But no matter, the sun was shining. Up there in the sky the great presider, greater than all the kings, emperors and ottomans, had come amongst his people to renew their courage and hope.

Strange thoughts for so early in the morning; strange thoughts for a man to have before he'd eaten his breakfast. He bent down and picked up another stone, but this time with a strong flick of his wrist flung it towards the far bank. He stood for a minute and retracing his steps, he headed back across the bridge and up the path back to the hotel.

As he entered the hallway he could hear the sound of doors slamming. The rattle and clink of china and cutlery

118

were quite audible now and there was a barrage of noise from the kitchen as the chef threatened and harried his staff.

He slipped upstairs to his room to get his cigarettes and matches before going into the dining-room. On the way back, at the foot of the stair, he bumped into John Mitchell, the proprietor.

'Well, it's yourself, Robert, and how are you this morning?'

'I'm fine. I've just been down to the river. I've never seen the water so low.'

Mitchell shook his head sadly. 'Aye, we could do with a bit of rain. You weren't thinking of having a go at the fish, were you?'

'Nah. I don't think so. Mebbe later in the week. Sandy was saying he might get me a day on one of Farquharson's beats . . . the big pool.'

'Oho. So that's the story. Well, if there's fish to be had that's the place for them. Yon was a right fine pair Mr Grant killed yesterday.'

'Aye, so I heard. Is he . . . is he staying here by the way?'

'What? Mr Grant? No, he's a place over Glen Isla way, though he's staying wi' the Colonel at the moment.'

'Ah, well, I'll away in and have my breakfast. I'm taking a trip into town later on. Must get some pipe tobacco or I'll be smoking myself to death with these fags.'

'What would you be doing that for? I've some pipe tobacco through in the public bar.'

'You must be joking, John. That stuff would burn the lungs out of you.'

'Too strong for you, is that it? Aye, Robert, I mind the day you used to smoke it and be glad of it. I hope a' that livin' in London's no making you saft.' Laughing to himself Mitchell went on his way into the kitchens.

Wishart had breakfast. By the time he had finished the local papers had arrived. He read through them and picked up an item in the readers' letters which immediately aroused his interest. Some land-owner had made the suggestion that it was time to do away with open fishing for trout and that all water should be private. He flung the paper away. God, how these people hated and feared the common man. 'Keep them out' was their slogan. They made him sick. That land, the basis of all life, should be held privately at all was a disgrace. But the thought of all the great estates and their absentee landlords, drawing profit from the land without shedding one single drop of sweat, was enough to turn his sickness to anger. Scotland,

119

already two-thirds of it no more than a playground for the wealthy sportsman, and there they were trying to deny the ordinary man his hard-won rights. Well to hell with it, when he saw old Sandy he'd tell him he wasn't interested in a day's fishing on the Colonel's water. He could keep his fish.

He lit a cigarette and went outside. The Aston Martin was parked up at the end of the hotel by the petrol pump. He climbed in and switched on the ignition, hearing the tick of the petrol pump. He waited till the sound had died and pressed the starter. The engine caught immediately. A minute later he'd swung the car round and was heading down the hill towards the little town no more than six miles away.

In the town he bought tobacco and *The Guardian* and the *Mail*. He would have liked to have had a pint but it was too early; it would be nearly an hour before the pubs opened. There was nothing else he needed so he set off back up the glen, driving at a moderate pace with the windscreen turned down. Even at thirty miles an hour he could feel the force of the air. It blew his hair about wildly and pressed the skin against his cheekbones. Enjoying the illusion of freedom he leaned back in the bucket seat, his eyes sighting along the length of the bonnet as he drove along the familiar road; a road which had hardly changed since he was little more than a boy.

Approaching the fork which led to the hotel he slowed down to let a hen-pheasant cross the road, and was just picking up speed again when he saw a figure in front of him. With the sun now directly in his eyes the figure was no more than a smudge of colour against the trees. He drew level, and as he turned his head he saw it was the girl he'd met in the hotel the previous night. His heart gave a little jump of pleasure and his foot came hard down on the brake pedal.

'Morning,' he said leaning over the cut-away door. 'Can I give you a lift?'

She came over, walking slowly and easily. He could see she was carrying a small knapsack.

'Good morning,' she replied. 'I'm going for a walk actually, but you could drop me at the hotel. It'll save me walking up that awful hill.'

Even in the strong light of the sun her grey eyes looked cool; twin deep pools hidden in some silent glade. He leaned over and opened the passenger door. 'Here, let me take your pack.' She slipped it off her shoulders and he took it from her and put it behind the seat as she climbed in neatly. He noticed she wasn't wearing any make-up. But, he seemed to remember, she hadn't been wearing any the previous night either. But there was something different about her. It wasn't the clothes – she was dressed in much the same way. Perhaps in the hotel he'd seen her as the daughter of Mr Grant, the successful angler and friend of Colonel Farquharson, but to-day he was seeing her as herself; a person without associations or attachments. Last night in the hotel she'd looked as if she might have been just as much at home in the cocktail bar of the Savoy, but now, with her skin beginning to take on a deep tan and her hair gathered at the back in a bow, she wouldn't have looked out of place seated on a tractor or carrying pails of milk.

'It's going to be hot for walking,' he said as she settled in the seat. 'Where were you intending to go?'

She shrugged. 'Oh, any place. I did think about going up the hill.'

He smiled at this and glanced around meaningfully at the hills on all sides.

She laughed as she caught on. 'I meant the one across the river; behind the hotel. I don't know its name, but there's a loch on the other side.'

He noticed that, despite her refined almost English-like accent, she had no difficulty in making the 'ch' sound. 'Well,' he said, drawing the word out, 'there is a loch on the other side, but it's a fair way. In fact, to get to it you'd have to go down the next glen for a bit when you'd crossed the hill and then back up through the forest. It's quite a long way from here.'

'Oh. Perhaps I'll just go up the hill then. I don't really care. In weather like this it doesn't matter, everything's so beautiful.'

He wanted to ask her how long she'd been staying, but the sound of the big two-litre engine as he engaged gear and pressed down on the accelerator pedal made conversation impossible. Within a few minutes they'd reached the sharp right-hander and begun the long climb up to the hotel.

He pulled up at the entrance, scattering the loose gravel as he used the brakes and swung the wheel round. She got out and he handed out her pack.

'Well, thank you,' she said. 'It was nice of you to give me a lift.'

He got out of the car. 'It wasn't much of a lift, was it?'

'It saved me that awful walk up the hill, at least.'

They stood around for a minute. He felt he should say

something but couldn't find the words, feeling hesitant and awkward.

'Well, thanks once more,' she said and, slinging her pack on she turned and made her way towards the path that ran from behind the hotel down to the river.

He opened his mouth to call after her but she'd already rounded the corner of the hotel. For a moment he stood gazing in the direction in which she'd gone, annoyed at his lack of decision and his inability to act naturally and freely. All he'd wanted to say was that he'd hoped they might bump into each other again. Well, so what? She was only another girl, a passing stranger who happened to have a nice face and a nice smile. Good God. He'd hardly spoken two words to her. Charm and good looks were nothing but sexual devices that seldom reflected the personality underneath.

He reached into the car for his papers and tobacco and, drawing the tonneau cover loosely over, went back into the hotel. In the public bar, Jock, the barman, was restocking the emptied shelves with bottles. He stopped what he was doing when he heard Wishart come in.

He mopped the sweat from his forehead. 'Well, Rab, looks like being another stinker the day. What can I get you, a pint?'

Wishart nodded. 'Better have one yourself, when you're at it, Jock.'

The barman poured the beer. He lifted his pint. 'Cheers, and whit's on the day, Rab? You'll no be goin' up the hill in this?'

'No, I've a couple of things to do, but right now I'm going to sit outside and read the papers.' Taking his pint with him he went out of the door of the public bar and sat down, reaching into his pocket for his pipe and tobacco. When he'd got the pipe going he opened up *The Guardian* but he found his mind straying as he tried to read. He found his thoughts returning to the girl. She had some strange and inexplicable quality about her that was new to him. It was as though she radiated some healing influence on his jangled nervous system. The sort of thing he imagined that people got in the presence of a great sage or philosopher. And yet she was quite young; in her early twenties.

He would have liked to talk to her. He felt she would be easy to talk to. A good listener, that rare quality, but at the same time with a mind of her own. But he was romanticising a perfectly ordinary situation. How could he, or anyone else, possibly deduce such things from a couple of brief meetings?

He finished his pint and took the glass back into the bar

122

and went up to his room, his mind suddenly made up. He was sickened by his own indecisive behaviour; it was time to get a grip. Do things and think about them after. Too much thinking about anything could be destructive. Thought should be a guide to action and not an exercise in itself. He got out his portable and, slipping in a sheet of paper, wrote to his publisher and the B B C producer.

He signed the letters, glancing at his watch. He would catch the twelve o'clock post from the village. Immediately he felt relieved by his action. That was the secret; keep yourself so busy that there was no time for introspection. In his new-found mood of enthusiasm he forgot he'd already tried all this before. It would work, for a while, and then he would be back on the tread-mill with his thoughts churning the same old familiar paths.

He looked at his watch again. It was still early in the day. There was plenty of time. He jumped up from the chair and from the wardrobe in the small room he pulled out his rucksack, throwing all its contents in a heap on to the bed. He wouldn't need much; just the boots, the flask and something to read. The books were in his case; a couple of hardbacks and half a dozen paperbacks. He flipped through them, once, twice, before he realised he was falling into the trap again. Make a decision and go along with it, he told himself. He selected Jack London's *Martin Eden* and piled the books back in his case.

Slipping the book into the pack he changed into his climbing breeches, thinking at the same time he would have been much better with a pair of lightweight slacks if he was only walking. To hell with it, he wasn't going to change again. He pulled on his boots and laced them up firmly. He was ready to go now. Leaving everything on the bed he picked up the pack and went downstairs.

There was a girl at the reception desk. A student who'd arrived the previous evening to help out for a few weeks during the busy season.

He gave her the vacuum flask, asking if she would mind going through to the kitchen to get it filled with tea and would she also get him a couple of sandwiches when she was there. She looked at him as if to suggest it wasn't a receptionist's job to do such menial errands, but she went. He couldn't help smiling to himself. She would learn soon enough that everyone in John Mitchell's hotel mucked in. The staff worked hard and tried to please the customers, but once a year, around Christmas time, the roles were reversed and the regular customers took over the bars and the kitchens and served the staff. It had become a tradition that everyone looked forward to.

Whilst he was waiting for the sandwiches he slipped into the public bar. It was empty but for one customer, old Hector, a retired shepherd, and Jock the barman.

Old Hector cleared his throat, spat and bade him the time of day. 'Man, you're no' goin' up the hill, are you?' he said, his old eyes peering at Wishart, noticing the breeches and the boots. 'You'll be fried to a frazzle in that heat,' he added, shaking his head.

'I thocht you said you were workin', Rab?' said the barman.

'Ach, I changed my mind. It's not a day for work.'

'It'll be damned harder work where you're going,' said Jock. 'What's it to be, a pint?'

Wishart nodded, and asked old Hector what he'd have.

The old shepherd pushed his glass across the counter. 'I'll ha'e the same; a pint o' heavy.'

'An' whaur'll you be headin' for? Up the glen?'

Wishart took a gulp of his beer. 'I'm not sure yet. I just thought I'd go for a bit of a walk.'

'Well, just mind your step,' the old man chuckled into his beer. 'The glen's so fu' o' they damned chicken factories you'll be fa'in' ower them. I've never seen the like; it's a' feathers now, ye ken.'

'So I'm told,' said Wishart.

'Told! Man, can you no' see? The bluidy place is fu' o' them. It's a fair disgrace. An' the taste o' them, like plastic bags stuffed wi' sawdust. Yuugh!' The old shepherd made a face and poured some beer down his throat, wiping his mouth with the back of his gnarled hand. 'Fowk dinna ken what they're eatin' these days. Nothing tastes the same. Even the tatties. I mind when I was a loon we used to get a puckle o' tatties on a plate wi' a lump o' butter an' it was a meal in itsel', but now . . .?'

The barman laughed. 'Christ, that must have been some time ago when you were a loon, Hector. I didna' think the tattie had even been invented then.'

The old shepherd spluttered in his beer.

Wishart laughed, finished his drink. 'I'll leave you two to sort it out. I'm on my way. See you later . . .'

He left the bar and went back out into the lounge. The receptionist had got his sandwiches and the flask was ready on the counter. He put the sandwiches and the flask in his pack, telling the receptionist to put it on his bill.

Outside the hotel he stood for a minute looking up and down the road. Everything was quiet and there was no traffic about. He was about to move off when he remembered the letters. He dumped the pack and ran back upstairs.

He posted his mail, and after a moment's hesitation made his way round the back of the hotel and picked up the path.

Crossing the bridge over the river he by-passed the saw-mill and headed up across the fields towards the neighbouring glen. Half a mile up the road he took a path which led round the foot of the hill to an old deserted cottage. From there the land canted upwards at a steep angle. Broken land, strewn with boulders and only fit for sheep. He skirted the hill before changing direction to take him up through a forest of young firs, the still air heavy with their scent. At the edge of the forest he came to a deer fence. He climbed over it to find himself in a dead forest. All around him the rotting trees thrust tortured limbs skywards as if in one last desperate plea for help. After its decimation in the first world war the forest had died. It was now no more than a silent reminder of the havoc of war.

The whole place had an air of sadness about it. A desolate spot in the midst of so much greenery. Even the calls of the birds here seemed to possess a different note, an anxious beseeching sound as if cut off from the surrounding world and destined to fly round this forbidding spot forever.

He was glad when he gained the fence at the far end. Below him little clusters of farm-buildings were dotted over the folds of the land and the fields were a rich green. Keeping to high ground he continued to head upwards and soon he'd reached the shank of the hill. From here the glens appeared to flow southwards towards the strath like tributaries spilling into a river.

The ground was wild and untended. Moorland mostly, with a coarse covering of bracken and gorse. An expanse of un-tenanted land with only the shooting butts to betray the presence of man. Soon it would become a battlefield, as the guns blazed away at the terrified birds, and in the evenings the sportsmen would gather in the mansion houses and the hotels, whisky flowing like water, the dead grouse already on their way to the best hotels in Europe in one last and final flight.

He headed up through the thick gorse, gaining height, but it was hard going. The near knee-high growth clung to his legs and he was hot and sweating by the time he reached the saddle and reversed his direction to come back over the hill from the east. He looked at his watch. It had taken him little more than an hour. He felt pleased, at least he was still fit and strong.

At the top of the hill he lay down by the small cairn of stones. Far to the south he could just see the glint of the sun on the river's estuary. The ancient Picts had stood on these very hills. Small dark men muttering in an unknown tongue and pointing excitedly towards the river as they watched the first slow advance of the Roman legions.

Long banners of cloud stretched across the horizon, heading east in steady convoy. Over the whole stretch of land down to the estuary the air rose in great wafts of heat as if some enormous subterranean door had been left open.

He got to his feet again after a short rest. It was stifling hot on top of the hill. He felt he had to find shelter from the sun and he headed back down in the direction of the forestry plantations. Here the trees grew tall, screening off the rays of the sun. Thankful to reach the shade he purposely chose a spot near a firebreak so that he would be able to see anyone come up the hill. He didn't want to bump into – come to think of it he didn't even know her name, he only knew her as Miss Grant, and he didn't like to think of her by that name; it sounded prim and stuffy – anyway he didn't want to see her on the hill, especially since she'd told him where she was going. It would seem as if he'd been deliberately following her.

He pulled out his pipe and was about to light up before he remembered where he was. He'd seen one forest fire and the damage it had caused; he hadn't forgotten it. With the land baked hard as clay and the twigs under foot as dry as old bones, it would only need one spark to set the whole place ablaze.

For a while he lay stretched out, enjoying the feel of the pine needles under his back.

It was some time before he got to his feet again. If he was going to visit the cottage it was time he got going. He went back up the hill and, skirting the cairn, made his way down the shallow slope of the saddle with its thick covering of gorse and broom. He was glad by the time he reached the burn that ran down into the glen, stopping for a moment and scooping up handfuls of cool water into his mouth before setting off again. An hour later he'd reached the cottage, keeping a wary eye open for the bull as he crossed the field and climbed over the fence.

The old farmhouse had a deserted air about it and he noticed that one or two of the heavy roof tiles had slipped. In fact one part of the roof had sagged considerably and would obviously need attention. Weeds had overgrown the garden and were thrusting up through the cracks in the stone slabs that he'd laid only the year before. The paintwork on the doors and window-framing was cracked and peeling, and a drain-pipe sagged brokenly.

A lot of work was needed if he was to put it in order. More problems. He opened the door – never locked – and went inside. The house had a dry musty smell about it and there was dust everywhere. On the ceiling of one of the bedrooms he noticed a large spreading stain. That would be under the loose tiling. He'd have to do something about that before winter set in. Next he tried the taps. No water. Then he remembered he'd shut the cock off the last time he'd been there. He went outside and opened the cock. Still no water from the taps. He shook his head. It could only mean the well up the hill, where the house got its water supply from, had gone dry again. It was the worst feature of the house – its inconstant water supply. He decided to have a look at the well, wishing now that he'd brought a rope with him. The well, some ten feet in diameter, was covered in planking rotting with age.

He had a thought and went into the wooden annexe that had been built on to the house. In a cupboard in one of the bedrooms he found an old nylon rope. The strands had furred and he'd chucked it away as being no further use for climbing, but it was good enough for his present purpose. Slinging the rope over his shoulder he went up to the well. The planking was green and covered with moss. Wrapping a few turns of the nylon round his waist he tied a bowline and secured the free end to the trunk of a nearby tree. Protected now, he crawled over the planking and lifted off the inspection cover, squinting down into the depths of the well. To his surprise, despite the long dry period it was quite full. It could only mean there was an air-lock in the system somewhere. Well, there was nothing he could do about it now. He'd have to see the estate manager about it. Replacing the manhole cover he went back to the house, a thought beginning to take shape in his head.

He wondered why it hadn't occurred to him before, and then he knew why. It was because of Carole. Carole? It was only a few days since he'd seen her and already she seemed a million miles away. It was like a fading dream. But then his life over the past few years had been a sort of dream – no, more of a nightmare than a dream. It was going to be different now.

He sat down on the steps in front of the house and opened up his pack of sandwiches. The layers of brown bread were thickly packed with salmon – fresh salmon – and chicken. He ate them hungrily, and pouring himself a cup of tea from the flask lit his pipe. He began to get the old familiar taste of tobacco again and resolved – for the hundredth time – that he'd give up cigarettes. But that was a minor problem for the moment. The idea that had come to him was growing, and the more he thought about it the more it appealed to him. It would cost a bit of money of course and his bank balance wasn't all that healthy, but he could do it. Puffing on his pipe he tried to figure out the probable cost.

First he'd have to get a generator and then the house would have to be wired. A second-hand 'genny' he could probably get for something like sixty or seventy pounds, and then there was the wiring. He could do a lot of that himself; say another fifty. That was around £120. Something would have to be done about the kitchen range. But there again he could probably get one second-hand for around fifteen or twenty pounds – a good one. After that it would be a simple paper and paint job with perhaps some additional bits of furniture. Say another £50. The whole total would be less than two hundred pounds. Two hundred pounds? He checked the figures again. They were right. Two hundred pounds and he'd have everything he needed. Why, his flat in London was costing him that a quarter and he had lighting and heating on top of that, to say nothing of the expense of living in London. Up here he could live on a few pounds a week.

He began to feel enthusiastic about the prospect. He could work up here for the rest of the summer and let his flat in London. He still would have to make the occasional trip south, but it would be worth it and it would be good to live in Scotland again.

It was worth thinking about. He decided to contact the estate manager. If he didn't see him in the hotel he could always phone and tell him of his plans. Graham would help. He might even be able to get his hands on a generator. Yes, that was it, he'd get in touch with Graham and see what he had to say.

128

Feeling easier in mind now that he had an objective, he made a vow he wouldn't let himself get clogged up again in fruitless introspection. Gathering his things up he had one last look round the house before closing the door behind him and setting back off over the hill.

It was late afternoon when he came down through the forest, his ears picking up the high-pitched whine coming from the sawmill. There was a heavy smell of resin and diesel fumes, above the sheds soft clouds of wood-dust hung in the air. He cut past the sawmill and down to the bridge. He was half way over when he saw a figure seated on the far bank. He looked again. It was her. He would have continued on but realised she'd caught sight of him.

Crossing the bridge, he hesitated. She hadn't given any indication she was aware of his presence, but he knew for certain she'd seen him.

She was only a few yards from the bridge, lying on the bank, her legs stretched. He could hardly go by without a word. He walked along the bank and stood above her. She looked up and smiled.

'Hullo.'

'Hullo. I see you're doing the wise thing. Have you been here all day?'

'No. I went for a walk.' She laughed. 'I didn't get up the hill, at least not to the top. It was too hot so I came down again and here I am, just sitting by the river.'

She looked so different from Carole. Her face had an expression of honesty and calm as if to say 'here I am, what you see is me, not a mask.' He wanted to sit beside her, it only needed a step, but something held him back. He was silent for a moment, feeling the old uncertainties in his mind. Go on, he said to himself, just sit down beside her if you want to. She's not likely to leap in the water and scream for help. After all, you just want to talk to her, don't you?

But his legs wouldn't move.

The silence grew and the more it grew the more conscious of it he became. He was freezing up again, his mind in conflict, robbing him of the power to think – or, more important, act!

She was looking at him with that calm measured look he'd already associated with her. Fearful what he said might be misinterpreted, he muttered something about the weather. Instantly he was aware of the inadequacy of his remark and sought to cover it up by saying something about the water and how low it was.

'Do you fish?' she asked.

'Yes, a bit,' he said and froze up. Nothing else would come. There was an unbearable silence. He was beginning to find the situation embarrassing.

'I don't suppose you have a match?' she broke the silence.

The question threw him for a moment, and his answering movements were so nervous and clumsy he almost dropped the box in the water. He bent down quickly to retrieve it and the next moment he was sitting down beside her, lighting her cigarette.

'I'm sorry,' she said. 'I didn't offer you one. Do you smoke?'

He shook his head. 'I won't have one, thanks. I'm trying to get back on the pipe again.'

'I think it's much better. Cigarettes are foul things, really.'

'Somehow I can't imagine you smoking a pipe.'

She laughed and he found himself laughing too. Really laughing. But a moment later he stopped. It hadn't even been a joke, and here he was laughing like an idiot. He grew silent again, embarrassed by his display of emotion.

She noticed it. 'Do you holiday here much?' she asked. 'You seem to know the country so well.'

She had a direct manner of speech that discomfited him. In his experience, frankness and candour were often assumed – he was thinking now about Carole's friends – a trick to impress people.

'I was born not far from here,' he answered briefly. 'I should know it.'

'And how do you find living in London after this?'

He shrugged. 'You get used to it eventually, I suppose.'

'I don't think I could live anywhere else now but London. If you have to leave home it's really the only place to live.' She sat up and, clasping her knees, stared at the river.

'Were you born there, er . . .' he hesitated, resenting the formality and the social implications of having to address her as Miss Grant.

She twisted round to look at him with open-eyed frankness. 'Joanna's the name,' she said. 'Though Sandy always insists on calling me Miss Grant. I wish he wouldn't . . . but you were asking if I was born in London. As a matter of fact I was born in India. My father was in the Army. But I was quite young when we returned to Scotland. We lived just outside Edinburgh, in Swanston, do you know it?'

'I don't know Edinburgh at all,' he gave a half laugh,

'except for Rose Street. You know that old bet about being able to have a drink in every pub in Rose Street . . .?'

'I've heard of it.'

'Well, I didn't make it.'

'Not even on half pints?'

'Not even on half pints.'

She laughed and he found himself joining her once more.

For an hour they sat on the bank talking. Joanna was puzzled by his manner. She found him quite articulate and then for some reason he would appear to withdraw into an embarrassed silence, seemingly lost for words. It was almost like having a conversation with two people. And all the time, expressed in the eyes and the twist of the mouth was this impression of inner conflict. She wondered what had happened to him to create such doubt and uncertainty. He reminded her of someone who had lost his identity somewhere and was desperately trying to rediscover it.

'What time is it?' she asked after a silence which had become all the more uncomfortable because of his awareness of it.

'Time?' He sounded almost grateful she'd asked. 'It's nearly five-thirty,' he said, shaking his watch and holding it up to his ear.

'Oh dear. I'd better be getting back or Mrs Farquharson will be lecturing me on the virtues of punctuality. Father didn't appear for dinner last night so he's promised faithfully to be on time this evening. It would never do if I'm late.' She got slowly to her feet.

'Of course, you're staying at the Farquharsons'. Look, I'll run you back.'

'Oh no. It's not all that far to walk.'

'But it's no trouble.' He picked up her pack and hefted it on his shoulder and set off up the path.

They arrived back at the hotel. John Mitchell was behind the lounge bar talking to the new receptionist. He looked up at their entry, his eyebrows momentarily lifting in surprise as he greeted them.

'I'll just run upstairs and get the keys,' Wishart said to Joanna. 'Would you like something to drink while you're waiting?'

'No, I don't think so. But, look, why don't you have one if you feel like it, you don't have to run me back . . .'

'No, no. Now just hang on while I get the keys.' He dashed upstairs and was back in a few moments. They went outside.

131

Walking towards the car Wishart asked her when she was going back to London.

'The weekend after next,' she said with a little sigh. 'I'm going to miss all this. Still, you can't have everything. When are you leaving?'

'That's funny.'

'What is?'

'That's when I'm going back. The weekend after next,' he said, feeling a sudden impulse to offer to drive her back with him, but when she told him she'd a sleeper booked he dismissed the idea, thankful he hadn't mentioned it to her.

'Isn't it beautiful,' she said as they drew up at the car. 'I had a funny feeling it was yours.' She gazed admiringly at the Aston Martin.

'You like it?'

'It's *beautiful.*'

'I bought it from a woman who owned a pub up in Ongar.'

'A woman!' she said in surprise.

'Yes, she was quite a character. She was more interested in getting a good home for it than anything else. I got a bargain.'

'You must never part with it,' she said seriously.

'You really like it?' he said, looking at her with a new respect.

'It's the sort of car you *should* have.'

'Well,' he said grinning with pleasure, 'I'm glad you think so.' He walked round and helped her into the passenger seat.

Ten minutes later they'd reached the driveway leading to the house. The road was full of potholes and he had to slow down. They stopped at the house. He got out of the car. She was standing with her pack slung over one shoulder. For the first time he realised how beautiful she was.

'Well, thank you very much,' she was saying. 'It was very kind of you.'

His mouth twisted in a grin. 'It's all part of John Mitchell's hotel service. I get a commission.' He paused lengthily, trying to keep his nervousness from showing as he asked her if she might be up at the hotel again sometime.

She smiled. Why didn't he just offer to take her? 'Perhaps,' she said.

'I mean . . . well, I thought we could maybe have a drink sometime,' he said with a nervous cough.

'Why don't you phone to-morrow evening. Colonel Farquharson will be back from Edinburgh so I suppose I'd better stay for dinner, but perhaps you could phone after nine.'

John Mitchell was checking through the hotel register when Wishart got back. 'You're back soon, Rab,' he said giving him a curious glance.

'Oh, I was only down the road,' he said looking around. 'Where's everyone?'

'I'll get you a drink, if that's what you want.'

'Good. I think I'm going to have a half pint and a drop of Chivas Regal. And you'll have something yourself, John!'

Mitchell hesitated. 'Well, I might just have a small one.' He reached behind him and poured the drinks. 'So you've had a guid day.'

Wishart shrugged. 'Well, you know.'

'I thought you'd caught a twenty-pounder by the look on your face when you came in.'

'Eh? What are you on about, John? I wasn't fishing, you know that. I was over at the cottage most of the day.'

'Oh aye?' Mitchell said, giving him a sidelong glance.

'What's the matter with you? Where do you think I've been?'

'Oh nothing. How's the cottage?'

'It's okay,' replied Wishart, puzzled by Mitchell's manner. 'It needs a bit doing to it, the roof's pretty far gone in one part . . . that reminds me, have you seen Graham? I'd like him to come up and have a look sometime.'

Mitchell shook his head. 'I havena seen Graham a' week. You know what he's like, you'll see him a puckle o' times and then you winna see him again for weeks.'

'Well, if he happens to come in to-night, tell him I'd like to see him, will you?'

'I'll dae that, Rab, if I see him.'

CHAPTER XIII

Mrs Farquharson was complaining about the cook. They'd finished dinner, but Mrs Farquharson looked as sour as if she'd just sat down to a plate of pig-swill instead of prime Scotch beef. Molly, the maid, cleared away the dishes.

'Help yourself to a drink, if you want one, Brigadier.' The mistress of the house always addressed Grant by his military rank in the same way as she always referred to her husband as the 'Colonel'. 'Or would you rather go through to the lounge and have coffee later?'

Grant nodded. 'Good idea. Let's go through to the lounge. What about you, Joanna? Perhaps you might even play the piano for us?' It hadn't been such a good day on the water and he'd much sooner have gone up to the hotel and had a few whiskies, but he felt he'd spent little enough time with his hostess. He didn't particularly like Mrs Farquharson, she was without real colour or personality. Nevertheless, as her guest, he owed her something.

'Father, I haven't played for years. I'm much too rusty to entertain.'

'Oh come, Joanna, you play beautifully,' interposed Mrs Farquharson. 'I heard you the other day. It was quite charming.'

Grant got to his feet. 'Come, Joanna. Mrs Farquharson would like to hear you play again, I'm sure.'

Joanna's lips pressed together and the soft grey eyes glinted momentarily. She knew only too well her father was blackmailing her. She realised that, rather than suffer the boredom of having to talk to his hostess, he was forcing her to play. She rose from the table. 'All right, but I warn you I've only a limited repertoire, and it's not very good.'

'Off you go then and I'll see to the coffee.' Mrs Farquharson elevated her large, awkward frame. 'Just help yourself to drink from the cabinet if you want.' She went off.

In the lounge Joanna turned to her father. 'You're a monster,' she said.

'What's that? What do you mean, Joanna? You used to like playing at one time, as far as I can remember.'

'You know what I mean. Anyway you can pour me a

brandy – a large one. And if I get drunk and fall off the stool you have only yourself to blame.' She crossed over to the piano and sat down.

Mrs Farquharson didn't reappear for nearly quarter of an hour. When she did arrive she was clutching her head. She exhaled deeply. 'Well, that's that arranged. The coffee will be here in a few minutes.' She managed to sound as if she'd just returned from the stockades having beaten off an attack.

Joanna stole a glance at the huge gilded antique clock that stood on the mantelpiece above the fireplace. It had gone half-past nine. That poor girl Molly, she was nearly run off her feet. She felt sorry for her and would have offered to make the coffee herself, but such a suggestion would only have sent chills of horror through her hostess's mind. She took a sip of her brandy as her right hand sought out the crashing diminished chord that began the 'Revolutionary' study.

Instantly Mrs Farqurharson came over, a forced smile on her lips. 'What's that, my dear? I hope it's not one of those dreadful modern things. I'm afraid I can't understand them. Perhaps I'm old-fashioned, but there you are, it wouldn't do if we all liked the same things, would it now?'

'No, I don't suppose it would,' answered Joanna, wishing she could have played the study the whole way through, but she was too much out of practice. With a change of key she switched to the much simpler E flat Nocturne.

Mrs Farquharson went over to sit by Grant. 'Ah, isn't that quite beautiful,' she said.

He nodded. He didn't really understand music, but the thing sounded 'syrupy' and effeminate to him. He settled himself deeper in his chair, looking over at his daughter. There was something different about her to-night. He'd noticed it at dinner. He knew she'd been worrying about him and his plans. But that was women all over. In a way it was their duty to worry about the menfolk. But it wasn't that. It was something else. And there was yesterday. She'd said she wanted to go back to 'Nanga Parbat' and then for no apparent reason had suddenly changed her mind. He was glad she had, but it still didn't explain her behaviour.

Molly came in with the coffee. Joanna stopped playing and got up from the piano as Mrs Farquharson poured. They drank their coffee in silence, and no sooner had they finished than Mrs Farquharson rose and excused herself, saying she had so much to do next day for her husband's return that she simply had to get to bed early.

'Aren't you going to play any more?' Grant asked his daughter when she'd gone.

'No, father. I'm going to have one more drink and go to bed. And you don't have to pretend you're disappointed, because I know you don't really like music.'

Grant frowned. 'That's not . . .'

'Father!' She looked at him with an expression of humorous reproach.

'Oh, all right. Perhaps I don't, but I do like to hear you play.'

She knelt down beside him. 'You know, not only are you a monster but you tell lies.'

He took her hand and smilingly shook his head in mild exasperation. 'You haven't told me what you've been doing to-day. Walking again?'

'Mmm, yes and no. I went up the hill behind the hotel, but it was much too hot.'

'So you found a sheltered spot and read, I suppose?'

'Yes, I read a little.'

'Don't you ever get lonely, going away on your own like that?'

'Sometimes, but I found someone to talk to to-day.'

His brows came down. 'Talked? Who with?' Like most men with only daughters, Grant suffered from jealousy. Whilst he often expressed the hope to himself that his daughter would get married, secretly he didn't really want her to. His motives stemmed from a sense of possessiveness, though he would never have admitted this to himself. It was one of the few areas of his mind where truth was barred. Looking at it sensibly, he realised that such a good-looking young woman as his daughter would inevitably get married some day. It was true to say he'd even encouraged Osborne's attentions, but his daughter in her own decisive way had made it quite clear she hadn't liked him. Pity; Osborne came of a good family, landed people, with money. She'd have done well there if she hadn't chosen to be so damned awkward. But who was this she'd been talking to? She didn't really know anyone in the glen.

'I was talking to Robert Wishart.'

His frown deepened. 'Robert . . . who . . .? Oh, the chap you met in the hotel the other night. Where did you meet him?'

'Down by the river, by the sawmill.'

'Hrrrmph. He spoke to you, I suppose?'

'No, I flung myself at his feet.'

136

Grant's exasperation was real. 'Really, Joanna. You must be more careful, you know. You can't just go about talking to complete strangers.'

'But we'd already met. Sandy introduced us. Remember? And I'll tell you something else. I think he's the Wishart you were talking about.'

'Who . . . you mean the mountaineering chap?'

She nodded decisively.

'Oh nonsense, Joanna. What would he be doing . . .' he broke off. 'I'm not going to listen to you any more. I think you've had too much of the sun to-day.'

'I've a feeling I'm right.'

'But you don't know for sure?'

'I think I know for sure.'

'Joanna, that's a contradiction in terms, or didn't they teach you logic at University?' Grant finished his brandy. 'Anyway, I'm going to have another drink and off to bed.'

She gave a little yawn. 'I think that's where I'll go.' She rose to her feet and started collecting the coffee things and piling them on the tray. 'By the way,' she said, 'is Colonel Farquharson having anyone else for dinner to-morrow?'

'No, not as far as I know. Why do you ask . . . and what are you doing there?'

'Oh, just taking the things into the kitchen.'

'Joanna . . .?'

'You might not have noticed, father, but that poor girl Molly's run off her feet.' She crossed over and kissed him on the forehead, and, picking up the tray, she made her way towards the door. 'Good night, father. See you in the morning . . . and don't stay up too late.'

With a shake of his head he bade her good night and, going over to the cabinet, poured himself a stiff brandy. He sat down again, letting out a deep sigh. He would never understand his daughter, her ways and motivations were beyond him. Though there were times when he admired her independence of spirit, he thought too much independence in a woman could be a bad thing. It wouldn't have surprised him at all if she'd taken the initiative and spoken to this Wishart chap. He felt a stab of jealousy. Who was he anyway? Some local chap, he supposed. Might even be the postman for all his daughter seemed to care. That was the second time she'd spoken about him in two days. And how long had she spent with him to-day? On top of that she seemed to have got hold of the crazy idea that he was the mountaineering fellow.

He took a sip of his brandy. Well, he would ask Farquharson to-morrow about him. Farquharson knew everyone in the glen.

Molly and the cook, Mrs Beaton, were having an early morning cup of tea. It was not long after seven and Mrs Beaton, who was the wife of one of the estate workers, had not long arrived.

'Looks like bein' a fine day again,' said the cook to Molly, offering her a cigarette.

Molly took it and produced a lighter from her apron pocket. She lit Mrs Beaton's cigarette, then her own. 'The Colonel's back the day,' she said. 'I'm just going to have this and I'll have to go. The old battle-axe will be up about eight, runnin' aboot like a hen that canna lay an egg.'

Mrs Beaton snorted. 'She's a fair dither o' a woman, that. You should have heard her go on last nicht. Nothin' was richt. If it wasna for the few extra shillings, I'd tell her where to stick her job.'

Molly puffed at her cigarette, holding it inexpertly between her fingers. She'd just taken up smoking. 'Miss Grant's nice, tho'.'

The cook snorted again. 'They're a' the same, they toffs. It's affy easy to say please and thank you when you've got the siller.'

'No, she's nice. You know what . . .?'

Mrs Beaton looked at the maid. 'Whit?'

'When I came down this mornin' she'd cleared a' the coffee things frae the lounge and washed them up.'

'Hrmmph. That'd be a fine change for her. It's fair enjoyable to dae things when you dinna ha'e to.' The cook got slowly to her feet, groaning as she took the weight on her legs. 'Well, must get on wi' it, I suppose.'

Molly sat smoking, her eye-lids half-closed to protect her eyes from the smoke curling from the end of her cigarette. 'And the Brigadier . . . there's a nice man for you. Always says good morning and thanks for this and thanks for that. Though mind you I widna like to see him wi' his dander up. I'll bet he's a fair temper on him.'

Mrs Beaton shook her head. 'They're a' nice when it suits them, lassie . . .'

Molly laughed and stubbed her cigarette out. 'How about the Battle-axe?'

The cook snorted contemptuously. *'Her?'* One word was sufficient for Mrs Beaton to describe her mistress.

Molly jumped up and cleared the cups from the table, washing them in the sink and leaving them to dry on the draining-board. 'Well, must go now. She'll be up any minute. Thank heavens they've nae guests for dinner. There's only the four of them. I might be able to get awa' early, there's a dance on at the village hall the nicht.'

Colonel Farquharson arrived home shortly after lunch. Having assured his wife he'd already eaten, he asked where everyone had gone. She told him that the Brigadier had gone fishing since early morning and that his daughter had taken the car to go into the town for some shopping, and after that she was going back up to Glen Isla to collect some things and wouldn't be back till six.

'Mmm,' Farquharson stroked his long chin. 'I really should go into town myself.' He made up his mind suddenly. 'Yes, I will, I'll go into town and I'll pop down to see Iain on the way. He'll be at the pools, is he?'

Farquharson's wife waved her hand as if such things didn't really concern her. 'I really don't know where he is, but he was away early this morning, just after breakfast . . . I hope you're not going to be late now, John. I've arranged dinner for eight . . .'

'Yes, yes, my dear. I'll be back in plenty of time. Now is there anything you want when I'm in town?'

'Well, perhaps . . . no, it doesn't matter. I'll have to go in myself to-morrow anyway.'

'Are you sure?'

'No, no. I'll get it myself. Don't worry. I'll manage.'

'Right, I'll be off then . . . I suppose Iain's taken the Land-Rover. Doesn't matter, I'll use the car. 'Bye then, my dear. I'll be back about four if anyone phones.'

Farquharson got into his car and drove off. Stopping half way along the drive he took a narrow lane which ran to the left, and half a mile farther on stopped the car and got out. Here the lane had been widened to allow vehicles to park. The Land-Rover was drawn up close to the fence.

Farquharson went through the gate and down the long steep slope which led to the river. The slope was heavily wooded, screening the river from view. It wasn't till he reached the bank that he was able to see Grant. Grant was fishing from a little platform which had been built above the pool. Behind the platform the ground rose easily with no trees or bushes to interfere with a cast.

Grant had just cast and was reeling in when Farquharson made his way up the platform.

'Well, Iain, how's the fish to-day?'

Grant turned. 'Oh hullo, John. I didn't hear you.' He pointed to the far end of the pool, a spot deep in shadow with scarcely a ripple on the surface of the water. 'There's a big chap over there. I've been after him all morning, but he won't take a thing.'

'What fly have you on?'

Grant reeled in and seized the end of his cast. 'I'm using a cinnamon and gold. But I've tried everything.'

'Mmm. Well, I'm not going to give you advice on how to kill fish, Iain. Craig's the man for that. I understand you had quite a catch the other day.'

Grant's tanned features spread in a smile. 'You might say that. Yes, you might say that.'

'Good! Well, Iain, I just popped down to let you know I was back. I've one or two things to do in town so I'll see you later. You know what time dinner is. I'll pop down after tea, if I have the chance.' He nodded towards the far corner of the pool. 'Hope you have him by then.'

'All right, John . . . and why don't you bring a rod with you?'

Farquharson shook his head. 'Not me. I'm not much of an angler as you know.' He turned to leave but Grant stopped him as he remembered something.

'By the way, John, do you happen to know a chap by the name of Wishart?'

Farquharson paused. 'Wishart? Well, there was old Wishart who used to have a smiddy over at Newbiggin, but that's a long time ago. I don't know what happened to him, but he's been dead a long time now . . . about ten years I would say. Why do you ask?'

'Nothing really. I just wondered. Did he have any family?'

Farquharson rubbed his chin. 'Yes, quite a few. I think there were about six of them, if I can remember, but they all left to go abroad. No, wait a minute, there was another one. He didn't go abroad. Let me see . . . that's right, when the smiddy got a bit too much for the old man, he took over. I can't remember his name but he gave it up eventually and went off to work in town. He was rather a clever chap with
140

his hands, used to repair watches and that sort of thing, you know.'

'So that was the end of them?'

'Hold on, just let me think. Ah yes, of course, it's amazing how you forget things. This engineer chap used to have two sons himself. A couple of little rascals they were too. I can remember them now. In fact I caught one of them poaching and not very far from here either . . .' he paused to rake his memory. 'That's right, there were two of them with only a year between them. One of them – here, you should know him, Iain, what am I talking about, he's one of your chaps, you know, a bit of a mountaineer . . . you must have heard of him. What was his name, now? Oh damn, this memory of mine.'

'Robert, was it?'

'What was that you said? Robert? That's right. That's the chap. Come to think of it, I believe he still visits the glen, has a cottage over on Archie Laidlaw's estate. So I'm told, but I've never seen the chap myself. But why do you ask? Have you met him?'

Grant threw a long cast to the far end of the pool.

'No,' he said, his eyes fixed on the distant fly. 'But I'm going to.'

Farquharson had seen that look on his friend's face before. 'Oh,' he said. 'Oh. Well, must be off. Good fishing. See you later.'

So she had been right. Grant reeled in slowly, his mind no longer on the big fish lying snug over at the far end of the pool. He was thinking of other things.

They were all sitting in the lounge after dinner when the phone in the hallway rang. Mrs Farquharson got to her feet, a worried frown on her face. 'Who could that be, ringing at this time?'

She was back a moment later. 'It's for you, Joanna,' she said in a voice stiff with curiosity.

Joanna went out. The receiver was lying on its side on the hall table. She picked it up. 'Hullo, Joanna Grant here.'

'Oh hullo. It's me . . .' there was a pause. 'What are you doing? I mean to-night.'

'Nothing, nothing at all.'

'Would you like to come over to the hotel for a drink? I could pick you up.'

'You're speaking from there now?'

'Yes.'

'All right. Do you mind coming over? I don't want to drive.'

'Mind? No, that's okay. Hang on and I'll be there in ten minutes.'

'I'll tell you what. I'll leave now and start walking. It'll save you coming all the way up the drive.'

There was another pause and the line crackled and a voice broke in. Everything was a confused jumble of sound before she heard his voice again.

'Hullo . . . hullo . . . is that . . .?'

'It's all right, it seems to have cleared,' she said. 'I'll go now. See you in about ten minutes. 'Bye . . .' She heard him hang up at the other end and she replaced the receiver back in its cradle, feeling pleasantly surprised he'd rung.

Colonel Farquharson was on his favourite subject when she got back in the lounge. He was talking about shooting and had leaned forward in his chair to demonstrate a point. Her father seemed equally absorbed, only Mrs Farquharson paid her any attention as she walked into the room.

'Sorry to butt in,' she said, 'but I'm going out. I hope you don't mind?'

Mrs Farquharson's eyebrows came up fractionally in an expression of disapproval. A young woman going out at this time of night alone? It was unheard of. She waited in the hope of some explanation, looking over at the Brigadier.

Grant turned round. 'What's that? Did you say you were going out, Joanna?' His tone was matter of fact.

'Yes. I won't be all that late.'

'Do you want the car?'

'I'm only going as far as the hotel. And anyway I'm being picked up.'

'All right, Jo.' So she was going to see this chap Wishart? He hadn't let her know her guess had been right. He wanted to find out a little more about him first. 'Have a good time and don't have too many drinks.' He turned back to Farquharson. 'You were saying . . . about this Russian rifle – what'd you call it – oh yes, the "Baikal". Well, I'm not surprised, they produce first-class rifles, John, after all, they didn't do so badly at Wiesbaden did they . . .?' He paused for a second as Joanna called goodbye from the doorway. 'All right Jo, and just remember what I said.'

'I'll stick to beer,' she replied with a laugh, and slipped out of the room, closing the door behind her.

142

Farquharson smiled and shook his head. 'Ah, these modern-day youngsters,' he remarked and returned to the more important subject of shooting.

His wife was mildly astounded. She found it hard to believe the Brigadier had allowed his daughter to go off just like that. She felt it her duty to say something. 'Are you sure Joanna will . . .' she began, but Grant cut in smoothly.

'I shouldn't worry about Joanna, Mrs Farquharson. She's well able to look after herself.' His tone, though polite, indicated there was no room for question or argument.

'Oh,' said Mrs Farquharson and sat back in her chair, feeling like a lone protester in a world that had gone crazy.

Joanna had almost reached the end of the driveway when she heard the deep note of a car engine. A minute later the Aston Martin appeared, its racing green colours looking even darker in the evening light. Scattering a small shower of stones it drew up beside her.

'Hullo,' greeted Wishart and leaned over to open the passenger door. 'I'm sorry I'm a bit late, I bumped into somebody I hadn't seen for a long time just as I was leaving the hotel.'

She climbed in. 'That's all right. I enjoyed the walk and it's such a nice evening. And how are you?'

'Oh fine,' he said, 'just fine.'

She smiled to herself at his shyness.

He was about to drive off when he stopped. 'You should have put a coat on. You'll be cold. Look, I've got an old anorak in the back . . .'

'Cold? But it's warm this evening,' she protested.

'Well, let me put the windscreen up,' he said reaching forward, but she stopped him.

'Please. I'm not in the least cold, and anyway I rather like the feeling of the wind blowing in my face.'

So had Carole at one time, he thought. 'Look . . .' he began.

'If we don't hurry the pub will be shut and I won't get that drink you promised me.' She snuggled into the seat.

He slipped into gear again. Letting in the clutch he suddenly turned to her, his mouth curving in a little smile.

'What's so funny?' she asked.

'It was just . . . well, it was just you saying the pub would be closed. Didn't you know that John doesn't agree with licensing laws . . . and anyway there's a dance on at the village hall to-night.'

'A dance,' she cried impulsively, sitting up. 'Can we go . . .
143

it's years since I've been to a ceilidh.'

His smile widened. 'Would you like to . . . but it's not a real ceilidh, you know. It's just a dance.'

'Oh, let's.'

'Okay.'

The front of the hotel was jammed with cars when they arrived. Even the car-park was full. He drove round the back, parking alongside the hotel pick-up. He cut the engine. 'Careful when you get out,' he warned, 'there's a big hole on your side.' He jumped out, but he was too late, she'd already opened the door and stepped out.

His arm shot out to grab her as she slipped. He pulled her back on to level ground. 'That was close,' he said, holding on to her arm and guiding her. 'That's John's compost heap at the bottom of that hole. I wouldn't like you to fall in there.'

She stood for a moment rubbing her arm where he'd grabbed it.

Immediately he became solicitous. 'Oh, I'm sorry. Did I hurt you?' He moved closer to her.

She made a pained sound, sucking air between her lips. 'Just a little,' she said, looking at him with a new respect. 'But don't do that sort of thing too often. It hurts . . .' She saw his expression of concern. 'Don't worry about it. If it helps, just let me say I prefer the pain to the compost heap.'

His expression eased. 'I *am* sorry,' he said. 'I just didn't think.'

Think? Think what, that he'd forgotten women were more fragile than men? He was such a strange person in some ways. There was this caged thing about him as though some part of his personality had been trapped and was trying to get out. And the eyes, with their sad look. Eyes that had probably seen a great deal of suffering. She wondered if he'd ever been married. 'I'll accept your apologies only if you buy me that drink,' she told him.

'It's a deal,' he said. His laugh pleased her.

The lounge bar was crowded so they made their way through to the bar at the back. It wasn't much better, but he managed to find elbow room at the far end and near the adjoining door to the public bar.

'Whisky?' he asked.

'Not to-night,' she replied, pleased that he'd noted what she'd been drinking the night they'd met. 'I'm going to stick to beer.'

144

The four waiters behind the bar were busy. Eventually one of them spotted Wishart. His flushed face was damp with sweat.

'Hi, Rab,' he gasped rather than spoke. 'Whit's it to be?'

'A pint and a half pint of heavy. You're busy to-night.'

Beads of sweat ran over the barman's forehead as he shook his head. 'Busy? We've never stopped . . . hang on till I see if I can get you a pint glass . . . we've run short o' them.'

'Oh look, don't bother, just make it three halves,' Wishart said.

'Okay, Rab.' The barman grabbed three glasses with one hand and pushed them under the beer tap, filling them to the brim and pushing them across the counter.

They had a few drinks at the bar. About half-past ten, he asked Joanna if she still wanted to go to the dance.

'Of course,' she said. 'I think it's a wonderful idea.'

'Okay,' he said and, catching hold of the barman, asked him for a half-bottle of whisky. Joanna looked at him in mild surprise. 'What's that for?' she said.

'When were you last at a Highland dance?'

'It's a long, long time ago.'

'It must have been. Have you forgotten it's traditional to take a half-bottle?'

'I'm afraid I was much too young, and my escorts were all too refined to drink out of bottles.'

'You must have been associating with the wrong kind of people,' he said.

She smiled back. 'Perhaps I still am.'

Leaving the hotel, they walked down to the village hall. Wishart paid at the door and they went in. The hall was crowded, the sound of pounding feet near deafening as the dancers whirled about wildly to an eightsome reel. As soon as the reel had finished they were approached by someone to buy raffle tickets.

'Let me get them,' Joanna said, enjoying herself.

'No, no,' he protested.

'Please. I have the feeling I'm going to be lucky.'

'Okay,' he said, giving in to her plea, 'I hope you're right.'

She paid for a book of tickets and gave them to him, just as the band struck up again. It was an old-fashioned waltz.

She turned to him eagerly. 'Can we dance this one?'

Wishart groaned. 'You're not going to thank me. I'm a terrible dancer.' But he took her by the arm and led her on to the floor.

145

His dancing was an odd mixture of balance and clumsiness, but she didn't mind, she was so excited by the whole atmosphere. After the waltz came the Gay Gordons. It had been years since she'd danced it but the patterns soon came back to her. Wishart got himself all tied up and she had to lead him into the figures. By the time the Gay Gordons had finished she was panting and breathless and had to lean on his arm. They found a seat and sat down; even the band seemed in need of a break. It was difficult to talk above the hubbub of noise; during the break everyone appeared to have something to say, and to make it even more difficult Wishart was interrupted continually as old friends came up to speak to him. She couldn't help noticing that they stared at her in an odd shy way, and also that he made no attempt to introduce her, thinking no doubt that introductions and the shaking of hands were fancy English mannerisms that had no place at a Highland dance. But she didn't mind.

Wishart got up to leave her for a minute. When he returned a few minutes later she saw his face was slightly flushed.

'Sorry I was so long,' he said. 'I met an old friend and had to have a drink with him.'

'A drink,' she sounded puzzled, 'where?'

'Oh, in the toilet,' he explained. She laughed. 'In the toilet? I suppose that's part of the tradition too?'

'Very much so,' he answered and sat down beside her again. 'Where else would you drink?'

She found it very amusing, the thought of men gathered in a toilet passing half-bottles of whisky around, and said so.

He was about to reply when there was a call from the platform for silence. The draw for the raffle was about to be made.

A young girl, she couldn't have been more than fourteen years old, drew the first ticket, and to a chorus of booing and cheering the M C announced the winning number.

Joanna leaned over to Wishart. 'The tickets . . . the raffle tickets . . .'

'Oh,' he remembered. He dug in his pocket and found them, just as the M C called the second number.

Joanna rifled through the stubs.

'. . . and now the third prize, ladies and gentlemen – a bottle of whisky – goes to number . . .'

Joanna gave a cry and turned excitedly. 'We've won . . . we've won.' She handed the winning stub to Wishart and clapped her hands together.

He checked the number. She was right. She'd won a bottle of whisky. He handed her the ticket back with a grin. 'Off you go and collect your prize.'

'No, you do it.'

'Me? But . . .'

'No, please . . . do you mind?'

He got to his feet and self-consciously walked across the floor to the platform. There were loud cheers as he reached up to collect the prize. His face slightly reddening, he returned to Joanna and sat down again.

'Is is good whisky?' she asked, looking at the label. 'I'm afraid I don't know one from another . . .'

'The best whisky is the same as wine; it's the one you like best.'

'Do you like that one?'

'No-o, not particularly. I prefer malt.'

'Malt? What's the difference? Father once told me but I forget.'

'Well, it's a long story, but basically . . .' his words were lost as the band struck up again. She leant closer to him and he caught the faintest trace of perfume mingled with the warm smell of a living, breathing, human animal. He felt a pulse quicken in his throat as he shook his head. 'I'll have to tell you some other time . . .' he made a hopeless gesture with his hands.

The warm grey eyes stared into his own. Open eyes that were so frank and trusting that they made him feel strangely clumsy and inarticulate, like a crude-handed giant examining a small and precious flower.

He couldn't hear the words but he suspected he knew what she'd said. It had sounded like: 'I'm sure there are lots of things you could tell me.'

Slowly he felt the colour mount to his face. He suddenly wanted to take this girl by the shoulders and tell her . . . tell her what? He shook the thought from his mind.

In his nervousness he nearly dropped the bottle of whisky as he reached for his cigarettes.

She refused one and, his own unlit, he found himself asking her if she'd like to leave. He was surprised at his own actions, but without hesitation she rose. They made their way towards the door, threading their way across the packed floor as she held on to his hand. Outside he lit his cigarette and to his surprise discovered his hand was shaking slightly.

They stood for a minute. It had gone midnight but the

air was still warm.

'What a beautiful night,' Joanna said, her eyes shining, and then, turning to him, eagerly added: 'Do you think we could go for a drive?'

'Would you like that?'

'Where shall we go?'

'Tell you what, we could drive up to the head of the glen if you'd like.'

'Marvellous. I've only been there once before and it was raining cats and dogs at the time.'

'Okay, let's go.'

A few minutes' walk found them back at the hotel. Inside, lights were still showing and muffled sounds of revelry came from within. He brought the car round and she got in, the deep throbbing note of the Aston Martin filling the stillness of the night as they drove off.

It was nearly two o'clock before they got back. He cut the engine and threw his head back, breathing the night air. Joanna turned in her seat to face him, her tanned face showing white in the moonlight. She sighed with pleasure.

'What a lovely night that was.'

'You enjoyed yourself?'

'Very much. And the glen, it looked so lovely. You know what the hills reminded me of?'

'No, what?'

'Just like peaceful old men. Indian chiefs sitting quietly around a camp fire.'

He laughed and got out his cigarettes, feeling her calm reach out and touch him soothingly. 'Would you like a cigarette before you go in,' he said.

'You know, I think I will,' she answered.

Smoking quietly they watched the slow drift of smoke, pale blue strands in the light. Joanna stubbed her cigarette out. 'I really must go now,' she said. 'It's been a lovely evening, thanks for everything.'

'Here, let me help you,' he said, getting out to go round to the passenger side. He opened the door for her.

She stood for a moment looking up at him.

Once more he felt awkward in the face of her assurance. He dropped his cigarette on the gravel and ground it out with his foot. 'Well,' he said, searching for something to say that would indicate his feelings, 'I'm glad you enjoyed it.'

She remained silent.

'Well . . .' he began again and then suddenly remembered,

'Hey, you've forgotten,' he reached into the back of the car and produced the bottle of whisky she'd won, 'you were nearly away without it.'

'You have it,' she said.

'No, I . . .'

'Please. I'd like you to have it as a present. Must go now, or I'm sure Mrs Farquharson will be coming out to look for me.' She turned to go.

He stood clutching the bottle of whisky. 'Look. I was thinking . . . look, would you like to have a walk over the head of the glen sometime?'

She hesitated for a second, and then said: 'Yes. I think I would like that. Could you ring me to-morrow evening . . . and now I really must go. Good night, and thanks once more for a lovely evening.'

'Good night.' He waited till she had gone before climbing back into the car. He was still holding the bottle of whisky: her present to him. He laid it down on the passenger seat, feeling the leather warm to his touch. For some time he sat without moving.

He realised something very strange was happening to him. He felt at peace with himself and yet in his mind there was this strange turbulence, a state of emotional bewilderment which, though frightening, was also exciting.

He shook himself free of his reverie and switched on the ignition.

Joanna, in her bedroom, heard the sound of the engine start up. A contented smile on her face, she reached over and switched off the bedside light.

CHAPTER XIV

Grant split the middle of the eighteenth fairway with a drive. It was a long, climbing ball, and his partner Colonel Farquharson shook his head sadly as he teed up. Joanna watched the expression on her father's face. He made no secret of the fact he was conscious of his ability to hit a golf ball a long way.

It was Sunday afternoon, and there being no fishing that day Farquharson had suggested a game of golf. After church service which Grant – a confirmed atheist – only attended out of deference to his hosts, they'd had a snack lunch and driven down to the local golf course. Joanna had decided to join them for the walk. Mrs Farquharson had offered to lend her a set of clubs but she had refused, despite the fact she was an excellent player with much of her father's ability to hit the ball hard. She'd excused herself by saying it was too hot, and now like Colonel Farquharson she was beginning to feel it. But her father, though sweating heavily, never altered his stride and attacked the ball venomously with every shot.

Farquharson hit an indifferent drive, pulling his ball in to the gorse on the left of the fairway. Joanna had been pulling his trolley for him, but now he took it from her as they set off up the long gradient. He came up to his ball and selected a three wood to play the shot. Grant stood by, making no comment.

Farquharson slashed at the ball and it ran weakly along the fairway for about eighty yards. He played another shot with the same club leaving himself just short of the large dip in the fairway in front of the green.

It was Grant's turn to play. He was only carrying a few clubs and laid his bag down on the grass, selecting a long iron.

'I think you'll need more than that, Iain,' Farquharson cautioned. 'It's a long way, you know . . . and you've got to carry the dip.'

It looked a long way to Joanna, but Farquharson's advice only seemed to inflame her father's determination. It was the sort of thing he thrived on – a challenge. She knew that look well.

He took up his stance, squeezing his feet into the turf and
150

kneading the club in his powerful hands. He had a short, quick backswing, but he got his weight well over and was able to put the power into the shot where it was needed.

Whoosh! The ball took off like a missile and a large slice of turf flew out of the ground.

Farquharson shook his head again as he watched the flight of the ball. 'Good God, man, you've cleared it. How in heaven's name do you do it?'

Grant grinned with child-like delight. 'Cleared the dip? I'll bet you five shillings that ball's on the green.'

They walked up to Farquharson's ball. Joanna handed him a five iron. The colonel's shot sailed over the dip in a high arc.

'Shot,' Grant cried. 'I'll bet you another five shillings I'm nearest the pin, right?'

They walked round the edge of the dip which was about the size of a large bomb crater. There was one ball on the green. Grant was first to reach it. He bent down and slowly straightened up, a frown on his face. 'It's yours, John,' he said, 'now where the devil has mine gone?'

Joanna was the first to spot it. It lay at the back of the green. 'What's that?' she cried, pointing.

'Good heavens, good heavens,' Farquharson gasped, 'you went right through the green, Iain. What a grand shot!'

Grant's disappointment vanished in a flash. He'd not only done what he'd set out to do but he'd done it only too well. 'That's ten shillings I owe you, John, right?'

'I don't think I should take it after such a magnificent shot.'

Grant was checking his card. 'I think you'd better. I have three to get down in and win the match. In which case you'll still owe me ten shillings.' Grant walked round to the back of the green and with a look of intense concentration on his face chipped up to lay the ball dead. Farquharson's approach putt was miles away and he picked up.

'You're much too good for me, Iain,' he said on his way back to the tiny clubhouse. 'I wish I knew how you manage to hit the ball so damned far.'

Grant smiled with self-satisfaction. 'It's all a matter of balance and timing. All sports are the same. A batsman hitting a ball, a boxer throwing a punch, it's timing, and balance. Balance, my dear John, and knowing when to apply the effort.'

Farquharson put his arm on Joanna's shoulder. 'What can't this father of yours do? He catches fish, he climbs like a goat and hits a golf ball a mile. He even shoots better than me when it comes to it.'

'I know,' Joanna said. 'Some people seem to have all the talents.'

'Oh, come now, Joanna, I'm not having that. You have a talent all of your own,' Farquharson protested.

'I wish I knew what it was!'

Grant slipped his arm around her. 'For being just what you are, Jo – yourself.'

After tea Mrs Farquharson announced that her husband and she had to go into town for a couple of hours, but they would be back in time for dinner. Joanna and her father went out on the lawn to read the Sunday papers.

Joanna had got as far as the book reviews and was reminding herself to talk to Sandy Craig about the book she had in mind when the phone rang. She jumped up.

'All right, father. I'll get it.'

She came back a few minutes later. It had been a call for the Colonel. She must have looked a little disappointed, for her father said: 'What is it, Jo? Something the matter?'

She sat down again. 'No, it was for John. I told them to phone later.'

Grant rebusied himself in the Sundays, but a few minutes later he put his paper down.

'There's something on your mind, Joanna. Now don't try and hide it from me, after all I should know my own daughter by now.' He looked at her intently as if he could prise the truth from her.

'I was just thinking, that's all.'

'You haven't started that again, have you? I've told you to stop worrying about it. After all . . .'

She sat up. 'Father, I read the papers. I know how dangerous it is. I wish you wouldn't try and minimise it; I've outgrown my childhood, you know.'

'Papers, papers. papers. Surely I don't have to tell you what they're like. They exaggerate everything. Their business is sensationalism.'

'Perhaps, but there are some things you don't have to exaggerate. They're real and terrifying enough in themselves. Anyway, father, there's no point in arguing about it. I've told you what I think often enough, and I promised I wouldn't bother you with it again.'

'Then what are you worried about?'

'Oh,' she cried in exasperation. 'It doesn't mean to say

152

because I promised not to bring the subject up again that I can just put it out of my mind like that. Don't you . . .' The phone rang again. 'I'll be back in a moment,' she said, getting up and going indoors.

Molly had got there first and handed her the phone. 'It's for you, Miss. He didn't say who he was.'

'Thank you, Molly,' she took the receiver from the maid. 'Hullo . . . oh, it's you. What's that? Oh, I'm sorry, perhaps I do. I've just been having an argument with my father . . . what? No, not very often.' There was a long pause as she listened. 'To-morrow . . . and we would be back Tuesday afternoon . . . all right but not later, we're probably going home Tuesday . . . right, you'll pick me up then about nine . . . I'll be ready . . . 'bye now . . .'

She hung up and walking slowly went back out to the garden.

'Who was that?' her father asked when she'd sat down again.

'Robert Wishart,' she answered.

'Wishart?'

'Yes, he's asked me to walk over the hills to Braemar with him.'

'And what did you say?' Grant eyed her closely.

'I said yes. He's picking me up to-morrow.'

Grant folded his paper. 'It's quite a long way you know. It must be all of twenty-eight miles there and back. That's quite a lot for one day. I would have thought this chap Wishart realised that.'

'Oh, we're not going to do it in a day, father. We'll be staying in Braemar overnight.'

Grant put his paper down. 'You say you'll be staying overnight?'

'Yes, we'll . . .' She stopped when she saw the expression on his face. 'Oh, father,' she chided, 'I'm not going to jump into bed with him, or anything like that. But we've got to stay some place.'

He frowned heavily. 'I wish you wouldn't use such an expression. You make the whole thing sound so casual.' He leaned forward in his chair. 'Look, Joanna, I'm not trying to interfere in your private life, I don't think I have the right to, but after all I am your father and have some responsibilities. You've met this chap only a couple of days ago and here you are going away with him to stay overnight. Do you think that's wise? Don't misunderstand me. I have no doubt of your intentions, but can I be assured of his?'

153

Joanna's face paled. 'Father! That's an unkind thing to say. You don't even know him and yet you practically accuse him of being a smooth-tongued seducer.'

'No, Jo. I didn't imply that at all. I'm only saying what any father would in my position. Of course I don't know the man, but neither do you for that matter and that's why I ask you if you think it's wise.'

Her lips tightened. 'You must have little confidence in my ability to judge people, and after all the responsibility will be mine, won't it? And another thing you might as well know, he did ask how you might feel about it.'

'Very thoughtful of him, I'm sure. Well, Jo, all I can say is that it's up to you, but don't expect me to feel happy about it.'

Her anger vanished and she got up from her chair to walk over to him and run her fingers through his thick grey hair. 'Can't you trust me, father? He's a very nice person really. You'd like him if you met him, I know you would. He's honest and quite straightforward.'

'And also much older than you,' Grant couldn't resist saying.

She stepped back. 'How do you know that if you don't know him?'

'I think I do know him.'

'I'm sorry. I don't understand.'

'I'm pretty certain now he is the mountaineering chap I mentioned earlier to you, in which case I do know something about him.'

So her guess had been right. 'When did you find all this out?' she asked.

'John told me.'

'I see. What else did he tell you about him?'

'What do you mean?'

She crossed her arms. 'You've been doing a little checking up, haven't you?'

Grant made an explosive sound with his lips. 'Really, Joanna.'

'Well, never mind, if this is going to upset you that much I'll tell him I've called it off, but I'd hoped you'd much more confidence in me than that.'

Grant rose to his feet to unfold her arms and take her hands in his. 'I'm only thinking of your welfare. Please try and understand,' he pleaded.

She gazed into his eyes. 'I do understand.'

154

He smiled resignedly and letting go of her placed his hands either side of her head to rock it gently. 'You've always been able to get the better of me, haven't you? John was so right when he said you have a talent all of your own. Now you just go ahead and do what you think is right . . . that will be good enough for me.'

'Thank you, father,' she said, leaning forward to kiss him softly on the cheek.

'There is one thing you can do for me.'

'What is that?'

'Your friend Wishart. Bring him to supper one evening . . . over to Nanga Parbat.'

'I'd be glad to,' she said. 'I think you'd like him, you know. You're bound to have lots in common.'

Grant was far from sure of this but he tried to put his daughter at ease by saying, 'I'm certain we do. I'll leave it to you to fix up.'

Joanna sat down again and he picked up his paper. But he no longer felt like reading. Joanna's apparently growing friendship with this chap Wishart worried him. It was quite possible he was everything that she'd said about him and to be such a fine mountaineer, he realised, demanded unusual qualities of mind and spirit. Nevertheless it was impossible to dismiss the fact that his parents had been working people. He wished Joanna could understand what this meant. Democracy was a fine conception, but in terms of harsh reality it just couldn't work. All men were not born equal. Nature selected some to lead and others to follow and these qualities were best maintained by selective breeding, in the same way you bred a horse for speed or jumping. It was simple really, nothing complicated about it, though apparently not for his daughter with her modern generation brand of radicalism and protest. And yet she was such a sensible young woman in so many other ways. Couldn't she understand all this marching and banner-waving was a waste of time? Society had always been and always would be divided into classes. Of course, he agreed with her, poverty was a bad thing. People *should* be well-housed, well-fed and well-clothed, but it had to be as a result of their effort; not as unearned rewards. Each man should stand on his own two feet without all this pampering and cosseting by the State. A good example was the Gurkhas and Sherpas. You couldn't wish for a finer body of men, displaying excellent qualities once given the right leadership.

He sighed inwardly. Perhaps it had been his fault. He

155

should have spent more time with his daughter at an earlier age. He would have been able to counteract some of these extraordinary ideas of hers. What in heaven's name did she want to concern herself with politics and such things for anyway? She'd be far better off getting herself married and raising a healthy, lusty family. And there was Osborne, it was obvious he was itching to marry her and she'd turned him down absolutely flat. And the next thing, she meets a complete stranger and is prepared to go off with him for a couple of days. A man much older than her and with no kind of background at all. What did Farquharson say his father had been, a blacksmith or an engineer or something?

Yes, he should have spent more time with her. He'd allowed her to take too many decisions on her own, decisions that required experience and judgment. Still, it wouldn't do to say too much about this chap Wishart, it would increase her determination to see him.

'I'd give a *shilling* for those thoughts,' the voice broke in.

'What was that, Jo?'

'You were far away some place.'

'Oh, I suppose I was. I was thinking, Osborne said he'd phone some time over the weekend. He's trying to get a friend of his interested. They might even come up for a few days later if he does.'

'Here – to Scotland?' she asked with a little frown.

He noticed the tone in her voice. 'Well, yes. It is possible.' Why in heaven's name didn't she like Osborne?

The phone rang again.

'I'll get it.' Grant rose. 'That could be him now.' He came back a few minutes later, an expression of disappointment on his face.

'What's the matter?' Joanna asked.

He shook his head irritably. 'Oh, nothing. That was Osborne. Seems this chap isn't interested or hasn't got the time or something. Osborne's with him up in North Wales at the moment. He's going to have another go at him to-morrow but he doesn't think there's much hope.'

Joanna couldn't disguise the relief in her voice. 'And you can't get anyone else?'

'I wouldn't say that, but we're running short of time. I want to have everything arranged before winter's here. By the time we have snow I want the team all ready to start our working-up programme.' He sat down again and picked up his paper, frowning.

Joanna had been reading the book reviews. 'I've been thinking, father . . .' she said, breaking the silence.

'Yes.'

'It's something I might need your help with.'

'Oh?'

'It's about Sandy.'

'You mean Craig? What about him?'

'Well, it occurred to me that there might be a book there. His memoirs. Not just the usual rod and gun book but the changes he's seen in his lifetime and . . . well, something of his own outlook. He must have lots of stories locked away in that wise old head of his. I don't think it should just be memoirs of a gamekeeper, if you know what I mean.'

'My dear, you mustn't refer to him as a gamekeeper, he wouldn't thank you for that. He was head stalker on Lord Colme's estate at one time before he came down here. There's a big difference, you know.'

'All right, I'll remember, but what do you think of the idea?'

'Hasn't there been a lot of that sort of thing lately? I seem to remember reading a review recently in *The Field*.'

'I'm not sure. I'll have to check when I get back to London. Not that it really matters, a good book on a good subject will always sell.'

Grant looked doubtful and said so. 'Hasn't that sort of thing been done to death?'

She laughed. 'You're a pessimist at times. Have you thought of Western films? I would say they've been very much "done to death" and yet they still keep making them.'

'Well, Jo, you know best. I wouldn't presume to advise you there. Why don't you talk to him about it?'

'Uh-huh. It would be much better if the suggestion came from you.'

'All right, if you think so. I'll bring it up with him tomorrow, but I shouldn't expect too much. He's an independent old devil and mightn't take kindly to the idea. He's not the sort of man that would seek publicity and I must say I agree with him. Why are you smiling?'

'I was just thinking about this horror of publicity thing. It's so Scottish. We're never very far removed from the Old Testament, are we?'

'I don't quite follow you, but there's a lot of good things in the Old Testament we would do well to copy.'

CHAPTER XV

It was still early morning as they approached the head of the glen. The narrow twisting road could only take one vehicle at a time, and Wishart had to pull up on the bank to let the Post Office van past. The driver gave him a wave as he drove past.

Wishart was about to drive off again when Joanna gave a cry. He stopped.

'Look. There. It looks like an eagle.'

'Where?' His eyes followed the direction of her outstretched arm. 'I've got it. Yes, you're right. It is an eagle.'

In silence they watched the great bird circle overhead, the slow, occasional beat of its wings sweeping the air like galley oars.

Wishart knocked his pipe out on the side of the car. 'That's odd.'

'What is?' her voice was excited.

'Well, I was talking to "Dyke" Bruce the other day and he was telling me this pair might have shifted their eyrie. They used to be farther up the glen, but he reckons they've moved farther down. It's very unusual if they have.'

'Why would they do that?' she asked, watching the huge bird with fascination.

'I don't know. Last winter was pretty severe. We had a lot of storms and heavy snowfalls. It's possible there was a rockfall where they were nesting. I can't think what else would cause them to shift.'

'Look, look!' she cried standing up in the car. 'It's flying straight into that cliff.'

'Where? I can't see.'

She pointed again. 'Just there . . . where you're looking now.'

'Hurry,' he said. 'There's a pair of glasses in my pack.' His eyes were glued to the spot where the eagle had alighted on the rock face.

She searched in the pack and found the binoculars.

He focused them, surveying the cliff before handing them back to her. 'Here. Have a look.'

For a long minute she peered through the glasses. 'It looks . . . it's their nest, isn't it?'

'See anything else?'

She concentrated. 'Just a minute . . . there's something in the nest. It's – it's alive.' She lowered the glasses, a troubled look spreading over her features. 'Oh, Robert, it isn't something they've caught, is it?'

He shook his head. 'No, it's an eaglet. They must have hatched recently.'

She breathed a sigh of relief. 'For a moment I thought . . .' her voice tailed off and she gave a little shudder.

His hand went out to rest on her shoulder. 'You shouldn't think like that. Animals don't have emotions like us.'

'I know,' she said, slightly ashamed of her response. 'But they do suffer. Doesn't it seem cruel to you at times?'

'Don't think about it. It doesn't get you any place,' he said, starting the engine. Joanna sat down again as they drove off. A few minutes later they'd reached the old quarry at the top of the glen and turned left through a gate into a farm. He drew the car up alongside a bright red Fordson tractor. 'Just look at that. A new tractor. Jock must be doing well.'

'Who's Jock?' she asked, handing him the packs and getting out.

'Jock? Oh, he rents the farm.'

'Are you leaving the car here?'

'Yes. It'll be okay. I'll just stick my head in the door and say hullo to Mrs Black. I'd better let her know we're here. Jock'll be away some place. I won't be a minute.' He crossed the yard and knocked at the door of the farmhouse. From inside, a dog barked and Joanna heard a woman's voice as the door opened. 'Oh, it's you, Rab,' she heard the voice cry. 'Come awa' in, man.' She didn't hear his reply but she caught a glimpse of the woman peering over his shoulder in her direction; a short stout woman with a high complexion and wearing a floral print apron.

The voices continued for a minute and then she heard him bid the woman goodbye and recross the yard.

He picked up his pack and slung it over his shoulders. 'Okay, Joanna. Here, let me help you on with yours.'

'I can manage, Robert. I'm not a hothouse plant, you know,' she said, her smile dying as she saw his face colour slightly. Instinctively her hand went out to touch his arm. 'Now I've offended you.'

He jerked his head away from her gaze.

'Robert?' she said. 'You mustn't be so serious all the time.'

He faced her again, his mouth twisting into a wry smile. 'I

am a bit at times, I suppose.'

'Well, you shouldn't be,' she admonished. 'You should learn to laugh more.'

'Okay, I'll take your advice. You can put it down to my fire and brimstone upbringing. Ca . . .' he almost said 'Carole', but checked himself in time. 'A friend of mine used to say it was the Puritanism coming out.'

'Aye,' she said, mimicking his accent which seemed to have got broader since she'd met him. 'It's a terrible thing the Puritanism. But what else could one expect with a name like Wishart?'

He frowned for a moment before realising she was joking again. 'You know, that's a pretty good Scots accent you've got there,' he said, falling into her mood, 'for an English-woman.'

'What?' she said indignantly. 'I was born and brought . . .

He stopped her in mid-sentence. 'Aye, right enough, Miss Grant, but I would be asking you not to take me too seriously at times.'

She jerked her arm away with a laugh. 'Monster.'

Beyond the farmhouse the glen divided into two. Walking along by the river they came to a bridge and took the track to their right. The glen which lay in front of them was a flat expanse of moorland with the hills climbing sharply on either side. In the winter it was swept by fierce winds and covered in deep snow, but now its verdant colouring was slowly turning brown in the heat of the sun.

They kept to the Forestry road, the dust kicking up from their boots, and soon passed an old stalker's house on their right. Wishart stopped and pointed upwards to the hill. 'You wouldn't believe it,' he said, 'but you see that hill . . . well, I knew a chap who used to take his motor-bike across there.'

Joanna looked, an expression of disbelief on her features.

'Aye, and what's more there was a man took a horse and cart over the same hill.'

'Seriously?' she asked, her eyes twinkling.

'I know it's difficult to believe, but that's the truth.'

'But whatever for?'

'Well, I'm not sure about the horse and cart, but the chap with the motor-bike was courting a girl over by Ballater and that's the only way he could visit her.'

She looked again at the hill and shook her head in wonderment.

'Just wait till we get up the glen a bit and I'll show you something else that might interest you.'

They walked on for nearly a mile. When they came to a large boulder Wishart halted. 'We'll rest here a moment.'

Joanna sat down. Wishart put his foot up on the boulder and resting his arm across his knee pointed to the hill that fronted them. It was very steep and scarred by broken outcrops of rock. 'You see that hill? Well, a few years ago, during a bad winter there was a herd of deer crossing over when either one of them slipped or the snow avalanched, but the whole herd was caught up in an enormous snowball and finished up at the bottom of the glen.'

'Were they killed?'

'The lot. There were about forty or fifty of them . . . all killed.'

'Oh, how awful.' Joanna got to her feet. 'Let's go, Robert. I don't think I want to stay here much longer. It makes me feel sad.'

'Okay,' he said. 'We haven't far to go now and we can have a break when we get to the top of the hill.'

It grew hotter as the sun climbed higher. There was hardly a breath of wind and the glen was like a huge oven. Overhead a few curlews beat their wings as if to fan the still air, their melancholy cries and the occasional bleat from high-grazing sheep the only sounds in the glen.

The ground began to steepen and the path become more broken, twisting and turning as it followed the contours of the slope. Boulders and tree roots blocked the path, making the going more difficult. Wishart halted to allow Joanna to catch up.

'All right?' he asked.

'Phew! It's this heat.'

'How's your feet?'

'It's not my feet, I'm being fried, that's all.'

'Keep going,' he encouraged. 'We'll have a short rest when we reach the bridge. From there it's not far to the top; it'll be cooler on higher ground.'

They were right at the head of the glen now. On either side rocky crags rose steeply as the glen narrowed. They entered a narrow ravine with the starving water course far below. As they went on, still climbing steeply, the high land took on a tumbled appearance, reminding Joanna of a ruined temple, long covered by mosses and grass. And everywhere tall larches were in profusion. This was old forest land, the last before they reached the wide expanse of ground that formed a great table-top at the head of a series of parallel glens.

The ground became even steeper and he found he had to stop continually to allow Joanna to catch up. At last they came to the old wooden bridge spanning the gorge. In normal times the surrounding air would be filled with a cooling spray and the thunder of falling water, the sunlight broken by the prismatic action of the suspended water globules, but now the waterfall was no more than a thin trickle; like a tap that had been left running.

Joanna stopped on the bridge to look down. He glanced at her. She looked so natural and at ease in the surroundings, he found it difficult to imagine she worked in an office.

He gestured towards a spot shaded by larches. 'We'll have a spell here.'

She nodded thankfully and, walking past him, flopped down on the grass. 'I thought we were never going to reach it,' she gasped.

'Well, we're not quite there, yet,' he cautioned.

'How far have we to go, now?'

'Oh, not all that far. Another fifteen or twenty minutes should bring us out on the tops.'

'And then?'

'We'll head across towards the loch then, and come down by the side and follow the shore line till we get to the bothy. That should be enough for one day.'

She sat up slowly as the implication of what he'd said dawned on her. 'You mean you intend to stay there? I thought we were going over to Braemar.' A shadow of suspicion lurked in her mind.

'Did I say that?'

'Yes. You said we'd go over the hill track to Braemar.'

'Oh, I see, now. What I meant was that we'd take the Braemar track. I didn't actually mean we'd go there.'

'So we're supposed to stay in this bothy.' She felt a little annoyed. He should have made himself clear. Why hadn't he? They'd be all alone in a remote part of the hills. She couldn't rid herself of her suspicions and yet she felt she was being unfair to him.

He saw her look. 'Joanna,' he hesitated. 'There'll probably be others there. The bothy's used by climbers . . .' his voice tailed off in embarrassment.

'I wish you'd told me,' she said. 'I haven't a sleeping bag or anything.'

'That's okay, I brought one along for you. But look, Jo, if you'd rather we went on to Braemar . . .'

'No, it's all right. I don't mind, really.'

They crossed the plateau and made their way down the steep sides of the loch, stopping to have a sandwich before circumnavigating the loch. At the end of the loch the path led through a forest of pines. She enjoyed the feeling of walking on the soft carpet of pine needles, the quiet and peace of the forest. Clearing the trees, they stopped for a moment to look at a giant ant-hill nearly four feet in height. She found herself fascinated by the sight and only tore herself away when he reminded her it was getting late and they hadn't had a proper meal all day.

It was nearly seven when they reached the bothy. From the bent chimney-stack a column of soft blue smoke rose straight up in the air. There wasn't a breath of wind. Half of the old barn had been gutted by fire, exposing gaunt blackened timbers, but part of the roofing remained and one of the windows had even managed to retain a few panes of glass.

The door hung at a drunken angle, resisting his first efforts to open it with a protesting groan.

They went in. A solitary table was the only piece of furniture, and the bare floorboards were covered with bracken. At the far end, by the fireplace, two men and a girl were seated cross-legged round a primus stove. They looked up as Wishart and Joanna entered.

'Hullo there.'

'Hullo,' Wishart returned the greeting.

One of the men rose. He was thickset and bearded, with long powerful arms. 'Would you like a cup of tea?' he asked.

Wishart and Joanna dumped their packs and Wishart got the mugs out. The man – Joanna had already mentally christened him Trog – took the mugs and filled them with a dark brown liquid, adding condensed milk from a tin. 'Here,' he handed the mugs back, 'help yourself to sugar.'

'Thanks.' Wishart spooned sugar into Joanna's mug and, moving the packs over, beckoned her to sit down.

'Where are you heading for?' Trog asked.

'Oh, just a bit of hill-walking. We came over from Clova,' he answered, noticing the climbing gear scattered around. 'Where have you been? Lochnagar?'

The man nodded. 'Uhuh. Black Spout Buttress.'

The girl opened a tin of biscuits and offered them round. 'Staying long?' It was the other man who spoke.

'No, just the night and then we're heading back to Clova.'

'We've got a week, but we're thinking of heading for Aviemore.'

Wishart lit his pipe and threw the match away in the empty fireplace. 'Walking over, are you?'

'We've got a car down at the farm. We thought we'd drive up to the Linn of Dee and walk over.'

'It's a good walk.'

Wishart got to his feet and started emptying the packs. He got the primus out and started assembling it.

'You can use ours if you want,' one of the men said.

'Thanks,' Wishart said, 'but I might as well get ours going anyway.' He fixed the stove up.

Joanna wanted to help.

Wishart smiled at her. 'Here, you can fill that, if you want something to do.' He handed her a billy can. 'You'll find a burn just outside the door.'

Using the two stoves he had a meal ready in less than half an hour. Joanna looked after the soup whilst Wishart threw everything into a large pan, a legacy from some climber who'd apparently got tired of carrying it around. Eggs, bacon, sausages, tomatoes, beans, everything went in, and when Joanna had cooked the soup he prepared a dixie of dried potatoes.

They ate hungrily, and after washing up Wishart laid out the sleeping bags alongside the three others. The two men and the woman had gone out for a walk, leaving them by themselves.

'It's a bit primitive,' Wishart said, wondering what she thought about it.

She rubbed her hands on her jeans. 'I think it's marvellous . . . and that meal!'

'Fancy a walk?' he asked when he'd fixed the sleeping bags.

'Okay.' She slipped off her moccasins and pulled on her boots. 'Where shall we go?'

'Not far. Just down to the loch and back. How're you feeling anyway, we did quite a few miles to-day.'

'I'm feeling wonderful, full of beans.'

He smiled at her enthusiasm as he pulled on his own boots. They were gone about an hour, and when they came back one of the men had produced a guitar and was strumming softly.

Someone had lit the fire and brewed tea. Joanna and Wishart were offered some.

'Just a minute.' Wishart went to his pack and produced a half-bottle of whisky from the side pocket. 'Here,' he said, 'would anyone like a drop of Scotch in their tea?'

He poured whisky into four mugs – Joanna didn't want any – and next time round finished the bottle off. In the mountain shelter the act had the effect of drawing the group together. It was near midnight before anyone turned in, but up till then they'd sung and talked their way through the hours.

Wishart was first up next morning. He got the stove going and made tea, going round each sleeping bag with a warning to be careful not to knock the tea over or let it get cold. It was an old tradition: the first up made the tea and got the fire going.

Joanna raised herself on one elbow and pushed back her hair from where it had fallen over her eyes. She made a sleepy contented sound as she sipped her tea. 'Mmmm . . .'

'Breakfast'll be ready in ten minutes, Jo,' he called to her.

'Righto.' She finished her tea and got up and, slinging a towel over her shoulder, went down to the loch-side to wash.

Breakfast was ready when she got back. She seldom ate breakfast, but this morning she was hungry. After she'd eaten she helped Wishart to clear up and pack. It was still early morning when they said farewell to the others and left.

'I thought we could go up Lochnagar and then over to the Tolmount,' he said as they stopped for a moment to watch the birds rise off the water. 'It's a long drag,' he warned, 'but when we get to the top the worst of it's over. From the Tolmount it's downhill all the way.'

'I'll take your word for it,' she said.

'Okay. We'll stop half way up for a break. We should be at the top before twelve, and back down the glen in time for tea.' He looked at her for a minute. 'You're not tired, are you? That was a fair walk we did yesterday if you're not accustomed to it.'

'Robert, I'm not delicate you know.' She wished he wouldn't be so over-considerate.

'I'm sorry, it's just that . . .'

'Look, I'm a perfectly healthy girl.'

'Okay. We'll get moving then,' he said, setting off at a slow pace.

They crossed over a bridge and, passing the old shooting lodge, made their way up the hill. As the morning wore on the going got harder. On the baked slopes of the hill the heat was stifling. By the time they'd reached the spring known as the Foxes' Well, Joanna was glad to take a rest.

After ten minutes they moved off again. From here it was a long pull to the top, the path zigging and zagging as if struggling to make the gradient. Three and a half hours after leaving the bothy, the flowering heather glowing pinkly in the strong sunlight, they reached the top.

Joanna felt her legs going and she was glad when they reached the indicator set on top of the mountain.

She sprawled out. Wishart leant an elbow on the flat top of the indicator, gazing across the tops of the hills to the west, his eyes screwed up. She looked up at him, noticing the tiny wrinkles round the eyes, the deeply tanned skin and the lips beginning to crack in the heat, and felt something stir within her, he seemed so lonely and isolated.

She got to her feet just as he beckoned to her.

'Come and see this, Jo.'

She walked over to the indicator. He pointed to the table. 'Look along the sight-line. You can just see it in the haze: King Arthur's Seat.'

She bent down to peer along the sight-line and a second later gave a little cry. 'It must be miles away.'

'It is. Now look to your right, you'll see Ben Nevis, it's quite clear.'

She picked it out from the line of blue hills to the west. They spent a few minutes identifying other landmarks before sitting down again to have sandwiches and coffee. But half an hour later he was back on his feet.

'Ready to go?'

She groaned. 'You're a slave driver, you are, Robert Wishart.'

The cracked lips widened in a grin. 'Come on, you'll be all right once we get going. We haven't all that far now to the Tolmount. From there it's a free-wheel.'

It was hard going in the heat, but they reached the Tolmount and began the descent to the glen which would lead them to the farmhouse where they'd left the car. The path was well-defined; steep at first but the angle tapering off to run all the way to the foot of the basin of the glen to meet the water. To their right as they descended the path, dark cliffs guarded the entrance to a huge corrie, but on the opposite side the hills were softer in contour and covered with broom and heather.

166

Eventually they came to a small clump of forest. The path had widened to a Land-Rover track, barred by a forestry gate. From here the road led to a shooting lodge which had been converted into a youth hostel. The hostel was quiet as they passed it and made for the bridge which spanned the water.

Joanna halted for a moment.

'What's the matter?'

'My feet, they're burning. I'm going down to the water.'

'Okay. Here, follow me, this way.' He led her away from the bridge towards a pool.

Reaching the bank she pulled her boots and socks off. 'That's wonderful,' she cried delightedly as she dipped her feet in the cool water. 'Aren't you going to join me?' But he'd walked away farther down the pool, peering over the bank.

She dried her feet and slipped her boots back on. 'What are you looking for?' she asked as she rejoined him.

'Fish,' he said. 'Salmon. There's not enough water for them to have got up. There might be some trapped here.'

'Here? In the pool?'

He nodded. 'They'll probably be tucked away somewhere under the bank.'

She joined him in walking up and down, not exactly sure what she was looking for but peering down at the undercut bank. Suddenly she stopped and looked again. Jammed between two rocks in the pool there was an odd, triangular shape. 'Robert,' she cried, instinctively lowering her voice. 'Come here.'

He came up to her quietly. 'What is it?'

'Look,' she said, pointing. 'It's the tail of a fish. It must have been caught in the rocks falling from the bank.'

'Ssshhh,' he bent down quickly, holding his hand up for her to be silent. In a moment he had straightened up. 'It's a salmon,' he whispered.

'Are you sure?' she asked breathlessly.

'Go and get my pack, will you? Quickly,' he whispered.

She didn't pause for an explanation but ran off. She was back in a moment. He had his knife out and was cutting a deep notch in a stick. He put it down and, taking the pack from her, opened up the side pocket and fished out a length of light-weight nylon. He fastened one end to the stick and with the other end formed a running noose.

'What are you doing?'

He jerked his thumb towards the bank. 'The salmon.'

'But isn't it dead?'

He shook his head. 'No, it's only resting. There's a few of them lying under the bank.'

Her eyes widened. 'A few . . . what are you going to do?'

He grinned. 'Don't you like salmon?'

Her mouth fell open. 'You're not . . .?'

He silenced her with a wave of his hand. 'I want you to hold on to my feet when I lean over the bank. I'm going to slip the noose over its tail and when I say "now" I want you to hang on to my feet like grim death. He'll fight like mad once he feels the line hit him.'

'But . . .?' She felt alarmed now. 'Supposing anyone sees you.'

'That's another thing—keep a good look-out. I wouldn't like to be caught poaching, they'd impound the car.'

'Robert, do you . . .?'

He ignored her protests. 'Right, Jo. Here we go. Just remember to hang on to my feet.'

With the stick in his hand he crept up to the bank carefully and lay his full length. The salmon hadn't moved. Cautiously he brought the stick forward, but once in the water the loop in the end of the line slipped. He wriggled back again and sat up.

'No good,' he said, 'I need something to keep the loop from closing.'

She thought for a minute, caught up in the excitement.

'How about a hair-grip?'

'A hair-grip? You know, it just might do.'

Joanna loosed one from her hair and handed it to him.

He fixed it over the nylon line just below the slip knot, holding it up to test it. He shook it about. The loop remained open. 'Joanna, you're a genius,' he grinned at her. He wriggled back to the bank with a further whispered warning to her to hold on to his legs and not let go.

Again he let the nylon down slowly, but this time, though the loop held open, the oily line floated on top of the water. He cursed softly, and with a sign to Joanna to let go of his feet he crept away from the bank.

'The line won't sink . . . I wonder . . . stay there, Jo, and let me know if he moves. But be quiet, there's another three of them farther up the bank. Wait there.' He moved off quickly down the pool, and leaning over soaked the nylon thoroughly in the water, testing it to see if it would sink before returning.

'You okay?'

168

She nodded, glancing around to see that there was still no one about. Once again he lay down and crawled to the edge of the bank. The tail was still visible between the rocks. 'Okay,' he whispered, and let the line down slowly. It broke the surface of the water and sank slowly, but, though the loop held open this time, the thin nylon was too flexible to retain its shape and folded over itself in a figure of eight.

'Damn it,' he muttered softly and withdrew again. 'It's no good, Jo. The line's not heavy enough. We'll have to think of something else.'

They sat down together to hold a council of war. 'Haven't you anything else that would do?' she asked, enjoying her sense of complicity now.

He shook his head. 'Not a thing. It's no good, we'll have to go back to the car and get a bit of wire. Damn it,' he swore, 'they could be off by then.' He sat for a minute biting his lip before getting to his feet. 'You stay here, Jo. I'll be back in about ten minutes. Here, we'd better hide this,' he picked up the crudely fashioned rod and made for the long grass beyond the river bank. 'Just in case anyone comes, we . . .'

'Robert?'

He stopped. 'What's that?'

'Your torch.'

'Eh?' His face twisted in a puzzled frown. 'What . . .'

'Your head torch. The wire extension lead.'

He looked at her in admiration. 'You know, I think you've got it, Jo. Why didn't I think of that? Get the . . .'

But she'd already opened up the ruck sack and pulled out the head torch. It was just an ordinary torch with a detachable reflector fitted with a head band and a long flexible plastic-covered lead.

He took it from her. 'Do you think it will do?' she asked.

'Joanna, you're a . . .'

'I'm an accessory. I can just imagine what Colonel Farquharson will say if we're caught.'

'Plead ignorance, or say I forced you.' He bent down quickly and, breaking open the torch, removed the plastic-covered lead, and using a fisherman's knot secured it to the nylon line, forming a running noose in the wire.

They were ready again. Joanna felt her heart begin to thump with excitement.

'Now, remember, hold on to my legs. In fact, you'd better sit on them. I'll need all the weight I can get.'

This time the loop sank cleanly into the water, poised over

the unsuspecting fish.

Slowly, hardly daring to breathe, he lowered it inch by inch. He'd judged it nicely. The loop was just big enough to fit over the tail and no more. He got the lower half over the underside of the tail and halted to let the salmon get accustomed to the strange feel. When he was sure it hadn't been alarmed, he carefully eased the loop over.

He had it now. If only the wire would hold.

The noose circled the lower girth of the body where it met the tail. Gently he applied pressure, and now it fitted snugly touching the body and no more.

He raised a warning finger to Jo, and taking the rod in both hands, whispered: 'Now!'

He felt the violently exploding body hit the noose as he jerked upwards. The water thrashed wildly, boiling over like a hot-spring as he heaved with all his might.

He was drenched, but there was a heavy thump on the ground behind as the fish landed on the bank. He jumped to his feet, sending Joanna flying, and without pausing seized a stone and flinging himself bodily on the frantically threshing salmon pinned it to the ground.

One sharp blow just above the eye was all that was needed. The salmon lay still and lifeless.

Jo picked herself up from where she'd been sent flying. She got to her feet slowly, brushing the grass from her jeans, her mind still in a whirl; everything seemed to have happened so quickly, it wasn't till she saw the dead fish lying in the grass she realised what had happened. It made her feel ill. She didn't like to see things killed and all she wanted to do was get away from the spot. But Wishart had grabbed the fish and, moving quickly, went farther down the pool and put it back in the water. He jammed it in between stones just underneath the bank.

He came back, wiping his hands on his trousers. 'It'll be safer there. In case anyone comes.' He stopped to laugh as he saw her expression. 'I'm sorry, Jo. I hope I didn't hurt you . . . look, you're soaked to the skin.'

'So are you,' she said.

'Well never mind, it's only a drop of water. It'll soon dry out in the sun. Let's go. There's another three farther up the pool.'

'Robert . . .' she began, but he'd already moved off, clutching the rod in his hand.

She followed him. 'Robert, do you think . . .'

He turned, his eyes narrowing as they searched about. 'You didn't see anyone, did you?'

'No. I was . . .'

'Ssshhh. Now remember what to do, but keep your eyes peeled. You never can tell, there might be somebody about with a glass or a pair of binoculars.'

Before she had time to protest he'd dropped to the ground and wriggled up to the bank. Reaching the bank, he squirmed round and held his finger to his lips. She crawled up to join him and sat on his legs.

He was still for a long time, muttering under his breath, and once or twice he drew back and, twisting round on his elbow, fiddled with the wire loop at the end of the rod.

The minutes passed. He seemed to be having difficulty. He was right over the bank now, his body leaning out over the water. At that moment she heard a car and jerked up. His legs free of her weight, his body see-sawed towards the river and he had to twist round convulsively to reach the safety of the bank.

'What – !'

'It was a car passing,' she whispered.

'Never mind that. Just hang on to my legs, that's all you have to do. The only thing to worry about is someone coming across the fields or down the bank. Okay?'

She felt the reproachful tone in his voice and she was tempted to reply sharply, but checked herself. She couldn't have it both ways. She'd agreed to help and she couldn't draw back now.

Once again he'd eased himself over the water. Joanna had to exert more force to resist the upward thrust of his legs.

She heard him mutter to himself, then he was still again, his long frame frozen into immobility, only the hands moving gently and stealthily.

Immersed in his actions she forgot she was supposed to keep a look-out, and she'd just turned her head when out of the corner of her eye she saw his hand slowly come up in a warning gesture. Immediately she thrust her weight against his legs, her heart beginning to pound again as she waited.

'Now!' he cried and she flung herself against him with all her strength. His legs kicked out madly as if he were trying to free himself, and the air seemed to be filled with water. Great gouts erupted, drenching her to the skin. She no longer reasoned or felt, but clung on, feeling the muscles of his legs jerk with convulsive power. Water was everywhere and her vision was a kaleidoscope of arms, legs, earth and sky all rolled together in a crazy whirl. From somewhere behind her she heard a dull thud and next there was a wild cry and she was free, rolling back on the grass, her head buzzing where his boot had caught her.

There was the sound of a heavy splash as she twisted round, facing away from the river. Something was leaping about wildly in front of her. It was trying desperately to get back into the river. Instinctively she blocked it with her body, fighting it, pushing it, using her knees and her arms, her feet – anything that would prevent this thing from returning to the water.

She fought it away from the bank, driving it backwards. It still threshed wildly but there was no direction now to its movements. There was a noise behind, and she turned fiercely to meet this new challenge. For a moment she was stock still, unable to grasp the meaning of what her eyes saw, and then all her wild frenzy was gone and she was herself again, looking at the strange figure standing in the pool, hair plastered over his face, water dripping from his clothes.

'Robert!' she gasped, springing forward. 'What . . .?'

A broad grin covered his face, water running down his cheeks and dripping from his chin and the end of his nose. His chest was rising and falling with silent laughter. 'What happened to the fish? Did we land him?' he managed to say as he scrambled back up the bank.

'The salmon?' She'd forgotten all about it. She wheeled about. It was still threshing but its movements were subdued and lethargic.

He brushed past her and, picking up a stone, flicked the salmon over with his boot and hit it on the head.

The whole thing had only taken seconds. She still couldn't understand what had happened. He came up to her. 'Well done, Jo,' he said putting his hand on her shoulder and giving her a playful shake.

She didn't know what to say. She hadn't done her job properly, and he'd fallen in the river. It was . . . suddenly she burst out laughing, unable to control herself. He looked so funny standing there, soaking wet, his teeth showing white against the wet brown skin as he grinned like a schoolboy. Suddenly she was aware she was soaked to the skin herself.

They stood looking at each other and laughing, enjoying this wonderful private joke of theirs. It was theirs alone and no one else in the whole world had any share in it.

Looking into his eyes she saw he was happier at that moment than he'd been for a very long time. Her action was natural and impulsive as she took a step forward and put her arms round him, pressing her head against his wet shirt.

He was smiling, but the eyes were filled with a sad, serious expression as he bent down and kissed her on the forehead.

'Joanna . . .' She could feel his body trembling as he tried to find words. She shook her head and put her finger to her lips.

His arm went round her shoulder. She felt his gentle strength and then he was holding her in both his arms and his mouth was against her own.

She felt her knees go, but every cell in her body was alive with an enormous awareness of herself as she sank slowly to the ground.

The hands, so bony and strong, had become instruments of exquisite finesse: sentient and exploratory. She felt her skin was burning all over and her breath was a hot furnace suddenly gone out of control. Her mind cried a warning, but an older hierarchy had taken command, undermining her reason.

She felt herself going, a detached spirit, a bodyless entity seeking union with the oceans which thundered and broke in her ears.

And then the limbs which had clung with such a fierce tenacity now reflexed in rejection as she struggled to break free. 'No, Robert. Please, please, no.'

She felt the arms release her and the weight which had been pressing her to the ground had gone. She sat up, her chest heaving, her mouth wet and her hair in wild disorder. She didn't look at him as she buttoned her blouse. Nor did she when she asked him to get her pack.

He got it and handed it to her without a word. Fumbling inside, she found her brush and comb. He held up the mirror for her as she combed her hair into place. When she'd finished she put her things away again, feeling a sudden coldness of spirit as if she'd been found out in some misdemeanour and hadn't the courage to admit to it, nor the strength to lie.

She got to her feet. Her body was still quivering with shock but she was in command again. Reality was all about her, a tangibility of familiar sights and sounds; ordered and reassuring. Only then did she dare look at him. His face had a grave, carved expression.

'Joanna . . .' he began.

'Please don't say anything, Robert,' she broke in, and watched the light in his eyes die as he shrank into himself.

'Okay, Jo,' he said, 'okay.'

Immediately she felt miserable. It wasn't what she'd meant. She'd only wanted time to think, and now he thought she was accusing him of having tried to take advantage of her.

He handed her the pack. She slipped the straps over her arms, the same arms that only a few minutes before had been circling and clinging, and stood waiting.

He bent down and picked up the salmon. 'Might as well bring this along,' he said, taking an old oilskin from his pack and wrapping it loosely round the dead fish.

They stopped farther down the pool to retrieve the other salmon. With both fish in his pack he made for the far end of the pool away from the bridge. She didn't query his actions, but followed him. Crossing the boulders at the end of the pool, he turned for a moment to speak.

'It's quicker this way,' he remarked briefly. 'There's something I have to do, anyway.'

She wondered what he meant, but when they got to the long grass beside a little inlet he slipped his pack off again and, throwing the fish in the long grass, got out a small trenching tool and dug a hole. A moment later he took his knife from his pocket and bending down, with swift easy movements had gutted the fish. Burying the entrails in the ground, he covered up the spot, taking handfuls of grass and spreading it over the disturbed earth.

When he'd finished, they crossed the field to come out at the farm. No one was about when they reached the yard. Joanna got in the car and he went across to see Mrs Black. She heard raised voices and a minute later the sound of a door closing, and then the soft crunch of his boots as he crossed the yard.

He got in the car beside her. 'That was Mrs Black. She wanted us to come in and change into something dry.'

She'd forgotten he was soaked from head to foot. 'But why didn't you . . . you could have gone in, I wouldn't have minded waiting.'

He shook his head. 'I'm okay. A little water doesn't harm.'

They drove down the glen in silence. At last they came to a steep hill with the road curving away to the left at the bottom, before levelling out. They'd reached the hotel. He drew the car up outside and clambered out.

'I won't be long,' he said, lifting the pack out from the back of the car. 'I want to give these to John.'

She must have looked at him in a funny way because he said: 'I'd be glad to give you one, but I don't think the Colonel would take kindly to the thought of you aiding and abetting a poacher.' He slung the pack over one shoulder and with long strides went round the back of the hotel. He was back in a minute.

'I'll take you home, now. You should be in time for tea.'

'What time is it?' she asked, knowing that something had happened she didn't want to happen, and aware she'd helped to bring it about.

'Time? It's just gone five.'

They drove off again. It was only then she remembered it had been their original intention to have tea at the hotel. So she'd hurt him that badly. She knew she wasn't being herself, but the incident on the bank of the river had upset her. Unwittingly she'd made him feel guilty. She'd been at fault and she knew it, and it was all because she didn't want him to get the wrong idea about her. If only she'd spoken when she'd had the chance, before he'd withdrawn into himself, but it was too late now.

The Land-Rover wasn't in front of the house when she arrived. She was glad. She didn't want to see her father or Colonel Farquharson at that moment, in fact she didn't want to see anyone.

He got out of the car and opened the door for her. She climbed out and was about to say something, but he'd gone round again to the driver's side and got back in. He'd even left the engine running.

She walked round to him, feeling strangely unsure of herself. Come on Jo, she said to herself, remember what your father taught you: give it to people straight; they may hate you but they'll respect you in the end. The difficulty was there was nothing that she could put in words, not here anyway. Well, she'd just have to do the next best thing and hope the chance might come later for a bit of straight talking.

'Robert,' she said. 'I want to thank you for a really wonderful time. I enjoyed every minute of it.'

He nodded in silence. She thought he was never going to speak, and then he said: 'Every minute?'

She looked him in the eye. 'Yes. Every minute.'

He nodded again. 'Good. Well, I must be getting back to the hotel . . .'

She put her hand out to touch him on the arm. 'Look, Robert, what happened this afternoon . . .'

'Is there any point in talking about it? Okay, so I behaved like an idiot. I'm sorry but . . .'

'Just a minute, Robert,' she said firmly. 'I don't think you behaved like an idiot. It was me. It was my fault . . .'

He shook his head. 'Look, Jo, it's not a thing you can talk about, okay? Just let's say we behaved like a couple of idiots if that makes you feel any better.'

She bit her lip. 'All right, Robert, but will you phone me to-night? After dinner. Promise me.'

'I promise.' He revved the engine.

'Don't say any more now, please, just ring me to-night.'

'Okay.'

She watched him reverse the car and drive off, before running into the house, hoping she wouldn't bump into Mrs Farquharson. But there was no one about as she went upstairs to her room.

Wishart went back to the hotel, changed into dry clothing and went downstairs for an early dinner. Afterwards he went through to the bar. It was nearly empty at this time of evening and he was able to move into his favourite corner. He pulled up a stool and ordered a pint and a nip of whisky. He had an hour or more before he phoned Joanna – if he phoned. He was not all that sure he would after what had happened that afternoon. Okay, he'd lost his head, but she didn't have to reject him as if he'd been a leper. He felt his old sour mood return and he knocked back his whisky at one throw, thinking how the affairs of men and women could change with such dramatic rapidity. And yet he couldn't get her out of his head. She had given him a sense of peace and the first hint that some of his old self-confidence had returned. And then she had to destroy everything by a single disruptive action.

He had a few more drinks, his eyes continually straying to the bar clock, checking the time against his watch. When eventually the hands showed quarter past nine he rose from the stool, his mind made up. He made his way to the phone booth in the lounge.

A man's voice answered the phone and for a moment he was tempted to hang up, thinking she'd deliberately got someone to answer in her place.

'Grant here,' the voice was assured and confident.

He introduced himself and asked if he might speak to Joanna.

There was just the suggestion of a pause and then the voice again. 'Ahh. Wishart. Joanna's been telling me about you . . . I'll go and get her . . . look, why don't you come over and have supper with us one evening? Speak to Joanna about it . . . see if she can fix a convenient night . . . what's that? Fine . . . hang on, I'll get Joanna . . .'

Wishart waited on the other end. So that was Jo's father. He wondered what he was like. He certainly sounded friendly enough, though the invitation to supper had sounded like an invitation to some kind of inspection. It irritated him slightly, at the same time giving him a thrill of pleasure as if his relationship with Joanna had been given some sort of recognition. But the feeling was short-lived as he waited.

Joanna sounded a little breathless, as if she'd been running. 'Hullo . . .'

'It's me . . . you asked me to ring,' he said, feeling unsure and nervous and unable to take the initiative.

'Robert, I'm sorry, but I can't get out to-night. The Farquharsons have some guests and . . . well, I really must stay in.'

It was what he'd been half expecting. He was getting the brush-off. 'Oh, that's okay.' He tried to make his voice sound casual. 'Mebbe some other time. I'll give you a ring,' he said, sorry now that he'd phoned and feeling he'd made himself look slightly ridiculous by his attentions. He should have known better, she was just another example of the upper classes seeking relief from boredom. But her next words changed his mood abruptly.

'No, don't bother ringing . . . just come round. I'll be free to-morrow evening.'

'What time . . .?' he asked, feeling his throat go dry and his pulse beat faster at the prospect of seeing her again.

'Nine, if that's all right with you?'

'That's fine. I'll meet you in the drive . . .' He hung up and opened the door of the booth, nearly bumping into Jim Anderson as he stepped out.

'What are you looking so bluidy pleased about?' Anderson said. 'Anyway, auld Sandy's been asking for you. He's through in the bar.'

Wishart went through to the public bar.

'Ah, there you are, Robert. I was just asking . . .'

'I know. I just bumped into Jim.'

'It was aboot that day on the water. I haven't had the chance to speak to the Colonel yet, but I'll have a word with him soon's I can.'

He didn't want to offend the old gamekeeper. 'Look, Sandy, could we leave it till some other time? I've a few things I want to do over at the cottage and I haven't all that much time left. Mebbe the next time I'm up. Do you mind?'

'No, no, man. Suit yourself. But I must awa' now. Not to worry. Anyway by next time you might even be getting an invite from the Colonel himself.'

'Me? You must be joking . . .'

The old gamekeeper waved his pipe and his eyes twinkled. 'I'm no' so sure. Miss Grant and her faither's bidin' doon at the big hoose, and from what I hear you and her's quite chief . . . now, now, Rab, you're no' to tak' offence. Miss Grant's a fine lass. You'll forgive an auld man for his bit joke . . . I shouldna have spoken.'

Wishart shook his head. 'Forget it, Sandy.' He paused. 'So it's all over the glen already?'

'Well, Rab, you should ken by now what country fowk are like.' Sandy knocked out his pipe. 'Must awa'. The auld wife's expectin' me. And just forget what I said. I must be gettin' as bad's the rest o' them in my auld age. Good night to you, Robert.'

'Night, Sandy.'

He picked her up next evening. They decided to go for a drive. Cutting down through the glen, he headed east towards the distant coast. The land was flatter here, neatly patterned fields falling away in gentle slopes to the sea. It was rich land, with evidence of its wealth to be seen in the abundance of farm machinery and equipment; the combines glowing redly and the tips of the silos glinting in the evening sun.

The road ran between two hills. He stopped the car, pulling in to the side.

'You're going to tell me something,' she said.

'What made you say that?'

'I'm beginning to know you. Well, am I right?'

He felt flattered by her perception. 'Dead right.' He pointed to the hills on either side. 'Know what these are?'

'Mmmm . . .' she thought for a moment. 'Burial grounds, ancient burial grounds.'

'No, not quite right. They're ancient all right, but not burial grounds. They were Pictish settlements. If you look, just there round the bottom, you'll see little dug-outs.'

She looked. 'Yes. I think I can see what you mean.'

'Those were the sentry-boxes, you might say. The hills were a defensive position, you can see the ring of stones at the top.'

'I wondered what those were.'

'From the top you can see the estuary. The Picts would be able to see the Romans disembarking and marching up through the glens.'

She was excited by the thought. 'Oh, let's go to the top, shall we?'

He grinned at her enthusiasm. 'Okay.'

They got out of the car and climbed the path leading to the top of the northernmost of the two hills.

They reached the top and Joanna sat down on a heap of piled-up boulders, her eyes glowing with excitement. To the south the estuary of the river was shining like beaten silver. 'And they actually lived here, the Picts?'

'It was a long time ago,' he said sitting down beside her. 'It's difficult to imagine.'

She shook her head slowly in wonderment. 'I can almost feel their presence. The women busy cooking, the children playing around and . . . down there the men standing guard. And now they're all gone.' Instinctively she drew closer to him.

'I wouldn't let it upset you,' he said, beginning to understand her extreme sensitivity to atmosphere and environment.

'It doesn't . . . I mean it does and it doesn't. It makes you feel you're part of something much more than yourself. It's like being a part of a river. No matter what happens to you as an individual, it just keeps flowing on. You're yourself and you're also something bigger than yourself. Does that sound silly to you?'

'No. I understand what you mean, Jo,' he said, feeling at ease with her again for the first time since the previous day.

They sat for a long time quietly absorbed in their surroundings. The light changed and a chill wind came up from the distant river as the sun went down behind the hills.

He got to his feet. 'We'd better go, Jo.'

She got up reluctantly. 'I could stay here all night.'

'You'd be awful cold.'

They went back down to the car and drove back towards the house. It was still early when they pulled into the driveway.

She leaned over and shouted something in his ear. He stopped the car. 'What was that?'

'I don't want to go home yet. Let's go down to the pools.'

'All right.' He drove off again and took the turning off the driveway. They came to the spot where the narrow track widened. He swung the car round to face the direction in which they came and cut the engine. 'I'd better take a torch,' he said, 'it gets dark quickly down by the pools.'

They got out of the car and picked up the path that wound down through the trees. Taking her hand he guided her along by the edge of the pool. Protected by the trees, the air was warm here. Below the pool was a thin patina of light, its mirror-like surface broken occasionally into concentric luminous rings as a fish rose to take an evening fly. The air was still, as if the earth had stopped breathing. Only the faintest sounds disturbed the cathedral-like quiet as they climbed the steep path towards the platform overhanging the pool.

They sat down.

'Isn't it beautiful,' Joanna said in a low whispery voice.

He nodded silently, gazing into the still depths of the pool where a long, long time before he'd poached his first salmon. Life had been magical then: a thing full of wonder and mystery. And then somehow, before you were aware of it, the magic went out of it.

No more rising with the sun to throw off sleep with a shake of the head, to run barefooted in the still wet grass with the sun just lifting its head above the hills. Nothing left but the drudge of one's daily life. Yes, the magic went and in a vain effort to recapture it you turned to tobacco, alcohol and drugs. Chemical stimulants to make up for the lost joy of living.

Was it that he'd allowed himself to become too self-centred, pursuing his own dream in isolation from the rest of the struggling masses? Penny had thought so, and he'd ignored her and gone his own way. She wasn't interested in the dream. All she'd wanted was a home, marriage and children and the security of seeing her husband every day. But he'd gone off on long climbing expeditions and hadn't listened.

She must have worried herself sick at times. But he'd got over that by assuring her that nothing would ever happen to him. How arrogant – and how prophetic – that had been. No, it hadn't to him. It was Joe who got it in the end. He'd have been better with a mistress or a housekeeper for all the emotional security he'd given Penny. And yet, looking back on it, he'd loved her in a way, but it had been a selfish love, and when she'd complained he'd told her it was impossible for any man to demonstrate his affection every hour of the day. He'd pointed out with cruel logic that her demands had been unreasonable; and he'd been right in the sense that she'd been asking for something he wasn't prepared – or able – to give. And always he'd kidded himself his ambitions had been noble, inspiring. Such mundane vulgarities as a regular job and a regular income were not for him. He should have had the sense to realise the marriage couldn't have lasted.

'What's the matter, Robert?' Joanna stretched out her hand to touch his.

He shook his head. 'Oh, nothing, Jo. Just dreaming, that's all.'

'A dream is the enemy of action.'

'Eh?'

She smiled. 'Oh, it's just something father said.'

'Want a cigarette?' he said extracting one for himself.

'No, thanks.'

He lit his own. How good this girl was for him, how relaxed she could make him feel. Not like Carole. Carole? He realised with a shock he'd almost forgotten all about her. Still, there was no point in worrying about Carole, she'd be all right. In fact he could see now that she hadn't really been interested in him as a person. It was his reputation, the big-time adventurer and mountaineer, she'd been fascinated by. But since he was being honest with himself, it would be as well to admit he'd been more interested in her physical beauty than any mental or spiritual qualities she may have possessed. He'd tried to make his relations with her into something sentiment-ally unreal, when all he'd really wanted, to be brutal about it, was to go to bed with her. And even that had backfired on him in the long run, for all the use he'd been in the last few months.

Unconsciously he rubbed the scar on his temple. So there it was: a catalogue of errors with little to offer by way of self-redemption.

He felt the hand on his arm again. A touch that brought him back to the present and an awareness of Joanna and her effect on him.

'You're very quiet, Robert.'

He smiled wryly. 'Mebbe it's because I've nothing to say.'

She leant her head against his shoulder. 'Perhaps you won't let it come out.'

'What do you want to hear?'

'Nothing – everything.'

'Okay.' He found himself stirred at her physical contact, and tried to keep his voice light as he replied, 'I'm an un-frocked priest, a left-wing supporter who never even supported a banner, a hater of the rich and defender of the poor – '

'Don't be cynical,' she gently chided. 'I want you to be honest.' She paused. 'Tell me, were you very poor, I mean really poor when you were young?'

He gazed at a spot between his feet, angry with himself for his juvenile flippancy. He took a breath. 'I suppose there were lots poorer. We had a new pair of boots every year . . . we never had to go barefoot. And we had meat on the table at least once a week. I can't remember getting new clothes. It was always cut-downs. I'm sure my mother ruined her eyesight stitching and sewing by the light of paraffin lamps.'

'How dreadful it must have been.'

He shook his head. 'Strangely enough, it wasn't. It's never that bad when you're kids. I can't even remember ever being hungry, but I suppose that's because the folks did without.'

She leant closer. 'Tell me more.'

'There's nothing to tell. I grew up, got some sort of education, had a spell on a newspaper in Aberdeen when I left school, and that's about all there is to tell.'

'But what made you . . .'

'What made me become interested in mountaineering, is that it? Well, I couldn't really give an answer to that. All I know is that since a boy I'd been climbing. It just sort of grew in me. And then one day, out of the blue, I was asked to take part in an expedition. It happened after that. I'd like to think it was a burning ambition since boyhood, but it wasn't. It just happened, that's all.'

'It means a lot to you, doesn't it?'

'Climbing? Yeh, I suppose it does in a way.' His lips parted in a wry smile. 'After all I've spent my life at it. It gets a hold of you.'

She lowered her head. 'I know,' she said softly.

He laughed. 'Do you?'

She looked up at him, her head canted to the side. 'I should have told you earlier perhaps, but it didn't seem important at the time.' She watched the smile fade slowly from his face and she wondered what had happened to cause him to be so guarded and suspicious. 'It's about my father.' She paused. 'I think you might have heard of him. He's Brigadier Grant.'

He was silent for a moment. 'Brigadier Grant . . . you don't mean . . .?' A look of bewilderment spread over his features. 'Brigadier Grant. You mean *the* Brigadier Grant?' he repeated. 'But why didn't you tell me before, Jo? I had no idea . . .'

'Does it matter?' she said. 'Anyway you'll meet him soon. I'm sure you'll like him.'

But he hardly listened to her, still shaking his head in disbelief. Brigadier Grant, Joanna's father? And here in Scotland, the more he thought about it the more incredible it was.

She laughed at his expression. 'I can see I've given you quite a surprise. I suppose you imagined a Brigadier's daughter had to be one of those toothy, lantern-jawed Englishwomen, prancing about in riding breeches between debs' parties and hunt balls.'

'I just didn't think . . . I mean . . .' but he couldn't find the words and his voice tailed off.

'Well, don't worry about it. Now, when do you want to come over to supper? Father has promised to go some place with Colonel Farquharson on Thursday, and Friday, of course, I'll be going back to London. It looks like it will have to be Wednesday, if that's all right with you?'

He'd picked up a twig and was tracing patterns on the ground. 'Wednesday?' he muttered. 'Sure, that'll be okay.' He was silent for a long minute. Finally he said: 'Jo . . .?'

'Yes?'

'Am I going to see you in London?'

She was amused and yet strangely touched by his gravity. 'But of course. I'd be disappointed if you didn't.'

'Jo . . .?' He put his arm round her and drew her close.

She felt her blood leap and she twisted away, frightened by her response to his touch. 'Please, Robert . . .'

He released her. 'I'm sorry, Jo . . . it's just that . . .'

'There's no need to explain,' she broke in. 'I suppose you think I'm being silly, but I'm selfish enough not to want to get hurt. It might sound Victorian to you, but . . .'

He cut her off peremptorily. 'I know, I know. We've only known each other a few days and you don't even know a thing about me. You don't have to spell it out, Jo.' He bent down and picked up the twig again, twisting it in his hands. His voice was strained when he spoke again: 'I don't know how to tell you, but you do something to me . . . it's not just physical . . . I don't know how to . . .'

She reached out and put her hand on his. 'I've told you, there's no need to try and explain it. I understand.'

'Do you?'

She looked at him searchingly. 'You sound so bitter at times. Why are you so unhappy?'

He ran his fingers through his hair. 'Oh, I don't know. I just get screwed up. I . . . I . . . let's not talk about it, Jo . . .'

She squeezed his hand. 'All right, Robert, if you don't want to. Shall we go now?'

CHAPTER XVI

Brigadier Grant leaned over. 'Here, let me fill your glass. It's a damned fine wine this . . . a château bottled '58 Haut Brion. Though I'm not very sure if it's the thing to drink with jugged hare. What do you think, Joanna . . . claret with jugged hare?'

Joanna stole a secret smile at Wishart, who held his glass out for a refill. 'Someone once said that the best wine is the wine you like best.' His eyes exchanged a glance.

'What do you think, Wishart? Have you any ideas on the subject, since my daughter doesn't seem to know?'

'I don't know much about wines, but I don't think I've ever tasted better jugged hare.'

'It *is* very good. Joanna's excelled herself. You know, it's a funny thing, but it's something that seems to have vanished from the menu these days.'

Wishart hadn't felt at ease since he'd arrived. There was something about Grant's manner that made him feel uncomfortable, as if he was being secretly examined. And yet Grant had done everything to make him feel welcome from the moment he'd arrived. In fact he'd been treated like an honoured guest. He took a sip of his wine and said: 'John Mitchell's is the only place I know where you can still get it.'

'That's interesting,' Grant said. 'We haven't eaten there much, but I must make a point of trying it next time I'm over that way. I must say he keeps a good inn, Mitchell.'

'There's not many better,' Wishart agreed.

After the jugged hare they had fresh fruit salad with cream.

Mrs Robertson, the house help, came in to clear away the dishes. Joanna got up and followed her into the kitchen.

'Just leave everything, Mrs Robertson. It's getting late. Off you go. I'll make the coffee.'

Mrs Robertson piled the dishes into the sink, turning on the tap. 'It's a blessing this hot water,' she said, 'instead of having to boil everything. On you go, Miss Grant, and mak' the coffee, it'll no' tak' me a minute to do these.'

'All right, but when you're finished, I'll run you home.'

Mrs Robertson snorted. 'You'll dae nothing o' the kind. I can walk fine. So you just mak' your coffee and awa' ben the

185

hoose and enjoy yourself wi' your guest.'

Joanna sighed resignedly and made the coffee. There was no point in trying to argue with Mrs Robertson when her mind was made up. Thinking how lucky her father had been to get such an excellent house help, she went back into the dining-room with the tray of coffee things.

She poured the coffee and sat down again before noticing she was still wearing the apron she'd put on when she'd gone into the kitchen. She removed it and put it over the back of her chair. They'd just finished coffee when Mrs Robertson poked her head round the door. 'I'll be awa' then. I'll be round at the usual time to-morrow, unless you'd like me to come a bit earlier?'

'No, that's all right, Mrs Robertson,' said Joanna, getting to her feet. 'Thanks for all your help.'

'Away with you. You did maist of it yourself . . . well, I'm off now.'

'Why don't you let me . . .' Joanna was about to offer.

Mrs Robertson shook her head fiercely. 'You'll do nothin' o' the kind. I could do with a bit walk, anyway. So I'll just bid you good night and see you in the morning.'

When Mrs Robertson had gone, Joanna cleared the table. In the kitchen she washed up and laid out the cups on the tray again, should anyone want coffee later.

Her father and Wishart had gone into the lounge. They were standing looking up at the mounted stag's head above the fireplace, when she returned.

'My first stag,' her father was saying. 'Not a big beast but my first one. He gave me quite a bit of trouble. In fact I must confess I missed him with my first shot . . . got him in the shoulder, and he rose and was off again on three legs and a swinger before I was able to bring him down. Do you shoot at all?'

Joanna arrived back from the kitchen in time to hear the question. She stepped in quickly, knowing the two men would never agree on the subject. 'If you both sit down I'll get you a drink,' she said. 'Now, what are you going to have?'

Grant was the first to sit down. 'I think we've some of that Chivas Regal left,' he said. 'How about you, Wishart, or would you prefer a brandy.'

'Whisky'll do fine.'

Joanna poured the drinks and a brandy for herself. She brought them over. 'Help yourself to water,' she said, putting the carafe down. 'What is it, Robert?'

Wishart had half-risen from his seat. 'Do you think I could have a separate glass for the water?'

'But of course.' She brought him a glass. 'All right?' she said, putting it down on the coffee table.

He thanked her.

Grant was curious. 'Is that how you drink your whisky?'

'Well, not always, but I prefer it this way.'

'Mmmm . . . I must say I've never tried that. Joanna, do you think . . .?'

'I'll get you a glass.' She got up again and got him a glass.

Grant took a sip of his whisky and followed it with a drink of water. 'I must say that's rather good. You get the full flavour of the whisky, the water even seems to revive it. Yes, I like that.'

Joanna settled in her chair. 'We were over at Robert's place yesterday,' she said to her father, 'did I tell you?'

'You did mention something about it.'

'Well, the cottage – sorry, farmhouse – has the most marvellous spring water. I've never tasted water like it.'

'Yes,' Grant addressed Wishart, 'Joanna was telling me you have a place over at the other side of the glen.'

'Well, it's not much of a place really. It needs a lot doing to it. I'll get round to it one of these days. It's only a couple of miles from the hotel, over the hill. I stay there when I'm up from England, but this time I thought the hotel would be better.'

Grant laughed. 'Yes, yes. I suppose we mountaineering chaps are entitled to our comforts. We have to put up with so much at other times.'

Joanna could see her father was itching to get on to the subject of climbing with Wishart. He could be as wily as an old fox when he wanted to.

'Of course,' her father went on, 'when I decided to settle in Scotland and bought the house, I just had to name it after our expedition to Nanga Parbat. You can have anything you want in Kashmir or the Himalaya but I'll never forget our Nanga Parbat days. I think you knew some of the team . . . yes, of course you did . . . I remember now, particularly our medical chap, Dr Thow. He mentioned your name – said he'd climbed with you.'

Wishart nodded smiling. Dr Thow? He'd never thought of him as that, it had always been plain Andy. 'Yes, that's right,' he answered. 'I remember him well. Those long skinny legs and arms of his, and the way he used to tape his glasses on with Elastoplast to keep them from falling off.'

'Yes, he was a bit short-sighted, but a damned good man on the hill for all that. I don't know how he managed at times.'

'He didn't. There was one time on Nevis, we'd just done one of the gullies and we'd reached the top when he dropped his glasses. He went to look for them and walked straight over the edge of the cornice. He just about had the lot of us off.'

Grant laughed. 'I didn't know he was as bad as that. Here, let me fill up your glass. No, you stay where you are, Jo. You've done enough for one evening.' Grant got up and walked over to the cabinet. He was wearing a pair of cavalry twill trousers and a wool shirt with a cravat at the neck. Wishart noted the width of the shoulders, the strong back and the thick, powerful legs. No wonder they called him the 'Tank' in climbing circles. He looked the part. Once set in the right direction he'd just go on and on, surmounting every single obstacle in his path.

Grant brought the bottle back with him. 'We'll have it on the table.' He topped up Wishart's glass and leaned back in his chair. 'There's nothing like a good whisky to finish off a good meal.'

Wishart lit his pipe. He hoped the Brigadier wasn't going to dwell on the subject of climbing. It had been his one fear since accepting the invitation to supper. He took a swig of his whisky and made an effort to relax.

'Joanna was saying you had a good walk over the weekend,' Grant went on. 'She was telling me all about it.' (All? thought Wishart. I hope she didn't tell you about the salmon.) 'You seem to have covered quite a fair distance. Tell me, since you obviously know the country so well, are there any fish up in the hill lochans?'

'You get the odd trout, nothing much over half a pound, though. I know one shepherd who said he'd taken over fifty one night,' Wishart said.

'Hmmm . . . that's quite a catch, quite a catch.' Grant was silent for a moment. Then he spoke again. 'Tell me, how far is it over the hills to Braemar?'

'From Glen Clova?'

'Yes, from Clova.'

'About eighteen miles, I would say.'

'Very good.'

'Good walking country?'

188

'Mmm. Must try it some day. And of course from there you can go up to Glen Derry and pick up the old drover's track into Aviemore, is that right?' Grant was about to ask something else when he saw Joanna open her mouth as if intending to speak. 'Go on, my dear. What was it you were going to say?'

'Just that Robert was telling me that a friend of his had done the whole thing in fourteen hours.'

Grant frowned as he always did when someone else's feats were mentioned. It was not that he was jealous so much as that he was ever on the look-out for a challenge, something he could try and better. 'Oh, how far is that in all, would you say?'

Wishart thought for a minute. 'I'm not all that sure, but it must be the best part of forty-two miles.'

'Hill country all the way?'

'No-o. You pick up the road into Braemar and on the way out again. But most of it is hill country.'

'Well, I must say that's good going. Sounds a very creditable time. I daresay he climbs too, this friend of yours.'

'One of the best,' Wishart replied.

'That's what I like. A chap who can do a really hard day's march over the hill and can climb into the bargain. I don't know about you, but this modern school of steeple-jacks we seem to be producing are not really mountaineers in the true sense of the word. What do you think?' It seemed Grant was determined to talk about climbing.

'I've done a little "tension" climbing myself,' Wishart said. 'It's okay, but I think you miss a lot. You never really get to know the hills. I suppose it had to happen. You can hardly take a single mountain in the British Isles that hasn't had every bit of rock climbed over and over again. So once you run out of new routes, it's inevitable you're going to use artificial aids and do what used to be considered the impossible. I wouldn't say I'm for it, but I'm not against it either. After all, the old "Tricouni" nailed boot was, in a way, an artificial aid; you could say the same about the piton.'

Grant eased forward in his chair. 'Joanna,' he said, 'I think I'm going to have a cigar. Do you know where they are? I can't remember where I've put them.'

She looked at him in surprise. Only on very rare occasions did he ever smoke. She got up and walked over to the sideboard and opened the drawer. The cigars, half a dozen,

189

were in a box. She gave him one and offered the box to Wishart, who refused.

'Thank you, Joanna,' Grant said. He clipped the end and lit up, blowing out a plume of smoke before addressing Wishart again. 'Well, I suppose you do have a point there. But I much prefer the old-fashioned way of climbing, if you want to call it that. It's more personal. It puts the greatest demands where they should be; on the man himself. It's like all this damned nonsense in modern skiing. All these chair-lifts and things making the hills look like a fun-fair. When I learned to ski in Germany after the war, we used to trudge for miles. We really earned our fun. Nowadays you're dragged or carried up a hill and, whoosh, you're down again. That's no fun.'

'Perhaps not, but it's produced a lot of good skiers. Just think, a few years ago the instructors were mostly Austrian or Swiss, it's different to-day; the local lads are taking over and a lot of that is due to lifts and tow-bars. They save time, you can get in more hours in a day now than you could ever get before.'

Grant shook his head. 'If a man wants to do something hard enough, he'll find ways and means of doing it. I'm not fond of artificial aids in principle.'

Oh yes, thought Wishart, the old argument – you either had it or you didn't, and it was supposed to have nothing to do with education, training or background. He felt there was something neo-fascist about such reasoning, with its suggestion of an individual being superior to society: the myth of the 'superman'. But he didn't want to argue about it. Already they'd got on to the subject of climbing and he knew argument would only involve him more deeply. That was the last thing he wanted. He tried to steer the conversation away. 'Have you ever skied up in Aviemore, or Glenshee?'

The Brigadier shook his head. 'To tell you the truth, I haven't skied for years. The last time was out in the Lebanon, of all places.'

Wishart didn't know what to say next. The Brigadier was obviously one of those people who always had to have his teeth in something, relentlessly brushing small talk aside.

Joanna watched the two men. She sensed the confrontation of ideas and motivations. She hoped Wishart wouldn't take her father too literally; he often said things just for the sake of argument, to feel out the opposition, as he put it. Still,

190

they were both capable of taking care of themselves, and she remembered she'd promised to phone her friend Henrietta in London. She looked at her watch, having taken to wearing it again since returning to her father's house. It was nearing eleven. She'd better do it now before it was too late. She got up and excused herself, saying she had to make a phone call and she'd make coffee afterwards.

It was the first time Wishart had seen her in a skirt, or rather a dress; she was wearing a softly patterned mini-dress. He was pleased to discover she had good legs, strong athletic legs, peasant legs. He hated fashionable skinny types, all angles and bones.

'Here, let me have your glass,' he heard the Brigadier's voice cut in on his thoughts. He looked at the glass in his hand noticing with surprise it was empty.

Grant took his glass and filled it, handing it back to him with a friendly smile. 'It goes down very smoothly, the Chivas Regal. How do you find it?'

'Well, to tell the truth I usually drink malt, but there's nothing the matter with the Chivas.'

'Ah, so you're a malt man. Not very keen on the stuff, myself. Bit too strong in the flavour for me. Still, every man to his own taste. Farquharson's a malt man, you know him, do you?'

'I've never met him, not to speak to.'

'He's a grand chap. He was telling me he knew your grandfather.'

'Was he?'

'Yes, he knew him when he had the smiddy, apparently. John was a great horseman in his day. I daresay your grandfather did a lot of shoeing for him.'

Wishart looked at Grant. Was this a reminder of the social gulf that separated them? He felt like replying 'I only bloody well hope he got paid for his work', remembering the struggle his grandfather and subsequently his father had to get their money; and it hadn't always been the poorer farmers that had been in default. The gentlemanly credo of 'paying one's gambling debts and let the tradesmen wait' seemed to have been specifically designed for people like his grandfather, and he could remember the old man, with his work-thickened hands, sitting at his desk by the light of a paraffin lamp, making out bills in his oddly meticulous long-hand; bills that were sent out repeatedly and often fruitlessly. But Grant's features bore an innocent expression.

Wishart merely nodded in reply and waited to hear what the Brigadier had to say next.

Grant's blue eyes had a far-away look – Joanna must have taken after her mother's colouring – as he spoke: 'Pity so many of the old ways have gone. We might have gained a lot, but it's also true we've lost a lot. It's all machinery now. People are leaving the land, going to get jobs and big wages in the towns. The feeling's gone; the love of the thing.'

'It's difficult to love the land when you have a pittance of a wage and a tied house,' Wishart said impulsively.

Grant sighed. 'Yes, you're so right. It was a bad thing, that. It robbed men of their dignity and gave them nothing to work for but their daily bread. How stupid we were. A little thought was all that was required. Had it been given, we wouldn't have the sort of troubles we seem to be suffering from to-day. You know, I often think the worst crime we were ever guilty of was the depression in the thirties. Skilled men out of work in their thousands. We could have given them *something* to do. There were roads, bridges, all sorts of things we needed. We could have found them work. A man is no good unless he has something to do. The Army taught me that. Boredom and trouble always went hand in hand. We should have had discipline then, organised the men into communities . . .'

'You mean like labour camps?' Wishart was unable to check his response.

Grant frowned. 'You make it sound nasty.'

'I think the credit for that must go to Hitler and Mussolini.'

Grant took a long, slow draw on his cigar. 'Surely the question of what you call labour camps depends on purpose and motivation. After all, didn't Upton Sinclair try to do the same sort of thing in California? You're not objecting to the organisation of communities, are you?'

Wishart shrugged. 'No,' he began, telling himself to go carefully and not get embroiled in a political argument, 'but I hardly think the kind of Government we had at that time had *any* interest in the unemployed. I can't help feeling that any camps they might have set up would have been surrounded by barbed wire.'

'Isn't that a bit strong?' Grant said.

Wishart told himself to shut up. He'd said enough. But he couldn't help himself, the words seemed to come of their own volition. 'From my reading of it, it seems the ruling classes . . .' Ruling classes? Hell, why had he used that phrase, it was exactly the right thing to say if he wanted to provoke further argument. 'Well, it seems they were having a loving courtship with Hitler and Mussolini. Many of them in fact were suggesting that the sort of thing we needed at home were strong men who would stand no nonsense from the dissident masses.'

Grant puffed at his cigar. 'I'll grant you there were people in this country who thought that way, but it's an exaggeration to say they reflected Government policy – though, God knows I had little faith in our Government at the time – I think the real proof of that lies in the fact that in the end we declared war on the Germans.'

'And having done that, proceeded to convince them it was all a mistake and that they, the Germans, were facing in the wrong way – the phoney war.'

'Well, it wasn't all that phoney. I don't think the Navy, for instance, would agree with that,' Grant replied.

'No, you're right there. I had a good friend killed at sea within the first three months of the outbreak of war. I wonder what he'd think now if he had the chance to look back on it all?'

'I'm sorry about that,' Grant said. 'But I see we won't get anywhere on that subject. Let's agree to disagree for the moment,' he said, and then, swiftly changing the subject, went on: 'Tell me, Wishart, what do you think is the greatest challenge in Europe? I'm talking about climbing now.'

Wishart ran his tongue over his lips. Grant was full of little surprises. He thought for a long moment. 'I'd say it was the North Wall,' he replied, speaking very slowly.

'I had an idea you'd say that.' Grant nodded his head. 'It is a ferocious brute.'

'You've climbed in the Oberland?' Wishart asked.

'Not much. Been there a couple of times, I suppose. To tell you the truth, Alpinism has never really appealed to me. I prefer the planning and organising of bigger things. That's why the Himalaya and the Karakorum have appealed so much. You know what I mean?'

Wishart nodded, relieved they'd got away from the subject of politics, but still not happy about their present topic of conversation.

'One of the great rewards on a big expedition is the comradeship you form with the chaps you climb with. There's nothing quite like it. It brings out the best in a man. But to get back to the Eiger. Tell me, you've been on the North Wall. What do you think of it?'

Wishart hesitated a long time before replying. He exhaled deeply. 'Well, it's very hard in places, but the real trouble is the weather. Conditions can change so rapidly. And of course you're never free from the danger of avalanches and falling stones.'

'Supposing you climbed the thing in winter?'

'That's what Toni Hiebeler did. He reckoned in winter conditions were much more stable on the Wall. It's certainly one way of escaping the stone barrage, but I don't know if I'd like to try it. It's a pretty tough snow and ice climb.'

'Yes, I read about that. It was a pretty good show.'

Wishart wondered what Grant was leading up to, and for the first time he realised he'd had a fair amount of whisky – Grant kept filling his glass up – and he was beginning to feel its effects. It occurred to him it was a pretty odd sensation to be sitting here in a Scottish glen, drinking whisky with a man he'd recently met and talking about the Eiger. The last time he'd discussed the Eiger had been in North Wales over a pint of beer with Joe. He could remember Joe's enthusiasm, his confident grin: 'Let's have a go at the bugger, Bob.' He also remembered knocking back his pint and saying: 'Okay, Joe – you're on.' They'd got pretty drunk after that, reminding each other with each successive pint to keep their decision secret. And they had, until the day they hit the headlines and Joe had lost his leg. It all seemed so far away now, and there were even times he could forget about it, but he could never forget about Joe.

'What do you think of it, I mean as a winter climb? How would you rate it?' Grant was speaking again.

Wishart blinked and looked at his whisky glass. No more after this, he reminded himself. This is the last one. And what's happened to Joanna? Where has she gone? She's been away for hours.

'What do I think of it?' Wishart repeated the question. 'What do I think of it as a winter climb?' An interesting question, but how did you answer it? By saying, winter or summer, the North Wall of the Eiger was the father and mother of all bastards, that it was evil and hellish? But that would be no answer. All the descriptive words in the world would never describe the terrifying reality of the North Wall. He rubbed his chin, trying to think of his reply.

'Well,' he began slowly, 'there's not much I can say. The whole thing's different in winter. It'd be very hard. Only the strongest party could hope to do it,' he went on, wondering at the same time why Grant should be asking him all this.

'Hmm. I see,' muttered Grant, sensing Wishart's reluctance to talk about it. Had he taken a dislike to the Eiger since his accident? He'd known it to happen to climbers before. They'd get it into their heads that some particular climb or mountain was possessed by a 'hoodoo'. Understandable enough amongst simple primitive peoples, but quite irrational for twentieth-century man. He felt disappointed as he examined his guest with his shrewd eyes. There was something odd about the man; underneath the relaxed manner he could see there was tension – a suggestion of suffering. He'd have to watch Joanna. She was far too responsive towards lame dogs, with her over-developed sense of compassion. It would be quite possible for her to become serious about this chap. The idea had to be faced. But it was important that there should be no direct confrontation with her. Knowing his daughter, he realised that such a thing might well send her flying off in the opposite direction. She was much too self-willed to take easily to commandments, especially when voiced by authority. He looked at Wishart, trying to guess what was going on behind those flat, grey-green eyes and the seemingly changeless expression. He decided to test his emotional reactions.

'You had rather an unfortunate time on the Wall yourself, by all accounts,' he remarked, watching the eyes carefully.

Wishart sipped at his whisky. 'It was just one of those things,' he answered levelly, but Grant noticed he'd avoided his eyes.

'You were caught in a storm, if I remember rightly?'

'That's right,' the voice was flat and unemotional.

'Pretty ferocious, I should imagine.'

'It wasn't pleasant.'

'Tell me . . . have you ever thought about making another attempt?'

There was a long pause before Wishart replied.

'No,' he said simply.

Now that was interesting. When you set out to do something and were defeated, you simply went back again and had another try. How long ago had it been, two years or more? Certainly long enough to have organised another

195

attempt. So why hadn't he? Grant was interested.

'I take it you have no plans for another crack at the Wall?' he said.

The pause was even longer this time. 'I hadn't thought about it.'

'Ah well.' Grant leaned over and reached for the whisky botle. 'Perhaps one of these days.' He held the bottle up. 'Let me fill your glass ...'

Wishart shook his head. 'No thanks. I'd better not have any more. I've quite a few miles to drive back.'

Grant didn't press him. He filled his own glass, feeling certain now that Wishart was suffering from an irrational dislike of the Eiger. It was amazing what the human imagination could do when it was allowed to roam unchecked. Here was one of the most brilliant snow and ice climbers of his day, and it was plain he'd got himself into an emotional state about a mountain; or was it that he was suffering from a sense of failure? But if so, why hadn't he done anything about it? He'd have liked to know the answers to these questions, and was about to probe more deeply when Joanna returned.

Wishart looked at her with a sense of relief.

'Sorry to have been so long,' she said, 'I had to phone London.' She sat down and almost immediately got up again. 'Anyone like coffee?' she asked.

Grant shook his head. 'Not for me, dear. I'll have one when I get back. I'm just going for a stroll to the end of the road and back with the dog.'

'How about you, Robert?'

'No, don't bother. I'll have to be off soon, anyway.'

'But it's no bother, I'm going to have one myself.'

Grant excused himself, saying he'd be back in a few minutes, and Joanna went into the kitchen to make the coffee. Left alone, Wishart got to his feet. He was standing with his hands in his pockets, looking at a framed print of her father together with the other members of the Army expedition to Nanga Parbat, when Joanna came back with the coffee tray.

She put the tray down on the table as he turned. 'I think that's his favourite photograph.' She saw that Wishart had shifted his gaze. 'Except for that one,' she added.

'I thought it was your mother,' he said. 'You're very like her.'

'Do you think so?' she said.

'Very much so,' he replied.

She smiled wistfully as she poured the coffee. If only her mother had still been alive, perhaps she would have persuaded her father against . . .? But she broke off her thoughts. She'd gone over this problem a thousand times before.

Wishart sat down again and spooned sugar into his coffee.

'I suppose you were having a right old natter, you two?' she said to him, wondering at the same time how he'd got on with her father, and hoping they hadn't got on to politics. Because she knew her father and was aware of his basic sense of honesty and justice, she was able to tolerate his odd mixture of liberal conservatism. Others didn't recognise this so readily, as she'd learnt in the days when she'd introduced him to some of her friends at University. 'What were you talking about?' she asked, when she'd sat down and helped herself to coffee.

He shrugged non-committally. 'Oh, nothing . . . nothing much.'

'You're being devious. I bet it was mountaineering.'

'We spoke about it a bit.'

She laughed. 'A bit?' And then she suddenly grew serious, looking round as if to make sure there was no one else in the room. 'Tell me, Robert . . .'

Her manner was unusually hesitant and he looked at her questioningly. 'Yes, Jo?'

'I know you may not like talking about it, but what . . . what's the Eiger really like?'

He was more than surprised now. 'Did you say the Eiger?' First her father and now her. What was happening?

She nodded.

'Why do you ask?'

'I just wondered, that's all.'

He was silent for a moment, considering the question or rather her reasons for it. 'Do you mean, what do I think of it?' he replied guardedly.

'Is it as bad as the papers make out?'

He laughed dryly. 'The "killer mountain" and all that, is that what you mean?'

'Yes.'

'Look, Jo . . .' He stopped, as if searching for words. 'Look, Jo, all mountains can be dangerous. Even here in

197

Scotland there's lots of accidents every year. Someone's always getting hurt and mostly it's a result of carelessness or inexperience.'

'But surely some can be more dangerous than others?'

He shook his head thoughtfully. 'I wouldn't say that. More difficult perhaps, but more dangerous? I mean, anything can be dangerous if you don't know how to handle it. Electricity and gas can be lethal until you learn how to handle them.'

'Then the Eiger's no more dangerous than any other climb, is that what you're saying?'

He shifted in his chair uncomfortably. 'It depends. I mean it depends on the party, the weather conditions, things like that.'

'But it's very difficult?'

'Sure, it's difficult, and it's not just a question of being a good climber that counts,' he said, wondering again what was behind the questions. Was she merely going a roundabout way to ask him about his own experiences on the Eiger? No, she was much too direct for that, and besides, her father had asked him much the same questions; there had to be a reason. 'Tell me, Jo, why do you . . .?'

She shook her head. 'It's nothing, Robert. Forget I asked. It's my feminine curiosity, shall we say.'

He saw that she didn't want to talk about it any more, and for his own part he was glad to let the subject drop. He finished his coffee. 'It's been a great evening. I suppose I'd better be thinking about getting back,' he sighed ruefully. 'To-morrow's Thursday . . .' He left the sentence unfinished.

She understood. The last few days had gone by with bewildering speed and they would be back in London soon.

'Do you think you could get out to-morrow evening, Jo?' he asked. 'We could go some place for a bite to eat.'

She shook her head regretfully. 'Not to-morrow, Robert. It'll be my last night here and I don't want to leave father . . .'

'Of course, I should have realised.' He got to his feet. 'But how about during the day – are you doing anything?'

She got up from her seat and put her hand on his arm. 'I can't, Robert, I . . .'

'I know, it's your last day with your father.'

'You understand, don't you?'

He shook her by the shoulders with mock severity. 'No, I don't.'

'We'll see each other in London.'

'It's not the same.' His tone was bantering but she knew what he meant.

'Do you miss home very much, Robert?'

'Sometimes. I don't think I've ever really been able to get over feeling home-sick.'

'But you could stay up here, if you wanted to.'

'I've thought about it.'

'And . . .?' she asked, gazing at him directly.

'It wouldn't work out. I've got to be in London. It's too bad, but that's the way it is.'

'But couldn't you do your work up here? That script you were telling me about, for instance, you could easily do that up here.'

He shook his head. 'I've thought about it, Jo, but it would mean an awful lot of travelling back and forwards, and anyway . . .'

'Yes?'

'Well,' he began in embarrassment, letting go of her, 'you know . . .' He broke off again as he heard the sound of a door open and shut. A moment later Brigadier Grant came into the room.

'You're going?' he asked, slipping out of his coat.

'Yes, it's getting a bit late and I've a lot to do to-morrow.'

'Joanna was telling me you're going back to London the weekend. Well, I've enjoyed our little chat. You must come and see us aagin sometime. You know where it is now.' Grant followed them to the door.

'I won't be a minute, father,' Joanna said. 'I'll just walk out to the car with Robert.'

Grant shook hands with Wishart. 'I hope to see you again sometime. It's not often we have guests here. You're welcome any time.'

Wishart thanked him and bade him good night, unaware they would meet again in circumstances he would at that moment have believed impossible.

Joanna saw him to the gate.

'You'll phone me to-morrow?'

'In the evening, okay.'

They stood looking at each other for a moment. He was the first to break the silence. 'Jo . . . about London? Are you sure you want me to . . .?'

She cut him off. 'Of course I do,' she said, annoyed by his sudden lapse of self-confidence, and noticing how on occasions it would drain away from him like quicksand. 'If I didn't, I

199

wouldn't have said so.' She saw she'd hurt him and was immediately contrite. 'Robert?' She fought against her feelings of exasperation. 'What is it . . .? What is it that makes you so worried?'

He looked at the ground and shook his head. 'It's nothing.' He seemed confused and uncertain. 'It's just . . .' He didn't finish.

'Why don't you tell me?' she pleaded.

'It's nothing, Jo. Let's forget about it.' He bent forward and kissed her clumsily. 'Good night, Jo.'

She watched the tail-lights of the Aston Martin recede into the distance and finally vanish. Shaking her head sadly, she walked slowly back indoors.

CHAPTER XVII

It was both good and bad to be back in London. The good things were associated with Jo; the bad things, the price everyone had to pay for living in a big and overcrowded city. And of course the wet, Novembry weather. Since his return he'd been working hard. He'd finished the script for the B B C and was on the last stages of the mountaineering book, and he had begun a piece about rock-climbing in Britain for one of the weekly supplements. His bank balance was in a healthier state, and he was eating and sleeping in a way he hadn't been able to for a long time. He was beginning to feel something like his old self again; and it had all happened since his meeting with Jo. She seemed to have given him something to live for.

They saw each other regularly, going for long walks in the country at the weekend and getting in a bit of dinghy sailing. Every day he phoned her, and any time he was in town he'd meet her for lunch in a little Italian café in Wardour Street near her office.

Looking back on the period before he'd known her, he wondered how he'd managed to get through the ordinary, everyday business of living. He felt like a man recovering from a major operation; every day saw little improvements in his health and mental attitude, and one morning he'd been pleasantly surprised to find himself whistling while he shaved.

But there was one thing troubling him deeply. He couldn't put it off any longer. He took the plunge and phoned Dr William Black, a friend of his. Black said he'd see him that same evening if he'd come along after surgery.

Wishart rang the bell. It was Black himself who opened the door. He was a man of middle height, with shoulders like a middleweight and a pair of shrewd, penetrating eyes behind thick spectacles. 'Come in, Robert, come in.' He led the way through to the surgery and pointed to a chair, sitting down himself at his desk. He looked across at Wishart, eyeing him closely from behind his glasses. 'Well, what can I do for you, Bob?' He knew it must be something unusual to bring Wishart to his surgery.

Wishart hesitated, uncertain how to begin.

Black waited. He decided Wishart probably needed encouragement if he was going to speak about his problem. 'I must say you're looking well. Certainly a great deal better than when we last met.' Wishart had borrowed his Dormobile to go abroad earlier in the year, and he remembered how ghastly he'd looked on his return.

'Do you mind if I smoke?' Wishart asked.

'If you want to shorten your life span, go right ahead.'

Wishart lit up, blew the match out and put it in the ashtray on Black's desk. He blew smoke through his nostrils. 'I don't know how to begin, Bill,' he said.

'Are you ill?'

'No, it's not that.'

'You don't think you're suffering from some terminal disease or other?' Black, recognising his friend's nervousness, was being deliberately humorous.

'No, it's . . . well, it's . . . I'm impotent, Bill.' The words came out in a tumbling rush.

'Mmmm. How long has this been going on?'

'Oh, I don't know . . . eight or nine months, something like that, mebbe a little longer.'

'And this is the first time you've decided to do anything about it?'

Wishart shifted in his seat. 'Well, you know . . . I thought it was just a temporary thing.'

Black was silent for a minute, doodling on his blotting-pad. He spoke again. 'Are you still going with that girl – I forget her name?'

'No . . . I . . .'

'Yes?'

'Well, no. I haven't seen her for months.'

'Because of your trouble?'

'Look, Bill. It was nothing to do with that. I came here . . .'

Black cut him off. 'I know why you came here, you've already told me. All I'm asking you is, did you have normal sexual relations with her?'

'Yes . . . I mean no. I mean, not in the end, anyway.'

'Was that her fault or yours?'

Wishart exhaled deeply. 'Mine, I suppose.'

'Are you going with a girl now?'

'Y-es.'

'And you're finding difficulty with her?'

Wishart flushed. 'You don't understand, Bill . . . it's not like that.' His mouth snapped shut.

'How interesting. Not like what?'

202

'Look, Bill, do you have to . . .'

Black stopped him. He leaned forward in his chair. 'You're a mountaineer; I'm a doctor. When I want some advice on climbing I'll ask you, but meantime you happen to have come to my surgery, so let's get on with it, shall we?' He shook his head despairingly. 'You know, that damned Puritan attitude of yours has been responsible for more human unhappiness than all the bugs put together. What's so wrong about sex that you can't talk about it? Believe me, it's something that's here to stay. And furthermore, as it's also responsible for our presence on earth, it's a subject worth some consideration. Now, since you've chosen to bring this matter to my notice, it is my duty and responsibility as a doctor to help where I can, so let's forget your delicate feelings and try and find out what's behind this.'

Wishart breathed out hard.

'Now, can I ask you a simple question?'

'Go on,' Wishart answered in a tight voice.

'Right. Have you discussed your problem with this girl?'

Wishart grunted unintelligibly.

'I take it this means you have. And what did she have to say?'

'Nothing.'

'Nothing? Nothing at all?' Black feigned surprise.

'Well, she mentioned I should see a doctor.'

Black threw himself back in his chair. 'My God, Bob, you're the limit.' He shook his head despairingly. 'Anyway, I'm glad she showed considerably more sense in the matter than you did.' He leaned forward again. 'You're in love with this girl, aren't you?'

'What's that got to do with it?' he flared.

'Only that I presume you have some kind of regard for her feelings.'

'Of course I do, but the way you're going on you'd think we were just dying to get into bed with each other. There's more to it than that . . .'

Black got to his feet and sat on the corner of his desk. 'I would hope so, but that in no way precludes the normal and natural desires of two people of opposite sexes. I can tell you, I'd be somewhat concerned if you *didn't* want to go to bed with each other.'

'Perhaps I should have gone to a head-shrinker,' Wishart replied with heavy sarcasm.

'I don't think that will be necessary, but if I'm going to

help you I've got to try and find out the emotional background to your problem, if any. So we've established you're in love with this girl and she's in . . .'

'I didn't say that.'

'No, that strange ego of yours wouldn't allow you, would it?' Black paused. 'Sleeping all right and that sort of thing?'

'Yes.'

'And how's your work?'

'It's okay.'

'No problems there?'

'Only the usual.'

'Right. We'd better have a look at you. Whip off your shirt and lie down.' He gestured towards the examination table.

Wishart removed his top things and was about to lie down. Black stopped him.

'Just a minute.' He came over. 'I'll just check your blood pressure.'

Wishart sat down.

'Okay, you can lie down now,' Black said a few minutes later. 'Your pressure's normal and your ticker's as sound as a bell.'

Wishart lay down. Black checked him over. 'Right, Bob, that'll do. You can get dressed again.' He went back to his desk and sat down. Wishart followed, buttoning up his shirt.

'Sit down, Bob.' He waited till Wishart had finished dressing. 'Now look, as I expected, you're in pretty good physical shape. Excellent, in fact. The problem lies elsewhere, but we might just as well have a blood check. I want you to take this along to the Pathology Department at this address. It's a simple matter, just a few tests, it won't take long.' He scribbled something on a piece of paper and addressed the envelope. 'By the way, that pipe of yours, you don't smoke a lot, do you?'

'Not much. About four ounces a week.'

'Mmmm. There's some indication that heavy smoking could be a factor, but that's all right.' He handed Wishart the envelope and a prescription. 'I want you to take a course of these pills, three times a day.'

'What are they?'

'Methyltestosterone, if you want to know the name. I've found they can be helpful in such cases. But what I want you to understand, Bob, is that in most cases this condition seldom has a physical origin. It's a very complex thing, you know, this sex. It's not just a simple series of spinal ennervations, by any means. Emotional states have an enormous bearing on the

204

subject. As I said, you're in good shape, but I have the impression you're suffering from nervous tension. Stress can create havoc with the organism. The problem is how to relieve it, but this is the domain of the head-shrinkers as you call them.'

For the first time since entering the surgery Wishart managed a smile. 'You sound as if you don't like them either.'

'Well, psychiatry is a very specialised subject. Let's say I look upon it as an area of considerable interpretation. We G Ps are much more pragmatic. When you have to deal with all sorts of people and their infinite variety of problems, you can't help learning something about the species. Human beings need food, shelter and clothing, but they need something more than that. The emotional factor is extremely important in health. Not that I'm recommending you should start reading medical books, but if you have a few hours to spare you might find it worthwhile dipping into the work of Hans Selye. You could learn something there if you're prepared to accept the argument on a non-technical basis.'

'Selye?'

'That's right. You see – and don't think I'm presenting a psychological evaluation, I'm not qualified – I think you're suffering from a considerable degree of stress. You're coping with it, and it hasn't as yet had any noticeable effects on your physical condition, but if you allow it to become chronic you mightn't always get a clean bill of health. In a word, sort out what's troubling you and find some means of resolving it.' Black got up from his desk and stuck his hand out.

Wishart shook hands with him. 'Thanks, Bill, sorry I lost my duster a bit, but, well, this hasn't been easy for me.'

'I know how you feel. Impotency in either sex can so easily produce devastating feelings of inadequacy. That's no good for any of us, life has enough problems normally. Anyway, you did the right thing coming along to see me. Try not to worry about it – it's a lot more common than you might think; and take the pills, you'll find them helpful. Good luck, Bob, and I'd like to see you again in about three or four weeks, okay?'

Wishart thanked him again and left.

Next day he felt much better as a result of his talk with his friend. He phoned Joanna.

'You sound very cheery,' she said.

'I'm okay,' he answered. 'What are you doing to-night? I thought we might have a meal later on. I'll have to work till around nine, but I could pick you up after that.'

He met her later that evening and they went to a small bistro in Primrose Hill.

'Why aren't you drinking your wine?' she asked over the meal.

He rubbed his forehead. 'I don't know. I don't feel like it somehow.'

She put her hand up to his head, feeling his brow. 'You're fevered, Robert. I think you should get straight back home and into bed.'

He shook his head. 'No, it's nothing, I'll be all right.' But he felt lousy, his head ached and he had a feeling of nausea in the pit of his stomach.

When she saw that he wasn't even eating, she insisted he should go home straightaway.

'I'll be okay, I'm telling you,' he answered testily, annoyed that his earlier feeling of well-being had vanished.

'You're not all right. You're sickening for flu, or something,' she persisted.

Eventually he gave in with reluctance. Flu? He'd never even had a cold he could remember. He drove Joanna home and went back to his flat and got to bed. In the morning he was running a high temperature and his body ached all over.

He got up and tried to work but it was hopeless, and he went back to bed. Joanna came round in the evening and insisted he should get a doctor right away, but he wouldn't have it. Next day she sacrificed her lunch and came to the flat to see how he was. She took his temperature. One look at it and she said: 'I'm getting the doctor, and no arguments.'

He was too weak to argue with her and lay back in the bed feeling miserable, as she made him a cup of broth.

Black came round in the afternoon. He didn't say much, but warned him that he was to stay in bed for the rest of the week. In the next few days Joanna visited him regularly, coming up during her lunch hour and again in the evenings.

'You'll be knocking yourself up at this rate,' he croaked as she dashed around cooking, washing and tending to his housework and mail. But she wouldn't listen to him, and he had no strength to oppose her determination.

It was a whole week before he was back on his feet. The experience had shaken him. Apart from a dose of jaundice he'd picked up in India some years before, he'd never been ill in his life. He recalled what his friend Doctor Black had said about the long-range effects of stress, and once more resolved to do something about reshaping his life.

Two days later he'd recovered sufficiently to walk about. He started work again, and the same evening Joanna and he went out for a meal. Leaving the bistro later, they went for a walk on Primrose Hill.

It was a clear night with just a touch of chill in the air. They sat down on a bench at the top of the hill. Below London was a vast sea of coloured lights reflected in the atmosphere as a pale rosy glow.

'I like your doctor friend,' Jo said to him, leaning her head against his chest as he slipped his arm round her shoulder. 'He seems very capable and understanding.'

'Bill? He's okay. He knows what it's all about.'

'Have you known him long?'

'Ten or twelve years, I suppose.'

'He's nice.'

He was silent.

She twisted her head to look up at him. His face had taken on the haunted expression she'd known when she'd first met him. She could see he was deeply troubled. 'What's the matter, Robert? Aren't you happy?'

He sighed. 'I'm a bit of a dead loss to you, aren't I, Jo?'

She sat up. 'What do you mean? Don't say things like that.'

'It's true, Jo. I seem to be all twisted up inside and now this . . . you know, this problem of mine . . .'

'You're not to worry about it, not to-night. It's been a nice evening. Don't let's spoil it. And anyway,' she looked up at him, her eyes filled with compassion, 'it's not your problem, it's *our* problem.'

'That's not true, Jo.'

'Look, Robert, there's no point in talking about it. You'll get over it. Anyway, it's perhaps just as well at the moment.'

'What does that mean?'

She reached up with her hands to finger the lapels of his jacket. 'It doesn't matter. Let's not talk about it to-night.'

'What did you mean, it was just as well?' There was an angry, frustrated note in his voice.

She sighed. 'Basically, it's because I'm a bit old-fashioned I suppose, but I have my feelings, and at least this way I'm saved the risk of complications.'

'It's a helluva way to achieve that, isn't it? How do you think I feel?'

The calm eyes looked at him steadily. 'I can only guess how you feel, Robert, but I *know* how I feel. I know it must be pretty awful for you, but you mustn't feel bitter about it.' She was silent for a minute before going on: 'There's something else, isn't there, something that's bothering you deep down? I've known it all along. But don't you see, it's all part of the same problem. Don't you see that, Robert?' Her voice was soothing and gentle.

'You make it all sound so simple,' he answered.

She ignored the bitterness in his voice. 'Is it something to do with your friend Joe Bailley? I know you thought a great deal of him, but you're only destroying yourself going over it again and again in your mind. You couldn't help what happened; it was an accident. From what you've told me about Joe, I'm sure he accepted the risk the same as you all do. You mustn't cripple yourself because of his memory.'

He shook his head exasperatedly. 'You don't understand.'

'No, perhaps not, but I understand some of it. Don't you think I've worried about father? There were times when I couldn't even eat or sleep, worrying about him away in those awful lonely mountains.'

He sighed, rubbing his forehead with his hand. 'I don't know. I suppose you're right.'

'I'll tell you something, Robert. I've always been secretly afraid of mountains. Don't laugh at me, it's true.'

Afraid of mountains? That was funny – or rather ironic. You and me both, he could have said, but he hadn't the courage to admit his fears to her.

And yet why couldn't he tell her the truth? Was it such a shameful thing to confess to being afraid? Joe would have had the courage to say so. He wouldn't have kept it bottled up inside him.

'Jo . . .' he began, but even as he opened his mouth he knew he wasn't going to tell her.

'Yes?' she said, expectantly.

'Oh, nothing.'

'Tell me?'

'I was just thinking your worries were over now, as far as your father's concerned. You won't have to go through all that again,' he said, realising for the first time how his wife Penny must have really felt. She too must have worried herself sick, like Joanna.

She turned her head away and said in a voice that was barely audible: 'I wish they were . . . I only wish they were.'

He looked at her, recognising something strange in her attitude. 'What do you mean, Jo? Your father's in Scotland, at home.'

'Yes, for the moment.'

He swung her round. 'What's this you're trying to say? Come on, Jo, out with it. What do you mean "for the moment"?'

She gave a little worried sob. 'I shouldn't really be telling you this, he doesn't want anyone to know . . .'

'Go on.'

'He's – he's – well he and some others are planning to climb . . . the Eiger.' She got the words out.

'What's that?' He couldn't believe he'd heard her right. 'Did you say the Eiger?'

She nodded dumbly.

'Not the North Wall?' he asked, telling himself it couldn't be.

'Yes.'

He couldn't speak for a minute. Christ, the man must be off his head. What did he think the North Wall was? A long, interesting plod up snow and ice, a stimulating test of endurance? Had he any idea what it was really like? Didn't he know that the Wall was only for the youngest and the fittest? He almost spoke his thoughts out loud, and only checked himself when he realised it would upset her all the more. 'When did he tell you this?' he asked.

'Oh, a long time ago. Earlier this year. But he means it, he's determined,' she said, biting her lip.

So that was what all the questions about the North Wall had been about! It was clear now. He cursed inwardly. If only he'd guessed at the time, he might have done something to discourage him. No wonder Joanna had been worried. There was one consolation, however. It was a long way away from the following summer. A lot could happen in that time. He said something of this to Joanna, but she only shook her head.

'They're not planning to do it in summer, they're doing it this winter.'

He was too stricken to speak.

CHAPTER XVIII

Joanna read the letter from her father over again. On first reading it she'd let out a long sigh of relief. Osborne had broken his leg and would be out of action for months, and the other man whom her father had managed to interest in the climb – a man called Worthington whom she'd never met – had called off at the last minute. It looked like the end of her father's incredible plan to tackle the North Face of the Eiger, but on reading the short, terse sentences once more she realised the effect of these setbacks was only to increase his determination; so much, in fact, that he was coming to London within the next few days to contact some old climbing friends, in the hope they'd be able to help him get together a new team.

She put the letter down and bit her lip thoughtfully. She was aware a critical time element was involved. The original plan, which he'd told her about, was that Osborne and Worthington would join him in Scotland when the first snows fell and get in as much preparation as possible for the attempt on the Wall some time in January or February. It was now the end of November; possibly too late to organise a new team. It was a hopeful thought. If he had to wait another whole year till next winter it was possible the whole thing would be called off. It was a possibility that gave hope.

She met him at the weekend. Standing at the barrier in King's Cross Station it was easy to spot his athletic figure, the purposeful stride and the head held high.

She embraced him as he put his small travelling-bag down.

'Joanna, my dear. So good to see you again. How are you?'

'I'm fine.'

'You've no idea how good it is to see you,' he repeated, returning her hug.

They went outside to get a taxi.

'You know, I'm absolutely starving,' he remarked as they took their place in the queue. 'And you know what I feel like having for breakfast? Kippers. What do you say to that? Is it possible to get kippers in London at this time in the morning?'

She laughed. 'I wouldn't know.'

A taxi pulled in.

'Never mind. I'll ask this chap.'

The driver thought for a minute. 'I'm not certain, guv', but I think Joe Lyons do them. The Corner House in Trafalgar Square. Shall we give it a go?'

Grant nodded and they got in.

The taxi-driver had been right in his guess. Grant put his knife and fork down with a satisfied sigh. 'Delicious. Why didn't you have any, Jo? You used to like kippers.'

'I never eat breakfast.'

'Should, you know. Sets you up for the day.'

Joanna drank her tea. 'You didn't say how long you were staying?'

'I'm not sure myself. I don't want to be more than a few days. I'm having lunch with Tom Abercrombie at the club. He thinks he might be able to put me in touch with some chaps. I want to get back by Tuesday at latest, so it doesn't give me much time. Seems Tom knows somebody called Putnam who might be interested . . . we'll see, anyway.'

'You'll be staying at your Club?'

'Oh yes, I think so. They know me there. I'll be well looked after. Now how about this evening? I'm not sure what's happening, but we should be able to fit in dinner some place if you haven't anything else arranged.'

She thought for a minute. She'd have to put off seeing Robert that evening and possibly the next. Still, it couldn't be helped. It was not often she saw her father. 'That'll be fine,' she said.

They had dinner that evening, and the following night dined at his club. Her father looked a bit dispirited as he came back from the phone and piloted her into the coffee room.

She tried to cheer him up. 'What a charming room,' she remarked. 'It has an air about it.'

He grunted. 'It should. I don't know if I told you before, but this is where they signed away the colonies.'

She almost laughed, he sounded so like an old imperialist, but she knew he wasn't; it was only his bad mood.

He had a small cigar with his coffee. He seldom smoked, so she knew he must be quite upset. She waited to hear what it was about.

The waiter lit his cigar, and he leaned back in his chair. He muttered something and looked at the end of his cigar as if it was in some way responsible for his displeasure.

'You had no luck then?' she asked.

He shook his head. 'No, Putnam says he can't find the time. Pity. He sounds like quite a good chap. He's even been there once or twice. Never done the thing, of course, but he knows the country well. However, Tom says he might know someone else, but apparently he's in Greenland on some expedition with the Marine Corps. Won't be back for another fortnight at least. Tom's going to write him, but time's getting on.' Grant stared moodily at the end of his cigar.

Joanna was secretly glad, but tried not to show it. She knew how deeply disappointed he was now that it appeared his plans had fallen through. Robert, when she'd told him how things were going, had been of the opinion it was too late in the year to do anything about it. It wasn't just a simple matter of getting a couple of people together. A lot of special gear and equipment was required, and a lot of practice climbing was necessary before they became a proper team. Despite her sense of relief, she was sensitive enough to share some of her father's disappointment. This was to have been the last act in his career – one final expedition to finish it off with a flourish. She knew it meant a lot to him.

'What are you going to do now?' she asked.

'Do? There's not much I can do. If only Osborne hadn't broken his leg.' He shook his head. 'Still, there's no point moaning about it – he did, and that's that. I'm seeing Tom again to-morrow for lunch. He might come up with something.'

She knew her father's friend, Abercrombie, was an experienced mountaineer himself. Cautiously she mentioned the possibility of his joining her father.

'Tom Abercrombie?' he snorted. 'Good heavens, Joanna, Tom's a fine climber and all that, but you must realise he's getting on a bit. Tom must be nearly sixty.'

Joanna said nothing. It was clear that her father put himself in a special category. He wasn't far short of sixty himself, and yet he could discount his friend as being much too old. It gave her a feeling of disquiet. It was possible he was misjudging his own powers.

'Anyway, let's not talk about it for the moment, Jo,' Grant went on, 'we'll see what happens to-morrow. And about to-morrow, depending on what turns up I might not be able to dine with you, so just go ahead and make your own arrangements.'

'I thought I'd do something for you at home,' she replied.

'No, no. You've enough to do. I don't want you to start cooking in the evening after a day in your office.'

'It's no trouble, and I could always slip away about four. It wouldn't be very grand but . . .'

'No, Joanna. Perhaps I could come round after dinner. We could maybe have a drink some place.'

An idea had begun to form in her head. The more she thought of it, the more it appealed to her. She hadn't said much to her father about Robert, though he obviously knew she was still seeing him. If she could get them both round to supper, Robert might manage to convey something of his doubts about the possibility of organising the expedition in such a short space of time. She knew how much her father held Wishart in regard as a mountaineer. He'd be bound to pay attention to anything Robert said. It might not work, but it was worth trying.

'Look, why don't you come round to-morrow evening anyway, father? I thought about asking Robert round for supper. If you haven't eaten you could join us and if you have it doesn't matter anyway. I'm sure you'd like to see him again.'

Grant puffed at his cigar, eyeing his daughter shrewdly. She hadn't said much about Wishart, but then she didn't have to, her fondness for him was noticeable every time she mentioned his name. It was obvious, since her return to London she'd been seeing quite a good deal of him. It was also obvious that it was about time he gave their relationship serious atten-tion. Not that he had anything against the chap, despite his rather lowly origins, but he sensed a troubled air about him, an inner disturbance that somehow might spill over and engulf his daughter. He knew her weakness and didn't want her to get hurt.

'You see quite a lot of each other, do you?' His question seemed innocent, but Joanna wasn't fooled by the tone.

'Yes, quite a lot.'

He thought for a moment, wondering whether it was better to be subtle or use the direct approach. He looked at his daughter again. She had her mother's calm, grey eyes: honest and transparent. He decided to be direct.

'Are you sure you know what you're doing, Jo?' he said.

'You mean about Robert?'

'He's quite a deal older than you, you know.'

'It never occurred to me, but does that matter?'

'It could matter a great deal.'

'But surely you were much older than mother when you married.'

He nodded. 'That's true, Joanna. But your mother and I were in love.'

'Well . . .?'

Her reply brought him slowly upright in his seat. 'Well? You don't mean . . . Joanna, are you sure of what you're saying?'

'Yes, father, I am aware of what I'm saying.'

But Grant was shrewd enough not to press the point, knowing his daughter. He tried to disguise his alarm. He'd have to do something or she might even marry this chap Wishart and that would be the end of it. He pursed his lips thoughtfully. This problem was going to need a lot of careful handling. 'Well, Jo, I'm not going to try and tell you how to run your life, but you will promise me you'll give the matter a lot of thought before you do anything definite? Will you promise me that?'

'Robert isn't some kind of monster, father, I know what I'm doing.'

'I'm quite sure you do, Jo, but you will think of what I said? It's not much to ask of one's own daughter, is it?'

She smiled at him across the table. 'You're trying blackmail now, aren't you.' Her voice was gently chiding.

He frowned. 'I do wish you'd be serious. I have some experience of the world, and my motivations have your interests at heart.'

'Of course, father, I know that, but you must be able to trust me.'

'Very well, Jo.' Like a good soldier he saw it was time to withdraw. 'Now, let's leave it for the moment. What was that you were saying about supper to-morrow? I think I'll come, after all.'

'I'm so pleased. I'll ring Robert now and . . .' She looked at her watch. 'Good heavens, I'd no idea it was so late. I'd better dash or I won't be fit to cook anything at all to-morrow.'

Grant saw her to a taxi and returned to the lounge. He ordered himself a large whisky and sat back, his mind a smoothly-working logical machine, as he considered his problems. He had to face it, his dream of climbing the North Wall in winter was a rapidly-receding possibility. And now he had this other problem of his daughter to face. He sipped at his whisky, trying to consider the question calmly. It was quite late before he finally retired.

Joanna had got home early and started preparing supper. She intended to make a lasagne and it required quite a bit of preparation. About six o'clock she remembered she hadn't any wine at home. She dropped what she was doing, wiped her
214

hands and went to phone Wishart.

She spent a few minutes on the phone talking to him and, having asked him to bring a large bottle of Chianti, went back into the kitchen. By the time he arrived she had everything prepared.

He kissed her on the cheek as she opened the door, and held up the bottle of wine for her inspection. 'Hullo, Jo,' he smiled, 'how's it going?'

'I'm nearly ready.' She took the bottle of wine and he followed her into the kitchen.

'Mmm, smells great, what is it?'

'It's a secret.'

'Jugged hare?'

'No, it's not jugged hare, and I'm not going to tell you what it is, you'll just have to wait.'

'When's your father arriving?' he asked, and she noticed the nervous tone in his voice.

'He phoned me at the office to say he'd be here about nine.'

'Is there anything I can do?'

'Yes, you can pour me a drink. You'll find the gin in the cupboard. There's also some Vermouth there . . . just a minute and I'll get you some ice.' She opened the fridge and removed the ice-tray.

'Here, let me do it,' he said.

'Thank you, but not too much ice, please.'

'Don't you think I know how you like it by now?'

'Bob,' she called out as he was mixing her drink, 'how's the whisky? Do we need any?'

He looked in the cupboard again. 'There's the best part of three-quarters of a bottle here. If you think we need any more, I could nip out.'

She sucked her finger. 'That should be enough, what do you think?'

'I'll nip out for a half-bottle. Better to have too much than too little.'

'Just a minute,' she cried, 'wait, I'll get my handbag.'

'No, no, I'll get this.'

'Of course you won't.'

'But Jo, I was going to bring something anyway.'

'Well, you did. You brought the wine.'

She opened her bag and took out a couple of notes with a sigh. 'I just don't know where money goes to these days. I never seem to have any after the weekend.'

'Jo, I wish you'd . . .'

She handed him the notes. 'Don't be long. I hate drinking alone.'

He was back in five minutes. He put a whole bottle down on the table together with the change.

She frowned. 'You shouldn't have done that, Bob.'

He gave a small grin. 'I got a cheque to-day from the B B C. I was going to take you out to dinner, anyway. Don't look so worried – I'm actually saving money.'

She shook her head again and returned to the kitchen, calling over her shoulder: 'Help yourself to the whisky.'

He poured himself a small one and joined her in the kitchen. 'How's your father, Jo? Has he been able to fix anyone up yet?'

'No. There's some chap that Tom Abercrombie says might be interested, but he's away in Greenland at the moment and won't be back for two or three weeks.'

'What's his name?'

'Whose name?'

'This bloke in Greenland.'

'Oh, I don't really know. I don't think it was mentioned or else I've forgotten it.'

'And how's your father taking it all?'

She took a sip of her drink. 'Not too well. He's very disappointed.'

'Hmmmm.' Wishart would have liked to say he was relieved, but it was still possible that Grant might get someone and he didn't want to reveal to Joanna just how crazy he thought the whole scheme was. He'd thought a lot about it since she'd first mentioned it, and the more he thought about it the more wild it seemed. There weren't more than a dozen people in England he could think of that were capable of tackling the North Wall in winter, and Brigadier Grant, experienced climber though he was, wasn't one of them. Nor did he think this bloke Osborne, or the other one, what was his name, were capable either. He'd never even heard of them. Still, it was true the North Wall had been conquered by virtually unknown climbers before – but this seemed to him like a party that didn't know what it was letting itself in for.

Joanna finished in the kitchen, and taking her pinafore off went into the sitting-room. She went over to the radiogram and switched it on. 'What would you like to hear?' she said, bending down and shuffling through the pile of records.

'I leave it to you, Jo.'

'I'm going to play your favourite.'

'Which one?'

'The one you gave me.'

He grinned with pleasure. 'You mean Django . . .'

'Yes, Django, my favourite gypsy.'

'I told you you'd like him.'

'I admit I didn't quite at first, but now I'm mad about him. Henrietta was up one night last week and I played it, but I'm afraid she wasn't impressed.'

'It's all this "pop", does for the ears eventually.'

'I wouldn't say it's all bad.'

'I was only joking. I like some of it myself, though not twenty-four hours a day.'

'I know, even Beethoven couldn't stand up to that kind of treatment. Anyway sit back, close your eyes and just imagine you're in a small café in Montmartre.'

He shook his head sadly. 'You know, Jo, that's one of my great regrets.'

'What is?'

'Django. To think I had the chance to hear him and I put it off. What a pity it was he died when he did.'

'It is sad,' she agreed.

Wishart sat down with his drink in his hand, thinking for the moment of the strange gypsy genius who, despite a maimed hand, had taught himself to play with a technique unequalled to the present day. Still, Django would always be remembered, and that would be probably more than the world would do for him. Looking back on his life, what had he achieved? A few major expeditions and a few first climbs. That didn't entitle you to a place in the history books. It was just as well he'd met Joanna when he did or, God knows, he might have finished up an alcoholic. He had a lot to thank her for, but how long could he go on? Not long. She was a serious-minded girl who wanted to do something worthwhile with her life. Obviously she wanted marriage and children. But how could he possibly ask her to marry him the way he was? Perhaps later he would when he refound himself – if there was anything left to find.

He lay back and shut his eyes as the first few nostalgic augmented chords came out of the speaker, introducing the slow-tempoed 'Solitude'. There was a haunting quality about the music that never failed to move him deeply, and he listened in wonder to the genius of Reinhardt and the violin player, Grappelly.

'Isn't that just beautiful?' Joanna said in a hushed voice

when the first track finished.

He nodded, his eyes still closed.

They heard the record through and turned it over. After it was finished, Joanna sighed and sat down on the couch. He got up and joined her.

'Shall I choose something?' he said.

'Yes. But be careful, after Django you can't just put on anything.'

He went over to where the records were stacked. 'How about . . . no, that won't do . . . let me see . . . ah, here we are . . . some Ravel . . . The Pavane.'

'Mmm. I think that would be just about right. You should have been a disc jockey, Robert.'

'I think I like the open air too much.' He put the record on and rejoined her. She nestled close to him, cradling her drink in her hand and looking up at him.

'Tell me, Bob . . .'

'Yes?'

'What is it about this mountain thing? I mean, what is it that gets you?'

He looked at her. '*You* ask me that? Don't you like the hills, Jo? Remember that time we were on Lochnagar together? You thought it was marvellous.'

'Yes, I like the hills very much, but it's those awful desolate mountains. There's something not quite human about them. And yet you go back time and time again. And father too. What is it that gets you?'

He sighed. 'I've tried to explain it before but it's difficult. It's just something inside you. I don't even know what it is myself.'

'But don't they ever frighten you? Don't you ever get afraid of the mountains?'

He stared at the wall. 'Sometimes.' He inhaled a deep breath. 'Very much, sometimes.' He wanted to tell her the truth about himself.

She was looking down the length of her out-stretched legs. 'You're pulling my leg,' she said lightly.

He turned to face her. 'Jo . . .'

She saw his expression was serious.

'What is it, Bob?' She tried to encourage him.

Faced with her direct approach he could only shake his head helplessly.

She sat upright. 'I wish you'd tell me, Robert. What is it

that's troubling you? Don't be afraid to tell me, I'll try and understand.'

He got clumsily to his feet, reaching for the whisky bottle. 'It's nothing,' he muttered, 'nothing at all.' He poured himself a large whisky. His action both puzzled and frightened her.

'Can't you tell me?'

He sat down again and took a slug of whisky. 'It's nothing, Jo. Let's forget it, eh?'

'All right Robert. Excuse me.' She got up and went out into the kitchen. She had just returned after seeing to the lasagne when the door bell rang. She glanced at her watch. 'It must be father. He's a little early, isn't he?' She went to answer the door.

It was. Jo took his coat and ushered him into the room. Wishart got to his feet.

'Ah, there you are, old chap. Nice to see you again.' Grant's greeting was warm as they shook hands.

'Get father a drink, will you Robert?' Jo said as she popped back into the kitchen. 'And you can pour me another one when you're at it . . . a small one.'

'Whisky?' Wishart asked Grant.

'Excellent. Just the thing on a night like this. It's a bit raw out. I think it'll rain later.'

Wishart poured him a drink and they sat down. Grant bent down to pull up his socks before sitting back in his chair.

'Slainthe,' he toasted Wishart.

'Slainthe,' Wishart replied in the Gaelic.

Grant settled himself in. 'Well, it's been some time, hasn't it, since we last met? How time flies. It's getting on for six months, you know.' He paused. 'And what have you been doing with yourself, keeping busy?'

Wishart appraised the Brigadier warily. He couldn't get used to thinking of this man as Joanna's father. He didn't know why. It wasn't that the Brigadier looked so young, it was something else he couldn't put his finger on. 'Oh, so-so,' he replied. 'I've had a bit to do lately.'

'Well, it's best to keep busy. There's nothing calculated to bore so much as lack of goals or work. What do you say, Joanna?' he added as Joanna came back in.

'To what?'

'I was just saying to Wishart here that there's nothing worse than having nothing to do.'

'Well, sometimes. I often feel I could do with a week of

219

nothing else but lounging about in the sun.'

'What nonsense, Jo. You've always told me how you hated those holidays where you did nothing all day but strip off and lie in the sun.'

She made a mouth. 'Well, perhaps I may have said that in the good weather, but now that we're nearly into winter it doesn't sound such a bad idea!'

'But you used to like the winters.'

'That was at home. I remember I used to love the snow. It made everything look like fairyland and there was always that hushed feeling all round. I used to love the horses, that muffled sound of their hooves in snow.'

Grant turned to Wishart with a smile. 'I'm afraid Joanna's a bit of a romantic. I hope she grows out of it.'

Wishart couldn't help being suspicious. Was this a reminder of Joanna's age, and the suggestion she still had one or two silly notions she hadn't grown out of yet? 'I'd forgotten about the horses,' he said, 'but I used to love that sound myself. I suppose we had hard winters, but we never seemed to notice them at the time.'

'When you're young everything has an air of excitement; of adventure,' Grant said.

'That's true,' answered Wishart. 'It's a pity you soon lose your sense of magic. And yet I know an old man in his seventies at home and he still walks the hills, and to listen to him you'd think he was a boy, he's so enthusiastic.'

'Ah, that's the spirit. I like to see that in a man,' Grant agreed warmly. 'I can't stand these chaps who reach for their slippers by the time their children have grown up.'

'Would you like another drink or would you rather have supper now?' Joanna headed her father off from one of his favourite topics.

'Good idea. I am feeling a bit peckish,' Grant said.

'I thought we'd just have it in the kitchen, if that's all right? It's not much, really. Soup and lasagne, and there's fruit and cheese and things if you still feel hungry.'

Grant finished his drink and rose. 'Wonderful, Jo. I just adore lasagne, how about you, Wishart?'

'I'm mad about it.'

Jo smiled. 'Wait till you try mine before you say too much.'

'I'm sure it will be just perfect,' her father said, putting his arm round her waist and leading her into the kitchen.

Wishart followed, feeling shut out by Grant's act, but once they'd all sat down Joanna smiled at him across the table as she
220

asked him to pour the wine. It was as if she'd accorded him a position of authority in her home.

After the meal they went back into the sitting-room. Joanna put a record on and poured coffee.

'That was wonderful, Joanna,' Grant said, leaning back in his chair relaxedly. 'You're quite a cook.'

'And you're quite a flatterer,' she replied. 'I'm waiting to hear what Robert has to say.'

'I was always warned not to compliment your hostess on her cooking – not in England, anyway. It's expected that her cooking should be good. But in this case I'm willing to break the rule: Joanna, that was the best lasagne I've ever had.'

She laughed. 'You men, you're all flatterers.'

'Okay, I will admit to having had its equal, cooked by the wife of an Italian friend of mine back home.'

'How dare you?' she replied with mock indignation.

Grant listened to their banter, noting the way they looked at each other, the little signs and glances that could betray so much. It disturbed him. He had to return to Scotland the next day, and he still hadn't had time or opportunity to assess Wishart. He knew so little about him. Farquharson had told him something of his background, but beyond that he only knew him as a mountaineer who'd established a reputation internationally. And then, his name had been in all the papers after that affair on the Eiger.

The Eiger?

A thought struck Grant. A thought so bold that it caused him to pause in his mind. It was so obvious, he couldn't understand why it hadn't occurred to him before. He took a long sip of his whisky and leaned back in his chair.

Why not?

He'd been chasing all over the country, and sitting right here in front of him was one of the best climbers in Britain. And, furthermore, a man who had just the kind of experience he was looking for.

Yes, why not?

Why not ask Wishart to join him?

Grant didn't consciously reason that the man sitting opposite him might be – because of his relationship with Joanna – placed in a position where it would be difficult to refuse. He didn't allow the thought to get any farther from the place where it had originated – the back of his mind.

But first he'd have to get him on his own. He didn't want to put the question to Wishart in front of Joanna. Again, this

221

wasn't so much conscious reasoning as an instinctive feeling that his daughter might not approve.

Joanna was saying something to Wishart about Scottish poetry. She caught her father's glance. 'What is it?' she inquired.

'I just wondered if there was any more coffee,' he said.

'I'll make some more if you like.'

'Oh, it doesn't matter.'

'Of course it does, if you want more I'll go and make it now. Would you really like some?'

'Well, if you don't mind, dear.'

'How about you, Robert?'

'Well . . .'

'That means you do.' She got up and went through to the kitchen, leaving her father and Wishart alone.

Grant wasted no time. 'Remember we had a little chat about the Eiger last time?' he started off, leaning forward in his chair.

Wishart frowned. 'Y-e-es.'

'Did you ever meet Hiebeler?'

'Toni Hiebeler?'

'Yes, I thought you might have bumped into him sometime.'

Wishart shook his head. He was sure Grant wasn't just making idle conversation. He wasn't the type. The question had to have some meaning behind it. 'No,' he replied, adding, 'I'd like to have met him. He's a fine climber.'

'Hmmm. Do you think he was right in thinking winter's the best time for an attempt on the North Wall?'

'It would be pretty tough in winter.'

'Do you think it could be done?'

'It *has* been done.'

There was a short pause, and then Grant said: 'You're a very good snow and ice man. Do you think you could do it?'

Wishart's frown deepened. 'Me? Well . . .'

Grant leaned farther forward. 'Would you try?'

Wishart was so astonished at the question that he couldn't reply.

'Look, I'll tell you what it's all about.' Grant finished his drink and put his glass down. 'You might as well know I was planning an attempt on the North Wall this coming February. I had a couple of others interested, but one of them broke his leg and the other had to call off . . .'

Wishart was dazed. 'You mean you . . . you want me to join you?'

Grant nodded his head firmly. 'Exactly. Why not? You've been on the Wall before, you know the country well, you've done a lot of snow and ice stuff. Why not?'

Wishart felt as if he'd been hit by a club. He tried to keep his self-control, but Grant's outright question had stunned him. He took a deep breath. 'Look . . .' he began, but Grant checked him with a wave of his hand.

'Think about it. I don't expect an answer right away, but I'll be frank with you, there's a chap up in Greenland with the Marines who could be interested. Unfortunately he won't be back for a few weeks yet, and the time's getting on. There's a lot of work yet to be done as you can imagine, but this would be mostly practice stuff. I've arranged most of the other details – equipment and all that. But I don't want to bother you with this at the moment, that will be the least of our worries. Will you think about it?'

Our worries? Good God, he was speaking as if the thing were settled. He looked at Grant. To all appearance he seemed to be a rational, intelligent human being, and yet he was not only contemplating climbing the North Face of the Eiger at an age when most men would be glad to be pottering about in the garden, but had coolly suggested that he, Wishart, should accompany him! It was shattering and unbelievable, almost as if it were a dream. But it wasn't a dream. Joanna's voice brought him back to reality.

'There you are,' she said, putting down the coffee tray. 'Freshly ground with real cream.' She looked at Wishart and then at her father. Immediately she was aware that something had happened. Though her father looked composed enough, Wishart's face had gone white. What had happened? What could have happened in such a short space of time? She'd only been gone minutes, and the atmosphere was so charged she could feel it on her skin.

Her father calmly poured cream into his coffee. He looked up to catch her questioning glance. He stirred his coffee and sipped it carefully to satisfy himself that it was to his liking, before he spoke: 'I was just telling Wishart about the Eiger thing, Jo.'

'Were you?' she said in a small voice, sensing there was more to it than the simple explanation he offered.

'Yes, I . . .' and he paused for a fraction of a second. '. . . I told him about Osborne and all the chasing around and trouble I've had to get this thing going. Anyway, I've asked him to join me.'

Joanna felt the strength go from her legs. She sat down, no all too sure she'd heard her father correctly. 'You . . . you asked Robert if he'd join you?' she managed to get out in a voice she didn't recognise as her own.

'That's right.' Grant gave a short laugh. 'To think I've been flapping about all this time, and it only occurred to me this evening.'

'Oh?' Joanna turned to look at Wishart with a frightened questioning glance. He looked at her helplessly.

'Yes,' her father went on, 'can't think why it didn't occur to me before. I must have been blind. Anyway, he's going to think about it, isn't that so, Wishart?'

Wishart felt in need of a large drink. If he told Grant he considered the scheme dangerous and crazy, it would only create more anxiety for Joanna. And yet if he didn't say something, Grant might wrongly assume he was interested.

Both Joanna and her father were looking at him.

'Yes,' he said addressing her in a halting voice. 'Your father was just telling me about it . . .' He couldn't think of anything else to say, and dried up.

Grant came to his rescue. 'Well, look here, when you've thought about it you can get in touch with me. I'm going back to Scotland to-morrow, you know where we stay.'

The next hour passed with agonising slowness. Only Grant seemed unaffected by the air of tension which hung over the room like the warning approach of a thunderstorm. Even Joanna's self-possession appeared to have temporarily vanished.

At last Grant rose, saying it was time he went. As he'd forecast, it had begun to rain, a thin, cold drizzle. Joanna phoned for a taxi for her father and brought him his coat.

The door bell rang. Grant slipped on his coat. 'Well, I'm off, my dear,' he said, 'I've got one or two things to do to-morrow before I return, but I'll see you in the evening.'

She kissed him on the cheek, still dazed by his suggestion. 'Phone me at the office, will you?' she managed to say.

Grant turned to shake hands with Wishart. 'Well, 'bye old chap. Nice seeing you again. You'll let me know, won't you, but don't make it too long, we'll have to get cracking soon, and get some work in.'

When he'd gone, Wishart poured himself a large whisky and flopped down on the divan. Joanna joined him, her face pale and a perturbed look in her usually calm eyes.

'Let me get you a drink, Jo. You look at if you could do

with one,' Wishart said.

She shook her head slowly, reaching out to feel the coffee pot. 'I think I'll make more coffee,' she said in a distraught voice, 'would you like one?'

'I won't bother.' He'd never seen her look like this before. She was about to get to her feet when he stopped her.

'Jo,' he said earnestly, 'about your father. How serious is he?'

'About asking you?'

'Yes. *You* know him.'

She gazed at the coffee pot. 'I know that whatever he said, he meant it. He means everything he says. He's so . . . so determined. He's made his mind up and that's that. You know, I was almost glad to hear Osborne . . . had broken his leg. I thought that that would be the end of it.' She sighed despairingly. 'I might have known better. He just won't give in, nothing will make him change his mind.' She broke off, staring at the coffee pot. 'What did you say, Robert? What are you going to do?'

'I don't know, Jo,' he said, shaking his head as if in pain.

'You mean you're actually going to think about it?'

'No.' He put his arm round her, but she didn't respond. 'Why don't you tell me the truth, Robert?' she said firmly, sensing his hesitation.

The truth? Yes, why don't I tell you the truth, Jo, he thought. Tell you that I love you very, very much and I can't imagine life without you, and that I also love the mountains and I can't do anything about that either, because my life is all ballsed up. That would be the truth, Jo. Perhaps the real truth is that I'm incapable of the truth. He looked miserably at his feet.

'You're frightened to tell me, is that it? You think that this climb is too dangerous, and you don't want to say so because you feel you're protecting me.'

He shook his head in anguish. 'When did I ever say that, Jo?'

'Well, say it now, if that's what you really think. Don't try and spare me, that'll only make things worse.'

'Jo,' he groaned. 'What can I say? Of course it's difficult. I've been all over that before. But your father's an experienced mountaineer . . . and after all, it's been climbed before. What more do you want me to say?'

'My father isn't a young man. He'll be fifty-four soon. Don't you think that matters?' She removed his arm and got to her feet. 'I'm going to make coffee, Robert. Do you want any?'

He shook his head miserably. 'I think I'll go home.'

'All right, Robert,' she said and went into the kitchen.

He rose and followed her, standing in the doorway and looking at her beseechingly, as she busied herself making coffee.

'Do you want me to call a taxi?' she asked without turning.

'It's okay. I'll get one on the street. I feel I need to stretch my legs anyway.'

'It's raining, you know.'

'Jo . . .'

'Just a moment, I'll see you to the door,' she said, putting the coffee pot on the gas ring and wiping her hands. He looked at her hands. They were such nice hands – delicate, but strong. Capable hands that knew what to do. He felt something choke in his throat. God, why did he have to hurt her when all he wanted was to take her in his arms? But she'd walked past him into the tiny hallway and taken his coat down from the hanger.

She handed it to him. 'Good night, Robert.'

Wordlessly he put his coat on as she opened the door.

He stopped on the threshold. 'I wish you'd understand, Jo, I don't . . .'

She brushed away a strand of hair from where it had fallen over her forehead. 'There's no point in talking about it, Robert. But promise that you won't keep father hanging around. Let him know where he stands. It's a family trait, you know. We always like to know exactly where we stand.'

He winced at her words.

'Sure, Jo.'

'Night, Robert.'

She shut the door softly behind him.

He climbed slowly up the basement stairs to reach the street, feeling as if he'd been banished from her life.

CHAPTER XIX

He waited two days before phoning her, not sure of what her reactions were going to be. She was friendly, but with a suggestion of coolness in her manner he'd never known before. It shook him, especially when she told him she wouldn't be able to see him that week as she had a backlog of work to clear; nor would she manage at the weekend, as she'd promised earlier to visit her friend Henrietta at her parents' place in Haslemere.

Somehow he got through the week. But every time the phone rang, he'd leap to his feet, and the arrival of the post gave him anguished moments. The half-hoped-for letter never arrived.

By Saturday evening it became so unbearable that he phoned his friend the doctor.

'Are you doing anything, Bill?' he asked.

'No, apart from taking things easy. Harriet has gone down to her mother's with the kids. Why, what's the trouble?'

'Nothing. I just thought I might come round and see you.'

'By all means, Bob. Look, I've finished surgery, but I've one call to make. Why don't you come round about nine, okay?'

Wishart hung up, feeling relieved and guilty at the same time. The only time it seemed he ever visited Bill was when he was in need of something.

He waited till after nine and drove round.

Bill led him into the sitting-room. 'Make yourself at home, Bob. You know where the drink is. I'll be back in a minute.'

Wishart helped himself to a whisky and sat down. Black came back within a few minutes.

'Let's have this damned thing off,' he said, going over to the television, 'you don't want to see it, do you?'

'No, but I wouldn't mind seeing the football later on.'

Black switched the set off and, pouring himself a drink, sat down, removing his glasses and pinching the bridge of his nose. 'That was a hell of a day,' he said. 'I envy you, Bob. At least you get away from it all at times. The next time you're going abroad and need a medical man, let me know, I could do with a break.'

They had a few drinks and later watched the football. But Wishart felt restless and nervous, shifting about in his chair and smoking one cigarette after another. After 'Match of the

Day', he realised he just had to talk to Black about the new
problem he was faced with. He took the plunge. 'Listen, Bill
. . .' he began.

'Yes?' Black had guessed there was something on his mind
and had been half-expecting him to reveal it. 'I'm listening.'

'Have you ever heard of Brigadier Grant?'

'Brigadier Grant, can't say I have. Should I?'

'He's quite well-known. He's a mountaineer. He's led
one or two expeditions . . .'

'Oh, that one. I've got you now. A friend of yours, is he?'

Wishart shook his head. 'No . . .' He hesitated. '. . . He's
Joanna's father.'

'Joanna?'

'Yes, the girl I'm going with . . . but that's not what I'm
trying to tell you. What I'm trying to say is, he's one of these
crazy determined blokes, you know, he gets an idea in his
head and nothing will shift it.'

Black nodded. 'I've met the type, especially in the Army.
But what . . .?'

'You won't believe this, but he actually wants to . . .' He told
Black the whole story.

When he'd finished Black sat back frowning. 'And how old
did you say he was?'

'He's in his fifties, but it's not just that, I don't think he
knows . . . look, this Eiger's no joke, Bill. I know.'

'I can believe that. I've only read about it, but it sounds like
an ideal place for attempted suicide.'

'I'm beginning to think he's crazy.'

'I think you're all crazy. And when's all this supposed to
take place?'

'A couple of months or so.'

Black came upright. 'But that's winter!'

Wishart nodded.

'I think the pair of you should be locked up. You're in need
of care and protection.'

'Listen, Bill. It's not me. I'm not going.'

'But I thought you said . . .'

'Sure, he asked me to join him.'

'And you turned him down?'

'No, I mean I didn't turn him down flatly. I said . . .'

'Just a minute, I'm getting confused. Tell me one thing first
and you can go on. What does – what'd you say her name was?
– Joanna. Well, what does she think about it?'

'That's what I'm trying to tell you. It's because of Jo I

couldn't turn him down flat. Supposing I'd said what I thought about it, that the whole thing's mad, how do you think she'd feel? She'd be worried sick about her father. So I had to sort of go along with the idea when he asked me. I said I'd let him know.'

Black shook his head sadly. 'You're an idiot, Bob. You should have told him you wouldn't go within a hundred miles of the place if that's how you felt.'

'And how about Jo? How would she feel then? That wouldn't have helped, would it?'

'I don't see why you can't tell her the truth.'

'The truth? Look, have you any idea what the Eiger's like? Do you know the number of people that have been killed on the North Wall? How bloody difficult it is? You want me to tell her that?'

'Well, it wouldn't be easy.'

'The under-statement of the year.'

'Well, what *are* you going to do?'

'I wish to hell I knew.'

Joanna came back to town on Sunday evening. She'd had a quiet weekend with her friend Henrietta, going for a long walk on Saturday and just lounging about in the evening. But the weather had been dull, monotonous and cold, and hadn't helped to improve her mood. Back in her flat, she inspected the kitchen. The white painted built-in cupboards were streaked and grey. She'd been meaning to wash down the paintwork for some time, and in fact the more she examined the flat the more she realised it needed a good clean. It annoyed her to think she'd let things slip. She changed into an old pair of jeans and a woollen sweater and started scrubbing and polishing. It was nearly midnight before she finished, and then she remembered she'd intended to write to her father. It would have to wait till next day.

Making herself a drink of hot malted milk she went to bed, switched on the radio and tried to read, but she was too perturbed to concentrate. Her thoughts kept returning to the subject of Wishart and her father, and it brought her nothing but pain and anxiety. She knew Robert was keeping something from her and she resented it. It was as if he failed to put his trust in her. But why? What was he hiding? The question troubled her. She'd almost decided not to see him again. If they couldn't trust each other absolutely and completely it was pointless; it would only end in greater misery and she was miserable and worried enough. But in her own way she thought the whole thing over carefully, and came to the conclusion he needed her help. If he phoned her – and she knew he would – she would see him again. Life wasn't all blacks and whites. Chesterton had said: 'Everywhere in things there is this element of the quiet and incalculable.' There was truth there. Everything had its hidden and inescapable flaws.

But before putting out the light and trying to find sleep, she made a silent resolve that if he didn't learn to put his trust in her there could be no future for them. It might be a hard decision to make if the time came, but it was wiser and more honest to face up to the possibility.

He phoned her Monday, and she arranged to meet him that evening in a wine lodge in Baker Street. It was a place they often visited, sharing their liking for its old-world atmosphere and lack of plastic, chromium plate and Formica tops.

He was standing there at the bar, gazing moodily at the counter, when she arrived. She felt something grip her heart strings as he turned and gave her a slow, shy smile.

She smiled back, glad to see him.

'Hullo, Jo,' he said in his soft burr. 'What would you like to drink?'

'You know, I think that's the first thing you ever said to me – what would you like to drink?'

'Was it? Well, I'm glad I did. It was a good idea.'

She said she'd have a dry sherry.

'Want to eat afterwards?' he asked.

'We'll see, eh? I'm not very hungry at the moment, but the sherry might help.'

'Did you have a nice weekend?' he asked next.

'Oh, so-so. Didn't do very much. Henrietta and I went for a long walk on Saturday and just loafed around Sunday. What did you do?'

'Nothing much. Watched the box and did a little work.'

They finished their drink and went round the corner to a small Italian café she used to frequent before they'd met. It was some time since she'd been there, but immediately the proprietor himself came over, his dark skin wrinkling with pleasure when he saw her.

'Good a-evening, Miss Grant. It's a long a-time. How are you? You are keeping well?'

'Apart from this awful weather, I'm fine,' she answered.

The proprietor raised his shoulders and spread his hands. 'Ah, the weather, it's a-too bad, but never min'. You have a good meal and you forget all about it, yes? Now I get you something special.'

Over the meal neither of them said much. They were both feeling the strain of their last meeting.

Wishart shoved his plate away, the meal only half eaten.

'Aren't you hungry?'

'Not really.'

'But it was you who suggested eating,' she said.

'I thought you might be hungry.'

'Aren't you having coffee either?'

'I thought . . . I thought we might go to your place?'

She hesitated a moment. 'All right,' she said, 'but I mustn't be late.'

'Well, if you'd rather not . . .'

She rose from the table, feeling a sudden spurt of anger. He could be impossible at times.

He got the bill, but she insisted on paying her share. It nearly led to a quarrel.

'But why should you persist in this . . . this feudal attitude?' she said when they'd reached the street. 'Why shouldn't I pay my own way? I'm a working girl, you know.'

'Just say I'm old-fashioned, and anyway I'm never sure how far this female emancipation is supposed to go.'

There was a sneering quality in his voice and it hurt her. 'Just as far as we can be treated as human beings in our own right and not just as the playthings of men.' Immediately she felt sorry for the remark, but she was feeling jumpy and irritable.

He laughed bitterly. 'At least you can't accuse *me* of using you as a plaything.'

'I'm sorry. I shouldn't have said that.'

'It's okay, Jo. We're both feeling it a bit, that's all. Mebbe I shouldn't come back for that coffee. I'll just walk you round to the flat.'

She didn't reply, but walking along the street she linked her arm in his.

They reached her flat.

'You'd better come in.'

'Well, okay. But I won't stay long. For some reason I feel a bit whacked. I don't know why, I did nothing over the weekend.'

She opened the door and they went in. He hung his coat up and went into the sitting-room.

'I think you and father finished most of the whisky, but
231

there should be some left,' she called from the kitchen.

'No, I won't have one, thanks. How about you? Will I mix you one?'

'No, thanks. I think I'm still feeling the effects of that sherry.'

He sat down and picked up a copy of *The Guardian* lying on the table, scanning its pages idly and without real interest. Suddenly an item of news caught his eye. It was a down-page item, little more than a filler, but it caught his interest. An Anglo-French expedition to the Karakorum was about to be formed under the leadership of Marcel Roget, the internationally known mountaineer, the report stated briefly, and went on to say that the members of the party would be announced soon and that the expedition had the blessing of a number of sponsors.

He put the paper down. The Karakorum? It had been a long time ago, but for a moment he could feel the heat, the hot, dusty, winding roads, the babble of strange tongues, the swarming villages teeming with excitement, and then the cold howling winds as they reached the very roof of the world. Strangely, now that he felt it was all behind him, his regrets were no longer tinged with bitterness. Something had happened to him recently – he'd reached an important turning point in his life and he had Joanna to thank for it. With her, he'd been able to unwind some of the bandages he'd been keeping himself wrapped up in. The revealed scars had been ugly, but perhaps it wasn't too late for them to heal. What he required was faith.

Faith, in himself and Joanna. He should have been honest with her from the start. But for some reason he'd withheld something of himself. It was all inextricably bound up with his basic problem. He could see that. He also saw that Joanna was dangerously close to going out of his life. He had to make a decision and accept the fact he couldn't go back to the old way. That was gone.

It wasn't going to be easy. Nor was it going to be easy to tell Jo's father he wouldn't be joining his team. But it had to be done, and soon.

He started when he heard the phone ring.

'I'll get it, it's probably Henrietta,' he heard Jo call as she came hurrying out of the kitchen.

He sat down again. A moment later Jo came into the room. She looked agitated.

'What is it, Jo?' he inquired. 'Has anything happened?'

'I think I could do with that drink,' she said in a strained voice.

He went over to the cupboard and poured her a whisky.

'Thanks,' she said, and sat down.

'What is it, Jo? What's happened?'

'It's father. He just phoned to tell me he's found someone who's going to join him.'

Wishart frowned. 'Who is it, did he say?'

She shook her head. 'Oh, just a name, I've never heard of him before.'

He was silent for a minute. 'So he's done it. I didn't think he would.' He exhaled deeply. 'There's not much we can do, Jo. I know it's . . .'

'Robert, this chap he's found. He's quite young, he doesn't sound as if he's at all experienced or anything – he's . . .' she broke off, '. . . oh, I don't know, but it sounds madness to me, you can't just find someone like that. Surely you've got to get to know people first before doing anything like this. I mean it's not as if . . .' her voice broke off again.

'And that was all he said? How did he sound?'

'Oh, you know what he's like by now. He was full of enthusiasm, says he can't wait to get started and all that.'

'But didn't he mention anyone else? You don't mean to tell me there's to be only two of them?'

She looked at him with troubled eyes. 'Is that bad?'

There could be no hiding the truth from her now. He nodded. 'Very bad, Jo. It's asking too much. It's different in summer. Given the weather and a bit of luck, there can be advantages in only having two people, but in winter . . .' He left the sentence unfinished. 'What else did he say about this other fellow?'

'Not much. He's an officer in the Black Watch. He met him in Edinburgh and they've had a weekend in Glencoe together.'

'Anything else? No name?' he asked, thinking he could always check up later.

'He did mention it, but I've forgotten. Apparently, or so father said, he's done a lot of good stuff in Scotland, whatever that means. I can't understand . . .'

'Look, Jo, do you think you could find out this fellow's name and anything else that you can?' he broke in.

She shrugged despairingly. 'Does it matter now? He's going to go through with it, isn't he? He's got someone at last in spite of us, and he'll be all the more determined now to prove that we were all wrong.'

'But it does matter,' he insisted.

'But how . . . oh, I just don't know any more, Robert. I would have worried anyway, no matter who was with him, but I wish to God he'd been able to find someone who was a bit more experienced. It sounds crazy to me. From what you say, this sounds just about the most difficult thing he's attempted in his whole life, and he has to go and choose a man whom he scarcely knows.'

'You try and get me that information, Jo.'

'What good is it going to do? What can you possibly do?'

He shook his head. 'I don't know, Jo. I want to think about it.'

He thought about nothing else for the next two days. It was one thing for Grant to go ahead with his mad scheme; it was another thing that Jo should have to suffer.

He lit yet another cigarette, scarcely noticing the ashtray was full of stubs and it was still early afternoon. He hadn't been able to do a stroke of work. He'd sit down at the typewriter, but the moment he tried to concentrate, the blank paper would seem to cover itself in a series of question marks, and he'd have a mental vision of the worried expression on Jo's face. Then he'd rise, pace about the room, light another cigarette, sit down, and find himself going through the whole process again. It became so unbearable that he slipped the cover back on his machine and put his papers away. It was impossible to work.

He reached for a fresh packet of cigarettes. There was only one thing to do. Grant would probably tell him to mind his own business, but for Jo's sake he would have to try. He waited till nearly seven before phoning Grant.

After a lengthy time, during which he seemed to have got through to every exchange in Scotland, he finally raised Glen Isla. He let the phone ring for the best part of five minutes, but there was no reply. He waited half an hour and tried again. Still no reply. He cursed, feeling nervous and edgy. It was getting near eight, and he didn't want to phone Jo before he'd got in touch with her father. He'd tell her afterwards. Once more he tried, and still no reply. He gave up and phoned Jo. She sounded tired, and there was a note of dull resignation in her voice.

'Okay, Jo, if you want to turn in early. I'll ring you tomorrow at the office.' He bade her good night and hung up, standing by the telephone nervously biting his lip.

Around ten he phoned Scotland again. This time, Grant answered. It was a bad line making it difficult to talk. The right words just wouldn't come and a few minutes later, when he put the phone down, he knew he'd given Grant the wrong impression. He'd obviously think the idea of arranging a meeting in Edinburgh was to discuss plans for the attempt on the Eiger. Well, he was going to be disappointed, probably furious, but that was just too bad. Anyway, it would have been impossible to tell him on the phone. He could imagine what the reaction would have been. Grant would have hung up.

Next morning he phoned Joanna at her flat first thing. It had just gone eight o'clock, and she sounded as if she hadn't slept well.

'Look, Jo, I can't go into all the details now, but I'm seeing your father this evening.'

There was a startled gasp from the other end of the line. 'This evening . . .?'

'Listen, Jo, I don't have much time as I'm catching the ten o'clock this morning from King's Cross. We're meeting in Edinburgh to-night. I'm going to try and convince him the Eiger is not on. I'll phone you from Edinburgh later this evening. Now don't worry, just leave it to me. I just want to talk to him, that's all.'

'Are you sure you know what you're doing, Robert? He's not going to like it,' she said, her voice sounding faint.

'I know, he'll probably tell me to mind my own bloody business, but that's a chance I'll have to take. Look, Jo . . .' he took a deep breath, 'I didn't want to tell you before, but I don't think he's got a cat's chance in hell of making it with this bloke, and I've got to tell him. The least I can do is to persuade him to wait till he finds . . . well, at least another two blokes. If he still wants to go ahead, well, we've done our best, okay?'

'Bob?'

'Look, I'll have to go soon or I'm going to miss this train.'

'Do you want . . . do you think I should come with you?'

'You? Have you gone crazy, Jo? Can you imagine how he'd react if the pair of us appeared? His own daughter and a bloke he scarcely knows, offering him advice. He'd love that.'

She was silent for a moment. 'Perhaps you're right, but be careful, Bob, will you?'

'Now don't worry, we're not likely to come to blows or anything, and if the going gets too hot I'll beat a graceful retreat.'

'Look after yourself, Robert . . . and you know something

. . . thanks for what you're trying to do and I love you very much.'

He gasped. 'What was that?' But she'd put down the receiver.

He stood for a moment in bewilderment, unable to believe it was only half-past eight in the morning, and he was unexpectedly on his way to Scotland and that he had a train to catch, and that she'd said . . .? He shook himself. But she had said it, he wasn't just imagining things. Well, that was something else he would have to take up with the Brigadier when he saw him.

He hurriedly began to pack, feeling apprehensive and elated at the same time. He knew he'd reached a major turning point in his life.

Before leaving the flat he went back into the bedroom and from a drawer took out the one and only photograph he had of Jo. It wasn't a good photograph, it had been taken in too strong a light, but the expression in the eyes was there. He put the picture in the breast pocket of his jacket, feeling sure now he knew where he was going.

CHAPTER XX

He was glad when the train at last pulled in to Waverley Station. To be back in Scotland gave him a little thrill of pleasure. Even the faces of the porters looked familiar, and it gave him a sense of belonging to hear the familiar dialect all about him. It was beginning to get dark as he dumped his small carrier bag in a locker and headed up the steps. The sky to the east was a dark slate-coloured blue with a thin orange crescent of a moon. A cold wind blew the length of Princes Street, but he scarcely noticed it as he made for a small café he knew in Hanover Street.

He'd been too nervous and agitated to eat on the train, but now he felt the need for food. He had a quick meal and, leaving the café, turned off Hanover Street and into a pub. It was only when he ordered his second pint that he realised he'd unconsciously chosen the pub where he'd had a drink with the two lads he'd picked up last time he'd driven up to Scotland. He wondered, drinking his beer, how they'd got on in Skye.

He looked at his watch again as he finished his pint. Time to go, it was quarter to eight. He left the pub and headed for Princes Street. The hotel where he was meeting Grant was only a few minutes' walk. Mounting the wide steps, he went inside, looking around him, not too sure where the lounge bar was in this ornate reminder of the hey-day of the British Empire.

'Can I help you, sir?'

He turned round. The porter sounded helpful, but Wishart could tell by the eyes he was being shrewdly appraised. The suit, the accent, his business here. Only after the silent examination was made would the proper degree of deference be decided upon.

'I'm meeting Brigadier Grant,' said Wishart, purposely using the military title.

'And your name, sir?'

He felt like saying Field-Marshal Wishart. 'It's Wishart.'

'Ah yes, sir. The Brigadier's expecting you. He's in the lounge, come this way, sir.'

Wishart followed him into the thickly carpeted lounge,

feeling distinctly alien in this old-world sanctuary of th
Scottish ruling classes.

Wishart caught sight of the thick bulging neck muscles an
the silvery grey hair. Grant was alone. He turned round, a
smile on his face. He stuck his hand out.

'Ah, there you are, old chap. We keep meeting in th
oddest places. Nice to see you again, anyway. Do sit down
and let me get you a drink.'

Wishart sat down as a waiter unobtrusively appeared. There
was no queueing for drink here, no shouting to make yourself
heard, no jostling, no barging, everything quiet and orderly
a smooth-running machine brought into being by the needs of
a select society. Wishart didn't like the atmosphere. He would
have preferred to face the Brigadier on more neutral ground

'Well, to tell you the truth, I'd like a pint of beer,' he said
in a futile attempt to even the odds up.

Grant showed no sign of surprise or embarrassment. 'Jolly
good. I think I'll settle for another whisky. That will be a
pint of beer,' he said to the waiter, 'and a large Scotch. And
waiter, bring me a separate glass of water, will you?'

The waiter looked uncomfortable. 'Sir . . .' he said, 'I'm
afraid we don't serve *pints* in the lounge.'

'Oh don't you? Well, I'm sure you could make an exception
in this case. If you've any trouble ask the head-waiter to spare
me a moment of his time.'

The iron hand in the velvet glove. Wishart looked at the
Brigadier. He was a man who knew what he wanted and made
sure he got it. No offence, no harshness, no bullying, but
nevertheless it had been an order. Not only that, Wishart knew
that even if the waiter was forced into a position of having
to refuse, there would be no storming bombastics, no threats to
leave. No, nothing like that, but quietly and diplomatically the
management would be made aware of the fact that the
Brigadier's displeasure had been incurred. In spite of himself
he couldn't help feeling a sneaking admiration for the man.

But he got his pint without the need to call in the services
of the head-waiter.

'Your good health, old chap.'

'Cheers,' Wishart replied.

'You know, I've quite taken to this way of drinking whisky
and I have you to thank for it,' said Grant, taking a sip from
the tumbler of water. 'Jolly good idea. I've introduced the
habit to quite a few friends of mine.'

Wishart noticed he made no reference to Joanna. It could

have been a subtle way of not acknowledging the existence of their relationship. If so, it was something he would have to correct. There *was* a relationship, and he still had the memory of Joanna's parting words to remind him. But for all their differences of interests and outlook, there was still something about Grant he couldn't help liking. There was a quality about the man that came through.

'You'll have dinner with me, of course,' Grant was saying.

'Dinner? To tell you the truth I hadn't thought about it. In fact, I had something to eat a short while ago.'

'Surely you'll manage something? I'll tell you what, I was intending to have dinner here, but we'll dine out later if that suits you?'

'I'll try and work up an appetite,' he said, and realising there was no point in putting off the purpose of their meeting, took a deep breath: 'You're probably wondering why I'm here?'

Grant frowned. 'Should I? You said you'd let me know about the Eiger thing last time we met. I presume that's the reason for your visit?'

Wishart was about to reply, but a waiter had appeared by the side of Grant's chair.

'Yes?'

'You're wanted on the phone, sir.'

'Did they say who they were?'

'It's a Mr Barrington, sir.'

'Ah, Barrington. You'll excuse me a moment, Wishart.' He got up and went out into the reception hall.

Wishart saw that he'd nearly finished his whisky. He signalled the waiter.

'Yes, sir?'

'That'll be a large whisky and a . . .' No. He'd made his point and he didn't feel like another pint. '. . . and a small one, and bring me a McEwan's Blue Label, will you?'

'Certainly, sir.'

Grant was away quite a long time on the phone. He looked disappointed when he returned. He sat down, automatically reaching for his glass. 'Sorry to be such a long time,' he began and then noticed his glass had been refilled. 'Oh, you got one up, I see. Good show. Here's good health, and,' he raised his glass with a smile, 'to the Eiger.' Taking a sip of his whisky he ran his tongue over his lips. 'That was Barrington. I was hoping he'd be able to come to-night. Seems he can't manage, however he'll be down to-morrow. He hasn't far to travel, only from Perth.'

Barrington. Wishart had heard that name. Had he seen it in one of the climbing journals? He'd have to check up when he got back to London.

'Now where were we?' It was Grant again. 'Oh yes, you were saying . . .?'

Ever since his arrival Wishart had realised his mission was quite hopeless. He was only kidding himself. He'd never change this man's mind. So what was the old service adage: 'if you can't beat 'em, join 'em.'

He'd come to his decision. His nervousness had gone and he felt very calm. It would ease Jo's mind and that was all he wanted. But how ironic, he'd come to dissuade Grant and somehow it had worked out the other way.

In a perfectly calm voice he found himself saying to Grant: 'When do you intend to go?'

'I think February. We'd probably need the best part of the month, wouldn't you think, if we're going to make sure of getting a reasonable spell of weather. What's the matter, does that sound a bit too long for you?'

'Well, I wouldn't like to be away that long if it can be avoided. Hanging about the Kleine Scheidegg waiting for the weather to break can be a bit depressing. I thought perhaps we could be ready to go and phone through for weather reports. It would save a lot of hanging around. How did you intend to travel, by the way?'

'Oh, we'd fly out, of course. And now that you've brought the subject up, I would like to say that I'll be footing the expenses for travelling and equipment and that sort of thing.'

'It's going to cost quite a bit.'

'Yes it is, but it's my show and I want to bear most of the expenses anyway . . .' he paused to smile. 'Of course, that won't include such things as drink, though I promise you a champagne party on our return. But to be serious, a lot of the equipment we'll be able to get free. I've been in touch with a number of manufacturers and they're willing to support us.'

'How about the press?'

'Not a word. At least, till it's all over.'

'And how about Barrington?'

'He's a good chap. You'll like him. Plenty of go, young of course, but a damned good man. I've had a couple of weekends with him, one in Glencoe, the other at Nevis. There's nothing to worry about him. I mentioned your name to him, said you might be interested. He's very keen.'

'We could do with another one in the party.'

'Do you think so? No, no. Don't misunderstand me, it's not the additional expense I'm thinking about, this is to be my last fling, so to speak, so I'm not going to quibble over extra expenditure. After this it's the farm life for me. Of course, I shan't give up climbing altogether, but it won't be abroad – I'll stick to our Scottish hills. So you think a party of four would be best?'

Wishart nodded. 'Definitely.'

'Well, you know I've had a devil of a job as it is; to find another chap isn't going to be easy. Did you have anyone in mind?'

'I'd have to think about it, but there is one person I know who might be interested. I'll write him over the weekend.'

'Write? Phone him, let's not waste time.'

'I don't think he's on the phone.'

'Wire him then. Who is he, anyway? You've climbed with him, I take it?'

'Oh yes. Dillon's his name. He's a very reliable type, just the sort of bloke you need on the North Wall. Very strong and can keep going.'

'Wire him now.'

'Now?'

'Why not, you have his address? Let's do it right away and after that we'll go and have dinner somewhere.'

Wishart knocked off the remains of his beer and rose. Already he felt caught up in Grant's driving force, and realised how utterly useless it would have been to try and dissuade him. Well, he was up to his neck in it now; there could be no going back.

On his way to the phone booth to wire Dillon, he stopped for a second as the full understanding of what he'd committed himself to hit him. But he recovered his composure quickly as he thought of Joanna. What he was doing was for her, but he had to force himself to shut out from his mind the momentary and terrifying picture he'd had of the North Wall. There would be plenty of time to worry about that later.

He sent a brief message to Dillon asking him to phone or write soonest, and, leaving the phone booth, joined Grant in the reception hall.

'We'll just walk, shall we?' said Grant. 'I know a little restaurant not far from here that does a good stroganoff.'

The restaurant was no more than five minutes away, and though it was very cold, with most people going about wrapped up heavily, neither of them bothered with a coat.

241

'I'm glad to see you're like me,' Grant said as they walked along Princes Street. 'People wear too many clothes. You've got to condition yourself to cold. I used to plunge my hands into snow and keep them there, toughen them up. I was glad of it when we came to do the Nanga Parbat thing.'

Wishart was finding he had to force his own naturally long stride to keep up with the Brigadier. 'Hermann Buhl used to do that,' he said. 'He carried snowballs around in his hands.'

'Who was that you said?'

'Buhl, Hermann Buhl.'

'Oh, Buhl. Yes, he was some chap. Magnificent climber. Pity he was killed. Nanda Devi, wasn't it?'

'No, Chogolosa. He went over a cornice.'

'Ah, yes, of course.' Grant seemed matter-of-fact.

Turning off Princes Street, they reached the restaurant. It was quite small and obviously catered for a select clientele. The waiter showed them to a table.

Grant studied the menu and ordered for both. 'You know, I've a damned good mind to have a bottle of champagne. I don't mind telling you how pleased I am that you've decided to come along, Wishart. It's going to make quite a difference. I've done my homework on the Eiger, but I must say it makes all the difference having a chap that's actually been face to face with it, if you'll pardon the pun. Yes, I really am glad. Now, how about that champagne?'

'If you don't mind, I won't bother,' Wishart said. He found it impossible to share Grant's mood of gaiety, and wondered if Grant fully realised what they were going to have to face in little more than a few weeks' time. And yet he had to have some idea, after all he'd done quite a bit in the Himalaya. He could only suppose it was his colossal enthusiasm and supreme self-confidence that was responsible for his attitude. 'I think I'll just have a glass of wine.'

Grant smiled. 'That's typically Scottish, if I may say so. I mean, not to celebrate in advance, as if such a thing might incur the anger of the gods. I've noticed it quite a bit since I've returned to live here. You know, you get the sort of thing in a conversation where a chap might say, "It's been a grand summer, but wait till winter comes, we'll have to pay for it". I suppose it's a latent form of masochism, really.'

Wishart was only half listening. He was thinking about Joanna and what she was going to say when he told her what he'd done. She'd been worried enough about her father, and now she was going to have to worry about him. But, in the end, what he'd decided to do was the best thing. At least he was no longer a helpless bystander having to watch her suffering agonies of mind. He could just imagine how she would have felt if Grant and this fellow Barrington had gone it alone. God, it was fortunate she didn't really know just how mad that would have been. He wouldn't even have given them a fifty-fifty chance. But now with a party of four and the possibility of Dillon joining them, they had a chance. A chance? No, they were going to bloody well do it. They had to. Starting from now there were to be no negative attitudes, no doubts, no hesitations. He knew what he was in for, and he knew the reasons why he'd agreed to do it. If he had to drag himself up inch by inch he'd make it. It was for Joanna, and in a strange way also for Joe. Funny how it was that the scarcely believable position he found himself in was because of two people both called Joe.

'Did you say Barrington was coming down to Edinburgh to-morrow?'

'Yes, he's phoning to say what time he'll arrive. I think you'll like him.'

Wishart grunted between taking a mouthful of food. He didn't care if Barrington was the most objectionable person in the world, all he was concerned about was the man's ability *and* what experience he'd had. Personally he'd rather have taken a chance and cut the party down to three, than have two unknown quantities in its composition. With Grant in the middle of the rope, and himself and Dillon sharing the lead, it was just feasible, but with another man tied on – a man of whom he knew nothing – it would probably be more hazardous than helpful. One thing was clear, he'd have to stay over in Edinburgh now. Originally he'd intended to catch the late train and be back in London for Saturday morning, but if he was going to have a look at this Barrington it would mean he wouldn't be back till Sunday. Another problem was, should he phone Joanna and tell her what he'd done or should he wait till he got back. He thought about it, and decided to tell her when he saw her on Sunday.

After the meal, Grant accompanied him down to the station to pick up his bag.

Grant insisted he should stay in the hotel. He'd rather have had something simpler – a small bed-and-breakfast place would have suited him – but he didn't argue, though he refused

Grant's offer to put the room on his bill.

The next day was spent almost entirely in the lounge of the hotel, discussing plans. There was no doubt that Grant had done his homework with thoroughness. He had a whole folder full of maps, pictures and piles of notes. Wishart hoped Grant's ability as a climber was as good as his talent for organisation.

But perhaps he was being unfair, the Brigadier had an outstanding reputation, and like himself had spent years in the hills, and more than that, he had qualities like toughness and determination. Barrington was the real worry. From what Grant had told him, it seemed clear he belonged to the new school of young tigers. Probably an excellent rock man, but the Eiger's north face was a snow and ice climb, and called for a lot of experience, particularly in rope handling. The trouble was, they weren't going to get in many climbs together to help them knit a team. A couple of snow climbs in Scotland perhaps, and that would be all.

He began to think it might be better to adopt the Brigadier's original suggestion and spend a whole month in Switzerland and do some preparatory climbs on the Mönch and the Jungfrau. But then it was possible, more than possible in fact, that Dillon wouldn't be able to spare all that time – that's if he was able to manage, and if he wasn't, what then . . . he gave up, his mind showing signs of rebelling against the whole project. Why the hell did Joanna's father have to be Brigadier Grant? Or if he had to be, why the hell couldn't he have retired gracefully from the scene? He'd achieved plenty in his lifetime, but no, he had to go out in a blaze of glory by tackling the most dangerous and notorious face in the whole of Europe, a face that had already cost more than twenty people their lives and that had been responsible for more injuries and dramatic rescue operations than any other single mountain. Why hadn't he simply gone and done what his friend Osborne had done and broken his leg, and that would have been the end of it?

Barrington was late in arriving. He didn't appear till nearly nine o'clock.

He came into the lounge, breathless and apologetic. Apparently his car had broken down and he'd had to get a lift. Grant introduced him to Wishart.

Barrington grinned boyishly as they shook hands. 'I've been hoping to meet you,' he said, 'I think it's just great that you're ble to come along.'

Wishart eyed him as they all sat down again. He was tall, almost his own height, and probably not more than ten and a half stone. That was good in one way, bad in another; there wasn't much flesh to protect him from the cold. He had a nervous, excited look about him too, that went with his untidy red hair. Wishart didn't like that. He'd seen these types before: they could be absolutely brilliant, but when their nervous energy went they could literally fold up.

In discussion, he was surprised to find Barrington had done a couple of seasons in the Alps. Well, that was something. But why hadn't Grant mentioned it? He stole a look in the Brigadier's direction. Grant was smiling. He'd obviously been holding back this piece of information as a surprise.

'I didn't tell you,' Grant spoke to Barrington as he signalled the waiter, 'but we may have a fourth member joining the party. Wishart telegraphed him yesterday evening. We should know quite soon,' he said.

'Good. That would be better. Who is the chap? Perhaps I might know him?'

Grant left the question to Wishart. 'Brian Dillon. Comes from Manchester,' Wishart said.

'Brian Dillon, did you say?'

'Do you know him?' Wishart said, surprised.

'Well, I don't actually know him, but I've met him, if you know what I mean. You see, we used to live in Manchester before we moved up to Perth. I met him in North Wales quite a few times. He's a great chap; that's absolutely marvellous.'

'Isn't that a bit of luck,' said Grant approvingly. 'Everything's turning out just fine.'

'We haven't got his reply yet,' Wishart warned. 'He might not manage, you know. It was just an idea I had.'

Barrington looked disappointed. 'That would be a pity. He's absolutely first-class.'

That night, on the train back, Wishart slept badly. The nearer he got to London, the more he worried about Joanna and how she might react. He was also worried about Barrington's inclusion in the party. Instinctively he sensed he was the wrong type. Grant had allowed his enthusiasm to colour his judgment, or so he guessed. Most probably he'd been impressed by the younger man's climbing ability and infectious good nature: facile qualities that would be ruthlessly exposed by the Wall. He began to hope more than ever that Dillon would be able to join. In fact he was beginning to think he couldn't go through it without Dillon. Dillon was the linchpin. The problem was, would Dillon have enough faith or confidence in him after their last meeting in Switzerland? He hoped he would.

He was tired and edgy by the time they pulled into King's Cross. Unusually, he took a taxi home and plunged himself into a steaming hot bath, finishing off with a cold shower. After this shock therapy he felt a little better. It was still early but he decided to phone Joanna anyway, just to let her know he was back and pass on her father's regards. That had been quite significant. He'd meant to speak to Grant about himself and Joanna, but always the talk had centred about the Eiger and he hadn't had the chance. To his surprise, it was Grant who'd mentioned Jo. He'd come down to Waverley Station to see him off on the train. With a final shaking of hands, Grant had said to him to give Joanna his fondest regards. It had been trifling in its way but it had been an indication that for the first time Grant had acknowledged his relationship with Joanna. It wasn't exactly a blessing, but it wasn't a rejection either. He only hoped that this subtle change of attitude hadn't been conditioned by his decision to join the Eiger venture.

Joanna was eager to hear what he had to say. There was no point in keeping it from her.

There was a shocked silence on the other end of the phone when he'd finished.

'Are you there, Jo?'

She'd regained some control in her voice when she spoke again. 'Yes, I heard you, Robert,' she replied gravely.

'Well, look, I don't want to talk about it now. I'll see you to-night and let you know what's happening, okay?'

'All right. Just come round when you can. Would you like me to make something to eat?'

Dear, practical Jo. He'd just flung a bombshell at her, and all she'd done was to ask if he might be hungry. That was Jo all right. No matter what, the ordinary things in life still had to go on. That was the real source of her wisdom and balanced outlook: the recognition of necessity . . .

She poured a cup of coffee for him and one for herself, and sat down. Since arriving a few minutes before, he'd been watching her closely in an attempt to judge how deeply she'd been affected by what he'd told her.

Outwardly she seemed calm, but he could see a slight stiffening round the mouth and the suggestion of a crease in her wide forehead; the eyes too, that normally looked out on the world around her with a clear and untroubled gaze, were lightly clouded, reminding him of the expression a dumb animal bore when it had been unjustly punished. And yet there was nothing he could do about it, except try and convince her that she had less to fear now. They'd make it, and after that she had no further need to worry about her father, or himself. He'd decided that, along with a number of other things, over the weekend. He was finished with it all after they'd climbed the North Face.

Funny how it had worked out with a kind of Freudian predictability: it was almost enough to make him believe in fate, but the fact was that this was to be not only Grant's swan-song but also his own. From then on he would content himself with rambling over his native hills. But the strangest thing of all was how he found himself prepared to accept it. It was as if a new regime had taken over the workings of his mind. He couldn't really understand it, nor did he try, all he knew was that Jo was in some way responsible for it.

Meeting Joanna had changed his whole outlook.

He sat forward, elbows resting on his knees. 'Well, that's the way it happened, Jo. I knew it was impossible to try and talk him out of it. Don't ask me how, I just knew, that's all. I hadn't been there five minutes when I knew.'

She looked at him tenderly. 'You're doing this for me, Robert. You never would have even considered it otherwise,' she said. 'I know that and it makes me want to cry . . .'

'Jo,' he half got to his feet.

'No, it's all right. I won't. But I want you to know how I feel. I think what you're doing is wrong, but I'm not going to argue about it. I know how deeply you must have thought the whole thing out. You must do what you feel you have to do . . .' Her voice faltered, and for a moment he did think she was going to cry. He wished she would. It would release some of the tension that had piled up within her. But she caught hold of herself again. 'I don't know what more to say, Robert.'

He put on a grin and reached out to put his hand on her knee. 'Oh, come on, Jo. Look, I've got an old score to settle with the Eiger anyway, haven't I? It's about time I squared it up. I'm like your father in a way, I don't like to be beaten

that easily. After that I can hang up my boots and feel happ
about it.'

She was silent for a long moment. When she spoke agai
it was to say: 'You're frightened, aren't you, Robert? Some
thing happened to you to make you frightened, didn't it
That's what's been eating you up all this time.'

'Who, me?' he scoffed. 'You must be joking. Look, I'v
climbed things a damned sight tougher than the North Wal
And . . .'

'You don't have to pretend for my sake,' she cut in, her eye
filled with love and compassion in the knowledge of what hi
decision must have cost. 'Please try and understand that.'

'Who's pretending? Look, I've been on that bloody grea
hulk before, okay, so I respect it, but I'm not frightened of it
he lied. 'In any case,' he said, patting the telegram in hi
pocket, 'with Brian Dillon joining us, half the battle's over
You don't know Brian, but he's as strong as an ox. You shoul
see him on ice, he's like a machine, a steam-engine, in fact
and on top of that he's as safe as houses. I'd go any plac
with Brian and I'm not joking.'

'And how about this Barrington? Is he as strong as an ox
is he another steam-engine?' She purposely didn't mention he
father.

'Barrington?' He nodded his head speculatively. 'He's a
different type from Brian. He's good, all right. I looked up som
old copies of the *Climber* and some S M C Journals. For hi
years he's done quite a bit. He's got a few "firsts" to his name
too. And believe me, that's not easy to do to-day with al
these young "tigers" about. No, Barrington's okay,' he said
trying to put conviction into his voice. 'And then there's you
father. He's as strong as a horse too *and* he's fit, but more thar
that he's got this colossal mental thing. He's a real power
house . . .' He broke off with a laugh. 'I never told you before
but you know what they call him in climbing circles – the
"Tank". I tell you, Jo, the more I think about it, it doesn'
seem possible we could have got a better team together. We've
got power, skill and a whole lot of experience.'

Joanna jumped to her feet and fled into the kitchen. He go
up and went after her. She resisted his efforts as he took he
by the shoulders and tried to turn her round.

'Jo, love, what's the matter? Here, look at me, what's the
trouble?' he said.

She turned round, her eyes wet, her shoulders still shaking

He took his handkerchief out and put his hand under her

chin to raise her head. 'Come on. Where's that old family stiff upper lip?'

She took the handkerchief, smiling wanly through her tears. 'Come on, love.'

'I'm sorry. I'm behaving like a silly girl,' she said with a shake of her head, and dabbing her eyes.

His heart felt as if it would burst to see her standing there drying her tears. He'd never known such love for another human being.

He took a deep breath. He'd been going to wait till he'd got back from the Eiger, but his feelings were too strong to be contained any longer. Holding her head up he looked into her eyes. 'Jo?'

She gave a little sniffle that tore at his heart strings.

'Hang on for a shock, Jo.'

Her eyes widened, warning him that there wasn't much more she could stand.

He took another deep breath. 'I'm going to ask you . . . I mean I *am* asking you to marry me, Jo . . . don't answer now, just say I've given you notice.'

The grey eyes blinked, once, twice. She shook her head, smiling through her tears. 'We Grants don't like to put things off,' she said. 'I'm afraid I'm going to have to give you my answer now.'

He felt his body stiffen.

'The answer's yes.'

'Did you say yes?'

'Didn't you hear me? I thought you were never going to ask, and was wondering if I'd ever have the courage to ask you.'

'But . . . you mean . . . it doesn't worry you . . . I mean, the difference in our ages . . .'

She shook her head helplessly. 'You know, for a grown man, you can be downright silly at times.'

'But Jo . . .' he tried to speak, but something seemed to have gone wrong with his breathing.

She reached up, grasping the lapels of his jacket. The mocking gleam had gone from her eyes and her expression was serious. 'I want to go to bed, Robert.'

'Christ, I'm sorry, Jo. You must be feeling dead beat after all you've been through. I'll . . .'

'I want to go to bed, Robert,' she repeated.

It dawned on him what she was saying, and his lips twisted as if in pain. 'Jo-o,' he pleaded, 'Jo-o. How can you . . . you
249

know I can't . . .' He broke off in pain and embarrassment.

'It doesn't matter. Lovers should share each other's troubles It's going to happen to me at times too, you know, when we have children . . .'

'Jo . . .?' His voice was thick.

'Sshh . . . No matter what happens now, Robert, I'm your wife.'

He followed her slowly into the bedroom.

CHAPTER XXI

He felt very cold. He couldn't remember ever feeling quite as cold as this. Worse, his fears had returned with all their old strength and persistency, costing him valuable energy as he struggled to hold them in check.

Night had fallen to create an ethereal blue world. A silent world of snow and ice. From where he sat, or perched, he could see the dim outlines of the three others, grey, shapeless forms wrapped in their sleeping sacks, reminding him of hibernating animals. It was bitterly cold. He hated to think what it might have been like with a wind blowing. The last time he'd checked the thermometer, and that had been shortly before nightfall, it had shown –30° Centigrade. He'd forgotten, or perhaps he'd never really known, how to convert Centigrade to Fahrenheit, but he had no need of a formula to tell him how cold it was.

It was very, very cold. He'd never known such cold.

Far below, reminding him of a distant fun-fair, the lights of Grindelwald twinkled cheerlessly. And down at the Kleine Scheidegg he fancied he could make out the dark grey shape of the hotel where they had slept only the other night. He would have given almost anything to be safely tucked up there in bed right now.

Next to him, a few feet along the narrow ledge, he heard Dillon stir fitfully and begin to mutter to himself. In the whole expanse of this frightening alien world, Dillon's solid presence was comforting. There was no sound from the other two sacks. Grant and Barrington were obviously sleeping. Wishart knew there would be little sleep for him and it worried him; adding to his fears.

From the moment they'd arrived in Grindelwald from the UK almost a week before, his uneasiness had steadily grown till now his nerves felt like strands of barbed wire planted in his flesh.

Oh God, he recalled the moment when the train had stopped after the long pull up the valley. The others had gathered round the window, pointing eagerly, their voices betraying their excitement. He'd known what they were pointing to and what they were speaking so animatedly about; he'd seen it before.

251

It was the same when they switched trains for the Scheidegg. Grant, Barrington and Dillon had peered out of the window like schoolboys on their first plane trip. He'd sat quietly, pretending to read the opened paperback he held in his hands. Barrington, his eyes widening with respect, had remarked on his coolness, shaking his head in unbelief before resuming his hypnotised stare.

The higher they climbed, the more Wishart was able to feel its presence. By a near magical process it had become something more than a chance geological fold in the earth's crust. He could feel its substance, weight, mass and texture, in the way an animal can sense the presence of another. It was an awareness created by an aggregation of all the senses: tangible and palpable, it had frightened him.

When they got out of the train at the Scheidegg he left the others standing at the station and made straight for the hotel. Only when he dumped his pack in his room did he dare cross over to the window.

He stared for a long moment at the Eiger, before turning away.

He was sharing the room with Dillon and was lying on the bed smoking when Dillon appeared, lugging his pack.

Dillon dumped his pack on the bed and sucked in his breath. 'Ooohh! Did you get a look at that?' He rubbed his hands together. 'I can't wait . . .' He broke off. 'What's the matter Bob? Are you feeling all right? You're not sick, are you?'

Wishart rubbed his forehead. 'No, I'm okay. Bit tired, that's all.'

'Well, you'd better save your strength . . . I think we're going to need it. I'm going downstairs for a pint of that awful bloody beer, fancy it?'

Wishart shook his head. 'You go on, Brian. I'll be down later.'

Dillon came back in ten minutes. He stuck his head round the door, grinning widely. 'I saw the "Tank",' he said. 'He's like us all down for a meeting in the lounge . . .' he examined his wrist-watch, mimicking Grant, 'in exactly one hour's time. And here, Bob, you want to see the bird in the bar. She's a knock-out. Dutch, she was telling me. I asked her if I could be her Uncle but I don't think she got it. See you then,' he said, and vanished only to return a moment later. 'Here, Bob?'

'Yes?' Wishart said irritatedly.

'I forgot to tell you that anoraks will be worn.' He was off too quickly to notice Wishart's annoyance.

Wishart smoked another cigarette before rising. He walked over to the mirror, rubbing his chin. He decided to have a bath and a change of clothes and a shave. He knew he had to try and keep himself occupied and he prayed to God the weather – it had been fine all the way up – would hold and they'd get their practice climbs over and get started. He was in terror of losing his nerve and he knew if he had to hang around it would only make it worse.

He felt a little better after a bath and a shave. Taking unusual care over his appearance he went downstairs. The others were all in the lounge and the Brigadier had his folder with him. Christ! That damned folder! He felt like throwing it in the fire.

Grant ordered coffee for all of them and, seating himself at the head of the table, led off. 'Well, gentlemen, now that we are all here, I would just like to say a few words. We all know what our objective is, so we can leave that for the moment, but what I'd like to say, since we haven't a great deal of time at our disposal, is that, starting from to-morrow, we should begin our acclimatisation programme. I know all of us have had experience in high altitude climbing, but it is quite possible we have different adaptation periods, but perhaps even more important, it will give us our first opportunities to shape a team. I suggest, beginning from to-morrow, as I have already said, that we climb each day when we have the weather, and on the fourth and fifth days of our programme we should carry out an overnight bivouac. I repeat, then, our object is to acclimatise ourselves as quickly as possible to the local conditions, learn to think and work as a team, and at the same time test our equipment. The last item is important. We all know we have the best equipment that science and technology have been able to devise, but nevertheless we must guard against taking anything for granted. I can recall at least one occasion when a brand new karabiner was pulled out of shape from the effect of quite a moderate fall; as a result, the gate sprang open and I don't have to tell you we could have had quite a nasty accident on our hands under more severe conditions. Let me add that the possibility of this sort of thing happening is probably in the order of a million to one, but the lesson must remain for all of us. We take nothing, absolutely nothing, for granted.'

Dillon exchanged a glance with Wishart and winked as Grant went on.

'I realise, of course, that a week is not a great deal of time in

253

which to complete our warming-up programme, but against that we have a considerable amount of experience collectively, enough, I would say, to offset the disadvantages. Now as to our actual programme, and I know we have discussed this before, I'm going to leave the final choice of routes, etc., to Bob here.' (Since the first meeting of the four men in London some weeks before, Grant had insisted they should call each other by their Christian names.) 'Brian, I would like you to check the equipment against our list. You can do that perhaps later this evening, but make sure you do it in either one of our rooms – I don't want anyone in the hotel to see our gear, they may put two and two together and we don't want that. And of course this leads me to the question of secrecy. Whatever happens we don't want a flood of press and television people here, so we must be careful in what we say. Remember that the people here have been living with this situation over a great number of years now, they've developed unusual sensory equipment which enables them to smell out a "North Face" attempt a mile away. So the less said the better.'

'And how about all our gear? Surely they're going to wonder why we've got so much?' Dillon interrupted.

'I thought about that,' Grant said with a little smile, 'I've let the management know we're here to do some filming.'

'Will they buy it, do you think?' said Wishart.

'Perhaps,' Grant replied with a shrug. 'We can only hope, that's all.'

Later that evening Dillon, with Barrington's help, sorted out the gear. It made a massive pile in the small room. Dillon shook his head. 'There's enough here for an expedition,' he grunted as he began opening up the baggage.

'Well, that's what it is, you know. It *is* an expedition. The Brigadier's quite right, we should be thinking of it all the time in those terms.'

Dillon made a face. 'Seems a bloody waste to me. I think the old Brig's a bit potty on organisation.'

Barrington grinned. 'Did you do your thirty press-ups today?'

Dillon snorted. 'It's like a boy-scout camp. Press-ups, skipping, running. I can get all the training I need in the pub, heaving pints.'

'Do you know how long Hiebeler spent preparing?'

'Who?'

'Toni Hiebeler.'

'Oh, the German bloke.'

'He spent nearly a whole year.'

'Waste of bloody time. The same as all this acclimatisation stuff. What are we hanging about for? The weather's good. We should have a crack at the bugger right now, when we have the chance.'

Barrington looked at him in open-eyed astonishment. 'I believe you'd be willing to start out to-night?'

'Why not? It's there, we're here. What are we waiting for?'

Barrington shook his head wonderingly. 'Don't you think that all the work we've put in in the last two months, all the climbing we've done, hasn't been valuable?'

'Hrrmph,' Dillon grunted. 'It might have been if we'd all been climbing together.'

'Oh, I think what the Brigadier and I managed to do in Scotland was of immense value.'

'Mebbe, but I've climbed with Bob before, we don't need any practice,' Dillon replied, but secretly he'd been concerned about Wishart's performance. At times he'd be his old brilliant self, and then suddenly and for no apparent reason he'd go right off and they'd have to change over the lead. In fact, he'd had one or two bad moments causing Dillon to recall the time he'd 'come off' last time they'd been here. But Dillon wasn't given to brooding speculation and had a rock-like confidence in his own ability. He was able to convince himself that once they got cracking his old friend Bob would be all right. 'Anyway,' he said to Barrington, 'let's get this bloody thing over and get downstairs for a pint. Now, what's this we've got here?' He reached into a spare rucksack, heaving the various articles out on to the floor as Barrington checked them off against his list.

'Four miner's lamps with spare batteries . . .' Barrington read, ticking off the item. 'Three red S O S rockets . . . four electric torches . . . one pocket radio . . . one first-aid kit with penicillin syringes and morphine ampoules . . .' he broke off to shudder. 'Hope we won't be needing those. Now, where were we? Ah yes, one altitude meter . . . four pairs of Perlon gaiters and gauntlets . . . ah, four pairs of "special" climbing boots . . . what did you think of those, by the way, Brian?'

'Well, I hope they're as warm as they're supposed to be, because they're damned awkward to climb in. I'd rather use my own boots.'

'And get frostbitten. I think you're a bit of a conservative, you know, Brian.'

'Aye, that votes Labour, or what's supposed to be Labour.'

Barrington laughed. 'Don't let's get mixed up in politics. Now what was that last item again?'

Slowly the two men worked methodically through the list. At last they were finished. Dillon breathed a sigh of relief.

'Well, I'm off downstairs for that pint.'

'Okay, I'll just do a quick double check. I'll be down later. The Brig, I'm sure, will want to have a quick check himself.'

'But we've just done it.'

'You know what he's like, and I think he's right. You can't be too careful.' Barrington approved of most things Grant did.

Downstairs in the lounge Wishart was sitting with the Brigadier in the far corner. There weren't many people in the lounge, but there were some, and Dillon noticed that Grant and Wishart were keeping their voices down. He nodded in their direction and strolled across to the bar.

'Hullo, luv. Got any English beer in yet?'

The barmaid smiled and shook her head. She thought Dillon was amusing, as she thought the Brigadier impressive and Wishart strange; she hadn't made up her mind about Barrington yet.

'Oh well, just give's a pint, or whatever it is, of your own wallop.'

'Vot is wallop?' she asked in a heavy accent. 'I haf not heard.'

'It's beer, luv – English for beer. All beer is wallop, you know?'

She shook her head in mystification.

'Never mind, just let's have it.' Carrying his glass he went across to where Wishart and the Brigadier were sitting.

'Pull a chair up,' said Grant. 'Bob's been suggesting a few things, I'd like to hear your opinion.'

'If it's good enough for Bob, it's good enough for me,' Dillon replied.

'I'm afraid it's not as simple as that.'

Dillon pulled at his beer, wiping the froth from his lips with the back of his hand. 'No?'

'Not quite. What Bob's suggesting is that we should spend one day at least to climb as far as the exit gallery, but I'm not so sure. The moment anyone's spotted on the Wall, the phones are going to start ringing. And we don't want that.'

'We're going to be seen anyway, aren't we?' Dillon said. 'They can hardly miss us up there, stuck right in front of their oses. I don't see how you can avoid it.'

'Granted, but we'll be on the Wall by then. I wouldn't like the press johnnies to get hold of it before the show started. It could be upsetting for all of us if they come swarming about here.'

'Well, why don't you say . . .?' Dillon scratched his chin. 'No, that wouldn't do. I was going to say why don't you let it out we're just here to film the bottom part of the Wall. No, they'd spot it right away.'

'Look,' Wishart stubbed his cigarette out. 'I think it's important to get the feel of the Wall, both physically and mentally. You just can't believe the effect it can have on you. It can take over, sort of swallow you up. It's so . . . so domineering. I know it might sound crazy, but it's true. Most people that have been on the Wall have said the same thing. Believe me, the North Wall's something special, you can't really compare it to anything else.'

'It's an ugly-looking bugger,' Dillon contributed, while Grant went over Wishart's arguments in his mind again.

'You would rate it as important as that?' he said.

Wishart nodded firmly. 'I would. I'd say we'll just have to take a chance on the press finding out. It's more important that we all get the feel of what we're up against.'

'And what do you say, Brian?'

'Same's Bob. Bugger the press. We're going to have to face them anyway,' he answered, little realising how prophetic his words were.

'Right. I accept. So that's three of us in agreement, but I'll have a word with Barrington anyway. Where is he, by the way?'

'Oh, he's still upstairs,' said Dillon. 'He's checking over the gear again.'

'Was everything there?'

'Seems okay,' Dillon replied.

Grant rose. 'I'll just go up and have a quick check.'

'Were you serious, Bob?' Dillon asked when he'd gone. 'I mean about what you were saying about the Wall? You made it sound spooky.'

'It's a fact,' replied Wishart. 'And I'm not just speaking for myself. Remember what Toni Hiebeler had to say about it. Even Heinrich Harrer said that nobody he'd known who'd climbed it ever wanted to go back again. It's that kind of mountain. I'm not joking.'

Dillon flashed a grin. 'That makes you an exception, Bob.'

'You seem to forget we didn't make it,' Wishart replied soberly.

Dillon finished his beer. 'Well, we'll bloody well make it this time, Bob. Can I get you a drink?'

It all seemed a long way from here, now. So detached and removed in fact from the present that there was an unreal, dreamlike quality in its recall.

He wriggled in his sack, feeling the cold probe at his extremities. If only he could have got up and gone for a walk. But there was nowhere you could walk once you were committed to the Wall.

You either went up – or down!

They'd started off early morning. Shortly after two. It had been a long, weary drag across the snow slopes to the foot of the Wall. At that time in the morning the body resented being dragged from bed and forced to take part in strenuous physical exercise. Even Grant with his enormous driving power had found it fatiguing.

Mounting the Wall, they'd climbed steadily, though slowly, till daybreak, when they'd had a short rest. In the heavy, oppressive silence not a man spoke, hugging his thoughts to himself as he plodded upwards. By early afternoon they'd reached a point under the gallery exit. Up above the sky was clear, a hard metallic blue, with only little strands of cotton-wool clouds to mar its pristine appearance.

From here on the climbing became really hard. Luckily the snow was firm, but he found it difficult to keep up the lead. He had to keep forcing himself all the time. Barrington was next on the rope behind him, after that came Grant with Dillon bringing up the rear. From time to time he knew Barrington had looked at him questioningly as if offering to take over, but he'd ignored the looks and pressed on.

God, if this was how he felt like at the beginning, how was he going to feel after five – mebbe even six, or seven – days? It was unthinkable. Dillon could share the lead, of course, but he didn't want that. It wasn't just because he was the only one of the four who'd been on the Wall, but they expected him to take the lead, and if he fell down on it at the very beginning their confidence would be undermined in a way that might put them all in jeopardy. It was more important than anything else that they should keep faith in their ability to conquer what stretched, with seeming infinity, in front of them. No, whatever happened, no matter how he felt, he had to keep up front. He had to go on.

In the shallow confines of the ice-cave they'd dug out, he searched for his cigarettes, his fingers stiff and clumsy as he fumbled in his anorak pocket. With difficulty he got the pack out, his fingers chilled beyond refinement of movement. The cigarettes spilled out on his lap and it seemed to take an age before he'd gathered them up again and stuffed them back into the pack. He had the same trouble with his matches and managed to burn his fingers. The others stirred momentarily as the match sputtered and glowed.

Joanna would be sleeping now. He could imagine her lying still, calm as a sleeping child, her soft breath wafting the strands of hair fallen across her forehead in a gentle rhythmic movement. No, he was wrong. Her sleep would be broken and fitful. She'd be worried about them. It was amazing how she'd taken to Dillon. They'd been like old friends in a matter of hours and . . . and he'd been able to make her laugh; that was important. But there would be no more laughter for her till they all got back safely. God, how he hated her father at times. If it hadn't been for him and his colossal egocentricity, none of them would have been here now and she would be sleeping peacefully.

No, that was wrong, he didn't hate Grant, in fact in some ways he rather liked Iain – yes, it was Iain and Bob now; would it still be the same when all this was over and he told him he was going to marry his daughter?

No, it hadn't been his fault. It was something else, fate, destiny or whatever you wanted to call it, though he didn't believe in these things. No, he didn't believe in them, even though his grandmother had. He had a fleeting vision of her, silver-haired, dressed in black, with a pair of the most wonderful eyes he'd ever seen – except for Jo's, and even then he wasn't so sure – with always a kind and encouraging word for the souls she seemed to gather round about her like stray dogs. She'd been fey, as they said. Yes, she'd known things, his grandmother. He could still remember her warm gentle touch as she'd ruffle his hair, gazing at him with sad lovingness, wishing no doubt that she could protect him from the harshness of the world he was about to grow up in.

When she'd died something went out of his life.

He sucked deeply on his cigarette, watching the tip of it glow redly in the deepness of the night. Jo would have liked his Granny. They would have understood each other. The same kind of material had been used to fashion them both.

Rare material; rarer than gold or diamonds. Look at the time the girl had come running into the house behind the old smiddy, her face distorted with fright and pain. She'd managed to get a steel splinter in her eye, and his Granny had removed it simply and neatly. Not in the usual clumsy fashion with a handkerchief twisted round the tip of a matchstick, no, she'd taken it out with her tongue. With her tongue! Now where could she have learnt a thing like that? It was an act of pure wisdom. What a pity Jo had never had the chance to meet her. She'd have adored her, in the same way she'd have adored Joe, if she'd met him.

Hullo Joe, meet Jo. They'd have got on like a house on fire. No, he didn't believe in fate or anything like that, but it was strange that the two Joes – or should it be Jo's – in his life should have been linked together by a common factor.

Some common factor.

Looking back on it, he supposed it had been on the cards since he had chosen to re-visit Grindelwald earlier in the year. Had he been unconsciously seeking revenge for his defeat? Had the Wall triggered off dark forces within him that sought satisfaction?

God, it was cold. And this was only the beginning. How was he going to be able to face another week of it?

He peered out of the cave. Down below in the valley the lights continued to twinkle. There was a deathly stillness in the chill air. It was as if the Wall was listening to his private thoughts. Let it listen. He only wished he could find sleep, some relief from the continual churn of thoughts in his mind when he should be saving all his energies for the struggle to come.

For the tenth time in as many minutes he looked at his watch. The second hand was moving, it couldn't have stopped. And yet it was only two o'clock. How long was it bloody well going to stay two o'clock? Was this another trick of the Wall? Suspending time? Psychological warfare, was it? Another one of its tricks. Okay, but he was learning. Like the weather. When was it going to pull that one? He knew the answer to that. The weather would remain good. Good, that was, till they reached the 'Spider' – the point of no return. That's when the storms would come. That was the kind of thing the Eiger did to crazy people like himself who had the temerity to challenge it.

He almost cried out loud in protest at the sheer injustice of it. Once at the 'Spider' they'd never be able to get back down in a storm. From there it would mean they'd be inexorably committed to go on – or . . .?

If only they could have the storm now. A real savage one, the kind that only the Eiger can produce. They were only a short distance away from the gallery exit. Even in the very worst storm the mountain could throw at them they could make the exit. And then they would be safe and they could all go back to their homes and get on with the business of living and away from all this madness.

But that wouldn't work either. It would only mean delaying the inevitable. Yes, the inevitable. This was his cross, his punishment for a lifetime devoted to nothing more than the satisfaction of his own egocentric drives. For all the years of his existence he'd thought of nothing but himself. It had always been *his* aims, *his* desires, *his* wishes. No one else had really counted. He'd even tried to fool himself by marrying, but instinctively Penny had known. Right from the start, the marriage had failure written all over it. He'd given his love to the mountains and he'd nothing left over for her or anyone else. That was what Penny had known, that's what her instincts had told her. When the rest of mankind had fought its daily humdrum battles, he'd escaped to his magic world, a world far distant and removed from the commonplace. The only real marital contract he'd entered into was with the world of mountains.

Till death do us part!

He flung his cigarette away, watching it describe an arc, throwing off sparks as it vanished over the precipice.

Dillon, awakened by the noise of the spluttering petrol stove, stirred in his sleeping sack. He blinked, running a huge hand through his hair and pawing his face.

'S'time, Bob?'

Wishart gave the reluctant stove a bit more pressure. 'Time? It's late. It's near eight o'clock.'

The others moved.

Grant was next to emerge from his sleeping bag. He rubbed his eyes and licked his lips. 'What's the weather doing?' he asked typically.

'It's okay, holding,' Wishart said, pumping the stove.

'Good.'

Wishart handed them each containers of hot fruit juice. They drank it eagerly. After that they had a few spoonfuls of stabilised wheat-germ mixed with dried fruit and melted snow water. He handed round the vitamin pills. Breakfast was over.

Grant looked at him closely after inspecting the others.

'All right, Bob? Or would you rather Dillon gave you a spell with the lead to-day?' he said, noticing the tired expression.

'I'm okay. I'll lead,' said Wishart, tight-lipped.

'Fine. When we're ready then. I just want to take some photographs.'

A few minutes later they set off with Wishart in the lead position. Above them bulged the huge wall of the Rote Fluh, looking as if at any moment it would dislodge itself from the mountain and fall upon them.

Almost immediately he found himself in difficulty. Traversing the buttress the snow was firm, but the steep angle and his tiredness had combined to undermine his confidence. He made heavy weather of it all the way. The hours sped by and it was afternoon before they finally reached the Difficult Crack.

He looked up at it. This was going to be hard. They all sensed it. Once again Grant suggested that Dillon might give him a spell.

Wishart shook his head. He'd keep going as long as he could. Dillon could take over later for a bit, but not now.

The others watched anxiously as he led off. The crack was long and exposed; a hundred and fifty feet of ice-glazed rock. He'd gone no more than a few feet when Barrington, who was belaying, felt his heart somersault as he heard the ominous sound of Wishart's crampons tearing at the rock in a wild effort to obtain a foothold. From where he stood he saw the crampons on Wishart's left boot wave about like a strange bird searching for a place to alight.

He held his breath, but a moment later Wishart was moving up again. His movements were fluid and co-ordinated, and he climbed the rest of the crack in brilliant style.

The rest followed, and a few hundred feet farther on reached a steep snow slope. Grant decided they'd done enough for the day. They'd make this their second bivouac.

Dillon got the snow shovel from out of his pack and began hacking away furiously at the snow. It came out in large chunks. Grant and Barrington — Grant insisting that Wishart had done enough for one day — relieved him, and soon they had formed a platform big enough to take all four of them.

It was Barrington's turn to take over the cooking. Wishart got the stove out of his pack and handed it over when they'd

ettled themselves on the platform. Profiting from the experience of the others, Grant had had the foresight to have the
bottom of the stove modified to take three long screw-in legs.
Barrington fitted the legs to the stove and pushed it into the
now. He tested it when the legs had been driven home.

'It's perfect,' he said with a grin. 'You couldn't knock it
over if you tried.'

After a brew of hot soup, fortified with Marmite and
'econ – the Brigadier's and Wishart's idea – they had more
wheat-germ followed by a slice of pemmican to chew upon.

Grant worked his teeth into the dried meat hungrily. 'Mmm
. . Damned good lead, Bob . . . the crack . . . damned good.
Thought that was going to hold us up.'

Barrington grinned. 'I thought Bob was "off" at the start.
But after that, well, it was first-class. You know you did it in
an hour . . . an hour and a bit.'

Wishart grunted and chewed on his pemmican.

Yes, but how long could he keep it up? That was the ques-
ion. Physically he would be OK, he knew that, but the crack
had taken a terrible toll of his mental resources. He'd had to
clamp down on his fears every foot of the way. If once, only
nce, they'd gained control, nothing on earth could have forced
him to move. Dillon and Barrington would have had to come
p and take over. Only the thought of such humiliation had
ept him going – and also the tiny something else away at the
back of his mind that he didn't want to think about. To think
about Joanna would have hurt too much.

Dillon was fiddling about with the radio in the hope of
icking up a weather report. He listened for a minute to the
r ken, disjointed sounds and shook his head. 'Can't under-
tand a word. It's all that foreign lingo.'

'Here, give it to me.'

He handed the small set to Grant who put it close to his
ar, listening carefully. Like Dillon he shook his head.

Wishart looked at him questioningly.

'It's nothing. Some kind of talk on the Common Market.'

'You speak German, Brig?' Dillon alone amongst the others
had chosen to address him by this name. To Wishart's surprise,
Grant had accepted the title, and in fact even seemed to
njoy it.

After the meal they removed their crampons and boots,
covered their feet and got into their bivouac sacks.

Darkness spread over the valley like a flood tide, and the

temperature began to plummet. The four men settled them
selves as comfortably as they could and prepared to face the
long night. An unearthly silence settled over the Wall, broke
only by the animal sound of their breathing.

Soon Grant, Barrington and Dillon had dozed off.

Only Wishart remained awake, quietly smoking from time to
time.

CHAPTER XXII

Dillon awoke with a start. Wishart was tossing about in his sack, straining at the sling which anchored him to their snow-platform like a wild dog trying to slip a leash.

Dillon wriggled an arm free from his own sack. He grabbed Wishart by the shoulder. 'For Christ's sake, Bob. What are you doing?' he whispered.

Wishart came to life. He'd fallen off into a kind of drugged sleep, to enter the world of nightmare and terror. He shook his head. Dillon caught a glimpse of his face, a pale smudge in the darkness, carved by two deep lines running down either side of the nose.

'Okay, Brian. I'm all right . . . just dreaming.'

'Just dreaming? Christ, you were just about off.'

'Don't worry, that piton won't come out.'

Dillon sucked in his breath. 'You've got to get some sleep. Look, how about letting me take over the lead to-morrow? You must be near buggered after to-day. I'll take over to-morrow when we start, and you go last on the rope and take a breather.'

Wishart's head nodded wearily. 'We'll see how it goes to-morrow, Brian. Get back to sleep now.'

Dillon withdrew into his sack and in a few minutes he'd fallen asleep again.

Wishart lit another cigarette, trying to protect his exposed hands from the severe cold. Maybe Brian was right. Maybe he should let him take over the lead next day. He had to think in terms of the party. Could he face another day like to-day? The strain of leading was enormous. He knew it was all wrong, but he couldn't help thinking what might happen if he came off. It just wasn't possible to get sound belays all the time. Some of them, he knew, had been extremely thin. If he'd 'come off' on a belay like that, there would have been little hope for them. One by one they'd have been plucked off the face to plunge into the thin air.

For long hours he wrestled with the problem before managing to doze off.

The next thing he knew, Barrington was shaking him by the shoulder.

'Here you are, breakfast, drink up.'

He struggled out of his sack and took the cup from Barrington, feeling as if he'd only been asleep a few minutes. In fact he'd slept for an hour but it hadn't done much to allay his fatigue. 'Thanks.' He sipped at the hot liquid, ignoring the pain in his chapped lips. Breakfast was the same as before, the same as it would be next time, the same as it would be every day they spent on the Wall.

His body resented being forced out of the bivouac sack, but the sun was up and it was time they were starting again. He felt stiff and his body ached as he bent over to pull on his boots. Even with the quick-release bindings it was a struggle to put on his crampons. He didn't think he'd felt so physically exhausted on a mountain before, except for that time on Dhaulagiri. That had been ... what the hell was he concerning himself with Dhaulagiri for? They were here, on the Eiger! The North Wall! He heard a crackling sound, Grant was fiddling about with the radio again. He reached into his anorak and pulled out the aneroid and inspected it.

'All right, Bob?' Grant called over.

'Steady as a rock.'

'Good.'

'I'm feeling a bit bushed. Brian can take over to-day.'

Grant shot him a keen glance. 'Well, if you don't feel like it,' he said, switching off the radio and putting it back into his pack. 'All right, Brian?' he called out to Dillon who was seated on the far end of the ledge sorting out the rope.

'Sure. Ready to go.'

'Right. Let's get cracking then. We want to get over the Hinterstoisser as soon as we can. With a bit of luck we should make the second ice-field before we pack it in for the day. I'd like to. What do you think, Bob?'

Wishart shrugged. He was miserably cold through lack of sleep, and only wished they'd get on with it. 'Depends on the state of the traverse. Hiebeler's lot had a bad time on it.' He saw no point in adding that the leader had come off whilst negotiating the long, thin traverse which threaded its way under the Rote Fluh.

They moved off at last, Dillon in the lead.

He was slow at first, but in a short space of time began to work up a head of steam. Everywhere the snow was firm and presented no problems. They made good progress.

At last they reached the traverse and stopped. Wishart lit a cigarette and, making sure Grant and Barrington were firmly belayed, went to inspect it with Dillon.

'Not much snow, is there?' said Dillon peering along the traverse.

'Too steep to lie. You'll have to watch the ice. Make sure it's firm before you start banging pitons in.'

Dillon looked at him.

'I know, but it can be deceptive, sometimes there's a gap between the ice and the rock. Don't trust it too much, and be careful.'

'Right. See you all the other side.' Dillon hitched at his waist loop, waiting till Wishart had returned and had taken a belay before moving.

The three men saw the bulky figure, looking even more immense in his bright blue Duvet, step out on the near perpendicular slabs. He made about twenty feet and then he stopped. He called out over his shoulder. 'It's okay, Bob. The ice is firm.'

'Good.' Wishart felt some of the tension go out of his shoulders and neck muscles. The foot of the Wall was a long way down, nearly two thousand feet. Dillon was moving slowly, but his movements were confident and sure. They had one more glimpse of him, his body in a jack-knifed position, feet close to his hands, the points of his crampons and outspread fingers his only contact with the rock, and then he'd vanished as the long traverse curved away towards the ice-field.

After that the only indication of his existence was the sound of the piton hammer. An odd, out-of-place sound on the sepulchral quiet of the Wall.

It came to Wishart's turn to move. He was glad of the rope stretching away in front of him like a ship's handrail. The traverse was viciously exposed, and he was enormously conscious of the empty space under his feet.

The traverse – named after Andreas Hinterstoisser, a Bavarian who, together with his three companions, had been killed way back in '36 whilst pioneering the route – was extremely tricky and called for a high degree of concentration on thin holds. Wishart was a long time on it before joining Dillon on the other side. Barrington came next and then Grant followed.

Wishart watched, his admiration for Grant growing. Grant had a lot of trouble on the traverse, but what he may have lacked in skill he made up for by his incredible fitness and enormous mental drive. Wishart couldn't help thinking that to be climbing Grade VI stuff was an extraordinary accomplishment for a man of his years.

Barrington? He was okay. As a climber. But Wishart couldn't help wondering how he would stand up to the overall nervous strain the Wall would inevitably impose on them before they'd finished. Well, he'd have plenty of time to find out.

It was still early in the day and they had made good progress. What they faced now was a steep band of rock split in part by a stream of ice pouring over it from the ice-field above. En route they halted for a quick bite and a rest at the airy and exposed 'Swallow's Nest'. Barrington and Grant opened up their packs and unloaded 300 feet of spare nylon, slings, snap-links, pitons and a quantity of food; their insurance against retreat. Grant straightened up. 'Well, that's our line of retreat prepared,' he said, looking up at the cold blue sky above his head.

Barrington misinterpreted the look on his face. 'Yes,' he said, 'it seems such an awful waste to leave such good equipment behind.'

Grant's brows came down fractionally. 'The biggest mistake you can make is to take anything for granted. That sort of thing has cost a lot of people their lives on the Face. If Hinterstoisser had taken the same precautions we're taking now, he might have been alive to-day. Always cover your line of retreat.'

Barrington flushed slightly at the rebuke. To hide his discomfiture he looked away. A moment later he cried out: 'Look, down there at the Scheidegg.'

They all turned to look.

Far below, the cluster of buildings looking like match-box toys, they saw what had attracted his attention. Around the buildings they saw the glint of binoculars and telescopes.

'Damn it!' Grant swore. 'They're on to us. I suppose the next thing will be aircraft. They'll be bound to fly up in this good weather. What a damned nuisance.'

Wishart shrugged. 'They were bound to spot us eventually,' he said laconically and without surprise. So, they'd been spotted. What the hell difference did that make now?

They moved off again.

Surmounting the barrier to reach the second ice-field was a tough problem but, though it took Dillon a long time, he led it well, creating an impression of safety by the sureness and soundness of his methods. Wishart realised how valuable this was as a psychological factor. If even the hardest bits could be made to look safe, it was an advantage to those following.

But it was late by the time they'd gained the second ice-field.

Grant joined Wishart to have a word with him. It was agreed that they'd make their bivouac here for the night in spite of the fact they had almost another two hours of daylight in front of them.

Barrington couldn't believe they were stopping. 'But we could be across the ice-field in no time,' he remarked to Wishart as they unpacked.

'That happens to be three times farther than you imagine it is,' Wishart answered, and was immediately sorry for having spoken so abruptly. Barrington's attitude was understandable. He was young and under compulsion to keep going, without the need to give too much thought to what might lie ahead. He'd been like that himself at Barrington's age. If you were lucky you got away with it. If you were lucky enough to live through it, then it could be said you'd really learned the hard way. 'Look,' he added, 'distances are deceptive on the Wall. That's a lot farther than it looks. We'd end up climbing in the dark.'

Barrington's expression seemed to say, so what, he'd climbed in the dark before.

'Okay, suppose we get two-thirds of the way. We're in darkness and the weather changes. What then? On the Wall you play everything the safe way.'

Barrington turned away and began to unpack his kit.

Dillon leaned over. 'What was all that about?' he whispered. Wishart shook his head.

Dillon shrugged indifferently and got on with his own unpacking.

They had to hack out another platform. The snow was frozen to near ice – a much harder task to excavate. Despite having led all day, Dillon insisted on having first go at digging. Wishart signalled to Grant, who was about to protest, to let him get on with it. He knew how Dillon was feeling, and the exercise would help to release the inevitable build-up of tension that resulted from a hard lead. As long as he was still strong it was all right. And Dillon *was* strong, you only had to look at the way he swung the axe to realise the immense power locked up in his bulky frame. Chips of ice flew about everywhere, singing through the air like tiny frozen birds and launching themselves down the steep face in parabolic curves.

Barrington prepared the meal as they took their places side by side on the platform.

'Well, another good day,' Grant said when they'd finished.

269

'Well done, Brian. I must say I'm pleased with the way things are going up to now. Everyone in good health?' he queried. 'No complaints?'

'Yeh, me.' It was Dillon.

Grant bent forward on his narrow seat to catch a glimpse of Dillon. 'What is it?' he asked anxiously.

'I want to go on sick leave.'

Grant joined in the joke. 'I'm afraid that won't do. Sorry, Dillon, you're not going to be excused parades. Next man.'

Everyone laughed except Wishart. He'd been struggling to get his nerves under some sort of control. Dillon's leading had been a help and had taken a lot of the strain off him, but he knew he would have to take over again the next day. He couldn't leave it all to Brian. He wondered how he'd react to being on the ice-field again.

It had been a long time ago, nearly three years, but he could still shudder to think about it. That awful storm. How they'd ever managed to get back over the Hinterstoisser Traverse he couldn't remember, but it had been some kind of miracle. Well, here he was back on the Wall again, something he'd sworn he'd never do. This was it. With the rock-band and the traverse behind them they were irretrievably committed.

Even now, after all the long study and his experience at close hand, he still couldn't get over the Wall's terrifying magnitude and steepness. He'd read somewhere at some time that nuclear physicists had deduced the existence of anti-particles, anti-matter in fact; well, here on the Wall was anti-life. Not a single living thing was in sight, neither fauna nor flora, in the whole width and height of its desolation. It was a picture of Hell.

Well, he would have his own private hell to-morrow on the ice-field. Of that he was sure.

Once again it was well towards dawn before he managed to get any sleep, and once again he was wakened by Barrington with a hot mug of breakfast brew. His teeth were chattering as he took the cup from Barrington's outstretched hand.

Dillon, who was seated next to him on the ledge, asked: 'How's your feet, Bob? Okay?'

'Cold.'

'Why don't you take some of your Ronicol tablets? You don't want to get frostbite.'

Wishart shook his head. He had an aversion to tablets anyway, and would only ever use them in extreme emergency.

'I'll be all right,' he said, and seeing Dillon was still concerned, added placatingly: 'Mebbe I'll try a couple later.'

'Take them now, Bob,' Dillon urged.

But Grant had leaned forward so that he could see beyond Barrington who was blocking his view.

'What's the barometer say?'

With an effort Wishart got it out. 'Still steady,' he answered.

'Good. We're certainly having luck with the weather.' Grant sounded confident and enthusiastic. 'If it holds, we should be able to make "Death Bivouac" by to-night, shouldn't we?'

Wishart nodded. 'Should do.'

At that moment all their attention was diverted by a roaring sound which seemed to come from deep inside the face itself.

It sounded like an avalanche!

Dillon jumped to his feet, pointing.

It was so unexpected they couldn't believe it. At first they thought it was a giant bird. But passing within a hundred or so feet, the aeroplane dipped its wings in salute and they caught a glimpse of the pilot waving his arms. They were to see the plane twice more that day.

'Damned nuisance,' Grant said angrily. 'Why do they have to interfere?'

Wishart ignored the outburst. He turned to Dillon. 'I'll take over this morning.'

Dillon looked at the tired eyes, the expression of deep strain. 'Sure, Bob?'

'The ice-field shouldn't give us any trouble,' he said with a cracked grin. 'As a favour I'll leave the "Ramp" to you – if you want.'

'It doesn't sound like a favour the way you said it.'

'It's probably the hardest bit on the Wall. But we'll see how it goes to-day.'

They packed once more and fastened on their crampons, sorting out the seeming miles of rope. They could still hear the sound of the aeroplane's engine receding in the distance.

The snow was in near perfect condition. He had no need to cut steps and was able to crampon his way up the steep inclination. A great saving in time and energy. A hundred feet or more behind him Dillon came up on the double nylon, followed by Barrington, Grant bringing up the rear.

They made good progress, though the field, smooth as a starched tablecloth viewed from their last bivouac, was in fact broken into humps, mounds and depressions, with one rise no sooner negotiated than another one appeared to take its place.

But there were no real difficulties here. Steep, yes, but certainly the least troublesome part of the Wall.

Last time Wishart had climbed it, the three of them had been under a continual barrage of stones and rubble winging out from the 'Spider' high above, to plummet down the ice-field with the semblance of an artillery bombardment. But he didn't want to think about that.

The comparative easiness of the ice-field had given him a chance to bring his jangling nervous system under control, and for a brief period in time he came near to enjoying the old thrills of climbing and the sense of freedom and lofty detachment created by an eagle's-nest view of the world far below.

Some of this feeling communicated itself to Dillon, who waved his hand and gave the thumbs-up sign in a boyish gesture.

Wishart raised his hand fractionally in acknowledgement. He'd just turned and was about to go on when he heard a strangled cry. He swung round quickly. Dillon had flung his weight against his ice-axe.

Below them Barrington was a confused jumble of legs and arms as he slid down the polished ice-field.

Wishart felt no shock, no fear. In one quick glance he took in the situation and appraised it. Dillon and Grant would check the fall.

Barrington, somersaulting as the points of his crampons bit into the hard snow, halted. Grant and Dillon had him securely on the rope.

Barrington, his fall checked, regained an upright position. He bent down, shaking his head. To Wishart's horror he saw something dislodge itself from his boot.

He yelled out at the same time as Dillon.

One of Barrington's crampons had come out of its bindings, and with gradually increasing velocity was slithering down the ice-field.

Grant reacted quickly.

'Hold me!' he shouted to Barrington; at the same time he whipped his ice-axe free, and half running, half sliding, launched himself across the slope.

Barrington's crampon had been sent off at a tangent by the configuration of the ice-field. It was an act of good fortune.

Grant, plunging across the ice-field, was able to stretch out hand and grab it.

Unlike the older man, Barrington's reaction had been fractionally slow. Grant's sudden movement had thrown him off balance before he was able to get his ice-axe into the snow.

Wishart watched, helplessly, and both men slithered away, kicking wildly.

Everything depended on Dillon.

If Dillon 'came off', Wishart knew he'd never be able to check the fall of the three men.

But Dillon was like a rock. Thrusting his full weight against his anchored ice-axe, his body acting like a bollard for the rope, he was able to absorb the shock of the slip.

The danger was checked.

Grant was the first to recover. He climbed back up to Barrington and handed him back his crampon.

Barrington fastened it back on his boot, and both men climbed back to their original stance.

They were too far away for Wishart to be able to see their faces. He was sure Grant would be all right, but he was concerned about Barrington. Had the slip upset him? But, more important, how had he managed to fall anyway? The question worried him. Had it not been for Grant's quick – though risky – action, Barrington would have lost his crampon. That would have been serious! Without its aid he would have been little more than a passenger. And the North Wall was no place for passengers.

Thank God the powerful Dillon had kept his head. But for that, they'd have been at the very bottom of the Wall by now, smashed to pulp.

When they were ready, he set off again. He was glad to reach the arête under the Spider.

But here he found it hard-going on the snow-glazed rock of the ridge. He had to concentrate hard to keep going.

At long last he came to the spot known as 'Death Bivouac'. It was here that the first two men to attempt the North Wall – Sedlmeyer and Mehringer – had lost their lives. They'd been found frozen to death in their steps. But he put the thought from his mind as he halted and brought the rest of the party up.

He was feeling nervous and depressed again as they sorted themselves out at the bivouac.

Grant's mouth was a tight line as he unhitched his pack. Wishart guessed his thoughts. They were the same as his own. Why had Barrington slipped? He'd had a perfectly good

273

stance. He'd been belayed. So how had he managed to slip? There was no logical answer. And that was the worrying thing

Wishart decided to leave it to Grant. If he didn't say any-thing, then he'd forget about it. No, not forget about it. You couldn't forget about a thing like that. Barrington had made a serious error somewhere. From now on he'd have to be watched. You might get away with one slip on the Face. You wouldn't get away with two. But he'd leave it to Grant.

Grant's first intention was to have it out with Barrington as soon as they arrived at the bivouac. He was smouldering with anger. Anyone could have an accident. Despite the most careful planning, they happened. But this accident had been caused by carelessness. Yes, it had only been a momentary lapse, but it could have cost all of them their lives.

But when he looked at Barrington, prepared to blister him, he saw by the look in the younger man's eyes he was suffering agonies of guilt. Grant realised to serve him with a rocket would only further humiliate him. Nothing was to be gained by that. To apply the lash to Barrington now would only add to his misery, disturb his mental equilibrium further and, as a result, weaken the effectiveness of the party as a whole.

He decided to say nothing to him.

CHAPTER XXIII

During the long, cold night it snowed. Wishart, on the verge of an exhausted sleep, was wakened by the soft powder snow seeping into his sack. He opened his eyes in alarm, thrusting his head out of the sack. For the first night since they'd been on the Wall, he was unable to see the stars overhead. Something else was missing. It puzzled him at first, before the realisation came that the something missing was the lights of Grindelwald below.

A fresh wind had also risen, lowering the temperature even further. Fumbling in his sack, he found the torch and then the barometer.

To his dismay he found it was falling.

There was no point in waking the others. There was nothing anyone could do about it. He put the torch and the barometer back and snuggled into his sack, trying to find sleep.

Grant was the first to awake in the morning.

He popped his head out of his sack, frowning heavily.

The dry powder snow of the night had given way to large, wet flakes, dropping listlessly from the slate-grey arch of the sky. The wind had gone and there was an eerie, still silence.

Wishart anticipated his question. 'It's down a couple of points,' he volunteered.

'How long has it been snowing?'

'Three – four hours, perhaps. But the wind's dropped.'

'What was that . . . what's happening?' Dillon's head poked out. He saw it was snowing. 'Aw hell,' he cursed. 'What did it have to go and do that for?'

'How do you read it?' Grant asked Wishart, as Dillon looked about him in disgust.

'I don't know,' he replied guardedly. 'It was blowing earlier on, from the West.'

'Is that bad?' It was Dillon who asked.

'It's not good.'

Grant shook Barrington, and in a few minutes the little spirit stove was purring briskly.

Silently and anxiously the four men drank their hot fruit juice, cursing the weather in the privacy of their thoughts. Even the normally phlegmatic Dillon was affected. 'Blast this

bloody snow,' he cried, wriggling uncomfortably in his sack. '
gets in every bloody where.'

They finished off their breakfast and took their vitamin pill
one vital question dominating their minds. During the length
discussions prior to setting out, it had been universally agree
that if bad weather caught them before reaching the Spid
they would retreat.

What would they do now?

It was Grant who formulated the thoughts passing throug
their minds.

Rubbing his stubbly chin, he said: 'There's nothing we ca
do but sit it out for the moment. When this clears, we'll hav
to reappraise the whole situation.'

'And if it doesn't?' asked Barrington in a voice tinged wi
uncertainty.

'We go down. It'll be jolly hard in this stuff, but there yc
are,' he said, unable to hide his deep disappointment.

Wishart held on to his thoughts.

'How long do we wait?' It was Dillon's question.

'I propose we give it twenty-four hours. If it doesn't im
prove . . .?' Grant shrugged helplessly.

Wishart was aware that they were waiting for him to sa
something. He remained silent. What was there to say? Eith
the storm passed or it didn't. There was nothing any of the
could do. He lit a cigarette, peering into the soft whirling mas
feeling the intensity of the cold.

But by noon it had stopped snowing. Magically the sky ha
cleared. It was as though they had come through a long da
tunnel into the light. Everyone's spirits lifted.

Wishart looked at the barometer again. It had remaine
steady.

'All right?' Grant asked. 'We've lost a bit of time, but not
ing serious. Shall we get cracking?'

They sorted themselves out in preparation for the hard da
that lay in front of them. Ahead was the hardest part of t
climb – the Ramp. The great bulge of rock hadn't been improve
by the fall of snow. It was going to test them to the limit.

Wishart roped up.

'I thought I was going to lead?' Dillon reminded him.

Wishart hesitated. He'd been preparing himself mentally
morning, trying to force his mind to accept the unacceptabl
The thought of the Ramp scared him, and he felt tired ar
cold. Avoiding Dillon's gaze, feeling the guilt gnaw at him,
untied.

Dillon grinned, his lips blue and cracked. 'You did promise, Bob. Anyway, I'm dying to get warmed up.'

They moved off.

They knew it was going to be a hard day, as they started off, traversing the steeply-angled third ice-field. Fortunately the slope was too steep to retain the freshly fallen snow, but the surface, though clear, was as hard and as polished as marble. They had to piton their way across with great care.

By the time they had reached the projecting rock-buttress and made the slight descent to approach the beginning of the Ramp, they were all feeling the strain.

After a breather, Dillon led off again. The start up a long, narrow snow and ice-filled gully wasn't too difficult, but as the angle increased, progress became slower. Within the protective walls either side of the gully, the snow had found lodgement, and Dillon spent a great deal of time clearing away loose snow.

Coming up behind, Wishart had to wait for long periods. He felt frozen to the very marrow of his bones, the blood flowing sluggishly through his veins. There was an odd sensation in his right foot, the first warning sign of frostbite. He decided he'd better take some of his Ronicol tablets whenever Dillon found his next belay.

A few minutes later he heard Dillon's voice echo down the gully.

It was time to move again, but first, removing his two pairs of gloves, he managed to get out the packet of tablets from the top pocket of his anorak.

He'd taken one and was just about to take another when the packet slipped out of his hand. He watched it bounce down the gully, the tablets spilling out. Barrington made a grab for it but missed, and it was gone.

Wishart swore under his breath. He put his glove back on and, with a signal to Dillon that he was starting, moved off, wondering how many tablets the others had between them.

All afternoon they toiled up the Ramp. The light was beginning to fail and they still had a long way to go.

They halted.

Barrington and Grant came up to where Wishart and Dillon had taken their stance.

'Can't do much more to-day.' Grant looked about him. 'Hiebeler said there's a good spot for a bivouac here, but I'm damned if I can see anything, can any of you?'

'Mebbe it's a bit farther up,' suggested Dillon.

'All right. Let's give it another few minutes. If we haven
found anything by then, we'll just have to make the best o
it, but I can't say it looks all that promising.'

Once again they moved off tiredly, none of them relishin
the prospect of a long night without a good bivouac. They'
been lucky up till then. It looked now as if their luck wa
deserting them.

It was nearly dark before Dillon finally called a halt.

"S'no good,' he cried. 'We'll have to pack it in for the day
The others came up.

Grant shook his head. 'It's going to have to be here, then
he said, casting about him hopefully. 'I'm afraid we're in fo
a rather uncomfortable night.'

They unpacked. From below, Barrington was able to get i
an ice-screw and belay himself and Grant.

'Not much here,' grunted Dillon, looking for a belay.

Wishart felt like telling him to hurry up, but Dillon soo
found something. In a moment the noise of his hammer ran
out as he banged a small piton into the rock.

'Okay?' asked Wishart impatiently.

"S'not much, but it'll have to do. Can you see anything?'

Wishart, a few feet below Dillon, had been examining th
rock for some slight fissure or crack since arriving at th
stance. He shook his head.

'Well, that's it, then. We'd better take turns at sleeping.
Dillon said with a laugh. 'I wouldn't like to trust this littl
bugger too much.'

Wishart craned his head back to look up. He saw the smal
piton, only half its length inserted into the rock. 'Christ,' h
swore, 'is that all you could get, Brian?'

'It'll be all right, don't worry.'

Don't worry? He turned to shout down to Barrington: 'Ho
are you down there?'

'Okay. What's the trouble?'

'Look, bang another piton in, will you? It's a bit hairy u
here.'

'Okay.' Barrington selected another ice-screw from his slin,
and drove it home. 'How's that?'

'Fine.' Wishart bent down. 'Here,' he said, passing him
loop of rope, 'hitch this through, will you?'

Barrington slipped a snap-link over the eye of the lon,
metal screw and, taking the rope-end from Wishart, slipped
through the gate.

'Okay, that's fine,' grunted Wishart. He and Dillon wer

w anchored to both pitons. Next he took a spare sling from
und his shoulder and, forming it into two loops, stepped into
It was a sort of bosun's chair and provided a more com-
rtable support in their exposed position. Dillon did the same.

Barrington had got the stove out. He had some difficulty
ding a place to set it up, but finally, excavating some loose
ow, he was able to expose a flat piece of rock no bigger than
tea-plate. But it would have to do. There was no other place
r the stove.

Within a few minutes he'd got it going and brewed each
them a cup of beef essence.

Wishart cursed as he was forced to get out of his slings
ain to reach the cups Barrington handed up. Moving care-
lly so as not to spill any of the liquid, he passed a mug up
Dillon.

The hot beef essence was no more than a brief moment of
easure in the long night that followed. It didn't snow again
d the barometer was holding its own, but in their cramped
sition, half-seated, half-standing, it was impossible to rest
operly. Throughout the night all four of them kept turning
d twisting to ease their discomfort. But the hardest thing of
was in the morning, when they got out of their sacks to
sten on their crampons. Their limbs, stiff and frozen, resented
e acrobatic movements required for the task. Wisely, Grant
sisted on a 'one man at a time' procedure. In this way the
an nearest him was able to help, and should anyone have
opped his crampon – a disaster they didn't want to think
out after the near thing with Barrington the day before –
least it gave one or more of the others a chance to grab it
fore it slid down the narrow gully and ended up at the foot
the Wall, 4,000 feet below.

Wishart made no protest when Dillon offered to take over
e lead once more. He was very tired, and his limbs ached
ominably. The vicious cold and lack of sleep had taken a
out of him. It wasn't till they'd started off he remembered
hadn't taken his anti-frostbite tablets. And, having remem-
red, it took a few minutes for it to sink into his dulled mind
at he'd lost them. He'd have to ask Barrington or Dillon for
me of theirs. But though his right foot suffered from a
mbing sensation again – a warning of incipient frostbite –
forgot all about his trouble in face of the problems on the
per half of the Ramp.

The going was ferociously hard. He doubted if he could
ve led it. Dillon was magnificent, climbing brilliantly on

279

thin holds on ice-glazed rock, the 'lobster claws' of his cram
pons thrusting forward, seeking every little purchase li
probes, and where it was really bad he'd cut steps for t
others coming. It was exhausting work. Wishart wondered ho
long Dillon would be able to keep it up.

They were climbing at a snail's pace now. Every foot
rock gained, an effort. Despite the intense cold, Dillon w
sweating heavily. He mopped his brow as he brought Wisha
up to a stance just below an enormous bulge of ice whic
thrust out like the bulbous prow of a warship.

'All right, Bob?' Dillon said with a tired grin.

'How are you?' Wishart looked at him anxiously, knowin
how hard the lead must have been.

'Could do with a pint. Bloody hard work this. Must be ne
the top of the bugger by now, are we?'

'Not long to go now.'

'How's Barrington and the Brig? Any complaints?' Dill
laughed at his own joke.

'Okay,' Wishart replied, but in fact he hadn't liked the loo
of Barrington. Maybe he was suffering from the delayed sho
of his fall or it could be general fatigue, but whatever it w
he'd noticed the drawn strained expression, as if he were
pain. He wondered if Grant had also noticed it. 'We'll have
rest here,' he said to Dillon, 'we can bring the others u
There's room. How are you feeling?' he added.

'I'm okay.'

'You don't want a spell? You're not tired, are you?'

'Aaagh. Tired? I could do this bugger on roller-skate
Dillon snorted.

Barrington joined them and clipped on to Wishart's sna
link, shouting down to Grant to come on.

He was feeding the rope round his body as he belaye
the Brigadier.

Wishart leaned closer to him. 'You all right?' he sa
quietly. 'Didn't hurt yourself yesterday did you?' he aske
keeping his voice low.

Barrington half-turned, keeping his eye on Grant as he too
in the rope. 'No. I'm okay. Bit cold though,' he said ar
gave an odd, nervous laugh.

'Well, take some of your tablets,' Wishart advised, at t
same time remembering. 'Incidentally, you could let me ha
a couple when you're at it. I lost mine yesterday.'

Barrington gave him a frightened, guilty look.

Wishart frowned. 'What's the matter?'

Barrington looked down. The Brigadier was still some way below. He half-turned to Wishart again. 'I don't have any,' he said in a half whisper so's Dillon wouldn't hear.

'What do you mean, you don't . . . you don't mean to tell me you've finished them already?' Wishart asked with some alarm.

Barrington shook his head. 'I don't know what happened. I was sure I put them in my anorak . . .'

Wishart exhaled deeply. He called to Dillon. 'Brian,' he said, 'how many Ronicols do you have left?'

'Ronicols? Hang on.' He reached into his anorak and produced a small plastic container. 'Here you are. There's a lot left. I've only taken a couple. What do you want them for, anyway?'

'I lost mine yesterday.' Wishart jerked his head towards Barrington. 'He forgot his.'

Dillon unscrewed the cap and spilled them out. Wishart took half. Half of these he gave to Barrington. 'Here,' he said, 'don't do what I did. Look after them. You might need them. As a matter of fact, if you're feeling that cold, take a couple now.'

'Thanks. I will.' Barrington swallowed a couple of the tablets eagerly and carefully put the remainder in the pocket of his Duvet.

Grant came up. He looked like a man who had shed a lot of weight too quickly. He was obviously fatigued, and was forcing himself on by the power of his will. There was a grey look about his face that Wishart didn't like. Normally the Brigadier's skin was a healthy, brick-coloured red. He'd never seen him look like this before.

Grant paused to get his breath back. 'Magnificent, Brian,' he said. 'Absolutely superb, you know I don't think I've ever tackled anything harder than that.'

'It's not finished yet,' Wishart reminded him coolly with a glance upwards at the bulge of ice.

'Well, we'd better get on with it,' replied Grant. 'It's getting late.' He seemed to have recovered quickly, even some of his colour had come back.

Dillon looked at Wishart who nodded.

'Here goes,' Dillon eased his bulk on to the ice.

It appeared to all of them below that Dillon was climbing on virtually nothing. Only the very points of his crampons were in contact with the smooth, glistening ice. Despite this he still managed to cut an occasional step in the ice so that they would benefit when it came to their turn to tackle the bulge. He'd reached a point about thirty feet above their heads when he called out over his shoulder: 'Look out, Bob, I'm coming off!'

Wishart just had time to brace himself before Dillon came hurtling down. He hit the stance with a sickening thud, regained his balance momentarily, slid again and was off down the gully, the points of his crampons catching in the ice and somersaulting him over.

He'd gone another fifteen feet before Wishart was able to check the fall. Barrington's and Grant's features were frozen into agonised expressions.

Dillon regained his feet and came up the gully like an engine. 'Fuck it,' he swore, 'the bastard.' Without waiting, he'd launched himself again at the bulge before Wishart could restrain him.

Within a short space of time, so short in fact that it was possible for the three men to doubt the evidence of their eyes, he was back to the spot where he'd fallen and once more moving upwards.

Minutes later he sang out that he had a belay and that it was okay to come up.

Wishart, still not recovered from the shock, moved off nervously. The ice thrust at him and he had the greatest difficulty retaining his balance. The thick bulge was virtually holdless, all that could be said was that it contained a number of flaws in its otherwise smooth, unbroken surface. With the exception of the places where Dillon had cut steps, he had to kick the points of his crampons in all the way. His calf muscles ached and his breathing in the high, thin air was laboured.

Dillon's face was set in angry determination as if resolved to get even for his humiliating experience. He merely nodded to Wishart, and no sooner was he belayed than he was off again like a goat.

Despite their rapid rate of progress, occasioned by Dillon's furious burst of energy, it was darkening when they cleared the bulge.

They were all so exhausted that they could have flung themselves down where they stood. But there was no provision for such luxuries here. They had to go on.

A short but quite steep ice-slope led away to a band of rock above. It was a relief after the strain of the bulge, but even then their tired limbs made heavy weather of it. Dillon had finally run out of steam and was plodding his way up sluggishly and without drive.

'Keep to the right,' Wishart called out as he saw Dillon heading straight up. Dillon didn't hear him and kept plodding on.

'To the right,' Wishart yelled again, turning to Grant. 'He's going the wrong way. We'll come out too high for the Spider.'

All three of them yelled.

Dillon stopped.

Wishart flung his arm out, pointing. There was a long pause before the message sank in and Dillon began to traverse the ice-field, moving now under a large rocky overhang. He found a belay when he reached the rock and brought Wishart up.

'Are you sure we're right?' Dillon asked as Wishart joined him. He sounded doubtful.

'Go up that way and we'd only have had to come back down again.' He looked up at the sky around him, shaking his head despairingly. 'Not much good here for a bivouac. It's worse than last night's, and that was bad enough.'

Dillon muttered his agreement.

'Okay, we'll bring the others up first, then you can have a look. But we'll have to hurry, it'll be pitch dark soon, there's a lot of cloud about.'

Grant examined their stance. Like Wishart he shook his head. 'Not very pretty, is it?'

'We'll have to take a chance. Brian can push on a bit farther. If there's nothing doing he can come back.'

'Very well, but I shouldn't push it beyond a rope's length,' Grant said, switching to address Dillon.

'Don't worry, I'm not too keen on wandering about here in the dark, Brig.'

'Shall I go?' Wishart asked, feeling he should have volunteered anyway.

'Get off with you, I was only joking. See you.' Without another word he was off.

A few minutes later they could hear his voice calling. It sounded muffled and distant, but from the length of the rope out it was obvious he couldn't have gone far, sixty, perhaps seventy feet.

It was quite dark now.

'Be careful, Bob,' Grant warned as he prepared to join Dillon.

'Don't worry,' he replied, gripping the rope, though he felt far from happy. He should have had his lamp out, but the thought of removing his pack and having to go to all the

283

bother of fitting it to his helmet was too much for his tire
spirit. All he wanted to do was to find some place and res
His body was screaming out with fatigue. He would hav
given anything for one solitary hour of sweet oblivion, t
shut out this nightmare world and its oppressive atmospher
that he felt was slowly choking the life out of him. If h
didn't get some sleep soon he would be unable to go on
Gathering together what energy remained, he stepped ou
into the inhospitable, alien darkness.

Cautiously he made his way along the traverse. Dillon wa
waiting for him.

'It's okay, Bob. On you come. I've got a belay here tha
would hold the *Queen Mary*. Steady as you go, now, you'r
all right.'

A few minutes later, when he'd joined Dillon, a bobbin
ghostly light, oddly out of place here, indicated Barrington'
approach. Both he and Grant had taken advantage of th
time spent waiting to don their miner's lamps.

Where they now found themselves was on a narrow ledge
What lay beyond they could only guess at, for a few fee
farther on the buttress fell away back to create an empt
black void, merging with the vastness of space under thei
feet. Though weary and chilled to the bone, they took grea
care to fasten themselves to the rock.

Even had it been possible, they were much too tired to cook
Chewing on dried meat they wearily removed their crampon
and struggled into their sleeping sacks.

It was their fifth night on the mountain, and of all th
nights the coldest. Shortly after midnight it began to blow,
thin chilling wind with an edge like a knife. Wishart felt it
and it brought him out of a netherland half way between slee
and consciousness. His teeth were chattering uncontrollably. I
seemed to him that the relentless cold had invaded his bod
and was slowly and surely driving the force of life within hin
back to its last line of defence. If the cold ever reached ther
it would be the end. Already he felt that parts of him wer
dead: his arms, legs, the area of his back and shoulders. An
yet they couldn't be. He could still feel them, even though th
feeling was one of pain and the resentment of the flesh a
being subjected to conditions outside the range within whicl
life could reasonably hope to continue.

He couldn't understand why he was here. Was he bein
punished for some terrible offence he'd committed? Was thi
some terrible form of crucifixion? Why was he, of all th

millions of earth's inhabitants, lashed to the face of this awful precipice two miles above the surface of the earth. Why was he being punished in this way? And yet if he knew where he was, it followed he must know why he was there. That was logical. And where was Joe? What the hell had happened to Joe that he wasn't here? Why had Joe deserted him? They'd set out together, hadn't they?

He felt angry and disappointed about Joe. Joe had always been his closest friend and now he'd just pissed off and left him. That was a bit rough. You've no damned right to leave me, you know I'll never do it on my own, he felt like yelling out. But instead he frowned, twisting his head to try and bring into focus the thing that had entered his mind from such a disturbingly oblique angle.

So Joe had deserted him, but what about the other Jo, the one spelled without an 'e'? Had she deserted him too? No, that was impossible. This was no place for her. That's why she wasn't here. God, you couldn't expect *that* Jo to be here. But why hadn't she been in touch with him? Where was she, anyway? They'd been walking, they'd come down off the hill, and were walking along by the river and she'd pushed him in. Why did she do that? It wasn't like her. She'd pushed him in the river. He remembered he'd been soaking wet and Jo . . . she'd been laughing. He could see her there on the bank, standing laughing at him. But that was impossible, how Jo, with those incredible calm grey eyes, could do a thing like that when . . . no, of course she hadn't. He almost laughed in relief. It had been the salmon that had pushed him in, or rather dragged him in. Jo had in fact been helping him. How could he have thought that of her? Jo would always help him, if he gave her the chance. His Granny had told him. He could trust Jo, and who in the whole world was wiser or kinder than his Granny? But could that be right? Jo had never met his Granny. He puzzled over this for a long time, but gave up as a more significant problem occupied his mind. It was odd, but why did Jo remind him of a dolphin? A dolphin, did she remind him of a dolphin? Yes, she did, because she was warm-blooded, full of life, cheerful and the possessor of a great fund of wisdom and dignity. It was simple to understand, really. He'd read a book about dolphins somewhere. Such interesting creatures. They didn't destroy each other, like men, nor did they perform their playful tricks for material rewards. That was beneath their dignity. They performed because they liked performing. The dolphins were wise, clever and compassionate, perhaps they were the true inheritors of the earth. Well, that was okay with him, because Jo was one of them and she was only on loan to the race to teach them about living before it was too late.

Perhaps it was too late. Perhaps they were all lost. He'd been lost and look what had happened to him. He'd been taken to this awful place and left to die. Left to die in this awful cold.

Still, it wouldn't be long now. The pain and suffering would soon be over, though he still wasn't quite sure why he was being punished so cruelly. He'd never been selfish really, only self-centred. Surely there was a difference; it should be taken into account. Perhaps if he'd met Jo earlier . . . perhaps, perhaps. It was such a pity he wasn't going to see her again, he could have cried, only you weren't supposed to cry. Why are you shaking your head, Jo? You know I'll never make it now. We could have been married, too. I'd have liked that very much. Mebbe I would even have written that book – a real book – that you said I should. Too bad we didn't get married, Jo. Too bad about lots of things. If only I'd been able to . . . what was it they said in their legalistic jargon? oh, yes, consummate our love, that was the phrase, if only I'd been able to do that, it would have at least been something. It would have been our marriage without a marriage, you might say. So what all the confetti's about is not a very funny joke, is it? Confetti?

He shivered deeply. Inside his bivouac sack the snow had gradually infiltrated, and melted to add to the condensation, which in turn froze into ice owing to the difference of temperatures between the outer and inner walls of the sack. Then the ice would flake off and, coming into contact with his body, would melt once more to form condensation and repeat the cycle ad infinitum.

Fully conscious now, he opened his eyes with alarm. The snow, driven by the wind, swirled, changing direction constantly like a flock of birds. God, a snow-storm. And a heavy one by the look of it. He thought for a moment of reaching for his torch and inspecting the barometer, but he dismissed the idea. To know it had gone down again wouldn't help. There was only one thing to do – wait till morning and hope that it didn't worsen.

His teeth chattering uncontrollably, he shut his eyes in an effort to cut himself off from the icy world outside the flimsy boundaries of his bivouac sack. It was so cold he believed that
286

f he'd lit a candle it would have flickered out in an instant.

Somehow the long hours passed. He became aware of a lightening in the sky. He opened his eyes again. It had stopped snowing, but everywhere in the faint light it was a world of dull, uniform grey stretching away to infinity.

Barrington was groaning softly, half awake.

He turned to look at Dillon. The heavy form was slumped over, his weight pulling at the rope which anchored him to the rock and stretching the nylon to the tautness of a bar. Wishart was relieved to see he was sleeping soundly. He couldn't see Grant; Barrington, still groaning, was blocking out his view.

He nudged Barrington. 'All right?' he said, wondering why he had bothered to whisper.

Barrington moved. Strange sounds came from his throat, like a man who had just suffered a stroke. He half-straightened and slumped forward again.

Wishart shut his eyes in misery. He knew the previous day had taken a lot out of him, of all of them, and he wondered where he was going to find the strength to go on. Whatever happened they'd have to move. They couldn't stay another night here or it would finish them off. He didn't feel like going on, but the prospect of having to climb all the way back down was unthinkable. His eyes jerked open, alarmed that he'd nearly slipped off back into the safe world of the unconscious. In these conditions, it was a world he might not have returned from.

Once again he shook Barrington, this time roughly.

'Wake up, wake up, man!'

Barrington stirred and groaned as if in pain. Wishart turned to Dillon. 'Come on, Brian. Come on, we've got to get moving.'

At the far end of the ledge he heard Grant stir. He was glad that Grant had awakened. Turning to Barrington again he shook him fiercely.

He was more successful this time. Barrington awoke, his mouth hanging open slackly and his eyes rimmed with pain.

'Come o-on!' Wishart raised his voice.

'What's the trouble?' he heard Grant say.

'We've got to get moving. We've got to find somewhere where we can get the stove going.'

'It's my foot,' Barrington said. 'It's gone funny, and the other one's sore as hell.'

God, frostbite? 'Take a couple of your pills and let's get going,' Wishart said, urgency in his voice. 'And hurry, it might start snowing again.'

Grant got out of his sack as Wishart again tried to rouse Dillon. Dillon came to life. 'Shake it up, Brian,' Wishart urged

'For God's sake be more careful, man,' he heard Grant cry Wishart turned his head. Grant's features were flushed. Barrington was bent over, his hand to his mouth.

'Let me see,' Grant's voice was sharp. Barrington obediently stopped sucking and held his hand out, his eyes screwed up in pain. Grant had one look at it. 'I thought as much.' He let go of Barrington's hand and, reaching for his pack, opened it up and brought out the first-aid kit.

'What is it?' Wishart asked. Dillon had also stopped in the act of putting his crampons on to see what was happening.

'Bad ice-burn,' replied Grant brusquely. 'Apart from that,' he addressed Barrington again, 'you jolly well nearly lost your crampon. I know it's awkward, but you must keep your gloves on when you're handling metal in such temperatures as these.'

When he'd dressed Barrington's hand they were ready to move again.

'The barometer's going down,' Wishart said warningly.

Grant was silent for a long minute. 'Let's appraise the situation. Firstly, we must get out of here. Secondly, if we go back down – and I'm not suggesting we do – the nearest bivouac we can hope to reach by night, assuming the weather holds, is our previous one on the Ramp, but preferably below that. You'll remember there's an excellent bivouac spot there. But weather or no weather it's still a long way with particularly hard climbing involved. Yes, I know what you're going to say, Bob, we could rope down much of it. In that way we could probably reach the lower of the bivouacs by nightfall, right? But what happens if the depression is only a temporary one? We have to come all the way back, but worse, we've lost two whole days with an additional climb into the bargain.'

'We'd be able to put fixed ropes on the Ramp,' Dillon suggested.

'Yes, a good point. It would certainly make it a lot easier, but let's leave that for the moment and see what our alternative is. As I say, we must get out of here. We don't know what is ahead. In fact there's some confusion here. Harrer describes a bivouac at the start of the "Traverse of the Gods" as being the best one he was able to find on the whole face, on the other hand Hiebeler, who bivouacked at almost the same spot, had exactly the opposite experience. He considered it to be the worst bivouac on the Wall up to that point.' Grant shrugged.

'You takes your pick . . .' Dillon muttered.

Grant went on. 'However, I'm convinced we're bound to find something better en route. When we do, we'll stop and have a hot drink and some food. From there we can decide our movements in relation to the weather. Has anyone anything to suggest?'

Wishart had been thinking all the time Grant had been speaking. They'd climbed two-thirds of the Wall, with the worst — given fair weather — of their problems behind them. On any other climb he would have unquestionably opted for going on, but this wasn't any other climb, it was the North Wall of the Eiger. Nothing could be taken for granted here. Right up to the moment they reached the summit ridge they had to be on their guard. They couldn't afford to relax for one single instant. Even on the approach to the summit climbers had lost their lives. What could be termed as normal or expected were terms that didn't apply to the North Face. This applied especially to weather patterns. But, given all that, one thing was abundantly clear — they couldn't remain where they were. If they were caught by a storm in this badly exposed position it would be the finish.

He thought of the long climb down and the thought made him feel ill. It would be terrifyingly difficult even in good weather. Equally the thought of going on was almost as unbearable. But a decision had to be made — and now!

He argued that his decision was based on completely rational grounds, arrived at after much thought, but in fact the balance of the pros and cons which he weighed up so carefully were tipped in favour of continuing by a deeply hidden streak of stubbornness.

'I think we should press on,' he said looking at the others.

'You, Brian?' Grant put the question.

Dillon jerked his thumb up without hesitation. Grant smiled to himself, he'd expected that. Dillon reminded him of Bob MacGarry, the best sergeant he'd ever had. It was good to have chaps like Dillon around when you were in a bit of a jam. Wishart too, he had a cool head, and could climb brilliantly — on his day. It was unfortunately true that Bob Wishart, for all his qualities, suffered from inconsistency. He put it down to his sensitivity, a sensitivity he was obviously at pains to disguise. There was no telling what he might have achieved if he'd been possessed of the same kind of uncomplicated drives as Dillon.

Barrington? He had to confess he was rather disappointed in Barrington. Oh, he could climb, but that wasn't everything when it came to mountaineering. Lots of other things were required. Coolness, fortitude, faith, the ability to keep going when all seemed lost. And that slip yesterday, good God it was the day before yesterday, he was beginning to lose sense of time, that would never do – anyway, that slip had shown a carelessness and lack of responsibility that was disturbing. And then on top of that he'd given himself a bad burn by handling his crampons without gloves on and, worse, had nearly lost the crampon as a result. Sheer carelessness and not to be excused by lack of experience. He looked at Barrington now. What would his choice be? Though in practice, with both Wishart and Dillon opting to continue, he didn't have one. However?

Wishart was leaning against the rock smoking a cigarette, his expression serious but calm. Behind him Dillon was standing with a look of boredom on his face as if to say 'let's get on with it'. For some reason, watching the pair of them, one rangy and tall, the other not so tall but solid as an ox, Grant was reminded of his days as a youngish captain during the war when he'd led a commando group. Wishart and Dillon could so easily have been members of that group, the same unshaven chins, the same tough uncompromising look. Grant felt his spirits lift and his chest rose with pride. Nothing was going to stop them. They'd carry out their mission – successfully. But what about Barrington? He'd said nothing as yet?

Barrington coughed nervously as Grant continued to look at him. 'I don't fancy having to climb all that way back down. We've only the Spider, haven't we, and after that we'll be at the exit cracks.'

Wishart drew on his cigarette, watching through narrowed eyes. Only the Spider, only the exit cracks? He didn't say anything as Barrington went on: 'I agree with Bob and Brian. I think we should go on.'

'Good. So do I. We're all agreed then. We press on, find a decent bivouac, stop for something hot to eat and sum up our prospects from there.'

When they'd roped up, Wishart led off.

The snow which had fallen earlier had turned to ice, and he had to treat the traverse with great care. The buttress which flanked the Spider stood out from the Wall. On the narrow gangway they were directly poised above the snow-covered meadows some 5,000 feet below. It gave him the feeling of being suspended in mid-air, an airy, chilling sensation. It was impossible to believe that if he fell here he would touch nothing till he hit the ground. The wind blew, billowing out his heavy Duvet garment and sending little loose pieces of frozen snow into his face with painful force.

At the end of the traverse, where it began to get very thin, he arrived at a vertical crack. He felt his spirits shrink as, leaning out backwards, he surveyed it.

Dillon joined him.

'Ugly bugger,' he said, the wind snatching the words from his mouth.

'It's got to go,' replied Wishart tersely. He shook his head as Dillon offered to lead it. He began to climb the crack, so cold he could barely feel the ice-glazed rock with his hands. He'd made about a third of his way up the crack and was standing on small holds with only the leading points of his crampons supporting him, when his left leg began to tremble. He had to get a belay quickly. Unshipping a piton he reversed his ice-hammer and, holding the piton with one hand against the ice, gave it a couple of sharp bangs with the hammer. A hollow sound echoed back. He cursed. He knew what that meant. The piton was cracking the ice. He tried another spot with the same result. But it would have to do. His leg still trembling, he clipped on a snap-link and threaded the rope through, knowing it would never hold him if he came off. Aaahh! That had been close. The point of his crampon had lost contact for a brief second. Keep moving now, he forced himself to think. Keep moving!

The crack was no more than a hundred feet high, but he'd taken the best part of two hours on it. He reached the shelf at the top and lay down his full length, sure he would never get up again. His breath was coming in great gulps and he was shaking all over with exhaustion and fear. He was mentally and physically shattered. He'd have to give up after this and let Dillon lead. All right, it was cowardly, but every man had his limits. After what seemed an eternity he got to his feet again, stumbling, his legs robbed of all their strength. Somehow he brought Dillon up.

'What a bastard!' Dillon swore. 'That was a bloody sight worse than the Ramp.'

Wishart was too exhausted to reply.

It was getting dark again before the others were able to join them. Barrington was obviously suffering. He'd taken much longer on the pitch than either Grant or Dillon.

'It looks like this will have to do,' Wishart said wearily. 'At least it's better than what we had before.'

'Well, we'll have some place to sit down,' Grant agreed.

Barrington, his face twisted in pain, began to unpack. He got the stove out.

'Here,' Dillon said. 'Give's it over, you look bushed.'

Without a word Barrington handed him the stove. Dillon boiled up the fruit juice and, as a special treat, after that they each had a cupful of boiling beef essence. It did something to revive them. Once again it was the familiar, painful routine of removing their crampons and getting into their sacks.

'How's the barometer?' Grant asked, when he'd wriggled into his sack.

Wishart got the aneroid out, but it was too dark to read it without the aid of his torch. He got his torch from his pack after a lengthy search and switched it on. He shook his head. 'Still going down. Just a little, but it's definitely going down.'

'Right. There's nothing we can do to-night. I suggest we get what rest we can. We can make our decision to-morrow.'

Surprisingly enough the morning dawned fine. They set off at nine o'clock, too tired to have started earlier. As they headed for the 'Traverse of the Gods' the sun, which had been hiding behind a bank of light clouds, came out.

From their lofty and seemingly detached platform, suspended above the distant valley, they were able to see the vast bulk of the Eiger's shadow pull back across the meadows like a receding tide. The Kleine Scheidegg was clearly visible. Even at this time of day little clumps of figures stood around the hotel and railway station. As before they'd armed themselves with binoculars and telescopes, their lenses flashing and glittering in the strong light. And once again the wind had dropped to a gentle breeze, though at this height it was still bitterly cold.

Grant, who only the previous night had felt all in, was rejuvenated by the sight. He felt an enormous wave of well-being sweep over him to recharge his muscles. He was utterly confident now. All right, the barometer was still going down, but the weather hadn't deteriorated as yet and they'd soon be on the Spider. After that . . . he purposely checked his optimism. Maybe Wishart was a bit cautious. It was true they had quite a distance to climb yet, but with luck another two bivouacs and they would be there. Already he began to envisage his success. No, not his success – *their* success. He permitted himself to grin.

In contrast to Grant's outlook, Wishart had an uneasy feeling. He sensed the weather wasn't going to hold. God help them if it caught them now. Once they were on the Spider they'd be irrevocably committed to continue upwards: beyond the point of no return. But even the thought of returning was enough to make him shudder. No, they were wholly committed now. He knew that. There would be no return!

Dillon was leading the traverse. Like Grant he seemed to have recovered from the effects of the previous day and was forging ahead confidently.

But Barrington was making heavy weather. His left foot, which had been affected the most seriously by frostbite, was giving him considerable trouble. Something else had happened to him. It was as if a light had dimmed within him. He was no longer smiling or cheerful, and worst of all he seemed to have lost his earlier confidence. To Wishart this was the most serious thing of all. No matter how bad the physical shape a man was in, he could always be made to keep going if the spark was alive. If it wasn't . . .

Wishart prayed that the storm he sensed was coming would hold off.

Watching Barrington carefully, Wishart, as next man on the rope, tried to encourage him. It was essential that Barrington's spirits were kept up, but he got no more than monosyllabic replies.

They made the long traverse and at last, crossing a short ice-slope, stood at the foot of the Spider. From the perimeter of its 700 feet, long arms of ice spread out in all directions. It had been well named.

They gathered for a rest and something to eat.

Grant munched a piece of chocolate. 'What do you think now, Bob?'

'Should get beyond the Spider . . . we'll bivouac higher up.'

'I meant the weather?'

Wishart let his breath go in a long worried sigh: 'Don't know. There's something on the way, that's for sure.'

Grant eyed Wishart's stubbled features. Outwardly he looked calm, but Grant knew he was struggling with something. Perhaps it was frostbite, or was it that – he didn't like this idea – he was suffering from the memory of his last attempt on the Eiger when he'd been caught in a vicious storm? There had been another two with him then. From what he remembered of it they'd all finished up in pretty bad shape. Still, there was no good asking him about the frostbite, he'd only get a laconic reply. He turned to Barrington.

'How is your foot?'

'It's both of them now. One's pretty bad, I think.'

'We'll try and find a good bivouac and massage it to-night' Wishart said.

'Have you been taking your pills?' asked Grant.

'I haven't all that many left.'

'What?' Grant exclaimed.

'I lost mine on the Ramp, remember? Ernie shared his with me,' Wishart cut in.

'Of course,' said Grant, noticing the grateful glance Barrington shot Wishart. Odd, why should he do that? Still, it was no time for conjecture. They'd have to be on the move again. They had the Spider to climb and a bivouac to find after that.

To save time, it was decided to tackle the Spider as directly as possible, keeping their diagonal lines of ascent as highly angled as possible. Dillon had gained three ropes' length up the slope when Barrington slipped again. This time it was Wishart who had to check his fall. Fortunately he'd been half expecting it to happen and was taking more than usual care in belaying him.

The slip was a small one but it did nothing to improve Barrington's confidence, and inevitably it had its effect on the rest of the party. Without saying anything they began to look upon him as the weak link in the chain.

At last they'd surmounted the Spider. Standing at its rim Wishart felt the wind grow on his cheek. It was rising again. He looked up at the sky. It seemed a bit too dark for this time of day. He noticed, too, that farther up the valley and over to its northernmost side heavy cloud had gathered, though it was being pushed away by the wind. Not much could be deduced from that. Here the weather pattern could change violently and dramatically. And the Eiger was notorious – a law unto itself!

Still, there was that wind. It could hardly be ignored, especially since it was from the west.

'I think we should get going,' he said, a note of urgency in his voice.

'What's up, Bob?' asked Dillon.

'The weather. I don't like it.'

'Doesn't look too bad to me,' Dillon said, rubbing his chin and gazing upwards speculatively at the sky.

Barrington gave Wishart a worried look. 'Do you think we're in for a storm or something?'